*A Mother's Promise*

Dilly Court grew up in North-east London and began her career in television, writing scripts for commercials. She is married with two grown-up children and four grand-children, and now lives in Dorset on the beautiful Jurassic Coast with her husband and a large, yellow Labrador called Archie. She is also the author of *Mermaids Singing*, *The Dollmaker's Daughters*, *Tilly True*, *The Best of Sisters*, *The Cockney Sparrow*, *A Mother's Courage* and *The Constant Heart*.

# Dilly Court

## A Mother's Promise

arrow books

Published by Arrow Books 2009

4 6 8 10 9 7 5 3

First published in Great Britain in 2008 by
Arrow Books
Random House, 20 Vauxhall Bridge Road,
London SW1V 2SA

www.rbooks.co.uk

Addresses for companies within The Random House Group Limited can be
found at: www.randomhouse.co.uk/offices.htm

The Random House Group Limited Reg. No. 954009

A CIP catalogue record for this book
is available from the British Library

ISBN 9780099519348

The Random House Group Limited supports The Forest Stewardship
Council (FSC), the leading international forest certification organisation. All
our titles that are printed on Greenpeace approved FSC certified paper carry
the FSC logo. Our paper procurement policy can be found at
www.rbooks.co.uk/environment

Typeset by Palimpsest Book Production Ltd, Grangemouth, Stirlingshire
Printed and bound in Great Britain by CPI Bookmarque Ltd, Croydon, CR0 4TD

*For Jennifer, Maureen and Margaret*

# Chapter One

# Bow, East London, January 1888

Hetty stamped her feet in an attempt to bring them back to life. It was five o'clock on a bitterly cold winter's morning, and the queue of outworkers stretched from the gates of the match factory to the end of the street and far beyond. Women and girls, many of whom were little more than children, waited to collect the materials that they needed to take home in order to make matchboxes. The sleet-spiked torrential rain had eased to a fine drizzle, but the gutters were clogged with rotting straw and overflowing with evil-smelling water contaminated by horse dung. The feeble glow of the gaslights created monstrous shadows from the huddled shapes of the women as they crowded together in an effort to keep warm.

Hetty shivered convulsively, cupping her hands over her mouth and blowing on them in a vain attempt to bring some feeling back to her frozen fingers. Her teeth were chattering like a pair of magpies, and she wrapped her sodden woollen shawl a little tighter around

1

her thin shoulders; but for all the good it did her, she might as well not have bothered. A quick glance at her younger sister's pinched features and miserable expression made Hetty forget her own woes for a moment. She gave Jane's hand a squeeze. 'It shouldn't be long now before they let us in, love.'

Jane hunched her shoulders and shuffled her feet; her blue lips moved but her answer was drowned by a fit of coughing from the woman standing behind her. The harsh, hacking sound echoed down the street, generating a chain reaction of coughs and sneezes amongst the previously silent queue. Hetty could feel the icy water seeping through the thin soles of her second-hand, down-at-heel boots, but at least she had footwear. Others, less fortunate, had to watch their bare feet turning blue and then corpse-white as they waited for the factory gates to open.

'Ouch.' Hetty let out a yelp, spinning round to see who had tugged at her hair, which she wore in a thick plait that reached down to her waist. 'Oh! So it's you, Tom Crewe. I might have known it.'

Grinning mischievously, he dragged off his cloth cap, revealing a mop of curls, flattened and darkened by sweat but glistening guinea-gold in the gaslight. 'Morning, Hetty.'

She scowled at him, but her lips twitched

as she suppressed the desire to giggle. 'Do that again, and I'll have you.'

'Is that a promise, sweetheart?' Tom's teeth gleamed white in a face blackened with soot.

His companion, also covered in grime, chuckled and nudged him in the ribs. 'I'd have her sister, given half a chance.'

Hetty's protective instincts were instantly roused and she turned on him angrily. 'You don't half fancy yourself, Nat. My sister ain't interested in the likes of you.'

'Shut up, Hetty. I don't need you to speak for me.' Jane's pale cheeks flamed coral-pink. 'And there's no need to be crude, Nat,' she added, slanting a coquettish look at him beneath her long dark eyelashes.

'You wasn't so coy the last time we met,' Nat said softly.

Hetty opened her mouth to remind him that Jane was only just sixteen, but Tom was still fingering her braid and he brushed it against his cheek. 'Your hair's like black silk, Hetty, and your eyes are the colour of violets – I could eat you for me dinner.'

'Give over, Tom. You're embarrassing me.' Hetty forgot about Nat as she tugged her hair free from Tom's grasp. 'Get on home. You stink of the gasworks and you look like a sweep's boy.'

'Don't lower yourself to their level,' Jane whispered. 'It ain't seemly.'

3

Nat doffed his cap and bowed from the waist. 'Hoity-toity, Miss Jane Huggins.'

'I don't like a public show,' Jane said primly.

'You're a real lady, Janey.' Nat leaned towards her with a boss-eyed but charming smile. 'Will I see you tonight afore I goes on me shift at the gasworks?'

'Maybe. Maybe not.'

The woman standing directly in front of them turned her head and scowled at Jane. 'Fine goings-on, I must say. I've a good mind to tell your gran that you're carrying on with Nathaniel Smith. I seen you two canoodling beneath the gas lamps.' She jerked her head in Nat's direction, curling her lip in disapproval. 'His mother was a didicoi and his dad ended up in the clink. He'll go the same way, if you ask me.'

Hetty spun round to face her. 'That weren't called for, Mrs Briggs. I'll thank you to mind your own business.'

'Don't get into a fight,' Jane hissed.

'I'm not one for brawling in the street, as you well know, but I won't have my sister's name dragged through the dirt,' Hetty said, casting a withering glance at Mrs Briggs.

'Don't take that tone with me, young woman.'

'I won't let you or anyone else go round insulting my family, Eva Briggs. Your lot ain't so lily-white if it comes to that. I hear that Pearl

4

is in the family way again and still no ring on her finger.'

'You little bitch!' Mrs Briggs rolled up her sleeves and fisted her hands.

'Hetty ain't had breakfast yet,' Jane said hastily, stepping in between them. 'She's always like this before she's had a cup of tea.'

Mrs Briggs smiled triumphantly. 'Your own sister agrees that you're a mouthy cow. What have you got to say to that, Hetty Huggins?'

'Apologise,' Jane hissed. 'We can't afford to lose money just because of her.'

'Sorry, Mrs Briggs,' Hetty muttered, staring down at her boots. She knew that Jane was right. Any disturbance would invoke the wrath of the foreman and a hefty fine. Even so, it was common knowledge that Pearl Briggs was notoriously free with her favours and had three illegitimate offspring to prove the point. Hetty could feel Tom standing close by her side ready to leap to her defence and that was the last thing she wanted. She laid her hand on his arm. 'It's all right, Tom. I spoke out of turn and I'm sorry for it.'

Mrs Briggs snorted and opened her mouth as if to retort but the sound of the factory gates grinding on their hinges caused the queue to surge forward.

'Will I see you tonight then, Janey?' Nat asked urgently.

'I dunno. I'll think about it.'

'Maybe I'll see you too, Hetty,' Tom said, striding along by her side as the crowd moved as one towards the open maw of the match factory.

'I wouldn't count on it if I was you.' Hetty fluttered her eyelashes in an attempt to ape Jane's flirtatious manner but she couldn't quite suppress a giggle, which spoiled the whole thing. 'You're nothing but trouble.'

Responding with a chuckle, he rammed his cap back on his head. 'Meet me outside the gasworks and I'll prove you wrong.'

'Meet him outside the gasworks and he'll prove you're right,' Mrs Briggs called over her shoulder, emphasising her words with a suggestive wink.

'Ta, ever so!' Hetty retorted, refusing to rise to the bait. 'I'll bear that in mind, Mrs Briggs.' Swept onwards by the crowd, she turned her head and saw Tom waving to her. In spite of everything, she felt her spirits lift and she waved back. She could never be cross with him for long. He was a good friend; her best friend, if it came to that. She had known Tom for most of her nineteen years. He lived with his widowed mother and youngest sister in Dye House Lane, the next street to Autumn Road where the Huggins family dwelt in a single basement room. They had played together as children and had earned money as mudlarks, grubbing beneath the filthy waters of the River Lea for pieces of coal, copper or anything that might sell for a few farthings. Hetty had always thought of Tom as a big brother, although recently things had begun to change subtly. But there was no time to dwell on personal feelings now. 'No need to push,' she cried as she was shoved from behind, almost losing her footing on the wet and slippery paving stones. A fall could prove fatal as the desperate women and girls pushed forward to get a day's work for just a few pence pay.

Half an hour later, having stopped off at the bakery on the way, Hetty and Jane were back in Autumn Road, carrying their bundles of cardboard, paper and glue and a loaf of bread that was still hot from the baker's oven. It was not yet light and a grey mist floated just above the cocoa-coloured waters of the River Lea. The muddy foreshore was thick with pollution from the factories and the stench of coal gas and chemicals and the reek of the tanning works filled the air. Number one Autumn Road leaned precariously towards the river, as if the old building with its soot-blackened bricks was about to throw itself into the creek out of sheer desperation. Half the windows were boarded up and the rest were cracked or broken, with bits of rag and newspaper stuffed in the holes to keep out the bitter easterly wind that rampaged across the Essex marshes. Jane hurried down the area steps to the damp basement room they called home. Inside was barely warmer than outside, and the only light came from a single stub of a candle guttering in the middle of the table where their two younger brothers were perched on wooden stools.

'You've been ages,' Sammy complained. 'I'm hungry.'

'Me too,' Eddie said, banging his empty bowl with a wooden spoon. 'Where's our breakfast, Hetty?'

Hetty dumped her parcel of work on the table. 'Give us a minute, greedy boy.' She smiled at his downcast face and ruffled his hair. 'I stopped at the bakery and bought a loaf. It's in with the cardboard and glue.'

'I wants porridge.' Eddie's blue eyes filled with tears and his bottom lip trembled. 'I'm cold, Hetty. I want something hot to eat.'

'Well, you'll just have to make do this morning, Ed,' Hetty said, rummaging in the parcel for the loaf. Her heart was wrung with pity at the sight of her two small brothers' pinched faces and stick-like limbs, but she must not let them see how much it distressed her. She had to keep up the appearance of being calm and in control, even if she was as cold and hungry as they were.

Sammy jumped off his stool, making a grab for the bundle, but Hetty slapped his wrist; not too hard, just enough to make the seven-year-old think twice before he tore into the brown paper package. 'Hands off, you. I thought I told you to get the fire going while we was out.'

'The kindling's damp. It wouldn't light. I tried, Hetty. I really tried.'

'He did,' Eddie said, giggling. 'And when it went out he swore. Shall I tell you what he said?'

Sammy lunged at his younger brother, grabbing him round the throat. 'Shut up, big mouth.'

Jane took off her shawl and hung it over the back of the only chair in the room. She rolled up her damp sleeves. 'I'll get the fire going. You feed the little beasts, Hetty.'

'I'm not sure that Sammy deserves any breakfast,' Hetty said, winking at him. 'I should wash his mouth out with soap by rights.'

'Yes,' Jane said with feeling. 'That's what Ma would have done.'

'I wish she was here now.' Sammy threw himself down on his seat and laid his head on his arms. His thin shoulders heaved.

Eddie climbed up on his stool and began to snivel. 'M-me t-too.' Strings of mucus dribbled from his nose.

'Now look what you've done, Jane. You should have known better than to mention Ma.' Hetty wiped Eddie's nose on the corner of her apron, and she gave Sammy a sympathetic hug. 'Ma's in heaven now, boys. Up with the angels, and in a far better place than Autumn Road.'

Sammy wiped his eyes on his sleeve, suddenly curious. 'D'you think they mended her face – the angels?'

Hetty opened the drawer in the kitchen table and took out the bread knife, nodding emphatically. 'Of course they did. That would have been the first thing the angels did when Ma entered the pearly gates. I'll bet St Peter took one look at her and said "Hello, my dear. Don't worry; we'll fix you up good and proper now that you're in heaven. Just go over to the Angel Gabriel and he'll put your face back just as it was afore you got the phossy jaw in that damn match factory."'

Jane sat back on her haunches as flames licked round the kindling and twists of newspaper. She gave Hetty a withering look. 'How can you tell him off for swearing when you've just done the same thing?'

Hetty pulled a face which made Sammy and Eddie giggle. 'Oops! Sorry.'

Sammy rested his chin on his cupped hands, staring hard at her. 'Does that mean you won't go to heaven, Hetty?'

She cut the crust off the loaf and scraped it with margarine. 'Here, shove this in your gob and don't ask awkward questions.'

'I can't eat crust, Hetty,' Sammy said with fresh tears spilling from his eyes. He pointed to the gap where he had lost his top two baby teeth.

'I can.' Eddie snatched it from his hand, and took a bite as if to prove his point.

Hetty hacked off another slice and gave it to Sammy. 'Don't be a crybaby. Eat this and then we've got work to do.' She modified her words with a smile. 'There's a good boy.'

Jane had succeeded in getting the fire to light and she put the kettle on the hook over the feeble flame. 'I could murder a cup of tea.' She rose to her feet, and peering in the shard of broken mirror on the mantelshelf she patted her luxuriant chestnut locks in place. 'Just look at my hair – it's gone all frizzy with the damp.'

'Here's a slice of bread and scrape for you, you vain hussy,' Hetty said, chuckling. 'You're very pretty, Jane. But since it's only me and the boys will see you for the next twelve hours, it don't matter what you look like.'

Jane snatched the bread and bit into it hungrily. 'You're just as bad,' she said, swallowing a mouthful and licking her lips. 'I wasn't the one who almost started a fight because someone messed up her hair.'

'That was different. Anyway, you've no need to worry about your looks. You've got the face of an angel, didn't Ma always say so?'

Jane's sulky lips curved into a smile. 'I might be what they call pretty, but Ma always said you'd be a handsome woman when you was grown up. I'd kill for a straight nose like yours, and not one that turns up at the tip like mine. I've always wanted blue eyes like you and Sammy, instead of brown ones that look like puddles of muddy rainwater.'

'Never mind all that. We've got work to do, and you don't have time to go primping in the mirror every five minutes.'

'It's called keeping up appearances,' Jane retorted, smiling serenely. 'Ma would have approved. She always liked to look nice, no matter what she was doing or who she was seeing.'

'She was beautiful inside and out. Nothing could take that away from her.' Hetty slumped down on a stool at the table. 'Eddie, don't gobble your food, you'll make yourself sick.' She raised the slice of bread to her lips but her appetite left her as she remembered Ma's last days with the dreadful disease that had eaten half her face away. Phossy jaw was an occupational hazard amongst the girls and women who worked with the white or yellow phosphorus used in the manufacture of matches. On her deathbed, Ma had made Hetty and Jane promise that they would work from home, partly so that they could keep an eye on their younger brothers, but mainly so that they would steer clear of the hazards of working in the factory itself. Girls as young as fifteen often went completely bald from carrying heavy boxes on their heads. There were accidents with machinery and a high risk of burns from the matches themselves. The matchgirls' wages were scandalously low and outworkers were paid even less, but working from home had enabled Hetty to keep the family together. She had vowed to look after the little ones as though they were her own and she had kept that promise. Her eyes filled with tears as she thought of her mother, who had worked so hard to raise her seven children after their father had been killed in an accident at the gasworks. Betty, Ida and Fred had all succumbed to childhood diseases, diphtheria, measles and whooping cough, which had broken Ma's heart, but had made her even more protective of her surviving children.

Hetty nibbled at her slice of bread as she watched Eddie swallow the last crumb of his food, and, despite his missing teeth, Sammy was not far behind. They were eyeing the remaining half of the loaf like a pair of hungry wolf cubs, but that was for their dinner, and must not be touched until at least midday. Hetty tore what was left of her slice in half and gave it to them. 'Eat slowly and it will fill you up more.' She turned to Jane, who was standing so close to the fire that her skirt was steaming. 'Has the kettle boiled yet?'

Jane shook her head. 'Not quite. We're in desperate need of some more kindling and coal. We need matches and candles and goodness knows how we're going to find the rent on Saturday.'

Hetty glanced anxiously at Sammy as she heard his sharp intake of breath. 'Don't worry, Sammy. Jane and me will sort it out. If we can make three gross of matchboxes today, we'll have a fish and chip supper.'

Sammy beamed at her. 'Really, Hetty? Is that a promise?'

'Cross me heart and hope to die.' Hetty made the sign of the cross on her chest. 'Before we start work, you two take the bucket to the pump and get us some water.'

'Aw, do I have to?' Sammy groaned.

'Yes, you do. Or there won't be any fish supper for you, my lad.'

'Come on then, Eddie.' Sammy slid off his stool. 'You get the bucket. I'll open the door.'

Hetty watched them through the cracked windowpanes as they ran up the area steps. She could hear their childish laughter and yet again she was amazed by their resilience. The last few months had been truly terrible with their mother's dreadful suffering and subsequent agonising death. Money had been so tight that they had come close to being evicted from their one-room home. If she had not pleaded with the landlord, they would all have been out on the street or, worse still, in the workhouse. Hetty shuddered at the mere thought. Things were a little better now, although not much. They had borrowed money from Cyrus Clench, the tallyman, in order to pay for Ma's simple funeral and it would take months, if not years, to pay it all off.

Jane popped the last morsel of bread into her mouth. 'Put what's left of the loaf out of sight, Hetty. I'm still so hungry that I could eat the lot.'

'The kettle's boiling. You make a brew and I'll wrap the bread to keep it fresh. If we all work hard we should be able to earn sixpence three farthings today.'

Jane spooned tea into a chipped brown china teapot. 'This is the last of it, and these leaves have been used so many times I could read newspaper print through each one. They won't do another brew and that's for certain.'

'One day I'll buy me tea by the pound,' Hetty said, closing her eyes to shut out the cracked windowpanes, the fungus growing out of the brickwork and the worm-eaten beams above her head. 'I'll never use the leaves more than twice and if I wants two slices of bread for me breakfast, then two slices I shall have.'

'And jam every day,' Jane added wistfully. 'And cake on Sundays. I can't remember the last time we had cake.'

'I had jelly once, at Gran's house,' Hetty mused. 'Strawberry jelly. I never tasted nothing like it before or since.'

'Well Granny Huggins don't want nothing to do with us since Pa died, she made that plain, and she never even come to see Ma when she knew she was dying, so I'd rather you didn't talk about her.' Jane shook out her damp skirts. 'Anyway, there's no point going on about strawberry jelly and such; just the thought of it is making me feel faint from lack of nourishment. We'd best get started or we'll not earn a penny today, and the tallyman will be round tomorrow for his money. Don't forget that.'

'I ain't likely to forget him, the dirty old man.' Hetty shuddered; she had come to dread Clench's regular Friday morning visit to collect the next instalment on the loan. He never failed to make suggestive remarks and he had a nasty way of licking his lips as he stared at her breasts. She sighed and wrapped the loaf in the brown paper bag and placed it on the top shelf of the crudely fashioned dresser. Her pa had made that piece of furniture with his own hands soon after he and Ma were married, or so Ma had told them. A real labour of love, she had called it. It didn't matter that the shelves weren't quite straight and things slid to the end, or that the doors didn't fit exactly and often swung open on their rusty hinges. Ma always said it was the damp in the basement that had caused these things to happen; it wasn't a reflection on her Samuel's craftsmanship, because he was a perfectionist.

Hetty brushed the crumbs from the table and began setting out the makings of the matchboxes, just as Sammy and Eddie came clattering down the steps to the front door carrying the bucket between them and no doubt spilling most of it on the ground. She cast a warning look at Jane. 'Don't say nothing in front of the nippers.'

'As if I would. I ain't daft, Hetty.'

'No, far from it, but you forget sometimes that little pitchers have big ears.'

Before Jane had time to reply, Sammy and Eddie burst through the door, slopping water on the flagstones.

'Right!' Hetty said briskly. 'The sooner we

get down to it, the sooner we can have that fish supper.'

They worked all day, squinting in the poor light at the tiny matchboxes that they worked on so painstakingly, each one handcrafted to exact specifications. Hetty couldn't help noticing that Sammy held the work very close to his eyes and he often complained of headaches. She feared that the close work was making him nearsighted, but there was no way they could afford to have his eyes tested by a specialist, and, even if they did, there was no money for the purchase of spectacles. Perhaps it was just a growing thing. She had heard women talking in the queues outside the factory and they mentioned mysterious things like 'growing pains' and strange afflictions that might or might not disappear with the onset of puberty. So many infants died before they reached their first birthday that tiny coffins were as commonplace in East London as chocolate boxes were up West.

They stopped for a dinner break at midday. Even though she scraped the margarine on the bread, there was only enough for two slices and Hetty gave those to Sammy and Eddie. She and Jane ate theirs dry, washing it down with cold tea. The fire had long since gone out and they had run out of coal and kindling.

It was dark by mid-afternoon and the rain had turned to snow. Huge white flakes fell like feathers from a burst pillow, floating past the window and dissolving almost immediately on the wet ground. Sammy and Eddie were hugely excited and ran to the window to squash their noses against the grimy panes, begging to be allowed outside to play.

'No, I'm sorry, but you ain't going out there to get soaked to the skin and catch your deaths of cold,' Hetty said severely, even though she longed to let her brothers snatch back a little of their childhood. She could see them growing old before their time, but they had to fulfil their quota or there would be no payout at the factory this evening.

'Aw, go on, Hetty,' Sammy pleaded. 'Just a bit of a play in the snow afore it melts into slush, please.'

Jane cast Hetty a meaningful look, shaking her head. 'Don't let them.'

'No, you must sit down and finish your work,' Hetty said firmly. 'Maybe later, when we've finished the boxes, you can come to the factory with me to deliver them. If the snow is still around then you can have a play in it.'

Reluctantly, Sammy left the window and went slowly back to his place at the table. 'Don't forget you promised us a fish supper, Hetty.'

She smiled. 'Don't worry, love. I won't forget.'

At seven o'clock that evening Hetty and Jane were back in the queue outside the factory, but this time they had Sammy and Eddie with them and they were delivering the finished matchboxes. They had to wait for them to be checked and counted, and then they were given a chitty to take to the pay office, where they had to queue yet again to collect their hard-earned sixpence three farthings. The snow was falling heavily when they finally left the factory gates. It swirled around them in a dizzy dance, blotting out the harsh outlines of the buildings and softening the unremitting greyness of the pavements. Sammy and Eddie made snowballs, throwing them at each other and laughing gleefully. Hetty and Jane stopped for a moment, chuckling at their antics.

'I'm off then,' Jane said, brushing the snowflakes from her face.

'Where are you going?' Hetty stared at her in disbelief. 'What about the fish supper?'

'You know I promised to meet Nat outside the gasworks. You can keep me a bit of supper, although, if I'm lucky, he might take me to the pub for a pie and a glass of port and lemon.'

'I didn't think you would go,' Hetty said, hunching her shoulders. 'I thought you said . . .'

'Never mind what I said. I'm going and that's that.' Jane started to walk away but Hetty caught her by the sleeve.

'Hold on, Jane. What would Ma say if she knew you was going off to meet a fellow all on your own?'

'It don't matter, because she ain't here.' Jane shook off Hetty's restraining hand. 'We got to look out for ourselves now, Hetty. I have a good time with Nat, and he's been sweet on me for ages. As far as I can see, the only way you and I have of getting out of this miserable way of life is to find ourselves a husband.'

'You're only just sixteen, Jane. That's far too young to think about getting hitched.'

'Ma was sixteen when she married Pa.'

'That was different. Pa had good prospects at the match factory until he fell sick with lung fever. If you married Nat you'd have to get by on a labourer's wage. You could do so much better, love.' Hetty blinked away a snowflake as it landed on her eyelashes, but the chill was in her stomach as she thought of the risk that Jane was prepared to take.

'You need to live in the real world, Hetty. There ain't no knight in shining armour going to ride his white charger down Autumn Road to sweep you off your feet, nor me neither. We got to settle for what we can get, and if I can persuade Nathaniel Smith to marry me, then I'll be more than satisfied.'

'But – but he's cross-eyed, Jane. Sometimes when he's looking at you, both his eyes meet in the middle.'

Jane tossed her head. 'Well at least that stops his gaze wandering off and eyeing up other girls. I never said he was handsome, and maybe he ain't clever, but he's got a steady job and he's a hard worker. If I can get him to the altar he'll look after the lot of us, you and the boys included. Anyway, you're wrong, Hetty. I do love him in me own way. I really do.'

Hetty stared at her young brothers gambolling in the snow. She would have to rub Eddie's chest with goose grease tonight before she put him to bed, or by morning he would be running a temperature. She turned back to answer Jane but was just in time to see her disappear into a swirling mass of snow. She sighed. Well, it was Jane's life when all was said and done, but if Nat proved to be a bad choice she would have a lifetime of regret stretching out in front of her. 'Come on, boys. Stop that now and let's get to the shop to buy the things we need.'

Sammy dropped his snowball onto the pavement. 'And our fish supper.'

'That too,' Hetty said, smiling. A snowball, thrown by Eddie with deadly accuracy, hit her squarely in the face. 'Why, you little . . .' Half angry, half laughing, she wiped the melting ice from her eyes. 'Right, you little monster. You've asked for it.' She bent down and scooped up a handful of snow. Forming it into a ball, she tossed it at Eddie who screamed and ran away. Sammy responded by pelting Hetty with snowballs, and Eddie joined in, shouting gleefully. Hetty forgot all about being grown-up and sensible as she fought back, laughing and shrieking as loud as or even louder than her brothers.

'Hey! Two on to one – that's not fair.' Tom came striding towards them out of the darkness. He scooped up handfuls of snow and made a huge snowball.

'You wouldn't . . .' Sammy murmured, backing away.

'Oh, wouldn't I?' Tom lobbed it at them, but the snowball hit a lamppost, fragmented and fell harmlessly to the ground.

Hetty pitched a snowball at Tom, catching him squarely on the back of his head and tipping his cap over his eyes. 'Got you, Tom. That one's for me brothers.'

He spun round and caught her by the shoulders, giving her a gentle shake. 'Here, I was on your side.'

A snowball hit him on the head and another clipped his ear, knocking his cap to the ground.

'You see what happens when you take on the Huggins family,' Hetty said, laughing.

He bent down to retrieve his cap. 'Fainites!' he said, holding up his right hand and crossing his fingers. 'I'll go quietly.'

Sammy and Eddie pounced on him, grabbing his hands. 'We got him for you, Hetty. What shall us do with him now?'

Hetty angled her head. 'I think he should carry the bag of coal for us, for a start, and the kindling.'

'You're a hard woman, Hetty, but I know when I'm beaten. I'll pay my penance, gladly. But on one condition.'

'And what's that, Tom?'

'That you let me buy you a fish supper at Greasy Joe's.'

'I'll think about it.'

Sammy tugged at Tom's hand. 'And some wallies, please, Tom.'

'I think I can run to a wally or two.'

Eddie pulled Tom's other hand. 'How about a pickled egg?'

'Maybe, but only if you're a good boy and do everything your sister says.'

Sammy and Eddie whooped for joy and bounded on ahead as Tom linked Hetty's hand through the crook of his elbow and started off in the direction of the grocer's shop.

'You spoil them,' she said with mock severity.

'But thanks anyway.' Hetty knew that she ought to have refused his generous offer, but the thought of saving a few pennies was too tempting. She would be able to give Clench a little extra when he called next day. The sooner they paid him off the better. She smiled up at Tom. Although he was only just twenty-one, two years her senior, he had been labouring at the gasworks for more than seven years, and if she was being honest, she had to admit that he had matured into quite a good-looking young man. Any girl would be proud to be seen out with such a fellow.

The interior of Greasy Joe's café was filled with steam and the slightly rancid odour of hot fat mixed with the wet sheep smell of damp woollen clothes drying out in the fuggy heat. The other customers, all working men who had just come off shift in the gasworks or the carbolic acid factory on the banks of the River Lea, sat smoking hand-rolled cigarettes and drinking tea. Hetty prepared to queue at the counter, but Tom directed them to a bench, insisting that it was his treat and he had no intention of standing outside in the snow eating his supper from yesterday's newspaper. Sammy and Eddie took their places at one of the wooden tables, staring around wide-eyed. Hetty hid a smile as she watched them sitting primly on the form, unusually silent, as they absorbed their unfamiliar surroundings. She could not remember the last time she had sat down to eat in a café. Greasy Joe's might not be grand like the chop houses and restaurants up West that she had read about in old copies of magazines, but at least it was warm and cosy in here, and tonight for once they would go to bed with full bellies.

Tom threaded his way between the tables holding an enamel plate in his hand. He set it down in front of Sammy and Eddie. 'Here, boys. Get your choppers round them for a start. The fish suppers won't be long.'

Sammy grabbed the largest wally and bit into the sweet pickled cucumber with an expression of bliss on his face. Eddie snatched another and crammed it into his mouth.

'Steady on,' Hetty said sternly. 'You'll get bellyache if you gobble your food.'

'Let them be. They're enjoying themselves,' Tom said, taking a seat beside Hetty. 'This is most pleasant. We should do it more often.'

Hetty eyed him suspiciously. 'What d'you mean by that, Tom? I ain't a charity case, you know. I was going to buy us a fish supper tonight even if you hadn't offered. I can pay me way.'

'Don't get all huffy with me, girl. No offence intended. I just meant it was nice to have your company, and maybe we could step out together, proper like.'

Sammy paused with a wally halfway to his lips, scowling. 'Are you spooning with me sister, Tom?'

'Of course not, silly,' Hetty said hastily. 'Look, our supper's ready.' She half rose, intending to go to the counter to collect the food, but Tom pressed her back onto her seat.

'No, you sit there like a lady. I'll get the grub.'

Hetty watched him with a feeling of unease as he returned to the counter. She was fond of Tom, but she had no intention of getting tied up with a bloke, not yet anyway. She had ambition and it didn't involve getting hitched at nineteen and being saddled with a baby every year. She wanted something better out of life than the back-breaking daily grind suffered by her poor dead mother. She hadn't worked out how she would achieve her ambition, but there must be something she could do that would earn good money. The solution to all their problems would come to her one day, of that she was certain.

When Sammy and Eddie were so intent on stuffing fish and chips that the roof could have blown off without their noticing it, she turned to Tom, speaking in a low voice. 'I don't want you to get the wrong idea, just because I let you buy us supper.'

His smile faded into a puzzled frown. 'I ain't sure I get your meaning, Hetty.'

She laid her hand on his arm. 'Oh, Tom. We're good friends and always have been. I want it to stay that way.'

'And I do too, ducks. But that don't mean to say we can't be better than friends.'

'That's just it. I don't need any complications in my life. I got a family to raise and a living to earn.' She laid her finger on his lips as he opened his mouth to speak. 'No, hear me out. I got plans, Tom. Plans for a better future, and they don't include romance – at least not yet.'

# Chapter Two

Next morning, although dawn was several hours away, Hetty gazed in wonder at the moonlight reflecting on the surface of the snow and turning night into day. Standing beside Jane on the pavement outside the factory gates, she tried to ignore the bitter cold gnawing at her bones and hunger growling in her belly like an angry bulldog. Icicles hung from the factory roof, sparkling under the stars like diamonds around a rich woman's neck. The amorphous mass of darkly clad workers stood out eerily against the pristine whiteness of the snow. Some of the younger children were having snowball fights and their shrieks of laughter echoed off the high walls.

Hetty moved closer to Jane. 'What time did you get home last night?' she demanded in a low voice. 'I didn't hear you come in.'

Jane's soft lips curved in a smug smile. 'Can't say that I remember.'

'It must have been very late. I heard the church clock strike midnight before I fell asleep, and you still hadn't come home.'

'Me and Nat went to the Four Feathers for a drink. Then we had a pie and eel supper.'

'And then what?'

'That's none of your business, I'd say, Hetty.'

'I'm the eldest and Ma told me to look after you and the boys.'

'Well, when I'm Mrs Nathaniel Smith, I'll be the married woman and it will be me telling you what to do. He'll have to marry me now.'

Hetty felt her heart miss a beat and she seized Jane by the arm. 'What have you been and gone and done?'

Jane pulled her left hand from beneath her shawl and waved it in front of Hetty's face. 'We got engaged last night, me and Nat,' she said, her voice throbbing with suppressed excitement. 'Ain't you happy for me, Hetty? Nat wants to marry me as soon as he gets his promotion.'

'And when might that be?'

'I don't know.' Jane pushed her away, pouting. 'And don't look at me like that. You're just jealous because a man has asked me to marry him, and I'm younger than you. I'll be a married woman and you'll be an old maid.'

'It's not that and you know it,' Hetty said in a low voice. 'You – you didn't do nothing silly, did you, Jane?'

One of the almost unrecognisable figures in front of them turned her head to give Jane a long, searching look. 'I'd say she got more than just a cheap glass ring last night.' Mrs Briggs let out a loud cackle of laughter, causing heads to turn.

'Shut up, you old witch,' Jane cried angrily. 'Who asked you to stick your nose into our business, anyway?'

Mrs Briggs nudged the woman at her side. 'Jane Huggins will be needing your services in nine months' time, I'll wager.'

'Ignore them,' Hetty said hastily as Jane's lips began to tremble. 'They're having you on.'

'You don't think she could be right, do you, Hetty?'

'Oh, Jane, you never – you know what. Did you?' Hetty whispered.

Tears sparkled on the tips of Jane's long eyelashes and she nodded her head. 'But you can't get in the family way the first time you do it.'

Mrs Briggs doubled up with laughter. 'That's all you know, ducks.'

Hetty stifled a groan. 'How could you be so silly, Jane? Ain't we got enough trouble without you giving in to the first bloke who buys you a pie and eel supper?'

'He's going to marry me,' Jane whispered. 'Nat give me a ring and said he wanted to do it proper.'

'Oh, he's done you proper, all right, girl.'

Mrs Briggs uttered a derisive snort. She leaned over to Hetty, lowering her voice. 'If the worst comes to the worst, ducks, I know a woman who can fix her up. I shouldn't take too much notice of the ring neither. In my experience, blokes will say and do anything to get what they want.' She tapped the side of her nose. 'Know what I mean?'

Hetty drew herself up to her full height. 'When I want your advice, Mrs Briggs, I'll ask for it.'

'Well, don't say I didn't warn you.'

At that moment the factory gates swung open and the queue moved forward before Hetty had a chance to retaliate.

Later, when they arrived back home, Hetty sent the boys out to buy bread for breakfast, and she gave them enough money to buy a pot of beef dripping as a treat. As soon as they were out of earshot, she turned to Jane. 'How could you, Jane? How could you be so – so silly?'

Jane's lips drooped like those of a sad baby. 'You've ruined it. You and that old bitch, Briggs. Nat loves me, he said so, but you've made me feel dirty.'

Hetty hurried round the table to give Jane a hug. 'No, of course it's not dirty if you love each other, but you mustn't let him have his way with you again, not until you've got that wedding ring on your finger. We can't feed another mouth, even a tiny one.' She managed a wobbly smile. 'Cheer up, love. It might never happen.'

'That's right.' Jane mopped her eyes on her apron and she chuckled. 'I'm a woman of experience now, Hetty. I done something that you haven't done. At least, you didn't, did you? The boys told me that Tom bought you a slap-up fish supper and he saw you home.'

'Certainly not. I got more sense. I'm not going to live in this midden all me life. I got plans for all of us, so you keep your legs crossed next time, my girl.'

'I'll try,' Jane said doubtfully. 'But it won't be easy. To tell you the truth, Hetty, I really enjoyed it – after the first painful bit, that is.'

Hetty held up her hands. 'Ta, but I think I've heard enough.' She turned her head to peer out of the window at the sound of footsteps outside. 'Oh, blimey. It's Clench.' She picked up her purse and moved towards the door. 'I'll deal with him; you keep out of the way.'

'I can't help it if all the blokes fancy me,' Jane said, smirking.

'Clench fancies anything in a skirt. Just keep quiet and I'll get rid of him.' Hetty opened the door and held it, blocking his way as he was about to step inside. 'Good morning, Mr Clench.'

Cyrus Clench rubbed his mittened hands together and his knuckles made a sickly cracking sound. 'I wouldn't call it a good morning exactly, my duck. It's bleeding freezing out here. Ain't you going to invite me in?'

Hetty took a silver sixpence from her purse and held it out to him. 'Here's your money, Mr Clench.'

He snatched the coin and put it in his pocket, eyeing her up and down with a lascivious gleam in his pale eyes. 'Just a few minutes inside to get warm.'

Hetty held on to the door. Clench's gaze seemed to rip right through her shabby garments to the warm flesh beneath her shift. It was all she could do to remain civil. 'I'm sure you've got other business to do, Mr Clench. As we have. The matchboxes won't make themselves, and at twopence farthing a gross, we can't afford to waste time socialising.'

'But I was a good friend of your grandpa's when we worked at Tipton's Bank all those years ago, Miss Hetty. I remember the day he brought you there, sitting on his shoulders as bright as button. Who'd have thought you would grow up to be such a tasty morsel.'

'Please, Mr Clench. This ain't the time or place.' Hetty pushed at the door, but his hand shot out to hold it open. 'Five minutes inside to warm myself, or a big sloppy kiss. I'll settle for either.'

Hetty swallowed the bitter taste that flooded into her mouth at the thought of kissing him. She shook her head, forcing her lips into a smile. It wouldn't do to get on the wrong side of Clench; he could put up the interest if he chose to and they would be in debt to him for the rest of their lives. 'Maybe another day, Mr Clench.'

He put his foot over the sill. 'Just a little kiss, for old times' sake. It's not too much to ask when I'm letting you off paying at a higher rate out of the goodness of me heart.'

He was pushing so hard that Hetty knew she could not hold on much longer, but, just as her strength was giving out, a snowball caught Clench on the side of his head, sending his greasy bowler hat spinning to the ground. Sammy stuck his face through the area railings, poking out his tongue. 'Gotcha, you old bloodsucker!'

Uttering a loud roar, Clench snatched up his hat and raced up the steps after Sammy and Eddie, receiving a snowball in the face as he reached the top. Hetty closed the door and leaned against it laughing out loud. It almost would be worth paying an extra farthing a week for the sight of Clench staggering backwards wiping snow from his eyes and spluttering with rage.

'He might catch them,' Jane said, running to the window and peering out.

'Not a chance. Let's hope he gets some other poor soul to let him fumble her, the dirty old bugger. I swear I'll take the bread knife to him if he tries that one on either of us again.'

'We will do it though, won't we? Pay off what we owe him, and be free of the horrible brute.' Jane slumped down on a stool and began automatically sorting out the materials for making up the matchboxes. In less than a heartbeat she seemed to have forgotten Clench, and she looked up with a dreamy smile transforming her features. 'I'd like a new frock for me wedding, or at least a good second-hand one from the dolly shop. Maybe a straw bonnet too, with pink ribbons and silk flowers under the brim.'

Hetty bit back a sharp retort. Sometimes she thought that Jane lived in a different world from the bleak place that the rest of the people in Autumn Road inhabited. But perhaps it was better to be like that than to face the reality of their grinding poverty. As she moved to take her place at the table beside Jane, Hetty glanced upwards at the sound of footsteps pounding on the floorboards in the room above them. A shower of dust rained down on the table through the gaps in the ceiling plaster as one of the Brinkman children ran across the room upstairs. The family were immigrants from Russia, or maybe it was Germany, Hetty wasn't quite sure. When they first came to Autumn Road they had spoken very little English and any communication with them had to be accompanied by gestures, but Mr Brinkman had found a job on the docks and fourteen-year-old Sonia worked at Bryant and May, as did her younger sister, Anna. As their fluency in the language improved, Hetty had become quite friendly with Mrs Brinkman and the girls, or at least they passed the time of day and shared complaints about the state of the building and the inevitable problems with overflowing privies and vermin. There were several other families who rented rooms in the house: Irish on the top floor, French Huguenot and a Polish family on the first floor; and across the hallway in the back room on the ground floor were two spinster sisters who took in washing and kept cats. The pungent smell of feline urine seeped through the floorboards and their fleas rampaged throughout the building, but at least they kept the rat and mouse population down.

Hetty sighed. Maybe it was a good thing to have dreams like Jane, but she was of a more practical mind, and Jane's slip from grace had made her even more determined to get them out of this miserable place. If she did nothing, the boys would grow up stunted from lack of proper food, and half blind from working long hours in a poor light; they would end up labouring in the gasworks, the carbolic acid factory, or on the docks. She was determined to do something to get them away from here, although as yet she did not quite know what it would be. Hetty rolled up her frayed sleeves and started work.

'I don't believe you heard a word I said,' Jane said, frowning. 'You might pretend to be a bit pleased for me, Hetty.'

'I am, of course, but maybe you shouldn't get your hopes up too high. Nat may not get that promotion for a very long time, and you might change your mind, or he might . . .'

Jane thumped her hand down on the tabletop. 'Don't keep on about Nat letting me down. I know he's had other girlfriends, but it's different with me, he said so. He wouldn't have bought this ring for me if he hadn't been serious, now would he?'

'No, I don't suppose he would.' Hetty rose to her feet with a sigh of relief as Sammy and Eddie came clattering down the area steps. 'Thank God. I was beginning to think that Clench might have caught up with them.'

They burst into the room chattering and giggling, their thin cheeks tinged pink by the cold air and their eyes shining with mischief.

'We led him a real dance,' Sammy said, grinning from ear to ear. 'But he never caught us.'

'He fell over in a pile of horse dung,' Eddie chortled. 'Got it all over his trousers he did and he danced about shaking his fist and calling us names.'

'Fair turned the air blue,' Sammy added, handing the loaf of bread to Hetty.

She cuffed him gently round the ear.

'That's for knowing they was bad words. If I hear either of you repeating them, you really will get your mouths washed out with soap. D'you understand me?' Seeing their crestfallen faces, she relented and gave them both a hug. 'But you was brave boys taking on old Clench. It saved me from having to fight him off, so you shall have bread and dripping for breakfast and dinner. And if you work hard, you shall have bread and jam for tea, and a mug of cocoa.'

Jane snatched the loaf and began slicing it. 'Never mind the lecture, Hetty. I'm starving.'

'Take them jackets off,' Hetty said, eyeing her brothers' wet garments. 'Hang them on the clothes horse by the fire. We don't want you catching cold or lung fever. We've got work to do and we've lost enough time already.'

They munched their slices of bread and dripping while they worked, wiping their greasy fingers on the tablecloth that had once been

Ma's pride and joy, but was now threadbare and frayed at the edges. Hetty kept the fire going, but it only emitted a feeble heat, barely taking the chill off the room. They toiled in the dim light of a single candle until Eddie fell asleep and his dark curly head slumped down on the table, crushing a dozen or so match-boxes. Sammy rubbed his hand across his eyes, complaining that his head ached, and Jane got up stiffly to make a brew of tea. Only Hetty kept working, her deft fingers assembling the boxes at an amazing rate, but, with a sinking feeling in the pit of her stomach, she knew that they were not going to match their best effort of four gross in one day. They would be lucky to get as much as they had yesterday when she returned the finished work to the factory. The rent collector would call in the morning. She had one shilling and sixpence put by in a pot on the mantelshelf for that purpose, but once the rent was paid there would be little left for food, coal and candles. It was a never-ending struggle just to exist.

'Can we have our dinner now, Hetty?' Sammy tugged at her sleeve. 'I'll eat Eddie's if he don't wake up.'

She managed a weary smile. 'You can have yours, ducks. But we'll keep Eddie's for him, poor mite.'

Jane poured boiling water from the kettle

into the teapot. 'When I'm married to Nat we'll have a proper house and three meals a day. You'll see, Hetty. It will be all right when I've married my man.'

'Maybe we could pawn that ring of yours,' Sammy suggested, angling his head with a cheeky grin. 'We could have pie and pease pudding for supper every evening for a week if you did that.'

'Get away with you, you little monkey,' Jane said, cuffing him gently round the ear. 'It'll all be different when I'm Mrs Nat Smith. You'll see.'

That evening, after delivering two gross of matchboxes and collecting just fourpence, having had a halfpenny fine deducted for the materials damaged when Eddie fell asleep over his work, Hetty was in no mood to bandy words. Nat was waiting outside the factory gates and he lifted Jane off her feet, kissing her with undisguised ardour. Hetty marched up to him and tapped him on the shoulder. 'I wants a word with you, Nat Smith.'

He released Jane with a smacking kiss on the lips. 'What can I do for you, love?' With his arm still firmly clasped around Jane's tiny waist, there was a mocking twinkle in his green eyes, one of which wandered in to meet his nose, giving him a slightly comical expression which marred an otherwise hand-some countenance.

Hetty glared at him, unimpressed. 'I'd like a word in private.'

'Don't, Hetty. Please,' Jane pleaded.

'Just a quick word,' Hetty insisted. 'In private.' She moved away to stand beneath the street light, and Nat released Jane with a lingering kiss on the lips before strolling over to join her.

'I can guess what this is all about, but I mean to do the right thing by her, you know.'

The snow on the ground was frozen solid and Hetty could feel it cutting through the thin soles of her boots. She was cold and hungry and in no mood for small talk. 'I know what went on last night and it's got to stop, engagement ring or no engagement ring. Jane is only sixteen and you're her first, as I'm sure you know. Do you understand what I'm saying, Nat Smith?'

He nodded his head and his grin widened. 'My intentions is honourable, Hetty. I'll marry her when I've got me promotion.'

'That's not what I said and you know it,' Hetty hissed, well aware that Jane was straining her ears in an attempt to overhear their conversation. 'You treat her like a lady, or you'll have me to answer to.'

He tipped his cloth cap to the back of his

head. 'I wouldn't treat a duchess no different, Hetty. I swear it.'

Hetty eyed him suspiciously. 'Well, you'd better treat her right. If she's in the family way you'll have to marry her sooner rather than later, or I'll want to know the reason why.'

'Shut up, Hetty.' Jane pushed her aside. 'You're embarrassing both of us with that sort of talk. Leave us alone.'

Nat hooked his arm around her shoulders. 'Come on, love. Let's go to the Four Feathers. It's warmer in there and the company is better.'

With a sinking feeling in her stomach, Hetty watched them disappear into the gloom beyond the street lamp. She knew Jane only too well: affectionate, impulsive and head-strong. Her heart would always rule her head. It was not a combination that would easily withstand the persuasive tongue of a man like Nat Smith. She turned in the direction of home, clutching their hard-earned coppers in her hand. She had just reached Old Ford Road when the sound of heavy footsteps made her glance anxiously over her shoulder. She was not normally nervous, but she was afraid that Clench might have decided to come after her in reprisal for his loss of dignity that morning. Anyone could hide in the deep doorways or down the narrow alleys between the factory buildings. The pavements were as slippery as a skating rink, making running virtually impossible. She could stand it no longer and she stopped, turning round to see who was following her, but she let out a sigh of relief as she recognised Tom's substantial outline against the snow. She waited for him to catch up with her. 'You gave me quite a turn, Tom. I thought it was old Cyrus after me.'

'You shouldn't be out alone at this time of night,' Tom said breathlessly. 'I'll walk you home.'

She did not want to admit it, but it was a relief to have a big man who could use his fists if needs be walking by her side.'Suit yourself,' she said, trying to sound casual.

'Why are you afraid of Clench? What's he done to scare you?'

'Nothing more than the usual. He got a bit too familiar with me this morning. Sammy and Eddie threw snowballs at him and knocked his hat off. Clench went chasing after them but he couldn't catch them.'

Tom gave a throaty chuckle. 'Little monkeys! But it serves the old dog right. It's a crying shame you had to borrow money off him.'

'I know, but it was for Ma's funeral. I couldn't let them treat her like a pauper. It wouldn't have been right.'

Tom took her hand and squeezed it. 'No, it

wouldn't. The poor woman had enough to bear in life. She deserved a bit of dignity in death.'

'I knew you'd understand.' Hetty flashed him a grateful smile and she curled her fingers around his large hand. They walked on in silence until they reached the top of Dye House Lane. She slipped on the ice and would have fallen if Tom had not caught her. He held on to her longer than was strictly necessary, and for a moment Hetty allowed herself to lean against him. His jacket was rough against her cheek and the smell of the gasworks lingered in the coarse woollen fibres. His arms tightened around her but she drew away from him. 'You go on home, Tom. There's no need for you to be late for your supper. I can go the rest of the way on me own.'

'I said I'd walk you home, and walk you home I will.' He linked her hand through his arm. 'Ma will have put something by for my supper.'

Hetty stifled a sigh of relief. Any other man might have taken offence at being pushed away so abruptly, but not Tom. She gave his arm an affectionate squeeze. 'I must make time to visit your mum. She was always good to me when I was a nipper, but what with working such long hours I don't get out much these days.'

'Neither does she, poor soul. Since the accident at the factory she can only walk a couple of yards. She sits indoors all day making match-boxes, but her hands is bad too, so she can't make more than a gross a day. I tell her it's hardly worth her while, but she says it keeps her from fretting, and twopence farthing is better than nuppence. It means she can afford a quarter-ounce of snuff every so often, and that's her main pleasure. It's little enough when all is said and done.'

'Ma used to say that "what can't be cured must be endured", but that doesn't help when someone you love is suffering. I feel for you, Tom, and for your poor mother too.' Hetty glanced up at him and saw his jaw tighten as he struggled with an unspoken emotion. They walked on in silence until they reached Hetty's house.

'I'll wait until you're safely indoors,' Tom said, opening the gate at the top of the area steps.

'Thanks for walking me home. I dunno why, but I'm all jittery and jumpy this evening.'

He leaned over the railings to peer in through the window. 'You'd best go in quick; I think the nippers are fighting.'

'I'll put a stop to that.' Hetty was about to run down the steps, but Tom caught her by the hand.

'Hetty, will you walk out with me on Sunday

afternoon?' He dragged his cap off his head. 'Just to Victoria Park. We could listen to the band and go for a stroll.'

She could hear Sammy and Eddie yelling at each other like a couple of street urchins and she wanted to get to them before they hurt each other, but something in Tom's expression made her hesitate. She couldn't bring herself to disappoint him and she smiled. 'Ta, I'd like that very much.'

'That's splendid. I'll see you the day after tomorrow, then.'

'The day after tomorrow,' Hetty repeated. 'Goodnight, Tom.' She made her way carefully down the snowy steps and a wave of sound hit her as she opened the front door. 'What's going on here?' she demanded. 'Can't I leave you two for five minutes without you turning into wild beasts?'

Despite the blanket of snow covering the grass in Victoria Park, the sky was blue and the pale rays of the sun reflected off the frozen surface of the boating lake. Ducks waddled about on the ice, slithering and slipping as they searched for a patch of open water. Hetty and Tom walked along the path beside the lake, keeping up a brisk pace, while Sammy and Eddie raced about in a high state of excitement, shrieking and pelting each other with snowballs. In spite of the bitterly cold weather, the park was crowded with people out for a breath of fresh air in the only open space for miles around. Most of the trees were bare with their black branches forming intricate lacy patterns against the azure sky, but there were some evergreens and their boughs were drooping beneath the weight of the snow. The band had braved the weather and the strains of a military march filtered across the lake from the bandstand.

'Are you glad you came?' Tom asked, tucking Hetty's hand in the crook of his arm.

She took a deep breath of the ice-cold air, inhaling the resinous scent of the pine trees. The covering of snow seemed to have absorbed the noxious smells from the factories, abattoirs and the gasworks. This white oasis in an otherwise grey world was like a frosted heaven to Hetty and she smiled. 'It's lovely, Tom. I'm so glad I came.'

'Are you? Are you really?' His brown eyes shone with pleasure.

'Of course I am, and the boys are having a fine old time of it. Ouch!' A snowball had caught her between the shoulder blades and Hetty came to a sudden halt, turning on Sammy with a threatening glare. 'You little monster!' She bent down to pick up a handful of snow and pelted it at him with all her might.

It struck him on the head, sending a shower of snowflakes down his neck.

'That'll teach you,' Tom said, chuckling. He made a snowball and threw it, quite gently, Hetty was quick to notice, at Eddie. Soon they were in the middle of the best snowball fight ever, slipping and sliding and laughing until they were all out of breath and had to take a rest.

Hetty stamped her feet and blew on her cold hands. 'I think that's enough of that, boys. I'm freezing to death here.'

Tom hooked his arm around her shoulders. 'Come on then, let's have a nice hot cup of tea, and maybe I could even run to a sticky bun for the nippers.'

Whooping and giggling, Sammy and Eddie ran on ahead to the refreshment rooms where Tom treated them to mugs of cocoa and sticky buns crammed with juicy currants. They sat at a table in the window overlooking the gardens which in summer would be filled with flowers, and drank hot, sweet tea. Quite suddenly, so it seemed to Hetty, the grey-white daylight faded into a mystical dusk and the lamplighter was on his rounds with his long pole, igniting the gas lamps. The whole park was turned from silver to gold. She laid her hand on Tom's as it rested on the tabletop. 'This has been the best time I've ever had.'

'Me too,' Sammy cried, picking up the thick china plate and licking off the crumbs.

'And me,' Eddie echoed, copying his elder brother, his pink tongue giving the plate a good wash.

'Where's your manners, boys?' Hetty said, giving them a stern look.

'Oh, leave them be, Hetty.' Tom leaned back in his chair. 'It's been really spiffing as the toffs say. But it's getting dark and the park will be closing soon. We'd best be on our way.' He put on his cap and stood up, proffering his arm to her. 'Would you care to accompany me, my lady?'

She rose to her feet and laid her hand on his arm. 'Ta ever so, milord.'

Sammy pulled a face. 'Hetty and Tom have gone barmy. Next stop, Colney Hatch.'

Tom laughed. 'Less of your cheek, young Huggins, or I won't bring you here next time me and Hetty go stepping out.'

Hetty wound her shawl around her shoulders, flicking Tom a glance beneath her lashes. 'Who said there was going to be a next time?'

'Well, isn't there? Didn't you just say this was the best time you'd ever had?'

'I did, and I meant it.'

'Then you'll come out with me again?' Tom moved swiftly to open the door for her. 'Will you, Hetty?'

She linked her arm in his as they stepped outside. 'I'll think about it.'

As usual, Sammy and Eddie ran on ahead. Hetty and Tom followed more slowly. She was reluctant to leave this enchanted place, which was so far removed from Autumn Road or the match factory that it was like being in another world. They crossed the bridge over Sir George Duckett's canal, and Tom covered her hand with his as it nestled in the crook of his arm. 'Look at them stars, Hetty,' he said, pointing up at the sky. 'They look so big and bright you could almost reach out and touch them.'

Hetty was so deep in thought that she glanced up at him with a guilty start. 'Sorry, what did you just say?'

'I said the moon is made of green cheese and I can see the man in the moon laughing down at us.'

'You never!'

'No, I didn't, but I might have done for all the attention you was paying me.'

'I was miles away.'

'I could see that. Penny for 'em.'

'I was just thinking that they must make a fortune in that refreshment room.'

Tom chuckled. 'And there was me imagining that you was carried away with romantic thoughts about starlit nights and the moon shining on the snow.'

'I can't afford to have romantic notions. I was working out how much they must have taken on cups of tea, cakes and buns. Places selling food must make a good living. Take Greasy Joe's café, for instance. I bet he makes a small fortune every day.'

'What are you getting at, Hetty?'

'Oh, nothing really. I was just thinking that there must be better ways to earn a living than making up matchboxes, or working in the match factory until you die of phossy jaw.'

'Costs a lot of money to set up in one of them places.'

'Yes,' Hetty said, sighing. 'It's just a daydream, Tom. A silly old dream.'

# Chapter Three

On the following Sunday, Hetty needed no second invitation to accompany Tom to Victoria Park. It was not the frozen boating lake or the band music that attracted her, but the refreshment rooms. Ideas had been buzzing round in her brain like bees in a hive, and the idea of selling food and drink for a living had become more and more appealing. If she could begin in a small way, perhaps selling sand-wiches from a handcart outside one of the main railway stations, she might in time be able to get a proper coffee stall, and then another, which Jane could run with the help of Sammy. Eddie was too small yet, but he would soon grow.

She could hardly wait until the end of their walk, hoping that Tom would suggest a trip to the refreshment rooms. She couldn't very well ask him to take them. If he couldn't afford it he would be embarrassed, and she wouldn't hurt Tom's feelings for the world. But, as luck would have it, a fresh flurry of snow sent everyone scurrying for home or shelter and Tom suggested a cup of tea would be just the ticket. Sammy and Eddie were there almost before the words were out of his mouth. Tom, acting the gentleman, told them all to take a seat, but Hetty insisted on accompanying him to the counter. While they waited to be served, she studied the display of cakes glistening with sugar crystals beneath glass domes, the trays of sticky buns, studded with currants, and tarts filled with strawberry jam or lemon curd. There were ham sandwiches as well as cheese and cucumber, although the bread was curling a bit at the edges and they did not look too appetising. Hetty decided that she would make hers fresh, to order, and she would use butter and not margarine, with slices of the best ham and cheddar cheese.

Turning her attention to the woman behind the counter who was serving the tea and coffee, Hetty made a mental note of the equipment that she might need to start up a stall, in a small way of course. Her mind was so busy with figures that when Tom spoke to her he had to repeat everything twice. Even Sammy and Eddie noticed that her mind was far away, and they began to play up, earning a stern rebuke from Tom that quietened them for a few minutes.

On the way home, Tom took her by the hand. 'You're not still thinking about going into the grub business, are you, Hetty?'

'I'm thinking about it, but that's as far as it goes. We got no money and never likely to have any working from home, what with paying the rent and giving that bloodsucker Clench his dues.'

'I'd help you if I could, but apart from a few pennies a week for meself, everything I earns goes to me mum to help feed us all. What with Phyllis and Phoebe married and moved away, and Marie with her living-in job at the pub, there's only my wages and what Sally earns working at Bryant and May to keep us going.'

Hetty bit her lip, feeling horribly guilty. She had allowed Tom to spend what little money he had on her and the boys, and all because she had this grand idea of starting up her own business.' Oh, Tom. You should have said. There's me letting you treat us to buns and tea when you can't afford it.'

'I ain't complaining, Hetty. It's a pleasure to have your company, and I'm fond of the nippers. I was like them not so long ago, so I know the value of an outing or two.'

They had reached the house in Autumn Road and the snow was falling heavily, settling on the frozen ground and forming drifts against the walls. Hetty could barely see Sammy and Eddie, who were little more than shadowy shapes as they attempted to build a snowman. She called out to them. 'Sammy, Eddie, get indoors now.'

Tom squeezed her fingers. 'Can I come in and have a warm by your fire before I set off for home?'

She glanced down the area steps, but there was no telltale gleam of light in the window to show that Jane was at home. She had almost certainly gone out walking with Nat, and that worried Hetty. Nat was twenty-six, a good ten years older than Jane. He wasn't a love-struck boy who would be satisfied with a kiss and a cuddle. She could only hope that Jane would have a bit of sense this time, and not allow things to go too far.

'Can I, Hetty?' Tom urged when she did not respond immediately.

'All right then, Tom. Just to get warm mind, and no funny business.'

'Cross me heart, but if I stands out here any longer I'll turn into a snowman.'

Hetty giggled at the thought. 'Come on then.' She paused on the top step. 'Sammy, Eddie, if you don't come in right away there'll be no supper for you.'

She negotiated the area steps, treading with care as they were slicked with ice beneath the powdering of snow. Hurrying indoors, she lit a candle and went to riddle the embers in the grate. There was a only a small amount of coal in the bottom of the sack, but she added a couple of lumps anyway, even though she knew that there would be precious little left to light the fire next day.

Tom took off his cap and jacket. 'Is that all the coal you've got?'

'I'll send the boys out for some more in the morning,' Hetty lied, knowing very well that the cocoa tin on the mantelshelf where she kept the housekeeping money was empty. She placed the kettle on the trivet and swung it over the flames. 'It'll take a while.'

'Tell me the truth. Have you got enough money to buy coal?'

'Of course I have. Would I lie to you?' Hetty turned away from him as Sammy and Eddie burst through the door with their boots covered in snow. 'Take them wet boots off, and your jackets too. Come and sit by the fire and get warm.' She turned back to Tom and saw him staring round the room with a furrowed brow. 'What are you staring at? You know how we have to live. It's nothing new.'

'One day I'll get you out of this, Hetty,' he said, taking her by the shoulders and gazing earnestly into her eyes. 'We'll get wed and have a nice house with plenty of food on the table. You won't never have to wear yourself out making matchboxes ever again.'

'I told you, Tom, I got plans and they don't include getting hitched to you, or anyone else for that matter.'

'We was meant for each other, Hetty.'

'Is he going to kiss her?' Eddie asked in a stage whisper.

Sammy dug him in the ribs. 'Shut up, stupid.'

'No, he ain't,' Hetty said, hoping that the dim light hid her blushes.

Tom tightened his grasp on her shoulders. 'Yes, he is.' He drew her to him and kissed her full on the lips.

She pushed him away, covering her hot cheeks with her hands. 'Stop it, you silly thing. In front of the nippers too.'

'Go on,' Sammy cried, clapping his hands. 'Kiss her again.'

Tom held up his hands, grinning. 'I will, but next time she'll want me to do it.'

'Get on with you, you soft thing,' Hetty said, covering her embarrassment with a nervous giggle. 'Stop larking about and I'll make you a cup of tea.'

He shook his head. 'Ta, but I think I'd best make me way home. Will you come to the park with me again next Sunday?'

'I might, but only for a walk. You can't afford to keep treating us.'

'Don't be mean,' Sammy grumbled. 'I look

forward to a sticky bun on a Sunday afternoon.'

Tom chuckled and ruffled his hair. 'We'll see, nipper.' He moved towards the door, pausing with his hand on the latch. 'I shan't see you in the week, Hetty. I've got overtime.'

'All right then, Tom.' Hetty managed a smile, but she could still feel the pressure of his lips on hers. It was not at all unpleasant, but it wouldn't do to lead him on.

She turned away to make the tea.

The bitterly cold January weather gave way to a wet and chilly February. The whole family suffered from coughs and colds, chilblains and low grade fevers, but somehow they managed to continue working. Every Sunday without fail, Tom called for Hetty and the boys, and took them to Victoria Park. Jane always seemed to be out somewhere with Nat, and Hetty suspected that their relationship did not stop at a chaste kiss, but Jane was convinced that she would soon be married and refused to listen to her warnings.

At the end of a particularly wild and blustery March, Hetty's worst fears were realised when she went outside to use the privy in the back yard and found Jane whey-faced and trembling, having been violently sick. 'It must've been the stewed eels I had for supper at the pub,' Jane said, leaning against the brick wall. 'I don't feel too clever, Hetty.'

Hetty laid her hand on Jane's clammy forehead. 'You haven't got a fever. Has this happened before?'

'I been feeling a bit poorly in the mornings, but it passes off after a while.'

Hetty took her by the shoulders and shook her. 'You silly little cow. What did I tell you about going with Nat?'

Jane's amber eyes filled with tears. 'It was something I ate.'

'When did you have your last monthly? Come to think of it, I ain't seen you washing out your rags lately.'

'I dunno. I forget.'

'You're lying, Jane. You know very well what's wrong with you. You've let that bloke have his way with you once too often, my girl.'

'I – I can't be. I mean, he said he'd take care of me.'

'Well, he has. Good and proper. You're in the family way, unless I'm very much mistaken. Now what are we going to do?'

Jane dashed her hand across her eyes. 'Don't speak to me like that. My Nat will do the right thing. He'll marry me now. You just wait and see.'

'He'd better, or I'll want to know the reason why.' Hetty turned on her heel and strode back into the house, passing Mrs Brinkman and four of her younger children in the narrow passageway. 'Morning, Mrs B.'

Mrs Brinkman managed a faint smile and a nod as she shooed the chattering youngsters out into the yard. Hetty leaned her head against the wall and closed her eyes. 'Please, God,' she whispered. 'Make Nat Smith do the right thing by my sister.'

That evening, when all the work was done and their meagre supper cleared from the table, Jane arrived home with a slightly shame-faced Nat. Hetty stood with her arms folded across her chest, waiting for him to speak. He dragged his cloth cap off his head and grinned sheepishly. 'Hello, Hetty.'

Jane guided him to the chair by the fire. 'Sit down, Nat. We'll all sit down, shall we, Hetty? Let's be comfortable and friendly-like.'

Hetty perched on one of the stools at the table, casting a fierce glance at Sammy and Eddie who were lying down on the straw palliasse that they shared in the far corner of the room. They were supposed to be asleep, but she could hear their muffled giggles and whispers. 'Well,' she said coldly. 'What have you got to say for yourself, Nat?'

He reached out to clutch Jane's hand. 'It were a bit of a shock, Hetty, I can't say it wasn't, but I'll do the right thing by my Janey. I swear I will.'

'He will, Hetty.' Jane knelt on the floor by his side, smiling up at Nat with such a loving expression in her eyes that Hetty felt herself weakening.

'So I should hope,' she said. 'Have you set a date yet?'

Nat's smile faded. 'It's a question of finding the money. I'll put in as much overtime as I can, and we'll have to find somewhere to live.'

'We could live here,' Jane said, beaming. 'At first, anyway. Until we gets our proper little house, maybe somewhere nice like near the park, so that we can look out of our window at trees and grass and imagine that we're in the country.'

'Hold on, ducks,' Nat said, patting her hand. 'That sort of place costs money. We might well have to stay here for a while, since my lodgings is for gents only. My landlady wouldn't stretch a point, not even for a charmer like me.'

Jane slapped him on the wrist. 'There'll be less of that talk, Nat. You're going to be a married man soon.'

Hetty swallowed hard. They seemed to both inhabit the same dream world. If push came to shove, she supposed that Jane and Nat could have the bed that Ma and Pa had shared, and she could revert to sleeping on the floor. Plenty lived in even worse conditions, but it would be far from ideal. 'We'll just have to work something out,' she said slowly. 'As far as I can tell, the baby will come some time in September. That gives you a bit of time to find suitable lodgings and to save up some money. Until then, we'll just have to manage the best way we can.'

'You're a sport, Hetty,' Nat said, smiling. 'A real diamond.' He rose to his feet. 'I'd best be off, ducks. I'll have an early night and see the foreman first thing in the morning about getting more overtime.'

'You're going back to your lodgings already?' Jane sat back on her haunches, staring up at him in disbelief. 'I thought we was going to the pub.'

Nat ruffled her hair. 'We got to save money, Janey. From now on we'll have to make do with walks in the park on a Sunday like Tom and Hetty.' He bent down to drop a kiss on her forehead, and, with a cheery wave to Hetty, he left them staring after him.

Jane turned a tragic face to Hetty. 'He promised me a pie and pease pudding supper.' Her lips trembled and she burst into tears, rocking backwards and forwards with her arms wrapped around her thin body. 'It weren't meant to be like this, Hetty.'

Hetty shook her head, biting back a sharp

retort. It was no use saying I told you so; the damage was done. She got up to put the kettle on the hook over what was left of the fire. 'There's no use crying, Jane. We've just got to make the best of it.'

'But I'm hungry,' Jane wailed. 'I got to eat for two now.'

Hetty went to the dresser and peeled the brown paper off what was left of the loaf. She had been saving the stale crust for breakfast, but Jane needed some food now. She cut a thin slice and scraped the bottom of the dripping pot, spreading the dark brown meaty jelly onto the bread. 'Here, eat this and you'll feel better.'

Jane wiped her eyes on her sleeve and she took the slice of bread, cramming it into her mouth and barely chewing it before she swallowed. 'Is it always going to be like this, Hetty?'

'Here, that's not fair,' Sammy cried, snapping upright in his bed. 'Why has Jane got something to eat and we ain't?'

'I'm hungry too,' Eddie whimpered. 'She's eating our breakfast, Hetty.'

'Be quiet, the pair of you.' Hetty turned on them, covering her distress with an angry frown. 'You've had your supper and you should be asleep.'

They subsided instantly, but she could hear them grumbling as they huddled together for warmth. She glanced at Jane who was licking her fingers one by one and looking longingly at the remains of the crust. Hetty's stomach rumbled; she was hungry too, but that bit of bread would be the boys' breakfast. She and Jane would have to go without until dinner time. It was nothing unusual.

Later that evening when she lay on the lumpy, flock-filled mattress that her parents had once shared, so many years ago it seemed, Hetty was exhausted but she could not sleep. She could hear Jane's soft, rhythmic breathing by her side and the occasional snuffling sound from either Sammy or Eddie as they turned over in their sleep. Otherwise everything was quiet in the house. There was no sound from the room above, where in daytime the Brinkmans seemed to be constantly on the move, their combined footsteps resonating like an army on the march, or a troupe of clog dancers. In the early hours of the morning, Hetty had made her decision. She prayed that Ma would forgive her for going back on her promise, but she had made up her mind. They needed money desperately and they needed it now. There was only one way she could earn more than sixpence a day and that was to work in the match factory where she could almost double their combined income. It would only be a temporary measure until Jane was settled with Nat and the boys were big enough to go out and earn their own living. Just a temporary measure.

Next morning, when she told Jane what she planned to do, Hetty was taken aback by her sister's angry reaction. White-faced and trembling, Jane stamped her foot. 'If you do that, you're no sister of mine. What would Ma say? She'll be turning over in her grave if you break your promise to her, Hetty. You can't work in that place. I won't let you.'

Sammy and Eddie, awakened from their sleep and frightened by the sound of raised voices, flung themselves at Hetty, clinging to her and sobbing, even though they had no idea what the argument was about. In the end, Hetty gave in. She sank down onto the chair by the empty grate, holding her head in her hands. 'All right, I won't do it, Jane. Although, as far as I can see, it's the only way we can keep clear of the workhouse.'

'No!' Jane stormed, her eyes snapping angrily. 'My Nat will look after us all. Haven't I told you that again and again? He'll find us rooms in a better house, away from this slum. We'll have a fresh start and the boys can go to school, like they should. We'll be a proper family again. Don't you ever let me hear you talking about working in that blooming factory. D'you hear me, Hetty Huggins?'

Faced with this kind of resistance, Hetty

reluctantly gave up the idea, at least for the time being. She knew that she must not upset Jane in her delicate condition and they must continue the struggle from day to day.

The passing of spring into summer hardly made any difference in the brick and concrete canyons of Bow. The River Lea still oozed with foul-smelling muck and effluent from the factories, and the stench from the tannery hung in a miasma over the rooftops. The daily routine at the match factory was unchanging, but even the outworkers sensed a spirit of unrest amongst the twelve hundred or so women and girls who were employed by Bryant and May. Mutterings against the unhealthy working conditions, the poor pay and the fines imposed on the workers for the slightest infringement of the strict rules rumbled like an approaching storm.

On a fine June morning when the sun managed to force its way through the pall of smoke and industrial pollution, Mrs Briggs was in one of her rare conversational moods as they waited outside the factory gates. She told Hetty that the current unrest was coming to a head, and she wouldn't be at all surprised if they didn't just down tools and go out on strike. The matchgirls had done just this two years previously, but had been forced back to work by poverty and lack of support from outside. Now, she whispered, there was a lady, a Mrs Annie Besant, who kept coming to the factory and asking a lot of questions. The women were only too pleased to tell someone about their wretched working conditions, and the fines for talking, dropping matches or going to the privy without first asking permission. The lady was, they said, shocked to the core by their revelations and she was encouraging the women to take action against their employers. Mrs Besant was a good 'un, and she was on their side.

Hetty listened, but although she knew what Mrs Briggs said was true, she was not particularly interested in factory politics. She had enough on her hands coping at home. Jane was now a good five months gone, growing visibly larger and always hungry. She tired easily, and, although she still put in a twelve hour day, she often had to stop and rest, or simply get up from the table and walk about to ease her aching back. They did not see much of Nat who was working hard, putting in as much overtime as he could, saving his money. He was looking for suitable lodgings and when he had found them, Jane said, smiling proudly, they would be married. It shouldn't be long now.

Every Sunday afternoon without fail, Tom

came to call for Hetty and the boys. The walk in Victoria Park was now an established routine. It was the highlight of Hetty's week, and she sometimes thought that it was the only thing that had kept her going. Now that summer was well and truly here, the park was burgeoning with flowers and fresh green foliage. The scent of roses filled the air and the sound of birdsong was even sweeter than the music played by the band. Sometimes, if he had an extra penny in his pocket, Tom hired a rowing boat and took them on the lake and this day was no exception. Hetty sat back and trailed her fingers in the cool water while she watched the mallards and moorhens dabbling amongst the reeds. Some of them were diving beneath the surface with their tails and feet waggling in the air. Sammy and Eddie hooted with laughter, which in turn made Tom grin as he worked the oars. Hetty tried not to stare, but she couldn't help noticing and secretly admiring the way his muscles rippled with each powerful stroke. His shirtsleeves were rolled up to his elbows, and his bare forearms moved with a sinuous strength as his workmanlike fingers curled round the wooden oars. Those large hands, she thought dreamily, could stoke a boiler at the gasworks with coal in the making of coke, lay a man out flat on his back in a fight, or be so gentle that his touch was as soft as a moth's wings.

She closed her eyes, turning her face up towards the sun. All her problems seemed far away at this moment, until a loud splash and the sound of Sammy screaming brought her back to reality with a jerk. She sat bolt upright, opening her eyes in time to see Tom diving over the side of the boat after Eddie, who had tumbled overboard. 'Eddie!' Hetty leaned forward, catching hold of the seat of Sammy's pants as he hung over the side shrieking his brother's name. 'Don't, Sammy. You'll fall in too.'

Encouraging shouts were coming from onlookers on the bank, and a man ripped a lifebelt from its stand and tossed it into the water. Hetty covered her mouth with her hands. She could see Tom's head and his powerful arms slicing through the water, but Eddie had disappeared beneath the surface. She was sick with fear as she leaned over the side of the boat, peering into the lake, but the green depths were murky and filled with gently swaying water weeds. She held her breath as Tom surfaced, but he had not found Eddie. He shook the water from his eyes, gulped in air and dived again. Sammy threw himself into Hetty's arms, sobbing against her shoulder. She prayed silently to God to save her little brother. There was a deathly hush as those on the bank watched and waited. The surface of the lake had smoothed to a glassy sheet and the boat drifted aimlessly. The world had stopped turning. She was certain that both Tom and Eddie had been sucked down into the cold depths. She had a horrible vision of them both trapped by the long tendrils of waterweed, their faces upturned towards the light as they slowly drowned.

Then, so suddenly that everyone on the lakeside uttered a loud cheer, Tom's head broke the surface and he had Eddie in his arms. He reached for the lifebelt and the man on the bank, who had steadfastly held on to the rope, dragged them slowly towards dry land.

Hetty buried her face in Sammy's soft brown hair and held him close. Sometimes she lost her temper with her small brothers, but at that moment she realised just how much she loved them. 'Thank you, God,' she murmured. 'I swear I'll never shout at either of you, ever again.'

Sammy drew away from her, wiping his eyes on his sleeve and grinning. 'Is that a promise, Hetty?'

She hugged him, laughing from sheer relief. 'It is, but don't expect me to keep it.' She kissed him on the cheek and he pulled away, scrubbing at his face.

'Eddie will be all right, won't he, Hetty?"

She had been so relieved to see Eddie saved from the water that it had not occurred to her that his life might still hang in the balance. The boat had drifted a good way from the bank, but she could just see Tom kneeling over Eddie's inert figure. The crowd had gathered around them, watching in silence as Tom pumped Eddie's small arms up and down. 'Breathe, Eddie,' Hetty shouted. 'For God's sake, breathe.'

Afterwards, she was never certain whether she had actually heard Eddie take that crucial gasp of air, and the coughing and spluttering that followed, but she did hear the onlookers' sigh of relief and the sound of their clapping came to her clearly across the water. 'He's going to be all right, Sammy.' Laughing and crying at the same time, Hetty gave Sammy a hug, but he wriggled free from her grasp, pointing to the oars as they hung uselessly in the rowlocks.

'Can you row, Hetty?'

She slithered over to the seat that Tom had so recently vacated and gingerly took an oar in each hand. 'I dunno if I can, Sammy. But I'll have a bloody good go.'

Sammy's eyes widened. 'You swore, Hetty. You said a bad word.'

'I know I bloody well did,' Hetty said,

heaving on the oars. 'But don't you let me hear you using bad language, my boy. You do as I say, not as I do.'

Sammy chuckled. 'That's what Ma used to say. I remember that.'

Hetty managed a smile, although she had just missed her stroke and almost toppled backwards in her seat. She tried again. 'This might take a while, Sammy.'It was not as easy as Tom had made it look. After just a few minutes, Hetty's arms were aching and her back was in torment as she tried to synchronise her efforts. She realised that they were heading in completely the wrong direction and she attempted to turn the boat, very nearly capsizing them. Then, quite suddenly, and as if by magic, the boat started to move all by itself. The oars barely touched the water and yet they were moving towards the bank and the appreciative crowd of bystanders.

Sammy leaned over the prow to stare into the water. 'Hetty, it's Tom. He's towing us.'

Raising herself on her hands, Hetty could just see the top of Tom's head as he gripped the painter in his teeth and swam towards the shore. In a matter of minutes they were safe on dry land. Eddie was being comforted by a motherly lady. 'He had a lucky escape,' the woman said, smiling as Hetty flung her arms around her little brother. 'I saw him go toppling into the water and I thought he was a goner. But that man of yours is a real hero, missis. I'd give him a big kiss if I was you.' She shuffled off after her husband and four shabbily dressed children.

Tom had taken off his shirt and he was attempting to dry his hair with it, even though the garment was sodden. 'Well then, Hetty. What are you waiting for?'

The few people who were still standing round staring at them murmured encouragement. 'Go on, girl,' said a costermonger in his pearl-studded Sunday finery. 'Give him a smacker. He deserves it.'

Hetty felt herself blushing and she shook her head.

'Go on. Don't be mean,' shouted the coster's wife. 'If I wasn't a happily married woman, I'd kiss him meself.'

Glancing at Tom beneath her lashes, Hetty felt her heart give a little squeeze as she saw his muscular torso, glistening with droplets of water. She had never seen him bare-chested and she was suddenly ashamed of the feelings it aroused in her. She was about to turn away, but Tom seized her in his arms and kissed her soundly on the lips, much to the approval of those watching. Hetty placed her hands flat on his chest in an attempt to push him away, but the touch of his warm skin slicked with water was enough to take her breath away. She could feel his heart pounding away like a galloping horse, or was it her own blood hammering in her ears that she could feel through her fingertips? She did not know, but somehow she managed to wriggle free from his grasp. Covering her confusion, she turned to Eddie and swept him up in her arms. 'You bad, bad boy. Don't never do nothing like that again. D'you hear me?' She burst into tears.

Tom put his arm around her shoulders, leading her away from their audience. 'Come on, boys,' he called over his shoulder. 'Let's get your sister home. She's had a nasty shock, and you, young Eddie, need a change of clothes.'

'But I ain't got no change of clothes,' Eddie whimpered.

Tom chuckled. 'Well, at least those ones have had a wash. Come on, Hetty, let's get you home for a nice hot cup of tea. We can't very well go to the refreshment rooms looking like ship-wrecked mariners, now can we?'

'N-no,' Hetty said, sniffing. 'But I'm all right, Tom. Really I am, and I don't know how to thank you for what you done.'

Tom gave her shoulders a squeeze. 'Another kiss wouldn't go amiss.'

'You've got a cheek, Tom Crewe.'

'Come on, just a little kiss,' Tom said, stopping in the middle of the pathway and twisting her round to face him. His dark eyes twinkled mischievously. 'A little kiss for the hero.'

Hetty met his gaze and once again her heart thudded erratically inside her breast. She realised, in spite of the fact that Sammy was tugging at her sleeve and Eddie was complaining that he was cold, that she actually wanted Tom to kiss her again. The touch of his lips had lit a flame within her and she wanted more. She tossed her head. 'Certainly not. You're making a show of us, Tom.' Her pulses were racing and she could not look him in the eye. She walked off without giving him a chance to reply.

Seemingly no worse for his ordeal, Eddie ran on ahead with Sammy close on his heels. Hetty could hear Tom striding along behind, but she neither slowed down nor turned her head to look at him. She had no time for romance. If you let a bloke get close to you, the outcome was inevitable. Wasn't Jane a fine example of that?

Tom made no attempt to catch her up, and for a moment Hetty forgot all about him as she stopped behind a crowd that had gathered around a woman who was speaking from a soapbox. Hetty had heard the name of Bryant and May mentioned and she was suddenly curious. Could this be Mrs Besant, the woman who had been interrogating the girls at the match factory? Tom caught up with her but she brushed off his suggestion that they ought to head off home. 'Leave me be, Tom. You go on home and get dry. I'll only be a short while.'

There was something compulsive about Annie Besant's oratory, and Hetty listened intently to her scathing remarks about unscrupulous employers who put profit before the welfare of their workers. When she had finished speaking, Mrs Besant held up a newspaper. 'If you wish to learn more about the plight of the matchgirls and their appalling treatment by their bosses, then read my article in *The Link*, which will appear next Saturday, the twenty-third of June. In it you will find all the shocking details of the way in which these women, girls and even children have been exploited.'

'Come on home, Hetty,' Tom said softly. 'Let her talk, but don't get involved. We can't afford to listen to well-heeled, middle-class ladies like her. It's all right to have principles if you've got food on the table and the rent money in your pocket. She ain't got nothing to lose. We have.'

Hetty had almost forgotten his presence, but she knew that he was speaking sense. It was all very well for Mrs Besant to spout off about justice and moral rights, but she wasn't dirt poor like the workers in the factory. She turned to him with a reluctant smile and linked her hand through his arm. 'You're right, of course, and you'd best get home and into some dry clothes. We can't have our hero catching pneumonia or the like. What would I do without you, Tom?' She was rewarded by a broad grin, and she reached up to kiss him on the cheek. 'You are a hero. I'll never forget what you done today. Eddie would have drowned if you hadn't gone in after him, and me and Sammy would have been stuck in the middle of the boating pond until kingdom come.'

Tom fingered a strand of her hair which had escaped from the confines of a bun at the nape of her neck. 'You are beautiful, Hetty, and I love you.'

'Don't talk soft.'

'But you do like me, don't you, Hetty?'

'Of course I do, silly. But I ain't thinking about love and all that, not for a very long time.'

'I'll wait, Hetty. I'll wait until we're old and grey if that's what it takes.'

'You won't live to be old and grey unless you get out of them wet duds and into some dry ones. Come on, let's go home.'

On the following Saturday, Mrs Besant's article appeared in the newspaper, attacking Bryant and May for what she dubbed 'White Slavery in London'. Mrs Besant and a gentleman, who introduced himself as Mr Herbert Burrows, picketed the gates of the factory, distributing the article to the women. On Thursday, 5 July, the workers downed tools and went on strike.

'How on earth will we manage?' Jane demanded when Hetty came home on Friday to tell her that there was no work for them today or in the foreseeable future. 'How will we live without any money coming in?'

'I dunno, Jane, and that's the truth.' Hetty slumped down at the bare kitchen table. 'We can pay old Clench and I've got the one and six for the rent, but that leaves us with about threepence for everything else.'

Jane sank down on a stool, clutching her belly. 'My baby, my baby. It will die if I don't eat. We'll both die.'

'Nonsense,' Hetty said with more conviction than she was feeling. 'We'll manage, Jane. Mrs Besant said she would try to raise money for us all. She's organised a meeting on Mile End Waste for Sunday, where she'll champion our cause. You won't die, neither will your baby.'

Sammy tugged at Hetty's apron strings. 'If there's no work today, Hetty, can we go out and play?'

Hetty smiled and nodded. 'Go on then, but

keep out of trouble. Don't get in no fights with them Dye House Lane kids.' She watched them racing up the area steps, shouting and laughing as if nothing mattered. 'They're the lucky ones, Jane. They don't have to worry.'

'Neither do I,' Jane said with a wobbly smile. 'My Nat will look after us all. He'll just have to cough up some of that money he's been saving for our wedding and the new lodgings. If the worst comes to the worst, we can all live here.'

'Yes,' Hetty said doubtfully. 'Of course.' She was about to light the fire so that they could have a cup of tea, when she heard heavy footfalls coming down the steps to the front door. Someone hammered on it, calling out urgently. She looked at Jane and they exchanged worried glances. 'That doesn't sound like Clench,' Hetty said, hurrying to open the door.

It was not the tallyman who stood outside, but a stranger whose face and clothes were blackened with soot. He dragged his cap off his head and his knuckles showed white as he clutched it tightly in his hands. 'Are you Mrs Smith, ma'am?'

'N-no, but my sister is engaged to Nat Smith.' The bleak expression in his eyes frightened her, and Hetty stepped outside, closing the door behind her. 'What is it, man? Tell me.'

'It's bad news, miss. Nat, well – there ain't no easy way to tell you – I'm afraid there's been an accident at the gasworks, miss. He's a goner.'

# Chapter Four

After her initial outpouring of grief, Jane lapsed into a state of prostration, which worried Hetty far more than weeping or hysteria. Jane took to her bed and lay there, staring at the cracks in the ceiling with unseeing eyes. Nothing seemed to rouse her from her semi-comatose state. She would neither eat nor speak, but if Hetty lifted her head she would sip water from a cup like an obedient child. Then she would simply lie back, mute and unreachable in some silent nightmare of her own. Sammy and Eddie moved about the room like two small ghosts, speaking in whispers and tiptoeing around, as if terrified of awakening Jane and hearing those heart-rending sobs that had sounded more like an animal bellowing in pain than the grief of a human being.

Although Hetty had not previously known much about Nat's past, she now learned from Tom that Nat had been abandoned as a baby and raised in an orphanage. He had no known relatives and few friends. Tom made the funeral arrangements, but Hetty decided that Jane was in no fit state to be told, and on the day of the interment in the City of London and Tower Hamlets Cemetery, she gave Jane just enough laudanum to make her sleep. They had used Nat's meagre savings to pay the funeral expenses, but Hetty had insisted that this was only right and proper. At first, Tom said that the money ought, by rights, to go to Jane, but Hetty knew that when Jane came to herself she would agree that her beloved Nat should have had a decent Christian burial. She would not want his poor remains to have been flung in a pauper's grave where they might be taken by body snatchers, and sold to a teaching hospital for the benefit of medical students. If Nat was to go to heaven he needed to be whole, or he would not be admitted through the pearly gates, of that Hetty was certain. She was not an ardent churchgoer; for one thing she had no Sunday best clothes, and she knew that the upper-class worthies would look down on her shabby, threadbare garments, as if she were not fit to walk into God's house. Ma had always insisted that they attend Sunday school, and Hetty tried to live up to her mother's strict moral code. She had no doubt that Ma had gone straight to heaven. She had been a good and kind woman, who did not deserve her agonising disease and premature death, but

Hetty comforted herself with the belief that Ma was up there now, amongst the angels.

The funeral was the simplest and cheapest to be had. Nat was buried in a communal grave with only Tom, Hetty, Sammy and Eddie as mourners, and nothing to mark his grave, not even a simple wooden cross. Except for the child that was growing in Jane's womb, Nathanial Smith might never have existed at all, Hetty thought sadly as the vicar dropped a handful of earth onto the cheap pine coffin. She made him a silent promise that she would do everything in her power to look after his son or daughter, and to make certain that he or she had a better life than their poor, dead father.

Tom touched her on the arm. 'Are you all right, Hetty?'

She swallowed hard and just managed a weak smile. 'I was thinking of Jane and her baby.'

He slipped his arm around her waist. 'I know, girl. Best get on home then.'

She nodded her head, unable to speak for fear of bursting into tears. Sammy took her hand in silent sympathy. Eddie was also unusually quiet as they left the cemetery and walked slowly back towards Autumn Road, but, after a while, he began to snivel and that made his nose run as if he had a cold. He tugged at Hetty's arm, pointing mutely to his runny nose.

'Wipe it on your sleeve, Eddie,' Hetty said gently. 'One day, we'll be rich enough to have pocket handkerchiefs, just like the toffs. But until then, ducks, I'm afraid your sleeve will have to do.'

This made both Eddie and Sammy giggle, and Tom gave her an encouraging smile. 'Chin up, boys,' he said cheerfully. 'I reckon I got enough money to buy you a hot tater if we can find a bloke selling them this early in the season.'

Hetty's curiosity was instantly aroused. 'Is there a season to selling murphies?'

'There certainly is. I had a mate whose patch was outside Old Ford Station. Unfortunately he croaked last year from consumption, but he said he could make twelve to fifteen bob a week if he was lucky.'

'Did he now?' Hetty stored this bit of information in her head. With the strike still ongoing and no money coming in, she was going to have to do something drastic in the very near future, or they would end up in the workhouse. The mere thought of it sent a shudder down her spine. She was only too aware that the threat of that particular institution was a dark phantom which haunted the lives of the poor, filling their hearts with dread. To enter its grim portals was to abandon hope and endure a living hell.

'What are you thinking, Hetty,' Tom demanded. 'I seen that faraway look on your face before. What's going through your mind?'

'I've got to get money from somewhere, Tom, or else we'll end up on the streets. As it is I ain't got the rent for this week, or the sixpence for that old bloodsucker, Clench. I suppose I could borrow some more off him, but he'd shove the interest rate up sky high, and I'd never manage to pay him off.'

'Perhaps I can help.' Tom pushed his cap to the back of his head as he always did when he was thinking. That was one of the little habits that Hetty had noticed about him. Sometimes, if he was really stumped, he would take it right off, scratch his head and then put his cap back in place, as if he had gained inspiration by that simple act.

She squeezed his arm. 'Ta, but I know how you're placed at home. With your poor mum crippled and having lost her little bit of extra income from the match factory, you can't afford to give us money, and I wouldn't take it anyway. I got some pride left.'

'You could take it if we was married, Hetty. Just say the word and I'll marry you tomorrow. You could all move into our place in Dye House Lane. It ain't a palace, God knows, but we got two rooms. We'd manage somehow.'

'Marry him, Hetty,' Sammy urged. 'Then us can have hot baked taters every day, and trips to the park every Sunday.'

'And ham sandwiches,' Eddie chipped in, wiping his nose on his sleeve yet again. 'I could eat a ham sandwich right now, as well as a tater.'

Hetty laughed in spite of herself. 'Now see what you've done, Tom.'

'Is that a yes or a no?' Tom chuckled, but there was a serious question in his eyes. 'Will you, Hetty? Will you marry me?'

'No, Tom. Don't think I ain't grateful for the offer, and I am very fond of you, so don't feel bad about it, but it wouldn't do, it really wouldn't.' Hetty quickened her pace. 'Come on, I must get back to Jane and see if she's all right. What with the baby and everything, I fear for her, I really do.'

'Why won't you marry me, Hetty? I know you like me, and I love you.'

They had reached the end of Dye House Lane and Hetty stopped. She caressed Tom's cheek with her fingertips. 'I know you do. And, like I said, I'm very fond of you, but for one thing we got no money, and another thing, I couldn't lumber you with me family. There's Jane with a baby on the way, and these scamps, who need proper schooling to say nothing of food and clothes. It just wouldn't be fair on you.'

He grasped her hands in his, looking deeply into her eyes. 'Let me be the judge of that, girl. I just want to take care of you, and if that means taking on your family, then that's what I will do.'

Sammy and Eddie shuffled their feet and Tom put his hand in his pocket and brought out two halfpennies. He pressed the coins into their hands. 'Here, go and buy yourself a murphy from the baked potato man outside the station.' He took out another halfpenny. 'And get one for Hetty too. If she gets any thinner, she'll fade away.' He watched them running off with a smile on his lips. 'I'd be proud to bring them two up as me own, Hetty. And that's a fact.'

'Don't say no more, Tom. It might be fine for a while, but soon you'd be worn down with hard work and the problems of looking after a family that weren't your own. It would come between us in the end. It can't be. I'm sorry, but that's how it is at present. I've got to sort this out for meself.'

She was about to walk away, but he caught her by the hand. 'I ain't quite sure, but I think somewhere in there you might have meant that you care for me just a tiny bit.'

'I do, of course I do. And if I was to marry, I can't think of a better bloke to hitch meself to, but not at this present time. I'm sorry.' She turned away from him and broke into a run towards Autumn Road.

To her relief, Hetty found that Jane was still fast asleep. The laudanum had done the trick and rest was what Jane needed most, but Hetty knew she must look to the future. There would be none unless she acted very quickly indeed. She took the tin from the mantelshelf and tipped the coins out onto the tabletop. She had used one of the pennies to purchase a small bottle of laudanum, and that left fourpence three farthings, which would not go very far at all. Up above her, she could hear the Brinkmans moving round their cramped living space, but they seemed less lively than usual. She knew that the strike at the match factory must have affected the family badly. Sonia had worked there for some time and young Anna had started at Bryant and May just days before the strike began. Without their wages the family would have to survive on their father's meagre income. Hetty sighed. The strike might be justified, but there were many who would go under for supporting it. She was not going to be one of them.

Jane stirred and Hetty went over to her. 'I'm here, Jane.'

'I had such a lovely dream. I was walking up the aisle with Nat and I had on a new dress and a bonnet with pink ribbons. I had new shoes too and they didn't pinch one bit.' Jane's face contorted with pain. 'But it was just a dream. He's gone, hasn't he, Hetty? My Nat will never marry me, because he's . . .'

Hetty grasped her hand, holding it to her cheek. 'You must be brave, love. For the baby's sake, you got to go on.'

'I can't,' Jane whispered. 'We was to be married. I was going to have a nice house overlooking the park with a bit of a garden for the nipper to play in. But, Hetty, I can't raise a baby on me own. And now there's no work, we can't even feed ourselves. We're all going to die, just like my Nat.'

'Now you just listen to me, Jane Huggins. I don't want to hear none of that talk. You're going to get up from that bed, and you're going to have something to eat. You're weak with hunger, that's part of your trouble. We're going to be all right. I'm going to see to that.'

Jane raised herself on her elbow. 'But how? If we can't work, we can't earn any money.'

'That's true, and I ain't pretending things is going to be easy, Jane. But you and me is the eldest and we've got to keep our spirits up for Sammy, Eddie and your nipper when it comes. As I see it, there's only one thing we can do.

We got to pack up and leave here, afore the landlord has us thrown out on the streets for not paying the rent, or old Clench has me for his breakfast when I can't pay him his tanner on Friday.'

Jane sat up and the wooden pallet creaked with her movement. 'Where shall we go?'

'We'll have to beard the lion in his den, or should I say lioness?' In spite of everything, Hetty managed a wobbly smile.

'No, not Granny Huggins!'

'Can you think of anything better?'

Jane shook her head. 'Maybe the workhouse would be easier to take than asking Granny Huggins for help. She hates us, you know she does.'

'Hate us or not, she's our father's mother and she's family. She won't turn us away in our hour of need, not if I've got anything to do with it.'

Jane's eyes widened with horror. 'But you know what she's like, Hetty. What will she say when she knows I'm in the family way and unmarried?'

Hetty rose to her feet. 'We won't tell her. We'll buy a brass ring from the pawnshop and I'll tell her that you and Nat were married last Christmas. From now on, Jane Smith, you are a respectable widow.'

'My Nat will be turning in his grave,' Jane

said sadly. 'And your Tom won't think much to our moving away neither.'

Hetty sighed. She would have to go round to Dye House Lane and make things right with Tom. She just hoped that he would understand.

Granny Huggins' house in Totty Street was in the better part of Bethnal Green, as close to Victoria Park as the late Grandpa Huggins could afford on a bank clerk's wages. Situated in the middle of a row of terraced, red-brick houses, the two-storey dwelling boasted sash windows and a fanlight above the front door. There was no front garden, but Hetty could remember a back yard with a stunted, purple-flowering tree growing out of the wall, and a wooden gate which led into the busy thoroughfare of Grove Road. It was not a large house, although it had seemed enormous to Hetty on the odd occasions when Pa had taken her there as a child, but it was a miniature palace compared to their home in Autumn Road. She dropped the burden she had been carrying onto the pavement. Their few possessions had gone into two sacks with room to spare. Jane put hers down with a sigh of relief. 'Me back's breaking, Hetty. Thank the Lord it weren't no further. I can't go another step.'

Sammy and Eddie had their bedding rolled

up and strapped to their backs so that they looked like a couple of small snails. They shrugged off their loads, looking about them wide-eyed with curiosity. 'Is this it, then, Hetty?' Sammy asked breathlessly. 'Does our granny really live here all alone?'

Hetty ruffled his dark curls, smiling. 'She does, Sammy. At least she did. I hope the old girl hasn't moved house or gone and kicked the bucket.'

'Don't say that,' Jane said tiredly. 'Not even as a joke. She was sprightly enough at Pa's funeral.'

Hetty lifted the iron doorknocker, and then hesitated, clutching it in her fingers. 'That was six years ago, just before Eddie was born. Surely someone would have let us know if she had died?'

'There's only one way to find out,' Jane said, hopping up and down. 'Knock on the door, Hetty. I don't care who answers it, but I need to relieve meself something shocking. I'll wet me knickers if they don't come quick.'

Hetty knocked on the door. They waited, listening for the sound of footsteps. The narrow street was empty of people and traffic, although a few net curtains had been fluttered by unseen hands as they had walked past. The inhabitants might be invisible, but Hetty could hear sounds of activity coming from the Great

Eastern Railway depot on the other side of the Regent's Canal, which was just a street away. Shouts from men working on the canal banks floated over the chimney tops, and the rumble of cartwheels and the clip-clopping of horses' hooves came from the heavy traffic in Grove Road. Hetty crossed her fingers, praying that they had at least one relation still living, that is, if you could call Granny Huggins a relation. After all, hadn't she virtually disowned her one and only son for marrying beneath him? What sort of person would do a thing like that? The door opened and a tall, gaunt woman stood on the threshold, staring at them with a hostile scowl. 'What d'you want?' she demanded. 'No hawkers or beggars.' She was about to slam the door in their faces when Hetty put her foot over the doorsill.

'Granny, it's me, Hetty.'

Very slowly, Granny Huggins opened the door. Her eyes were hard as chips of granite as she looked Hetty up and down. 'Hetty who?'

Hetty's temper flared, but somehow she managed to keep her voice down. 'I know we haven't seen each other for six years, Granny. Surely you remember me and Jane? Sammy was little more than a baby when our Pa died, and Eddie wasn't yet born, but we are your grandchildren, and we – we . . .' Hetty could not continue in the face of such open hostility. She bit her lip, fighting back tears of exhaustion and disappointment.

Jane pushed Hetty aside. 'You know very well who we are, Granny Huggins. Are you going to keep us standing on the pavement all day? Because if you do, then I'll just have to piddle right here and now.'

'I see you are as common and vulgar as that woman my son was foolish enough to marry, and, by the looks of you, you're no better than you should be. Get off my doorstep, the lot of you. I said my piece twenty years ago to your father, and I haven't changed my opinion. Now go before I call a copper and have you arrested for begging.'

Hetty raised her chin and looked her grandmother in the eye. 'There's no call for that sort of talk. We know where we're not wanted, and I'm only sorry that my little brothers had to hear you speak to us so. As for Jane, well, I'll have you know, Granny Huggins, that she's a respectable widow.'

Sammy, who had been silently taking all this in, suddenly erupted into an angry frenzy and he head-butted his grandmother, so that her knees buckled and she staggered backwards into the narrow passage. 'I hates you, you old witch. Hetty said you was our granny, but you're just a mean, wicked old woman.'

'Sammy, don't.' Hetty grabbed him by the collar and pulled him away before he could lash out again. 'That ain't the proper way to behave and you know it.' She held on to him, even though he was wriggling like an eel, and she cast a warning look at Eddie. 'And don't you join in neither, young man.'

Granny Huggins clutched the door jamb for support, and, for a moment, Hetty thought she was going to scream for a policeman, but then something strange happened. Granny's lined face cracked into a grin. 'So you're Sammy, are you?'

Hetty prodded him in the back. 'What d'you say, Sammy?'

He scowled. 'Yes'm.'

'You know something, Samuel Huggins? You're the spitting image of your father when he was a boy.' Granny stood back, holding the door wide open. 'I suppose you'd better come in. But don't think I'm an easy touch, because I ain't.' She jerked her head in Jane's direction. 'The privy is outside in the back yard, and wash your hands after you've been. I don't want that trollop's dirty habits coming into my house.' She pressed herself against the door as Jane rushed past her. 'And you, boys! Behave yourselves in my house, or you'll get a clip round the ear from me. Understand?'

'Yes'm,' Sammy and Eddie murmured in unison as they filed past her.

Granny Huggins stood with her arms akimbo, glaring at Hetty. 'You can come into my parlour and tell me what the devil you mean by bringing your tribe here and disturbing my peace. I want no soft-soaping, just the plain truth. I can't stand liars or toadies, so you'd best come straight out with it and no nonsense. And don't think you're staying here, because you ain't.' She led the way down the dark passage to the room at the back of the house.

Hetty stood in the doorway, staring in amazement at the bright array of silk, feathers and ribbons that were littered over the table in the centre of the room. Despite the heat of the day, a fire burned in the range and a kettle hummed and bubbled on the hob. The mantelshelf was draped in faded green velvet and in the centre of it stood a large, black marble clock. On either side were two pot dogs, a spill jar decorated with cabbage roses and a framed daguerreotype of a bewhiskered gentleman whom Hetty recognised as Grandpa Huggins. He had died when she was just seven, but she remembered his kindness to her, his deep booming laugh, the way his whiskers had tickled when he kissed her and the smell of peppermint on his breath. He had always carried a poke of peppermint creams in his waistcoat pocket, and she could, if she closed her eyes, still taste the soft sweet confection.

'Well, then, sit down,' Granny said, picking up the poker and jabbing it at the embers of the fire. 'I suppose you want a cup of tea?'

Hetty went to take a seat at the table and immediately leapt up, realising that she had almost sat on a half-finished bonnet. She picked it up and put it on the table. 'Are you a milliner, ma'am.'

'No, I'm a chorus girl at the People's Palace! What do you think all this is? Ain't it obvious?' Granny Huggins took a knitted pot holder from a hook and picked up the kettle. She poured a little water into a brown china teapot and swirled it round, glaring at Hetty. 'How do you think I've supported meself all these years since your grandpa died? I certainly didn't have any help from my son. He was too busy with his own family to care what happened to me.'

'That's not fair. You disowned my pa when he married our mum, and you couldn't even bring yourself to speak a word of comfort to her at his funeral. You're a hard-hearted woman, Granny Huggins. I'm sorry we bothered you. I'll get the young ones and Jane and we'll leave right now.'

Granny tipped the contents of the teapot into a slop basin. 'Oh, sit down, and stop being so dramatic. You get that from her. My Samuel was always a down-to-earth, quiet sort of boy, just the sort to be led astray by a pair of big blue eyes.' She spooned tea leaves into the pot and added the boiling water. 'There, now. While that's brewing, you can tell me why you've come here today, and what it is you want from me.'

Reluctantly, Hetty sat down and told her as briefly as possible what had brought them to such straits. Granny Huggins listened with her head on one side, staring at Hetty with shrewd, dark brown eyes that gleamed like black boot buttons.

'So you see,' Hetty concluded, 'we need somewhere to stay, just temporary, mind you, until I can get together enough rent money for lodgings elsewhere.'

'I suppose you owe money to all and sundry. Let me tell you, young woman, I won't have debt collectors banging on my door,' Granny said, folding her arms across her flat chest. 'I'm a respectable widow, and my business depends on my good name. Also, I got my paying guest to consider. Mr Shipworthy is a clerk at the Bethnal Green branch of Tipton's Bank, just like my Harold was, God rest his soul. Mr Shipworthy has a very good position, and he pays his rent and minds his own business.'

Hetty bit back a sharp retort. 'We would do our best to keep out of his way, ma'am.'

'And I wouldn't want them young hooligans aggravating him with their wild ways and noise. Boys are dirty, noisy creatures, all except my Samuel, of course. He was a little angel.'

Hetty put her cup down on its saucer. 'I promise that they won't misbehave, and we don't need much room. Why, this is a palace compared to the place we've just left.'

For a moment, she thought that Granny Huggins was going to smile, but she merely nodded her head, as if to agree that her home was vastly superior. 'All right. Seeing as how you are my blood relations, I can't very well turn you out on the street. But it's only temporary, mind you. A few days at the most. You can have the spare bedroom upstairs. Mr Shipworthy has the downstairs front room, and none of you must ever intrude on his privacy. I want that fully understood.'

'Yes, ma'am. I promise to keep the boys in order.'

'You'd better, or you'll be out on your ear.'

Someone knocked on the door and it opened just far enough for Jane to peep into the room. 'Can I come in?'

'You can, but you may not,' Granny said severely. 'That's another thing. You both speak like costermongers' girls, and the boys are dirty little street urchins. If you're going to stay here, I want you to speak properly, wash regularly, and one hint of fleas, bedbugs or head lice, and you'll have to go on your way.' Granny stood up, smoothing down her starched white apron. 'You, girl – Jane. Take your brothers out into the washhouse and give them a good scrub down. They are not coming into my house until I'm certain that they are not infested. That goes for both of you too. You can heat some water in the copper, wash your hair with carbolic soap and then throw all your clothes in to boil. I keep a clean house. Cleanliness is next to godliness, as you will soon discover.'

They found out that this was no idle threat. Granny stood outside the washhouse, issuing instructions while the boys were stripped of their clothes, scrubbed until their pale skins were lobster-pink, and had their hair washed with strong-smelling carbolic soap and rinsed with vinegar. Then, wrapped in bed sheets, they were sent into the yard to dry off in the sun.

'You girls next,' Granny said, poking the boys' clothes with a copper stick as if expecting vermin to leap out at her. 'Everything has to go in the copper and be boiled. If you don't do your hair properly, I'll shave your heads. That goes for you girls as well as the boys.' She stamped off into the house.

Jane stood in her shift with her arms wrapped protectively around her bulging belly. 'I never been so insulted in all me life.'

Hetty stepped out of her clothes and began to wash her slender body, shivering as the rapidly cooling water trickled down her legs. 'Just do it, Jane. Be grateful that the old besom has taken us in. I'll find us somewhere better, but first I've got to get work and earn some money. I'm afraid we'll just have to put up with things, for the time being at any rate.'

When they had finished their ablutions, Granny Huggins made them all line up in the yard, still wrapped in bed sheets, while she examined their hair for lice. When she was satisfied that there were none, she went back into the house to fetch a bundle of clothes. She flung a couple of yellowed cotton shirts at Sammy and Eddie. 'These belonged to your grandpa, so you take care of them. They'll cover you up until your rags are washed and dried.' She turned to Hetty and Jane, who stood with their hair dripping wet and the sheets tucked up to their chins. 'These dresses might be old, but they're clean, and are a sight better than what you were wearing. I want them back, mind! Washed, ironed and in the same state as they are now. And don't think you're going to have it easy while you're staying here. Each one of you will have to earn your keep.'

That night they slept in Granny Huggins's back bedroom. Hetty and Jane had to share the iron bedstead, which had a mattress that was as bumpy as a rutted cart track. The boys slept on their palliasses, which had been hung over the washing line in the yard and beaten until they began to burst at the seams. Jane had fallen into a sleep of complete exhaustion almost as soon as her head touched the pillow, but Hetty lay awake staring at the ceiling and wondering if she had done the right thing by bringing them all here. It seemed unnaturally quiet without the familiar sounds of the Brinkmans moving about overhead. The sheets smelt of mothballs and the whole house reeked of carbolic soap, but that was infinitely preferable to the stench of sewage which had often seeped up through the flagstones in Autumn Road. Hetty turned on her side and curled up small, so as to give Jane more room. Tomorrow she must find work. Tomorrow – Hetty closed her eyes and drifted off to sleep.

Next morning at breakfast, Eddie had his head bent over his food, but Sammy had

already finished his, and was peering myopically at Granny who was helping herself to a
bowl of porridge. Jane was too busy eating
to notice and Hetty was about to say something when Granny turned her head to glare
at Sammy. 'Lord above, what's the matter
with the boy? Why is he squinting at me like
that?'

Hetty laid her hand on Sammy's shoulder.
'His eyes are weak from working twelve hours
a day making matchboxes. I think he might
need spectacles.'

'Hmm!' Granny slopped a ladleful of the
thick gooey mixture into a bowl. 'That's what
comes of having a matchgirl for a mother.'

Hetty leapt to her feet. 'Is that all you can
say, Granny? You can't blame everything on
our poor mother. She was a saint if you ask
me, and she worked her fingers to the bone to
keep us after Pa died. I'd have bought Sammy
some specs if I'd had the money, but it was all
I could do to feed and clothe us.'

Granny's dark eyes narrowed to slits and
she pursed her lips. 'I'm sick of hearing about
her. But if the boy needs spectacles, then that's
what he shall have. I know where I can get
them cheap in the market. Sammy, stand up
when I address you, boy.'

He jumped to his feet, eyeing her nervously.
'Yes'm.'

'After breakfast you will come with me to the pawnshop in Grove Road, where we will find some spectacles that will help you to see properly. I won't allow Samuel's son to go blind for want of a few pennies.'

Sammy began to cry, but before Hetty could leap to his aid, Granny had grabbed him by the shoulder and given him a shake. 'None of that snivelling, boy. Pass me your bowl and you shall have some more porridge. Then we will go out.'

'Me too.' Eddie jumped up, holding out his empty bowl. 'Can – I mean, may I have some more, please, Granny Huggins?'

'Why, I believe you actually listened to something I said, you little ragamuffin. Yes, since you ask so politely, you may have some more. I might make gentlemen of you yet, given time.'

Granny filled the boys' bowls and then she filled a third, placing it on a small wooden tray next to a cup of tea and a small jug of milk. 'Hetty, you may take this in to Mr Shipworthy. Knock on the door and wait for him to invite you in. I don't want you embarrassing the poor man by catching him in his smalls.'

Eddie and Sammy sniggered, but were subdued by a frown from Granny. Hetty rose from the table to take the tray. 'Yes, Granny.'

'And you might ask him if there are any

suitable positions going at the bank. I suppose you can read and write, Hetty?'

'Yes, ma'am. Our mother taught us all our letters.'

'At least the woman did something right.' Granny took her food to the table and sat down in Hetty's vacated chair. 'Well, go on. What are you waiting for?'

Hetty picked up the tray and hurried from the room. Once again, she managed to hold her tongue, but it was with great difficulty. She went along the passage to knock on the door of the front parlour.

'Enter.'

'Could you open the door, please, sir? I have your breakfast tray and my hands are full.'

The door opened and a short, tubby man with mutton-chop whiskers stared at her in surprise. 'Who are you?'

'Hetty Huggins, sir. Mrs Huggins' grand-daughter.'

He stood aside to allow her to pass and Hetty placed the tray on a small table by the window. Her first impression of the room was that of impeccable tidiness. The bed had been made and Mr Shipworthy's hairbrush and comb were set at right angles on top of the washstand. His towel was neatly folded and hanging over the exact centre of the rail, and the faint scent of bay rum brought back memories of her Pa. She was about to leave the room but he barred her way. 'You are Hetty Huggins from Autumn Road?'

Hetty tried to sidestep him, but he was amazingly light on his feet for such an over-weight man. 'I am, sir. Please let me pass.'

He took off his steel-rimmed spectacles, pulled a white cotton handkerchief from his coat pocket and polished the lenses, eyeing her with a calculating gleam in his eyes. 'I have a friend who might be interested in your where-abouts, young lady.'

There was something about him that made Hetty's skin crawl, but she managed to sound unconcerned. 'I can't think who that could be, sir.'

He hooked his spectacles over his ears and his smile was not pleasant. 'He's told me all about you and your feckless family, Miss Huggins. I think that my very good friend Cyrus Clench would be most interested to know that you are here.'

# Chapter Five

Hetty found Jane in the back yard washing the dishes in the stone sink. She looked up and her face puckered with consternation. 'What's wrong, Hetty? You're pale as a ghost.'

Hetty snatched up a drying towel. 'That blooming man is a pal of Clench's.'

'What man? What are you talking about?'

'Shipworthy, of course. He knows Clench and he's threatened to tell him where we are.' Hetty picked up a bowl and scrubbed at it with the cloth. 'I'm sorry, Janey. I didn't mean to snap at you, but I just can't believe our bad luck. Apparently he knew Clench when he worked at Tipton's Bank and they're still mates.'

'He might not say anything. Perhaps if we asked him nicely . . .?'

Hetty shook her head. 'He's a nasty piece of work. I didn't like him the minute I set eyes on the fellow. I tell you, Jane, we're going to have to move on from here sooner than I planned, or we'll never be free of Clench.'

'I don't think Granny will be too pleased if

she finds out we're in debt to a tallyman. She's got a low enough opinion of us as it is. What shall we do?'

Hetty put the bowl down with a thud on the wooden draining board. 'I'm going to look for work.'

'Will you go back to the match factory?'

'Not with the strike still on. Anyway, I need to find something that will pay enough for us to live on.'

Jane cast a meaningful glance at Hetty's attire. 'You can't go out looking like that. Best see if your old clothes are dry enough to wear.'

Hetty hesitated, torn between the desire to look presentable and the need to escape from Totty Street before Granny returned from her trip to the pawnshop. She crossed the yard to the washing line where her old black serge skirt and much-darned cotton blouse dangled in the still air. They were bone dry but stiff as boards and in desperate need of ironing. Hetty took them down and hurried into the parlour where, after a brief search, she found a flat iron. She placed it on the fire to heat and was waiting impatiently when Jane brought the clean crockery into the room and began stacking the dishes on the dresser. 'It's no good staring at it, Hetty,' she said, chuckling. 'You know what they say - a watched pot never boils.'

'Yes, well "they" didn't have Granny Huggins breathing down their necks.' Hetty picked up the iron and spat on it. 'It'll have to do.' She laid her blouse out on the tabletop and began to iron away the creases. 'If she wants to know where I've gone, just tell her I'm out looking for work. Don't say anything about her lodger or Clench.'

'Ouch!' Jane sat down suddenly, wrapping her arms around her belly. 'Baby's kicking something chronic this morning. He's a lively one, all right, just like his dad.' Her bottom lip trembled and her eyes brimmed with tears. 'Oh, Nat. Why did you have to go and get yourself killed?'

'There, there, don't get upset,' Hetty said anxiously. 'You've got to think of little Nat now.'

Jane sniffed and wiped her eyes on her apron. 'Little Nat, that's what I'll call him. He'll be his dad all over again.'

'I'm sure he will,' Hetty said, hanging her blouse on the back of a chair and picking up her crumpled skirt. 'That's the way to look at it.'

'And we'll be all right, won't we, Hetty?'

'Of course we will. You mustn't worry, Janey. I'll take care of you and your baby. Everything will come right, you'll see.' Hetty tried to sound optimistic, but inwardly she was quaking. Life in Autumn Road had been hard, but at least she had known what to expect. Now she was going out to face the unknown. She thumped away at the threadbare material with the hot iron, smothering a sigh. No amount of washing and ironing would make this skirt look anything other than old and shabby. Giving the garment a final shake, Hetty slipped off Granny's old gown and dressed in her own clothes. 'Well,' she said, patting her hair into place. 'I may not look smart but at least I'm clean and tidy.'

Jane stood up slowly and she went to the shelf where Granny kept the finished bonnets. After a moment's deliberation, she selected the simplest creation, which was saved from being too severe by the addition of violet-blue ribbons. 'Here, put this on, Hetty. You can't go out looking like a poor servant girl.'

'I dunno, Jane.' Hetty fingered the fine straw and stroked the silky ribbon. 'She'll kill me.'

'She won't, not if you find yourself a good position. You got to look like a proper young lady, Hetty. Put it on and let's see.'

Hetty placed the bonnet on her head and peered into the mirror above the mantelshelf. She tied the ribbons at a jaunty angle and was both amazed and pleased with the result. The ribbon was exactly the same shade of blue as her eyes, and the pale yellow straw contrasted with her dark brown hair, making it look almost black.

'There!' Jane said triumphantly. 'That makes all the difference. Go now, and good luck, dear.'

Hetty walked the streets of Bethnal Green, Bow and Whitechapel until her feet were blistered and sore. She knocked on doors with a boldness she had never known she possessed. She went into factories, workshops and small sweatshops hidden in the basements of courts and dark alleys, where the smell of fried fish mingled with the stench of excrement, both human and animal, and the sour odour of unwashed bodies. The sound of pigeons cooing in their lofts, the raucous laughter of drunks who staggered in and out of the many public houses, and the cries of the costermongers all merged into an ear-splitting din. Everywhere she went, she met with rebuffs and rejection. She was only too aware that there were well over a thousand factory girls out on strike and many had been forced to find work; some of them, Hetty was told by a watchman at one of the factory gates, had gone to the country to pick fruit, but others had taken any kind of work they could find in order to tide their families over until the strike ended. His boss, he said, had taken on as many as he could, but there were no vacancies now. It was the same story wherever she went.

By mid-afternoon, Hetty was footsore, tired and extremely hungry. Her mouth was so dry that her tongue felt twice its size and she was lost in the maze of traffic-filled streets that teemed with people of all ages, colours and nationalities. She stopped at a barrow selling fruit to ask the way back to Totty Street.

'Excuse me, mister.' Hetty laid her hand on the coster's arm. 'I'm sorry, but . . .' She swayed on her feet as the barrow, the costermonger and the buildings all seemed to be whirling around her head, making her dizzy. When she opened her eyes she discovered to her surprise that she was lying on the cobblestones amongst squashed cabbage leaves and turnip tops. A man was bending over her. His face was close to hers and his lips were moving, but she couldn't make out what he was saying.

'Ups-a-daisy.' A pair of strong arms raised her to a sitting position. 'Are you feeling a bit better now?'

Hetty blinked and stared into his friendly open features. 'That's the ticket,' he said, grinning. 'Feeling more like it now, are we? You swooned at me feet, girl. Not that that's an unusual occurrence. Happens all the time to yours truly, George Cooper, costermonger and heart-breaker, at your service.' He slipped his arm around her waist and helped her onto an empty orange crate. 'Here, take the weight off your tootsies and sit down.'

'Ta, mister.' Hetty was in no position to argue. She perched on the crate rubbing her hand across her forehead. 'I must've fainted.'

'I should say you did.' George folded his arms across his chest, eyeing her critically. 'You still look a bit peaky. I'd say, offhand, that you was in need of a bite to eat.'

'Ta, but I'm fine now.' Hetty tried to stand up and found that her knees had turned to jelly. She sat down again, sighing. 'I am a bit thirsty, mister. I don't suppose you've got a cup of water to spare?'

'As a matter of fact, young lady, I was just about to eat me dinner when you threw yourself at me like a dying duck.' He produced a meat pie and a ham sandwich from beneath the barrow with the air of a conjuror pulling a rabbit out of a hat. He bent down again and picked up a bottle of beer. Undoing the stopper, he handed it to Hetty. 'Take a swig of that, girl. It'll put feathers on your chest, as they say.'

Too tired to argue, Hetty swallowed a mouthful of the strong beer. She wrinkled her nose at the bitter, hop-flavoured taste, but it had an immediate effect and she felt refreshed, if a little tipsy as the alcohol hit her empty stomach. 'Ta, mister.' She eyed the sandwich and her mouth watered, but, even so, she couldn't take his food. It might be all that he would eat that day. 'But I ain't all that hungry. Best be on me way now.'

George pressed her back on the crate and he wrapped her fingers around the ham sandwich. 'Not until you've had something to eat. Now be a good girl and sink your toothy-pegs into that.' He turned away to serve an old lady. 'Yes, ducks. What can I do you for today?'

The old lady cackled with laughter and nudged him in the midriff with her elbow. 'You're a one, George. But you always got a smile, that's what I like about you.'

'I know, ducks. It's me winning smile what gets all the ladies going.'

'Half a pound of onions, a pound of carrots and a bit less of your cheek, young man.'

The temptation was too great, and while George was busy weighing out the customer's order Hetty bit into the white bread, thickly buttered and filled with a slice of best ham with just a hint of mustard. She hadn't tasted a sandwich like this for so long that she had almost forgotten how good it was. She chewed and swallowed, barely able to stop herself gobbling the lot in a couple of mouthfuls. When George turned round to speak to her, she was licking her fingers, one by one. He threw back his head and laughed. 'Well, now. Who said she wasn't hungry?'

Hetty stood up. She was feeling so much better that she almost forgot her aching limbs and sore feet. 'I was hungry, and you was very kind to share your dinner with me, but now I really must be going.'

'Hold on a moment, girl. You still look done in. Won't you rest up for a bit?'

'I can't, mister.'

'Me name is George, like I said. And you are?'

Hetty took his outstretched hand, a little shyly in the face of such an ebullient nature, and she shook it. 'Hester Huggins, Hetty for short.'

'Well, Hetty for short, what are you doing walking the streets in this part of Whitechapel and falling in a faint under me barrow?'

She smiled. 'Looking for work, George. So I've got to get on.'

'You wouldn't be one of them matchgirls that I've read about in the newspapers, now would you?'

'I was. I mean, we were; me and me sister and our little brothers. We worked at home making up the matchboxes, but now we've had to go and live in Totty Street with our granny who doesn't want us, and Cyrus Clench will be after me for his money, so you see I got to find work.'

116

'My my, girl. You've left me quite out of breath.' George stared at her with a puzzled frown. 'Why don't your grandma want you, and who is this Clench fellow? Would you like me to come round your place and beat him up a bit?'

A gurgle of laughter escaped from Hetty's lips. 'It's a long story. I don't think beating up Mr Clench would fix anything, but ta for the offer.' She began to walk away but George followed her.

'Look, I don't like to see no one in trouble. A pretty girl like you shouldn't be wandering about alone, knocking on strange doors. There's bad places round here with some evil sorts who might do you harm.'

'I'm grateful for your concern, but I can look after meself.' Hetty was about to walk on, but he caught her by the hand.

'Wait. I'll knock off when all me stock is gone, and then I'll see you home. No, don't shake your head. You can help me on the stall, if that makes you feel any better.'

'I would, but there'll be trouble if I gets home late. Granny ain't in the best of spirits having us foisted on her. She hates us all, with maybe the exception of Sammy who reminds her of our dad, and we're only there on sufferance. If I was to be late for supper, she'd skin me alive and probably throw us all out on the street.'

'You help me, and I'll pay you in fruit and veg.' George led her back to his barrow, where he wrapped a hessian apron round her. 'I'll bet the old lady will look on you more favourably if you go home with a couple of pounds of apples, some oranges and bananas, not to mention a fine head of cabbage and some taters.'

Put like that, Hetty simply couldn't refuse. Besides which, she had taken an instant liking to George, and she needed someone to lead her out of the maze of backstreets and festering alleyways. 'All right, then. It's a bargain.'

She worked diligently, side by side with him, watching his every move and the way in which he dealt with customers, from pleasant little old ladies to aggressive cabbies who accused him of selling rotten fruit, and barefooted street urchins who tried to steal apples from his barrow. Mostly, she noticed, he turned a blind eye to the starving younger children, but the bigger boys, who were simply out to steal his goods and sell them on street corners, were dealt a sound cuff round the ear and a good telling off. 'There's all sorts round here,' George explained, after the first incident. 'You got to keep on your toes and be able to tell the good 'uns from the bad 'uns.'

Hetty had just weighed out two pounds of potatoes for a customer. She had taken the money and given the right change, and was feeling quite proud of herself. She wiped her hands on her apron. 'I've been thinking,' she said slowly. 'I've been mulling over in me mind the idea of selling hot taters. What do you think to that, George?'

She had spoken tentatively, half expecting him to laugh and tell her that it was a silly idea, but he put his head on one side, considering her words with a serious expression on his sun-tanned face. 'I should say it's a possibility. It's mostly blokes who sell taters, but I don't see why a girl shouldn't do it.'

'Really?' Hetty could hardly breathe as she served a drayman with two bananas and an apple. She took the money and slipped it in the money bag tied round her waist. 'Do you really think I could do it?'

'Why not? Although you'd need money to buy the equipment.'

'And do you know what that would be?'

'You'd need a can for the water, and a fire pot to keep the water and the taters hot. You'd have to have charcoal for the fire, and potatoes, of course; butter, salt and pepper, and a sharp knife. Then you'd have to find a baker who would bake the taters for you and a pitch where you could sell them.'

Hetty chuckled. 'And a reliable vendor of potatoes, such as you?'

'The most reliable chap in the business.' George tipped his cap. 'You'd need a bit of money to start up with, but the tin man in Ratcliff Highway makes up the cans for a couple of quid, so I hear tell.'

'Two pounds!' Hetty's breath hitched in her throat. He might as well have said two hundred.

'But you could make up to fifteen shillings a week, maybe more, if you was prepared to work into the late evening, standing outside the stations or theatres. You'd soon get your money back.'

'I couldn't raise that kind of money, but it was a pleasant thought. I'll just have to think of something else.'

'You don't look like the giving up sort to me, Hetty.'

'I'd best be going now. If you'll just point me in the right direction.'

'Just another half-hour or so, Hetty. We've nearly sold the lot, and I promised to walk you back to Totty Street. George Cooper always keeps his promises.' He gave her a saucy wink. 'And your granny will forgive you when she sees what you've brought for her.'

When the last apple had been sold, George packed up his barrow and trundled it to his lodgings in Cottage Green, which sounded wonderfully countrified, but in reality was a narrow street off Bow Road lined with smoke-blackened back to back houses, pubs and pie shops. The smell of onions, soot and stale beer was almost overpowering. Hetty said nothing as George parked his barrow at the kerbside, along with several other handcarts. He covered it with a piece of tarpaulin. 'There, that'll do. Now I'll walk you home, Hetty. Luckily we're only a short way from Grove Road and Totty Street.' He proffered his arm, and Hetty took it. She might have refused, but she was glad to have someone to lean on at the end of a long hard day. She hoped that the fruit and vegetables wrapped up in a piece of sacking would be enough to placate Granny, but she was not looking forward to explaining her absence. When they reached the end of Totty Street, she stopped. 'Ta, George. I'm really grateful to you for walking me home, but, if you don't mind, this is where we say goodbye.'

'I get it. You don't want the old dragon to see you out walking with a handsome young fellow like me.' He grinned, tipped his cap and winked at her. 'Say no more, Hetty. I'll stand here until you're safely indoors, and then I'll be on me way. Good luck to you, girl.'

Overcome with gratitude and relief that he had understood the position, she reached up to kiss him on the cheek. 'You're a toff, George. A real toff. I won't forget you.' She hurried off without waiting for him to reply, but when she reached the house she paused to glance over her shoulder. He gave her a cheery wave, shoved his hands in his pockets and sauntered off, whistling a tune. Hetty took a deep breath and knocked on the door.

Sammy let her in and his eyes looked huge behind the thick lenses of his newly acquired spectacles. 'Where've you been, Hetty? She's really got the hump.'

Hetty put the sack down on the floor, and she brushed his unruly curls back from his forehead. 'Never mind her, I'll sort her out. But just look at you in your new specs. You don't half look smart.'

He shook his head. 'I look stupid. Eddie's been teasing me all day. Jane said I look like an owl. I hates wearing these silly things.'

'But can you see better? That's the real point, Sammy.'

'Yes, but I don't like being laughed at, Hetty.'

She gave him a hug. 'Take no notice. I think you look like a proper little gent.' She took off the borrowed bonnet and hung it on a peg in the hallway. It wouldn't do to face Granny while she was wearing the evidence. Hetty picked up her peace offering, took a deep breath and went into the parlour, but she stopped short when she saw two men sitting at the table drinking tea out of Granny's best cups. One was Mr Shipworthy, but the other man, who had his back to her, was unmistakeably Cyrus Clench. Jane was seated by the fire, pale-faced but defiant, and Granny was standing by the table with the big brown teapot clutched in her hand. She glared at Hetty, nostrils flaring. 'So, what time of day do you call this? Where have you been since this morning? It's half past seven. You've missed your supper.'

Cyrus turned his head to give Hetty an appraising stare. 'Is this the way to treat the good woman who has taken you in off the street, Miss Huggins?' He rose to his feet. 'And did you think that by running away from your previous abode you would escape paying your debts? I call that shocking behaviour.'

'And so do I,' Mr Shipworthy agreed, nodding his head. 'Shocking. You are a disgrace to the name of Huggins. Your grand-mother is a saint to have taken you in.'

Hetty opened her mouth to protest, but Jane shot her a warning glance. 'You was looking for work, wasn't you, Hetty? Did you have any luck?'

'You should have sought my permission before you went gallivanting off for the day,'

Granny Huggins said, slamming the teapot down on the table. 'I might have had errands for you to run, or chores that your sister could not do in her delicate condition. And did you stop to think about the distress you might cause your young brothers by being absent all day and late into the evening?'

'It's not that late, Granny,' Hetty said, controlling her rising temper with difficulty. 'And what is he doing here, I'd like to know?'

'I felt it my duty to inform my good friend Cyrus of your whereabouts,' Mr Shipworthy said, tugging nervously at his mutton-chop whiskers. 'Your sudden appearance here smacked of a moonlight flit, and I could not allow you to tarnish this good lady's name by your nefarious deeds.'

'Thank you very much, Mr Shipworthy,' Granny Huggins said tartly. 'I don't need you to protect my good name. I am a respected member of the community and I gave shelter to these young people in good faith. If it has been abused, that is my business.'

'Absolutely, ma'am.' Mr Shipworthy subsided into his starched white collar, his cheeks flushing brick-red. 'No offence meant.'

'I'm sure it was just an oversight, ma'am,' Cyrus said, rubbing his hands together. 'I'm certain that Miss Hetty meant to let me know, but what with the strike and everything, it just slipped her mind.' He shot a calculating glance at Hetty and waited for her reply.

There was little that she could do other than agree with him. She nodded her head. 'That's right. Of course I was going to let you know our whereabouts, as soon as I had found work and could pay what we owe.'

'Huh! I find that hard to believe,' Mr Shipworthy snorted. 'That wasn't my impression this morning. You went as white as a sheet when I mentioned my friend's name.'

Hetty struggled to think of a suitable retort, but before she could answer, Granny Huggins had taken a leather purse from her pocket. 'How much, Mr Clench?'

He rose to his feet, blinking at her like a surprised owl. 'How much, ma'am?'

'Yes, you silly man. How much does my granddaughter owe you?'

Cyrus ran his finger round the inside of his collar. 'Why, that will be sixpence for last Friday and a further sixpence for this coming Friday. I could add on extra interest for non-payment, but I'm a fair man, ma'am.'

'You're a leech, Mr Clench. I know your sort.' Granny thrust two sixpenny bits into his outstretched hand. 'But never let it be said that a Huggins did not pay his or her debt. Now I'll thank you to leave my house.'

Cyrus closed his fingers over the coins and

he backed towards the doorway. 'There's no need to adopt that attitude. I'm only doing my job, ma'am.'

Mr Shipworthy clambered to his feet, his jowls wobbling as he puffed out his cheeks. 'I say, Mrs Huggins. This isn't the sort of treatment I would expect a friend of mine to suffer in my own home.'

Granny bridled, narrowing her eyes. 'This is my home, Mr Shipworthy. You are just a paying guest, and I can turn you out any time I please. If you don't like it here, I suggest you find yourself another place. I could fill that room ten times over and still have gentlemen queuing at my door.'

Cyrus hovered in the doorway, as if poised to beat a hasty retreat. 'I daresay that's true, ma'am. Especially now you have two young women who are known to be free with their favours. I expect the queue would reach as far as Piccadilly Circus.'

Hetty dropped the sack on the floor and she advanced on him with her hands balled into fists. 'Say that again and I'll throw you out meself.'

'It's true, Mrs Huggins,' Cyrus said, backing into the hallway. 'Ask Miss Jane where she got that wedding band. I think you'll find it's made of brass, ma'am. Ask her to show you her marriage licence. Ask . . .' His words were lost as Sammy charged with his head down and butted him in the stomach. The air exploded from his lungs and Cyrus staggered against the wall, clutching his belly, temporarily bereft of speech.

'Are you going to allow that kind of behaviour, ma'am?' Mr Shipworthy demanded, eyeing Eddie nervously as he pawed the ground with his feet, like a small bull making ready to charge.

Granny laid a restraining hand on Eddie's shoulder. 'I didn't see anything, Mr Shipworthy. I think your friend tripped over his own flat feet. I suggest you see him out.'

Hetty stared at her open-mouthed, and then the comical side of the situation struck her and she burst into laughter. After a moment's pause, Jane began to giggle. Mr Shipworthy snorted and marched out of the room, narrowly escaping being run into by Sammy as he returned slapping his hands together in triumph. 'I sorted the old codger out, Hetty. Did you see me?'

'I saw you,' Eddie said breathlessly. 'You went at him like a proper prize fighter.'

Sammy flexed his muscles. 'So you'd better not go on about me specs now, or I might have to wallop you too.'

Hetty wrapped her arms around him and straightened his crooked spectacles. 'Don't think I ain't grateful to you for standing up for us, Sammy, but fighting ain't the right way.'

'Yes,' Granny said severely. 'I'll let it pass this once, but we do not knock people down because they have offended us. This was an exception. I can't abide moneylenders, they're all bloodsucking leeches, and it shouldn't be allowed.' She turned to Jane with a stern look on her face. 'As for you, young woman, I can tell gold from brass, especially when the ring leaves a green stain on your finger. Are you a bad girl? Do you go with men for money or a cheap thrill?'

Jane blushed scarlet and she heaved her body off the chair. 'No such thing. I was properly engaged to my Nat, but he . . .' She covered her face with her hands and her shoulders shook.

Hetty shot a darkling glance at Granny. 'Her fiancé was killed in an accident at the gasworks. They were to have been married as soon as the last of the banns were read, but poor Nat died and Jane is left to bring up her baby single-handed. Not that she's on her own, Granny. She'll never want for anything as long as I have a breath left in me body.'

Granny Huggins lowered herself onto her rocking chair. 'Fine words butter no parsnips, my girl. You have no work, you are not trained to do anything other than make matchboxes, and I suspect that you have had very little in the way of education. How do you propose to support this family of yours?'

'I – I dunno really.'

Granny folded her hands in her lap, and her raised eyebrows almost disappeared into her hairline. 'You've been out all day. Did you find work?'

'Not exactly.'

'Well, did you, or didn't you? It's not a difficult question.'

'Leave her be, ma'am,' Jane said hastily. 'Can't you see she's fair wore out with tramping the streets?'

Eddie and Sammy huddled together at the table, their moment of elation chased away by the sound of angry voices. Hetty laid her hands on their thin shoulders, exerting a gentle, reassuring pressure. She met Granny's eyes with a defiant lift of her chin. 'No, I didn't find work, but I helped a bloke on his fruit and vegetable stall and he paid me in kind.' She bent down to retrieve the sack, and she tipped its contents out on the table. Sammy and Eddie murmured with delight as the apples and oranges rolled towards them. Their small hands reached out to grab the fruit, but they obviously thought better of it as they kept a weather eye on their unpredictable grandmother. 'Go on, boys,'

Hetty said. 'I'm sure that Granny won't mind if you share an orange or an apple. They was honestly come by.'

Granny Huggins waved her hand at them. 'Go on. I can't stand to see good food go to waste.'

Jane grabbed an apple, rubbed it on her skirt and sank her teeth into the sweet flesh with a sigh of pleasure, while Sammy and Eddie pounced on the oranges.

'That's right,' Hetty said approvingly. 'Enjoy the treat.'

'Aren't you going to have some, Hetty?' Jane asked with her mouth full of apple. 'Aren't you hungry?'

Hetty's stomach rumbled. It seemed a very long time since she had eaten George's ham sandwich. She glanced at Granny Huggins, half expecting to see censure in her eyes, but she was startled to see one of her grandmother's rare smiles. 'Oh, go on,' Granny said. 'Eat the fruit but don't complain to me of belly-ache afterwards. And, Hetty, there's some bread in the crock. Never let it be said that Mattie Huggins allowed her poor relations to starve. And you can pass me an orange, before the greedy boys eat the lot.'

After Hetty had eaten her bread and butter, finishing off her meal with an apple, she suffered a sharp pang of conscience when she saw the empty space on the shelf where the straw bonnet should have been. Granny seemed to be in a mellow mood, but she would almost certainly be mad as fire if she discovered that Hetty had taken the bonnet without asking. She decided to confess and get the worst over, and she was taken aback when Granny simply shrugged her shoulders. 'I know,' she said, wiping her fingers on a dish-cloth. 'I'm not blind and I'm not stupid, Hetty, as you'll discover if you stay here much longer. I know you took the bonnet, but I suppose I can hardly blame you for wanting to look your best when you went out looking for work. Luckily for you, that particular piece of millinery is not wanted urgently, or I might have been extremely angry.'

'I'm sorry, Granny,' Hetty said, hanging her head. 'I know it was wrong of me.'

'We'll say no more about it, but, next time, you must ask my permission before you borrow anything.' The clock on the mantelshelf struck the hour and Granny glanced at the time, then she pointed at Eddie and Sammy. 'It's time you two were in bed. Jane, go with them and make sure they wash their hands and faces before they get between my clean sheets.'

'Yes'm.' Jane shooed the boys out of the parlour. 'I think I'll go to bed too, I'm fair wore out and little Nat is kicking me to bits. Are you coming, Hetty?'

'I want a word in private,' Granny said, motioning Hetty to sit down.

'I won't be long, Jane,' Hetty promised. 'I'll try not to disturb you.'

Jane closed the door behind her, leaving Hetty and Granny Huggins sitting on either side of the fireplace, facing each other.

'Well?' Hetty said, expecting the worst. Granny had made it plain from the start that they were here on a temporary basis. She braced herself, waiting to hear that they must pack up and leave. 'What did you want to say to me?'

'I may have been a bit harsh with you yesterday when you arrived on my doorstep.' Granny held up her hand as Hetty opened her mouth to reply. 'No, let me speak. I will help you, because I can see that you are not to blame for your current situation. Don't expect me to become a doting grandparent overnight, that's not my nature, but you may stay here for as long as it takes you to get enough money together to find more suitable lodgings. I hope it will be before Jane's time comes. I can't stand squalling babies, but we'll meet that fence when we come to it.'

'Thank you, ma'am. I'm very grateful to you, especially since you stood up to old Clench earlier. He's a dirty old dog and that's for certain.'

'I could see that. I'm not a fool, Hetty. And you can stop calling me ma'am. You may call me gran or granny as you please. Just remember that I will stand no nonsense and I expect you all to abide by my rules.'

'Yes, Granny.'

'Now tell me how you propose to support yourselves while you are under my roof. I'm not a rich woman, and I can't keep you all indefinitely.'

Hetty looked her in the eyes, and she realised that honesty was the only way with Granny Huggins. 'I couldn't get work anywhere today. I tramped the streets from Bethnal Green to Whitechapel with no luck.'

'But you helped a costermonger on his barrow, and he paid you in kind.'

'Yes, and we talked about an idea that I'd had for some time.'

'Don't beat about the bush, girl.'

'I believe I could earn twelve to fifteen shillings a week selling hot taters in the street.' Hetty held her breath, waiting for Granny to make some scathing remark, but she was silent for a moment as if giving the matter due consideration.

'I suppose it's possible,' Granny said after a long pause. 'I've only ever seen men selling hot potatoes on the streets, but in my opinion a woman is capable of doing most of the things done by men, and probably better in most cases. However, you would need money to start up such a venture, and you would have to face the rigours and dangers of working on the streets. Could you do that, Hetty?'

'I was raised in Autumn Road – it ain't exactly Mayfair. I can handle meself, Granny.'

'I don't doubt it. But what about the money? How much would you need?'

Hetty did a rough calculation in her head, based on what George had told her. 'Two pounds nine and eleven. That would be everything, including a shilling to pay the baker for roasting the taters.'

'I see you may have inherited your grandfather's head for figures, my girl. Well, Hetty,' Granny leaned forward, lowering her voice, 'I have a little money saved for a rainy day. I'll put up the necessary to start you in business, but I shall want repayment at a set rate each week and five per cent interest on the capital sum. Do you understand?'

Hetty nodded, hardly able to believe her luck.

'You will pay me for your board and lodging and the boys will attend the school in Sewardstone Road. I don't want them to grow up uneducated with no prospects. You and Jane will behave yourselves while you're under my roof – no followers and no hanky-panky. What do you say, Hetty?'

# Chapter Six

Hetty accepted Granny's offer gratefully, but she worried about how Tom would take the news that he was not allowed to visit them. It seemed, however, that she had reckoned without his dogged determination to get his own way. He arrived in Totty Street one evening armed with a bunch of flowers which he presented to Granny, and asked very politely if she would spare him a few moments of her valuable time. Hetty and Jane exchanged amused glances, fully expecting her to send him packing, but she surprised them by saying she would be happy to speak to such a well-mannered young man. Hetty and Jane were banished to the back yard and they had to wait until Tom emerged, smiling and triumphant, with permission to call on them whenever he was passing by.

'How did you do it?' Hetty demanded in astonishment. 'Granny doesn't approve of gentlemen callers.'

'I said I had looked out for you since you was a nipper and that I had no intention of abandoning you now.' Tom winked and tapped the side of his nose. 'That's all you need to know, but Mrs Huggins and me have come to an understanding.'

Jane rushed over to give him a hug. 'Well, I'm glad. We would all miss you if you didn't come round regular.'

Hetty nodded in agreement, and she smiled. 'I don't know how you did it, Tom, but you certainly worked a spell on Granny.'

'I'm a part of this family, girl. You won't get rid of me that easily.'

'And I wouldn't want to.'

'Now what's all this I hear about you planning to sell hot taters? I think you'd best come clean, Hetty.'

Now that she had made up her mind to become a street seller, Hetty couldn't wait to put her plans into action. Life in Totty Street was far from easy. Jasper Shipworthy's continued occupation of the front parlour was a constant reminder of Clench and all that he stood for, but at least Granny seemed to have relented a little towards them. She was still as spiky as a holly bush and Hetty was conscious that they were only there on sufferance. It was all too obvious that Granny had little time for her or Jane, but she doted on Sammy and seemed to have grown quite fond of Eddie. It was fortunate, Hetty thought, that Jane was too wrapped up in herself to worry about what went on in the house. She seemed content to sit all day, dutifully stitching material for bonnets under Granny's strict supervision. For Jane the future was limited to birthing her baby. After that she seemed to assume that everything would naturally follow.

Sammy and Eddie started at the school in Sewardstone Road, reluctantly at first, but to Hetty's relief they came home on the first day with glowing faces and actually seemed to have enjoyed the experience. Sammy was a different child now that his new spectacles enabled him to see properly, and he said proudly that the teacher had held his ability to read up as an example to the other boys in the class. He had not, he said, told Miss that his first reading primer had been the labels for Bryant and May matchboxes. Hetty told him he was a clever boy, as was Eddie, who had also proved to be an apt pupil. She was glad now that she had searched the street markets for second-hand books, reading to them before they fell asleep at night and teaching them the alphabet in a sing-song voice by way of a lullaby. Ma had been very keen that they should all be literate, and Hetty could see that she had, as always, been right.

At the beginning of August, Hetty was almost ready to set up business as a huckster. She had ordered a can to be made by the tin man in Ratcliff Highway, and a fire pot to hang beneath it. She asked George if he could supply her with sacks of potatoes, and he advised her to use the cheaper imported French Regents, which were waxy and would not shrivel up when cooked. She walked the streets looking for suitable sites on which to start trading, and having watched street sellers at work she realised that there was something very important that she had overlooked. She would need some means by which to transport a heavy can filled with potatoes.

It was George who came to the rescue. He turned up in Totty Street one evening pushing a small handcart, which he said he had found half submerged in the canal. He had rescued it from a watery grave and had fixed the broken wheel. Now it was almost as good as new. He brushed aside all offers of payment and Hetty thanked him profusely. After he had left, having exerted his charm on Granny who fell instantly under his spell and invited him to call again whenever he was in the neighbourhood, Jane teased Hetty mercilessly. 'George fancies you,' she said, giggling. 'Hetty's got a fellah.'

The boys took this up immediately and ran around the yard chanting, 'Hetty's got a new fellah. George loves Hetty.'

Hetty felt her cheeks burning with embarrassment and she attempted to laugh it off, but she could see that Tom was simmering with resentment. She did her best to placate him. George was a good-hearted rattle-brain, she said, and not to be taken seriously. She did not add that she liked him immensely, or that he had an undeniable way with the ladies. He was not what most people would consider handsome, but his larger than life personality made up for a nose that was a shade too big, a chin that was a little too square, and a wide mouth that curled in a wicked grin when he was amused. His brown eyes, which seemed to vary in colour according to his moods, could glow with sympathy or twinkle with good humour and she could quite understand why women customers favoured his stall. She recalled the day when they had first met, and how his merry laughter had rung out across the market place, causing people to turn their heads and smile in a natural reaction. Yes, she thought, giving Tom's arm a companionable squeeze, George was good fun but not a man to be taken too seriously.

As the time for collecting the finished can drew near, Hetty approached the local baker and he agreed to bake a hundred potatoes at the cost of ninepence. She used the last of her money to buy butter, salt, pepper and charcoal, and when she collected the can she polished it until it gleamed like silver. She was now ready to launch herself in business, but Tom was becoming increasingly worried about her decision to work alone on the East End streets. He visited them almost every evening after work, and he did everything he could to dissuade Hetty from her purpose, but she turned a deaf ear to his pleadings, cajoling and downright sulks.

Their final argument, on the evening before Hetty was due to start work, was conducted in Granny Huggins' back yard, which was the only place where they could have a little privacy. Even so, Hetty had been aware of Sammy's and Eddie's faces pressed against the windowpane in the upstairs bedroom, and she supposed that Granny and Jane had overhead every word as they sat in the parlour, finishing off her new work clothes.

'You're an obstinate, stubborn mule of a girl,' Tom cried passionately. 'Don't come crying to me when you get bullied or worse by the other hucksters, or your takings are stolen by villains.' He strode out of the yard, slamming the gate behind him, and Hetty went back indoors. She was too angry for tears, but she was deeply hurt that Tom had not supported her. She tried to tell herself that she didn't care, and that he was just a stupid man, but somehow she felt betrayed. She did not feel like facing the family. If she had been a man she could have gone to the pub and drunk herself into oblivion, but she was a girl and she had no choice but to join Jane and Granny in the parlour.

Jane looked up from stitching the hem of the navy-blue linsey-woolsey skirt and her eyes were filled with sympathy. 'Are you all right, Hetty?'

'Of course she's all right,' Granny snapped, biting off a thread of white cotton with her yellowed teeth. 'I thought he was different, but that boy is an idiot, just like most of his gender, with the exception of my dear, departed Harold. He would never have behaved like that, shouting and storming just because he couldn't get his own way.'

'He wouldn't have dared,' Jane whispered as Hetty sat down on a stool beside her.

'What was that?' Granny fixed her with an angry stare. 'I hope you weren't being cheeky, miss?'

'No, Granny,' Jane murmured, suppressing a giggle.

Hetty was too emotionally drained to suffer yet more unpleasantness, and she leaned over to touch the crisp white cotton blouse that Granny was just finishing off. 'That's too good to wear for work, Granny. I ought to keep that for Sunday best.'

'It is a fine piece of work, although I say it myself. I've always been good with my needle. As to being kept for best, that is not the point. I won't have a granddaughter of mine going out to work looking like something the cat's dragged in. You're starting up in trade now, Hetty. You've got to look businesslike.' She fastened off the cotton on the last button, and handed the garment to Hetty. 'Wearing that and the new straw bonnet I made for you, you'll look respectable and people will have confidence in you. If you look clean and tidy, they won't be afraid to taste your wares.'

Next morning, Hetty and Jane took their wicker baskets to the bakery where they collected the hot potatoes. They wrapped them in green baize to keep them warm, and then hurried back to Totty Street where the can was wedged in the handcart waiting to be transported to Hetty's chosen pitch outside Bethnal Green station. Jane insisted on accompanying her, but it was a hot day and about halfway there she began to complain that her feet were sore and swollen. Hetty was sympathetic but eventually she could stand it no longer and sent Jane home with strict instructions to rest. When she reached the station Hetty found to her dismay that another potato vendor had already set up his pitch. He scowled at her and shook his fist. She did her best to ignore his threatening looks, but as she called out her wares her voice quavered and was lost in the blast of a whistle from a steam engine. She tried again, and was drowned out by her competitor's stentorian tones.

Hetty moved a little further away and this time she took a hot potato from the can, and slit it so that the fragrant steam wafted under the noses of the passers-by. 'Tasty hot taters. Come and buy.'

A man wearing a black city suit with a greenish tinge to it and slightly frayed at the cuffs stopped to make a purchase, and Hetty pocketed the halfpenny with a feeling of triumph. But, at that moment, the irate huckster came striding over to her. 'What d'you think you're doing, girlie?'

Hetty swallowed hard. He was a head and shoulders taller than she, and his face was scarred, causing the eyelid to droop over his left eye, which gave him an even more sinister appearance. 'I'm selling taters,' she said, hoping that she sounded more confident than she felt.

'Push off and sell them somewhere else. This is my pitch.'

She opened her mouth to argue, but his fists were as big as York hams and his broken nose suggested that he was no stranger to violence. She shrugged her shoulders. 'All right, mister. I'm going.' She could hear him swearing as she pushed her cart down the street. Tears of anger and frustration burned the backs of her eyes, but she bit her lip and trudged on, not really knowing where she was going, until she turned a corner and found herself in the middle of a street market. Taking a quick look round, Hetty couldn't see anyone else selling hot potatoes, and she set up her stand. 'Hot taters,' she shouted. Her voice was lost in the general hubbub of voices and costermongers' cries, but it was almost midday and the appetising smell of baked potatoes was enough to entice customers to buy. She did a brisk trade, and even the costers themselves began to wander up and make purchases.

By the time the crowds had thinned and the market stalls were closing down, Hetty had sold almost all her stock. Despite the heat, the flies and the stench of the city streets, Hetty pushed her cart homewards with a spring in her step. She did a rapid calculation in her head, and worked out that she had made one shilling and threepence profit. If she carried on at this rate she would be able to start repaying Granny as well as Cyrus Clench. If she worked even harder, perhaps taking her stand outside the People's Palace or one of the larger railway stations in the evenings, she could double her takings. Then, she thought, crossing the busy Cambridge Road and narrowly missing being run down by a carthorse pulling a dray laden with barrels, by the time the potato season ended in April, she might have saved enough to start up a proper stall and sell ham sandwiches and cups of tea and coffee.

She was sweating profusely and the sun beat down on her back, making her feel slightly sick. Her feet were swollen and sore in her ill-fitting second-hand boots, bought cheaply from the dolly shop, and she stopped at a communal pump to fill her cupped hands with cool water. She drank some and splashed the rest on her hot cheeks. Judging by the position of the sun, it must be after six o'clock; she would be late for supper, but Jane would be sure to have saved her some food. Hetty realised then that she was ravenously hungry. In her enthusiasm for trading, she had forgotten about her own needs and had eaten nothing since a bowl of watery porridge at breakfast. Her muscles were aching, but she pressed on, attempting to find a short cut by venturing down narrow side streets and alleyways.

When she reached the Regent's Canal she knew that she was heading in the right direction, but she found herself in a dismal jungle of industrial waste, bent girders, rusty paint cans and piles of slag. She was afraid to go on, but retracing her steps was not an option as she would almost certainly lose her way. She put her head down and concentrated on getting the cart through the debris that was littered all over the towpath. She had reached the bridge which carried the trains of the Great Eastern Railway over the canal when she realised that the echoing footsteps were not hers alone. She turned her head to see Cyrus loping towards her at a jogging pace. She wanted to run, but it was impossible to do so without upsetting the cart and damaging her precious can. She tried to ignore him and quickened her pace, but he was at her side before she reached the end of the tunnel. He clamped his hand on her shoulder. 'What's this, Miss Hetty? Have you grown too proud to speak to an old friend?'

She turned her head to give him a disdainful look. 'You are not my friend, Mr Clench.'

He struck a pose. 'That is a cruel thing to say, my dear. Who was it who provided you with the money for your late mother's funeral? And at a very reasonable rate of interest, I should add.' He tightened his grip, digging his clawed fingers into her soft flesh. 'I think you owe me a little civility, at the very least.'

She drew away from him in alarm, but he

moved even closer, leering into her face. 'No need to be afraid of me, girlie. I won't hurt you. On the contrary, I like you, Hetty.' He slid his hand down her arm to fondle her breast. 'I could make your life a lot easier if you would let me. If you were my woman, I wouldn't let you hawk hot taters like a common huckster.'

'Let me go, Mr Clench,' Hetty said, pushing him as hard as she could, but she was no match for him. Cyrus might not be a big man, but he was much stronger that she. He seized her round the waist, drawing her so close to him that she recoiled at the smell of beer, onions and dental decay on his breath. 'Just a little kiss and a cuddle, dearie. Don't forget you still owe me three weeks' money. I've been a patient man, but now I want some recompense for my good nature.'

Hetty struggled in vain. 'Let me go, Mr Clench. I'll pay you in full as soon as I am able.'

He pushed her back against the damp brick wall and he took her lips in a wet, slobbery kiss. Hetty kicked out with her feet and twisted her head away, but he pushed his knee between her legs, growling with laughter as his hot mouth travelled down her neck, biting, sucking and making animal noises as his excitement intensified. She screamed, and the sound ricocheted off the damp walls, and was carried away on the murky waters of the canal. She felt the buttons popping off her blouse and his fingers sought her left nipple, tweaking and twisting it until she yelped with pain. This only seemed to excite him further, and the more she struggled, the harder he pressed himself against her. He lifted her skirt, forcing her ruthlessly against the hard bricks, and his hand slid up her thigh. She screamed again, but he released her breast only to clamp his hand over her mouth. 'You will pay me the interest here and now, dearie.'

She felt him hard and warm against her bare flesh. She could scarcely breathe, let alone cry out for help. Then suddenly she was free. Cyrus was grabbed from behind and flung into the canal, where he landed in the murky water with a resounding splash.

'Hetty, are you all right?' George's face was close to hers, and his arms supported her as her knees trembled and gave way. 'Are you hurt?'

She leaned against him, sobbing as she fought to catch the breath that Cyrus had almost squeezed out of her, but she managed somehow to shake her head in answer to his question.

'The dirty old dog,' George said, holding her close. 'I saw what he was trying to do to you. Are you sure he didn't hurt you?'

'N-no, I'm all right, th-thanks to you, George.' Hetty steadied herself and turned away to fasten her blouse, although several of the buttons had been torn off in the assault.

George shook his fist at Clench, who was struggling ashore on the far side. 'I should set the police on you, you villain.'

Coughing and spluttering, Clench heaved his body out of the water. 'She led me on, the little trull. And she owes me money. You wait, Hetty Huggins. I won't forget this in a hurry.'

George waded into the canal. 'Come near her again, mister, and you'll get what you rightly deserve.'

'Come out of the water, George,' Hetty pleaded. 'It's filthy dirty.'

He turned to her and his angry expression dissolved into a sheepish grin. 'I got carried away.' He climbed out and shook himself like a wet dog. 'Now I got a bootful of the Regent's Canal. At least I won't need to wash me socks!'

Cyrus stomped away along the towpath, his muttered insults and threats drowned by the sound of a steam engine thundering across the bridge.

'He's gone,' George said, eyeing her with concern. 'You're very pale, Hetty. Are you sure you're all right? I mean, he didn't actually . . .?'

She shook her head vehemently. 'No, he

didn't. Oh, George, I dunno what I would have done if you hadn't come along when you did.'

'I saw you walking down Bethnal Green Road, but when you cut through the alleys and I knew you were heading this way, I thought I'd better follow you. This is a bad place, Hetty. Don't never come this way again.'

She managed a wobbly smile, even though her lips were bruised and swollen. 'Don't worry. That's the last thing I'd do. I wanted to get home for supper and I just didn't stop to think.'

He linked her hand through his arm. 'Come on, girl. I'll see you safe home.'

'At least he didn't find me takings,' Hetty said, thrusting her hand into her pocket and taking out the leather purse. 'When I deduct me costs, I'll have made one and three today, George. We was lucky to make sixpence a day making matchboxes.'

'That's a good start.' He took the handle of the cart, but had only taken a few paces when he stopped, turning to Hetty with a frown creasing his brow. 'But it ain't safe for a girl like you to walk home alone.'

Hetty's knees were still shaking and she could still taste and smell Cyrus. It would take a long time to put his brutal assault out of her mind, but she was not going to let on to George, or anyone at home for that matter.

'Don't worry about me. I'll be more careful in future.'

'I'm sure you will, but that fellow is dangerous, and I don't think he'll give up easily. What if he tries it on again?'

'I'll report him to the police if he lays a finger on me.'

'He's a crafty one, Hetty. He's got it in for you, of that I'm certain. You'll need to be extra careful, especially when it starts to get dark earlier and earlier. If you'll just tell me what time you'll be heading off every day, I'll meet you and see you home.'

She could see that his mind was set on it, and, after her encounter with Cyrus, Hetty was not in a mood to refuse. 'Ta, George. Maybe it would be a good idea, just for a while at any rate, until I get the hang of things.'

They parted in Totty Street, arranging to meet outside St Matthew's Church in Bethnal Green Road the next day after work. Hetty went indoors, determined not to mention anything about Clench, but Granny's eagle eyes immediately spotted the missing buttons on her blouse, and, as she peered closer, she saw the telltale marks on Hetty's neck. Granny sent Jane outside to fill the kettle at the pump and she gave Sammy and Eddie a farthing each to go to the shop on the corner of Grove Road to buy some sweets as a special treat. 'It's not every day your sister goes into business,' she said, shooing them out of the door. She turned to Hetty, frowning. 'So what happened to you, miss? Have you been making free with that coster-monger fellow?'

Hetty's breath caught on a sob. 'N-no, it weren't George.'

'Pull yourself together, Hetty. Stop blub-bering and tell me what happened. I may be old, but I know the signs when a girl has allowed a man to go too far.'

Reluctantly, Hetty told her what had happened. If she had expected any sympathy, she was disappointed. Granny pursed her lips. 'Well, what do you expect? Only a fool would cut down by the canal. That was asking for trouble, Hetty.'

'Yes'm. I know that now. It won't happen again.'

Granny folded her arms across her flat chest. 'So how much do you owe this creature all told?'

'I dunno exactly. He keeps adding on bits of interest. I think it's about two pounds.'

'We'll see about that. Now, not a word of this to that silly sister of yours. We don't want her having hysterics and going into early labour. I'm no midwife and we've got enough trouble on our hands without adding a squalling brat that comes before its time.'

Early on Friday morning, when Cyrus came for his money, Hetty had not yet gone to the bakery to collect the potatoes. Summoned by the rapping on the knocker, she went to open the door but was forestalled by Mr Shipworthy who gave her an icy stare. 'I know what you did, young woman. Cyrus told me all about it in the pub last night. Very upset he was, poor fellow. A girl like you gets a man into trouble.' Without giving her a chance to respond to this unexpected verbal attack, he opened the door and ushered Cyrus into the narrow hallway. 'Ah, Clench, old chap. I hope you've recovered from your nasty experience.'

Cyrus took off his greasy top hat and clutched it in front of him, baring his blackened teeth in an ingratiating smile. 'I have, but it's a wonder I didn't catch me death of cold, Jasper. However, it's kind of you to enquire.'

Jasper looked down his thin nose at Hetty. 'I hope you're suitably apologetic to this poor man, miss. Leading him on and then crying rape. Shame on you.'

'I never did that!' Hetty glared at Cyrus. 'You liar! What have you told him?'

'Exactly what he said, Miss Huggins. You

took advantage of my chivalrous nature.' He turned to Jasper, holding out his hands. 'See how she pretends innocence? She is the worst kind of tease, promising much and then screaming for help. I was never so embarrassed or humiliated in my whole life.'

'A liar and a coward, that's you, mister.' Granny Huggins stalked out of the parlour, advancing on Cyrus with her eyes narrowed. If she had been a cat, Hetty thought in astonishment, Granny's back would have been arched and her fur standing on end as she hissed at Clench.

His eyes opened wide in alarm as he backed towards the front door. 'Mrs Huggins, surely you haven't been taken in by that wanton girl's lies?'

'Get out of my house,' Granny said in a low, menacing tone. 'Get out and don't ever show your face in this street again.'

The front door was still open and Cyrus stumbled out onto the pavement. 'I've come on legitimate business. That little trull owes me two pounds fifteen and eleven. If she don't pay up, I'll send the bailiffs in.'

Granny put her hand in the pocket of her apron and Hetty heard the sound of coins jingling. She held her breath, not daring to speak. Jasper pushed past her and went to stand beside Clench. 'Mrs Huggins, ma'am.

Where is your sense of fair play and justice? My friend Cyrus is only doing his job.'

Granny hurled a handful of coins at their feet. 'There's your blood money, Clench. Take it, and go. If you ever come near my granddaughter again, I'll have the law on you.'

'He is the injured party here, ma'am,' Jasper protested, grovelling on the ground as he helped Cyrus to pick up the money. 'You are in the wrong.'

Granny stormed into the front parlour and reappeared seconds later with an armful of clothes, shoes and a china shaving mug which she tossed onto the pavement at Jasper's feet. The mug broke into shards and he let out a loud groan. 'Madam, you can't treat me like this.'

'Ho! Can't I? You can sling your hook too, Mr Shipworthy. If that creature is an example of the company you keep, then I don't want either of you in my house.' Granny slammed the door in their faces, slapping her hands together with a triumphant smile. 'That told them, Hetty. I think that's the last you'll see of Cyrus Clench. Let's put the kettle on and have a nice hot cup of tea before you go out to business.'

Hetty continued to go out on her rounds daily, with the exception of Sundays. After her clash with the huckster outside Bethnal Green station, she was very careful where she set up her can, but even so she still came up against serious opposition from some of the other hot potato vendors. It was heavy work, too, but gradually she became used to heaving about hundredweight sacks of potatoes and carrying wicker baskets to and from the bakery. Trade was reasonable considering the hot weather, and she continued to make at least a shilling a day profit, but she was determined to make even more.

Although Cyrus had been paid off Hetty was not convinced that he would fade into the background. She could still feel his malignant presence hovering over her like a great thundercloud, but she dared not voice her worries to Tom, who had always been unhappy about her plying her trade in the streets. He still called at Totty Street almost every evening, and they had resumed their Sunday outings to Victoria Park, much to the delight of Sammy and Eddie. Jane had accompanied them once or twice, but she was getting near her time. She found the heat exhausting and she spent most afternoons resting on the bed in the front parlour. After Mr Shipworthy's undignified departure, Granny had seen fit to allow Jane and Hetty to share his room, and she went so far as to purchase a cradle from the second-hand furniture dealer in Grove Road. Hetty wondered if this generous act indicated a change of heart, but she could not quite summon the courage to put the question into words. Granny had made it perfectly clear that she could not abide babies, but she had not repeated her threat to turn them out as soon as it arrived. Hetty now lived from day to day; hoping for the best, but prepared for the worst.

Towards the end of August, Jane began to get restless. Casting her mind back more than forty years, to the birth of her beloved Samuel, Granny concluded that Jane's time must be near, and she announced that arrangements had been made for the midwife to attend the birth. Hetty knew that all this was going to cost money and she still owed Granny a considerable sum. She had tried to save but with the boys attending school, and Jane unable to work outside the home, her profits were soon eaten away. She had tried to keep her worries to herself, but Jane had sensed that something was wrong and in the middle of a hot August night when sleep was virtually impossible, she demanded to be told the truth.'You should have told me before,' she said, pacing the floor of their room with her bare feet padding softly on the floorboards. She stopped for a moment to support her bulging belly and took a deep breath.

'Are you all right?' Hetty asked anxiously. 'It's not the baby coming, is it?'

Jane shook her head. 'I wish it was, but I don't think so. I'm so sick of being like this. I don't think I'll ever see me toes again and I hate being fat.'

Hetty scrambled off the bed and rearranged the tumbled sheets. 'Lie down and rest.'

'It's too bloody hot to sleep. Anyway, now I'm just as worried as you are, and it's all my fault. If I could earn some money we wouldn't be in such a fix. What if Granny throws us out because we can't pay the rent?'

Hetty put her arm around Jane's shoulders and guided her over to the bed. 'She wouldn't do that. She's not as hard as she makes out. You mustn't worry; it's bad for the baby. I'll see us right, Janey.'

'I'm sick of helping her make bloody bonnets. If she paid me it wouldn't be so bad.' Jane slumped down on the bed. She frowned thoughtfully. 'I could make matchboxes though. Even if I only earned a couple of pennies a day it would help to pay for the midwife.'

'I won't hear of it. I've already decided to go out in the evenings to sell hot taters outside the theatres and music halls. There's good profit there, so I hear. You've got to look after yourself and little Nat. Leave the rest to me.'

The following afternoon, after a long day of

trading in the blistering heat, Hetty had just wheeled the cart into the back yard when Tom burst through the gate, red in the face and panting. He clutched his side, struggling to catch his breath. 'Come quick, Hetty. It's Jane.'

'What? Where is she? Is it the baby?'

He nodded. 'God knows why, but she went to the match factory. Mrs Brinkman found her collapsed outside on the pavement. She managed to get her back to Autumn Road.' He took a deep breath. 'She sent her Sonia round to our place to find me.'

'Oh, my Lord.' Hetty clutched her brow. She knew exactly why Jane had gone to the match factory, and it was all her fault. She should have kept her money worries to herself and not burdened Jane with them. 'I must go to her right away, Tom.'

Sammy had wandered out into the yard. 'What's going on, Hetty?'

She took him by the shoulders. 'I think that Jane's baby is coming too soon. She's over at our old place in Autumn Road, but Mrs Brinkman's taken her in, so she'll be fine. I just want you to go in and tell Granny that Tom and me have gone there to make sure she's all right.'

Sammy's face paled and his eyes were huge behind the thick lenses of his spectacles. 'Is she going to die like Ma did?'

'No, of course not. You're not to worry,

Sammy. Babies come every day. Now you go indoors and don't frighten Eddie.'

Sammy did not look convinced. 'Granny says that lots of women die birthing babies.'

'Well Jane won't die. I promise you that.' Hetty watched him run into the house with a lump in her throat. 'I pray to God that I'm right.'

# Chapter Seven

Sonia Brinkman met them at the door of the old house in Autumn Road. Her small features were puckered with concern, and the scarf that she wore to conceal her bald patch had slipped to one side, revealing an expanse of white scalp. 'Thank goodness you've come, Hetty. Your sister very bad, very bad indeed.' As if to emphasise the point, an animal-like howl emanated from the depths of the house. Sonia held the door open. 'You come in,' she said, dragging Hetty over the threshold, 'but he stay outside,' she added, jerking her head in Tom's direction, which caused her scarf to slip off completely, and she righted it with a self-conscious giggle. 'Mama says birthing babies is not a man's business. She sent Papa to the pub.'

'Not to worry,' Tom said, backing away into the street. 'I'll go to the pub and keep Mr Brinkman company.'

Hetty followed Sonia down the dark passageway. As she entered the darkened room, she almost choked on the nauseous stench of cess filtering through a broken windowpane. The heat was almost unbearable and flies buzzed in angry circles above their heads. Jane lay on a blanket spread on the bare floorboards. She was naked from the waist down and her face was contorted with pain as a contraction racked her body. Mrs Brinkman knelt beside her, holding her hand and murmuring words of encouragement. She looked up as Hetty entered the room, and she managed a tired smile. 'Hetty, thank God you come. Jane, your sister is here. Baby come early, she say.'

Jane's cracked lips formed a word but then another scream was wrenched from her lips. 'Oh, God,' she murmured as the pain ebbed away. 'I'm dying, Hetty.'

Hetty threw herself down on her knees by her side. 'No, you're not, dear. It will all be over soon.' She cast an anxious glance at Mrs Brinkman. 'How far along is she?'

'Baby come when he is ready.' Mrs Brinkman turned to Sonia, who was hovering anxiously in the doorway. 'Fetch clean water, Sonia. And bring something to wrap baby in.'

Sonia needed no second bidding and she ran from the room.

Mrs Brinkman patted Jane's hand. 'Soon you will hold baby in your arms. Not long now.'

'It's all bloody right for you,' Jane gasped. 'You're not the one trying to shit a football.'

'Jane!' Hetty gasped, shocked to hear such words coming from Jane's prim lips. 'Watch your language.'

Mrs Brinkman chuckled. 'I been through this ten times. I know how it is.'

'Never again,' Jane moaned. 'I'll never let another man near me, ever again.'

'Yes, yes. So you say now,' Mrs Brinkman said, mopping Jane's forehead with a piece of damp rag. 'Haven't I said the same thing myself, and look where it got me.'

Sonia scuttled back into the room slopping water from a chipped enamel bowl. 'I couldn't find nothing clean to wrap the baby in, Mama.'

Hetty scrambled to her feet and stepped out of her calico petticoat. She folded the warm material and laid it aside in readiness to swaddle the newborn baby.

'Go, make us tea, Sonia,' Mrs Brinkman said as Jane uttered another loud groan.

Sonia backed towards the doorway, pale-faced and staring at Jane in alarm. 'I don't think she wants tea, Ma.'

'Not for her, silly girl,' Mrs Brinkman said impatiently. 'Tea for me and Hetty. Go!' Shooing Sonia from the room, she turned back to Jane. 'Brave girl. Baby come soon.'

'Hetty!' Jane gasped. 'Hold my hand.'

Kneeling beside her, Hetty had to bite her lip to stop herself from crying out as Jane, with seemingly superhuman strength, almost crushed the bones in her fingers as she rode the next wave of pain. Surely this could not go on much longer, she thought dazedly. How much pain could one slip of a girl bear?

Hetty lost all sense of time as the labour went on and on. Sometimes Jane was quiet, but then the contractions started up again and heart-wrenching screams were torn from her throat. It seemed to Hetty that no human being should go through this much agony in order to produce a child, and at times she thought that Jane really was going to die, but Mrs Brinkman simply smiled and murmured words of reassurance. After what seemed like an eternity, Mrs Brinkman exhorted Jane to give a final push, and Hetty choked back tears as she watched her sister being delivered of a squalling, red-faced infant.

'It's a girl,' Mrs Brinkman said with a triumphant smile. 'A beautiful baby girl.'

Jane raised her head and peered at the squalling baby. 'She's ugly. I wanted a boy, not a monkey-faced girl.'

Mrs Brinkman wrapped the baby in Hetty's shift. 'She'll grow into her looks, Jane. You hold her?'

Jane shook her head wearily. 'I just want to sleep.'

'I'll hold her while you do what you need to,' Hetty said, taking the baby from Mrs Brinkman.

'Take baby into parlour,' Mrs Brinkman said. 'I look after little mama.'

Hetty rose to her feet, cradling the baby in her arms. The fierce squalling ceased abruptly and Hetty found herself looking into a pair of violet-blue eyes. It was as though she and Jane's child already knew one another, and something almost mystical seemed to pass between them. At that moment, Hetty fell in love with the tiny, red-faced infant. She kissed the top of her fuzzy dark head. 'Hello, baby.'

Mrs Brinkman nodded with approval. 'She's a little flower, that one.'

'She should have been a boy,' Jane murmured drowsily. 'She was going to be my little Nat. I don't want a blooming girl.'

Sonia had crept back into the room unnoticed. She sidled up to Hetty and peered at the baby. 'If it hadn't been for Mama, Jane would have had baby on the pavement outside the factory. Baby should be named for my mama.'

Mrs Brinkman shook her head. 'Hush, Sonia. Jane don't want to name baby after old Russian woman who don't have no education.'

A flicker of interest momentarily lit Jane's eyes. 'What is your name, Mrs Brinkman?'

'Well, it ain't Brinkman for a start. My Colya changed name to sound more English; he say we get on better in this country if we sound less foreign.'

'But your first name, Mama,' Sonia said eagerly. 'Tell them what it is.'

'Natalia. My name is Natalia.'

'Natalia,' Hetty repeated, staring down at the baby. 'She can still be your little Nat after all.'

'I really don't care . . .' Jane closed her eyes and turned her head away.

Hetty was almost overcome by a wave of protective love for the helpless infant in her arms. She struggled to understand Jane's indifference to her own child, and failed.

'She is so beautiful, Jane. Why don't you hold her for a moment?'

Mrs Brinkman laid her hand on Hetty's arm. 'She don't know what she say. You take baby and leave Jane to me.'

Hetty carried Natalia into the Brinkmans' living room where she found Tom making an effort at conversation with Mr Brinkman who, judging by the smell of alcohol, had spent most of the day in the pub. The surviving Brinkman children ranged from a ten-month-old baby to Sonia, who was the eldest. Her younger sister Anna was busy slicing up a loaf for their supper, and seven-year-old Larissa was scraping the bread with margarine. The younger ones waited eagerly, but silently, for their food.

'So it's over,' Mr Brinkman said thickly. 'Another mouth to feed.'

'She's a beautiful baby girl,' Hetty said proudly. 'Jane is going to name her for your wife, Mr Brinkman. I'm ever so grateful to her for what she did today.'

Tom moved to Hetty's side. He lifted his hand as if he wanted to touch the baby's cheek and then he dropped it to his side. 'She's so tiny.'

'She's called Natalia. And you can touch her, Tom. She ain't made of glass.'

He shook his head. 'Not with my big mitts. I might accidentally hurt the little mite.'

Hetty frowned. 'How are we going to get them home, Tom?'

Mr Brinkman raised himself from his seat by the fireplace. 'I got friend with cart. He do it cheap.'

It was midnight when Tom lifted Jane off the rag and bone man's cart, and Hetty carried Natalia into the house in Totty Street. 'This is your home, Natalia Huggins,' she said softly.

'What sort of heathen name is that?' Granny emerged from the parlour holding up an oil lamp. She stared at the baby with unconcealed distaste. 'Put it in the cradle in the front room, Hetty.'

Sammy and Eddie appeared at the top of the stairs and came running down to peer at the baby. 'What's it called?' demanded Eddie.

'Natalia,' Hetty said, smiling. 'You and Sammy are her uncles. You must look after little Talia.'

'She should have been a boy,' Jane murmured, leaning her head against Tom's shoulder. 'Girls are nothing but trouble.'

'You're just worn out, Jane,' Hetty said as she opened the door to the front room. 'You'll see things differently when you've had a rest.'

Tom carried Jane over to her bed, setting her down gently. 'Anything else I can do for you, ducks?'

Jane turned her head away. 'No. Go away.'

'That's no way to speak to Tom,' Hetty said angrily. 'Where's your manners, Jane?'

'I'd best be off then,' Tom said, backing away from the bed as if he expected Jane to rise up and slap him.

'Thanks for everything, Tom.' Hetty flashed him a grateful smile as she laid the sleeping baby down in the cradle. She couldn't resist stroking Natalia's downy head. She was so perfect, even down to her tiny fingernails. How could Jane not love such a precious little girl?

She looked up and found that Tom was watching her closely, and she smiled. 'Have you ever seen such a beautiful little thing?'

'She's a proper little peach, all right. I'm glad I was there to give a hand, but anyone would have done the same.'

'No, that's just not true.' Moved by his modesty and with her heart bursting with gratitude for his unwavering support, Hetty threw her arms around his neck and kissed him on the cheek. 'A brother couldn't have done more than you did today, and I'll always be grateful, Tom.'

'A brother! I should hope I'm more than that to you, Hetty.'

'Oh, don't mind me,' Jane cried angrily. 'I've just been through hell and you two are spooning.'

'We was not. I was just showing a bit of gratitude to Tom for standing by us today. It wouldn't hurt you to do the same.' Hetty went over to the bed and pulled the coverlet up to Jane's chin. 'Now you get some sleep while I see Tom out.'

'You're too late, Hetty. He's gone.'

Hetty heard the front door open and then close. She had not meant to bruise Tom's tender feelings. It had been a manner of speaking when she likened him to a brother, but he had taken it completely the wrong way. She bit back the angry words that rose to her lips. After all, Jane had just been through a long and painful labour; she must make allowances for her. She brushed a lock of damp hair back from Jane's forehead. 'Best get some sleep. When the baby wakes up she'll be hungry.'

'I don't want her,' Jane said tearfully. 'She's not my little Nat. She's just a girl.' She buried her face in the pillow and wept.

There was nothing that Hetty could do or say that would comfort her, and she sighed. Perhaps Jane would see things differently when she had rested. Hetty left the room to find Granny and Sammy waiting outside the door. 'So, she's not best pleased,' Granny said, curling her lip. 'Well, she had the kid and now she's got to look after it. I can't abide babies, never could. I don't want to hear it caterwauling in the night, so you'd better see to that, Hetty. I've got to get my beauty sleep.'

Sammy and Eddie sniggered at this and Granny dealt out clouts round their heads. 'Get back to bed, boys. You've got school in the morning.' She stalked off into the parlour and slammed the door.

Worried that the noise might have awakened the baby, Hetty tiptoed back into the room to check on her. She stared down at Natalia with an almost suffocating rush of emotion.

'I love you, little Talia,' she whispered. 'I'll never let no one hurt you, my pet.'

The baby's eyelids fluttered, half opened and then closed as she gave Hetty a gummy smile. Hetty knew that it must just be wind, but it was still a smile for all that. She left the room, closing the door softly behind her. Jane would change her mind when she had rested. She would learn to love her little daughter.

Jane did not change her mind. She was as reluctant a mother as anyone could be and sometimes Hetty despaired of her. Jane could not seem to overcome her disappointment on giving birth to a girl. Hetty struggled to understand how a mother could turn away from her own child. She could only think that her sister had so desperately wanted a small replica of her lost love that she could not forgive Natalia for being born female. After a good telling-off from Granny, Jane made an effort to feed the baby, and she did everything necessary to nurture her daughter, but it seemed that she did it without any joy.

Hetty worked even harder now that there was another mouth to feed, and, as a warm September gave way to a chilly October, she started going out at night to sell hot potatoes outside Coborn Road railway station. On Friday and Saturday evenings she took a stand outside the People's Palace in the Mile End Road, which had been built to provide recreational activities for the poor. It was hard work and tiring, but doing the night shift was very profitable and Hetty was able to start repaying Granny, and even managed to save a little each week. Her customers ranged from housewives who wanted to take home a quick and easy supper, to weary workers who needed the hot murphy to warm their cold hands on their journey homewards.

Working at night was not without its dangers, but Hetty soon learned which areas were safer than others, and if she spotted trouble she would pack up her cart and head for home. She avoided the streets where drunks lurched out of public houses, and prostitutes touted for business. It was plain commonsense, she told herself, and there was no need for either Tom or George to know what she was doing. Matters were made easier for her as Tom was putting in as much overtime at the Gas Light and Coke Company as he could get. He told her proudly that he was saving for their future, and he was so convinced that they would one day be married that Hetty almost came to believe it herself. She was fond of Tom, and she doubted whether she would ever fall head over heels in love, as Jane had fallen for her Nat. Tom was safe and solid, and, Hetty thought vaguely, she could do a lot worse.

George, on the other hand, was a good friend. He could make her laugh even when she felt sad and low, and she enjoyed walking home with him every day, when he would tell her about the goings-on in the market in such a way that she was often breathless from laughing. He had never been remotely lover-like in his behaviour towards her; in fact he told her in great detail about his most recent conquests and she commiserated with him when his love affairs ended badly, as they almost inevitably did. George had a roving eye and a tender heart, but Hetty compared him to the colourful bird of paradise that she had once seen illustrated in a picture book. If George was a bird of paradise, then she likened Tom to the pigeons which were to be seen everywhere, working hard to fill their bellies and to raise their young in the harsh environs of the East End streets. She loved them both, in her way, and if she were to lose either of them, Hetty knew that she would be quite heartbroken.

She had not seen either Cyrus Clench or Jasper Shipworthy since Granny had thrown them out of the house, and for that she was extremely grateful. Sometimes, when she was trundling her cart home late at night, she had the feeling she was being followed, but it had always turned out to be either her imagination or some quite innocent pedestrian who happened to be going her way. Once, it was a feral dog, whose panting had made her hair stand on end, but when she spun round to face her fear, she had laughed out loud to see the cur slink away in the darkness with a crust of bread in its mouth.

The days grew shorter, the nights longer and the weather colder. Hetty continued to work and her savings grew. She was out in the foulest of the winter weather, except the pea-soupers that wrapped a blanket of yellowish-green fog around the city. The choking smell of coal tar and smoke clogged the nostrils of those caught in its clutches, and, with the exception of the trains, everything ground to a halt. On one occasion, Hetty had braved the fog to stand outside Bethnal Green station at the time when the workers were hurrying home; she had done a brisk trade, but she had caught a chill and had to spend the next couple of days confined to her bed.

When spring came with lighter evenings and milder weather, the potato season had just about ended, but Hetty had been planning for this all winter. She had asked George to keep an eye out for a two-wheeled spring barrow, such as the coffee-stallholders used in the market places. She had been watching them trade, and now she was ready to branch out, selling not only ham sandwiches, but boiled eggs, watercress, currant cake, coffee and tea. She had done her sums, saved her pennies and she was eager to start.

Late one Friday afternoon at the end of April, George met her as usual, and he was grinning from ear to ear. 'Hello, my lovely. Guess what clever George has done?'

Hetty stopped to rest for a moment; it had been a long, hard day, and, with the warmer weather, her takings had been down. 'What have you done, George? Who is the lucky lady this time?'

His eyes turned the colour of warm amber and he clutched his hands to his heart with a pained expression on his face. 'You ain't being fair, girl. You make me sound like a ladykiller.'

Chuckling at the thought, Hetty patted him on the cheek. 'You've left a string of broken hearts from Bow to Bishopsgate, don't deny it.'

His eyes twinkled with golden lights. 'Haven't I just? But that's another matter, Hetty. I've found your barrow. Old Skaggs the pie man dropped dead all of a sudden. They say as how he was poisoned by one of his own pork pies, but I say it was his heart what give out sudden-like. Anyway, I know his old lady, so I jumped in quick, made her an offer she couldn't refuse, and you've got your barrow.'

Hetty flung her arms around his neck and hugged him. 'George, I love you. You're wonderful.'

His cheeky grin faded and a dull flush spread upwards from his neck. 'Give over, girl. You're making me blush.'

'You're a toff, George.' She stood on tiptoe to kiss him on the cheek. 'Where is this barrow? When can I see it?'

'It's alongside mine in Spitalfields market. We can fetch it now, only you'll have to take your cart home first.'

'That would take too much time.' Hetty dragged the cart off the pavement into the doorway of an empty shop. 'It'll be safe enough here for a while.'

George shook his head. 'I dunno, Hetty. There are some light-fingered geezers around.'

'I doubt if anyone would bother with a can at the end of the season, and we'll only be gone half an hour at most.'

'All right, if you say so.'

'Lead on,' Hetty cried excitedly, falling into step beside him. 'This means so much to me, George. I was thinking I'd have to start my next venture selling ham sandwiches from a basket, but now I can start off proper.'

'Tomorrow a coffee stall - next year a coffee shop.'

'That's right. And I won't stop at one coffee shop. I mean to have a whole string of them circling the city like pearls round a rich lady's throat.'

George took her by the hand. 'Come on then, girl. There's no time to lose if you want to be a pearly princess. Best foot forward, Hetty.'

She was breathless from exertion and excitement by the time they reached Spitalfields market where the stallholders were packing up for the day. The ground was strewn with broken flowers, leaves and squashed vegetable matter, and everything was sparkling as the sun emerged from the clouds after a sudden shower of rain. Hetty gasped with pleasure as George pointed out her barrow. Raindrops hung from the striped canopy, shimmering like diamonds in the sunshine. She barely noticed the peeling paint or the broken spokes on one of the wheels; to Hetty it was a gleaming miracle, as smart as any of the carriages that the toffs might ride in with their noses stuck in the air. And it was hers. She covered her mouth with her hands, unable to speak.

George slipped his arm around her shoulders and gave her a hug. 'It'll clean up nicely. It just needs a few minor repairs and the old barrow will be good as new.'

'It's wonderful,' Hetty breathed. 'Oh, George, I can't thank you enough for getting this for me. How much do I owe you?'

He pushed his cap to the back of his head. 'Well, now. I got it at a knockdown price, Hetty. I ain't sure that I could rightly claim anything back in terms of hard cash. But I tell you what. How about me being what they call a sleeping partner in your business? I could be the "and Co." on the side of your barrow. Hetty Huggins and Co. That has a good sound to it, don't you think?'

'I don't know what to say, George.' Hetty traced the wooden surface of the barrow with her fingertip. 'I must pay you back what I owe.'

'I'll be more than satisfied with a free cup of tea every now and again, and you can buy your watercress and cucumbers off me. I can see you going far, Hetty. I'll be proud to be the one who gave you a start, and if you're that particular about paying me back, we'll talk about it when you're running at a profit. What could be fairer than that?'

Hetty grabbed him by the hands and danced him round in a circle, her skirts flying and her hair coming loose from the tight knot at the back of her head. 'Business partners it is then, George. Huggins and Co. I like the sound of that.'

'Oy, George, me old cock.' A large woman with red-veined cheeks and a pendulous bosom waddled over to them and slapped him on the back. 'What's all this, then?'

George doffed his cap with a flourish, bowing low to the woman. 'Nora, me love. You're a sight for sore eyes, and that's a fact.' He turned to Hetty. 'Hetty, this is Nora Jackson, the pearly queen of Spitalfields market. What she says goes, doesn't it, my duck?'

He pinched Nora's chubby cheek, and she uttered a great wheezing laugh. 'You and your soft soap, George,' she said, slapping him on the shoulder. 'I hope you don't let this man lead you astray, dearie.'

'No, ma'am,' Hetty said, bobbing a curtsey. It seemed fitting in the presence of royalty. She had seen pearly kings and queens all dressed up in their finery when the occasion called for it, but she had never actually met one before.

'No need to be formal,' Nora said, puffing out her chest. 'But I am the one you need to see before you starts up on the market. What's your trade, dearie?'

'A coffee stall, Nora,' George said, hooking his arm around Hetty's shoulders.

'Let the girl speak for herself, George.'

Hetty cleared her throat. 'If you please, ma'am – I mean, your highness – I want to run a coffee stall and sell ham sandwiches, cake and stuff like that.'

'Your highness, eh?' Nora let out a throaty cackle of laughter. 'I can see we're going to get on well, Hetty. But just Nora will do. I don't wear me pearly finery to work. I saves it for high days and holidays.'

'And very fine you look, my dear,' George said with his irrepressible good humour. 'A real duchess among women is Nora.'

Nora cuffed him round the ear but without any force behind the blow, and she was still smiling. 'Cheeky boy.' She turned to Hetty, nodding her head. 'Well, I don't see any problem. There are two coffee stalls, but they are on the far side of the market, one at the west entrance and one at the south. I see no reason why you can't set up over there.' She pointed to a space not far from where they were standing. 'When can you start?'

Taken aback and breathless at the rapid turn of events, Hetty did a quick calculation. She would have to get the barrow fixed up; a sign painted, and buy in the foodstuffs she needed to set up business. 'In a week's time.'

Nora shook her head. 'Can't have an empty space for a whole week. I'll give you two days, and if you can't set up first thing on Monday morning, the spot will go to someone who can. Good luck, dearie.' Nora winked at George and walked back to her own stall, swaying like a tea clipper under full sail with her corsets creaking at every move.

George tossed his cap up in the air with a loud whoop of glee. 'She likes you, Hetty. You're in, girl. Now all you got to do is push the barrow home, get it done up a bit and you're in business.'

As Hetty struggled to push the barrow homeward, she was beginning to wonder if she had taken on too much. It was both cumbersome and heavy. Easy enough for a strong fellow like George, but extremely hard work for a slender girl who only came up to his shoulder. By the time they reached Bethnal Green Road, Hetty was panting and ready to drop, but she would not admit it to anyone, least of all George. She came to a halt outside the empty shop where she had left her cart, but to her dismay there was no sign of it.

'Maybe this isn't the place,' George said, pulling his barrow into the kerbside. 'Perhaps it was further on?'

'No, it was here. I know it was, opposite the pawnbroker's. It's gone, George. Someone has pinched it and me can too. I can't afford another two quid for a new one and I was banking on that for hot water for making tea and coffee.'

George scratched his head. 'Maybe it was

kids, Hetty. You know what young limbs boy are. Perhaps they've taken it for a lark.'

'Some lark. That's my living they're playing with.' Hetty fought back tears of desperation. Everything had been going so well and now she was facing disaster. Even if she could afford to buy a new can and fire pot, it would take at least a week for the tin man to make one, and then she would have lost her site in the market place.

'Cheer up, love,' George said gently. 'You go on home. I'll get me barrow back to Cottage Green and then I'll go out looking for your cart. Ten to one it's down by the canal. That's where things usually end up.'

Hetty nodded her head. 'Ta, George, but it's my problem, not yours.'

He brushed a strand of hair back from her forehead. 'Well, now, I'm the "and Co" so I've got to do me bit. You go home and cuddle that little baby you're so fond of and leave the rest to me.'

It was a struggle to get the barrow through the gate into the yard of number ten Totty Street, and at one point the canopy became tangled in the washing line, but Hetty finally managed it with a good deal of shoving and pushing. She took the dry clothes off the line and carried them into the house. In the parlour she was surprised to see Tom sitting in a chair by the fire, bouncing Natalia on his knee. The baby gave a squeal of delight on seeing Hetty and held out her chubby arms.

Jane was standing by the range pouring boiling water into the teapot. She looked up and frowned. 'Baby likes you better than me,' she grumbled. 'You should be the one to stay here all day and see to her, Hetty.'

Hetty's heart gave a leap inside her chest as she took Natalia from Tom, and she kissed her downy head. 'If she was mine I'd be more than happy to look after her. She's a little pearl, aren't you, my poppet?'

Tom stood up, stretching his limbs. 'Why don't I get a greeting like that, Hetty? I've been sitting here for a good hour, waiting for you to come home.'

'With only me for company,' Jane said, slamming the lid on the teapot. 'However, I never heard him complaining about it.'

'No, of course not,' Tom said hastily. 'We had a good chat, didn't we, Janey? At least someone finds me interesting.'

Hetty tickled Natalia's tummy, smiling as the baby gurgled with laughter. 'Don't be such an old misery-martin, Tom. I suppose you'd like me to tickle you too?'

His frown dissolved into a grin. 'Well, I wouldn't mind, if you're offering.'

'Don't mind me, you two.' Jane put the

teapot on the trivet. 'That needs to brew for a while.' She bustled over to Hetty, taking the baby from her arms. 'It's time I changed her, she smells something awful. Anyway, I daresay you two want to be alone for a while.' She cast an arch glance at Tom. 'I'll knock on the door before I come back, shall I?'

'No need, Jane. I got a bone to pick with Hetty.'

Jane flashed him a brilliant smile. 'Well best get it over afore Granny and the boys get back from delivering her latest creations. She'll be complaining about her bunions and gasping for a cup of tea, so you'd better keep out of her way.'

'It won't take long,' Tom said, glowering at Hetty. 'You go and see to the baby, Jane. And ta for the tea.'

'My pleasure,' Jane said archly as she left the room carrying a howling Natalia, who had objected to being snatched from Hetty's tender embrace.

'What's up?' Hetty demanded as the door closed on Jane and the baby. 'Why the long face? It's me who should be looking like I lost sixpence and found a farthing.'

'Where've you been? Why are you so late, and why didn't you tell me that costermonger fellow sees you home every day?'

Hetty poured the tea. 'Because I knew you'd

make a fuss and turn it into something it ain't. George is just a friend, that's all.'

'If that's so, then why keep it secret? I'll bet he don't think of himself as just a friend. What's going on between you two?'

'Nothing.' Hetty handed him a cup of tea. She wanted to tell Tom everything, but when he was in this sort of mood there was no sense talking to him. He was so stubborn sometimes. Once he had an idea stuck in his head, there was no shifting it. She decided to change the subject. 'Anyway, why are you here so early? I thought you was doing overtime.'

'I've worked every night except Sundays for the past month, and I reckon I'm due a bit of time off. I come round early to see if you wanted to go to the music hall tonight. It's not too late. Will you, Hetty?'

She hesitated. She had never been to a music hall, or any kind of theatre come to that; it would be a rare treat indeed. But there was the missing cart and her precious can, and she ought to be here in case George found them. If she told Tom about the theft she would have to explain why she had abandoned her cart in an unsafe place, and then it would all come out. She would have to admit that she had gone against his advice and worked nights in order to save enough to start her coffee stall. He would be hurt and he would be angry. He was staring at her with a puzzled expression on his face, waiting for her answer. She managed a wobbly smile. 'Ta, Tom. I'd like that very much.'

They were about to leave the house when the sound of cartwheels rumbling down the street made Hetty pause and turn her head. In the flickering glow of the gas lamps, she saw George pushing the battered cart towards them. It was dripping muddy water and festooned in green slime. She bit back a cry of horror at the sight of the once gleaming tin can, which was now battered and dented. She snatched her hand from Tom's arm and ran to meet George.

'I found it in the canal,' George said breathlessly. 'Some bugger had tried to sink it with bricks, but the can floated and I waded in to get it.'

Hetty's voice caught on a sob. 'Oh, George, it's ruined. Now I'll never be ready to open up my coffee stall by Monday.'

# Chapter Eight

'What's going on?' Tom demanded. 'Have you been pulling the wool over my eyes, Hetty?'

'Steady on, mate,' George said, frowning. 'There's no need to take that tone with her.'

Tom pushed Hetty aside, squaring up to George with an aggressive out-thrust of his chin. 'And who are you to tell me how I should treat my girl? I'll not stand for you sniffing round her like she was a bitch on heat.'

'Tom!' Hetty slapped him on the arm. 'You've no right to speak to George like that. He was just doing me a favour.'

Tom turned on her, white-lipped and eyes blazing. 'Yes, and I know the kind of favour he'd like to do for you. I've met his type afore, Hetty.'

'You don't know what you're talking about,' Hetty cried angrily. 'George has done nothing but try to help me. He believes in me and encourages me, which is more than I can say for you.'

'Now, now,' George said pleasantly. 'Don't you two fall out on my account. Hetty and me are just friends, mate. There's no call to get yourself in a stew.'

'Hetty is my girl, d'you understand me, mate?' Tom clenched his fists, stressing the term mate with heavy sarcasm.

'Shut up,' Hetty hissed. 'I won't have this sort of behaviour, Tom. George is my friend and a sort of business partner. Yes, you can scowl at me all you like, but I am, or rather I was, going to start up a coffee stall on Monday. But now, thanks to some bugger who threw me cart and can into the canal, it looks like everything is ruined. So if you can't do something useful, then just sling your hook.'

Tom stared at her for a long moment. The silence between them seemed to stretch into infinity, and then, with a casual shrug of his shoulders, he strode off down the street.

'I'm sorry, Hetty,' George said softly. 'I never meant to come between you and your fellow.'

Hetty brushed the back of her hand across her eyes, flicking away tears of anger and frustration. 'You didn't. He takes too much for granted. We aren't engaged or nothing.'

'Didn't seem like that to me, girl.'

Hetty waved her left hand in front of his face. 'Do you see a ring on me finger? No, you don't, because there ain't one. Tom can think what he likes, but I've never promised him nothing, and right now I got more urgent things to sort out.' She stared down at the battered can, polluted by the filthy water of the Regent's Canal.

George angled his head, following her gaze. 'It needs a good scrub, but we can probably knock out the dents and it'll do until you can get a new one.'

'Even if that was true, I'll never be ready to take up me pitch on Monday.'

His serious expression melted into a grin. 'Who says?'

'I can't see how.'

'Leave it to me, girl.' George hefted the can onto his shoulder. 'I'll take this back to Cottage Green and see what I can do. Tomorrow's Saturday, so I'll be working late, but I'll be round on Sunday. You see to the vittles and leave the rest to good old George.'

Next day, enlisting Sammy and Eddie's help, Hetty went to the grocer's shop to buy butter, sugar, eggs, ham, mustard, tea and coffee. She ordered bread from the baker, and a large currant cake. She agonised over a seed cake and some sticky buns, but she had set a budget and she knew she must not overspend. When they arrived back in Totty Street, she put all her purchases on a marble slab in the tiny washhouse, wrapping everything carefully in butter muslin and covering the ham with an upturned pudding basin in case there were any flies about this early in the year. A fitful sun had pushed aside the rain clouds, but as Hetty examined the barrow she had to admit that it looked a sad sight, and she felt her heart sink as she inspected it more fully. Flakes of peeling paint had fallen off and were scattered on the concrete like blossom from the flowering cherry trees in Victoria Park. Sammy kicked at the broken spokes of one of the wheels and it snapped right off. His small features puckered as if he were about to cry. 'I'm sorry, Hetty. I never meant to break it.'

She patted him on the shoulder. 'Don't worry, Sammy. I don't think you can do much harm to this poor old barrow.'

'It's broke, Hetty,' Eddie said, shaking his head. 'And it stinks.'

At that moment, Granny came bustling into the yard carrying a bowl of slops, which she threw down the drain. 'A pig in a poke, that's what you bought, Hetty. That thing will fall to pieces before you get to the corner of Grove Road.'

'I pushed it here from Spitalfields market, Granny. And George has promised to come tomorrow to fix it up.'

Granny sniffed. 'It would take a small army to make that contraption look respectable.

You've wasted your money, girl. You might as well have gambled it away on the horses.'

Hetty had a nasty feeling that this was true, but as she glanced through the parlour window she saw Jane sitting by the fireside, feeding Natalia bread and milk. She had a faraway look on her face, as if she was dreaming of better days. Hetty hardened her resolve. Their whole future depended upon this and she was not going to give in so easily. She picked up a bucket and went to fill it at the pump. 'It will work, Granny. I ain't going to be beaten. I'll get this barrow fixed up to start trading on Monday if it's the last thing I do.'

'Better be careful that it isn't,' Granny said tersely. 'That cart is only fit for matchwood or a bonfire.' She stalked back inside the house and the brass doorknob rattled as she shut the door with a bang.

Hetty turned to her brothers. 'All right, there's a penny each if you help me scrub this barrow clean, and scrape off all the old paint. And a pie and mash supper with pease pudding if we get it done by the end of the day.'

It was hard work, hindered by intermittent showers of rain. By mid-afternoon they were still scrubbing and scraping with little visible sign of improvement. The groaning of the back gate on its hinges made Hetty look up, and she stiffened as she saw Tom walk into the yard. He came to stand beside her, pushing his cap back and scratching his head. 'You'll never manage it on your own,' he said, taking the rusty kitchen knife from her hands.

Hetty stood aside, rubbing her sore fingers as she watched his deft movements. The paint peeled off as easily as butter beneath his firm strokes. Sammy and Eddie stopped to stare in awe as Tom worked steadily and in silence. Hetty knew that this was his way of apologising, and, anyway, she could never be angry with Tom for long. 'I think a cup of tea would go down nicely,' she murmured, heading for the house.

'We will get our pie and mash supper, won't we, Hetty?' Sammy called out anxiously. 'I mean it ain't fair if Tom does us out of it.'

Tom looked up at Hetty and smiled. 'I wouldn't want to do anyone out of their supper.'

She felt her heart lighten; she hated not being friends with Tom. 'You won't, and I might even include you in the treat.'

Next morning, Hetty was up at dawn. She went out into the yard to inspect the barrow. It had not rained in the night, and, in the pale spring sunshine, the wood gleamed as white as bleached bones, but there was still a long way to go before the barrow was fit for use. There was little she could do, since she had no tools, and even if she had, she would not have known where to begin. She went indoors to get the fire going and put the kettle on. She was just making the tea when she heard the sound of voices outside in the yard. She ran to the window and looked out. There seemed to be a small army of men clustered round the barrow. George was at the front, pointing out the defects. She hurried outside to join them. 'George?'

He turned to her and smiled. 'These are my mates,' he said, encompassing them with a sweep of his hand. 'And this, boys, is our newest costermonger, Miss Hetty Huggins.'

Hetty bobbed a curtsey, suddenly feeling shy. 'Pleased to meet you all.'

The tallest and brawniest man in the group stepped forward, taking off his cap and holding out his hand. 'Pleased to meet you, miss. I'm Brush Barber. As you might guess, I sell brushes for sweeping, scrubbing and painting; mops, buckets, pails – anything in that line.'

'How do, Mr Brush.' Hetty shook his hand.

'Just Brush, miss. That's what they calls me.' He backed away, replacing his cap on his bald head.

George pointed to a short, fat man who was

busy measuring up the spokes on the broken wheel. 'This here is Joe Jenkins; he's a butcher by trade, but a carpenter by nature. Ain't that true, Joe?'

'True as you're standing there, George. How do, miss?'

Hetty nodded and smiled, but before she could reply George had thrust her towards a thickset man with a shock of ginger hair. 'This is Ginger Turner. He sells haberdashery and he's a demon with a needle. He was apprenticed to a sailmaker, but he didn't have a liking for the trade, so now he sells pins, needles, thread and materials. He's going to fix the canvas canopy for you. And lastly, here's Fred Dixon. He sells paint and wallpaper and everything anyone might need to decorate their home. He's going to paint the barrow and write Hetty Huggins on the side, not forgetting the "and Co."'

Fred waved a paintbrush at Hetty. 'Pleased to meet you, miss. I couldn't half do with a cup of tea right now, if it ain't asking too much.'

'Yes,' Hetty murmured, quite at a loss for words to thank them all. 'Of course.' She hurried back into the house. In the parlour, she took cups from the dresser and set them on a wooden tray with the best silver-plated teaspoons. Granny was very particular about doing things properly. Hetty hoped that she would not be too put out when she saw her yard filled with a raggle-taggle assortment of men working on the barrow.

George stuck his head round the door. 'Can I give you a hand?'

Hetty poured the tea. 'I'm truly grateful for everything, George, but I can't do nothing without me can.'

He pushed the door open and set the slightly dented but brightly polished can on the floor. 'There, it's as good as new. Well, almost. Anyway, it'll have to do for now. I've scoured it inside and out. You'll not find any tadpoles floating in your coffee, Hetty.'

'Oh, George!' Hetty rushed over to him and flung her arms around his neck, giving him a hug. 'I'll never be able to thank you enough.'

He extricated himself from her clasp with a rueful smile. 'Now, if another pretty young lady had said that, I would have known exactly what to do. But being as how you're my partner in this business, I think a hug will do nicely. For now, anyway.'

Sleep evaded Hetty that night. In the wakeful small hours she went over her plan of action again and again. She was excited, nervous and frankly scared that her big scheme would prove to be a failure, and that no one would want her ham sandwiches, or the eggs that she had spent all evening boiling in batches on top of the range. Granny had complained bitterly about the steam ruining her half-finished creations on the shelves, and Jane had said the smell was making her feel sick. Despite their grumbling, Hetty had filled a basket with four dozen hard-boiled eggs, and had put them with the rest of her stock on the marble slab in the outhouse. She had made up her mind to leave home at first light and get the stall set up in order to catch people on their way to work.

She lay on the lumpy mattress listening to Jane's rhythmic breathing, which was interrupted occasionally by a muffled snort as she turned over in her sleep. Natalia slept in her cradle, making no sound at all. Hetty made a silent vow - little Talia would not grow up in poverty as they had done. She would not have to spend twelve hours a day making matchboxes at the age of five. Talia would go to a good school and learn to be a proper young lady.

Hetty awakened with a start, her heart beating a tattoo inside her ribcage. She must have dozed off without realising it and the first light of dawn was filtering through the partially drawn curtains. She sat bolt upright in bed, gathering her wits. She was going to be late and now she would have to hurry. She slipped out of bed, dressed hastily, and went outside to the yard to make everything ready. An hour later, as the sun rose in a misty pearl sky, she was trundling her barrow along Commercial Street towards Spitalfields market. It was chilly, but her hands were sweating as she clutched the freshly painted handles of the barrow, although it was excitement rather than nerves that was making the blood pulse through her veins. Today was a new beginning. The tin can might be dented but it would do its job, and the sound of the china cups rattling together in their cardboard box was music to her ears. The bright yellow paint, so carefully applied by Fred, had dried to a satin sheen, and her name stood out in bold black lettering on both sides of the cart – *HETTY HUGGINS AND CO.* As she pushed the barrow into the market hall, Hetty was met with a hive of activity. It seemed as though she was not the only early bird in Spitalfields.

'Hello, love,' Nora called in her wheezy foghorn of a voice. 'You can bring me over a cup of tea when you're ready. Two sugars and a dollop of milk.'

Her first order – Hetty's heart swelled with pride. She began setting up her stall, lighting the charcoal in the fire pot and filling the can with water from the pump close by. She received cheery greetings from the costers who were busy setting out their stalls. Brush waved to her from his pitch, and a woman who introduced herself as Floppy Flora, the flower lady, came over to pin a daffodil on Hetty's straw bonnet.

By the time George arrived, Hetty had the water boiling and had served her first dozen customers, mostly the other costermongers who had arrived early and were now breakfasting off coffee and ham sandwiches. Hetty cut and buttered bread, sliced cooked gammon and spread mustard in response to the increasing demand.

'How's it going then, Hetty?' George asked, helping himself to a slice of currant cake. He tossed a halfpenny into Hetty's money bag. 'Looks like you're off to a good start.'

'I can't believe it, George. I never expected to be this busy so early in the morning. I've almost run out of bread.'

'I'm not surprised. Your sandwiches look good enough to eat, not like the stale old doorsteps that Biggins sells over the way.' George jerked his head in the direction of the coffee stall by the south entrance. 'Besides which, you're much prettier than he is. You'll do well, Hetty. I know you will.' He tipped his cap to her and sauntered off to set up his stall.

Things quietened down a little after the early

morning rush, and Hetty was able to leave her pitch in order to get fresh supplies from the bakery in Spital Square. She bargained hard with the baker and left his shop with a tray of freshly baked loaves, cake and buns, and she gave him a repeat order for the following day, obtaining a most satisfactory discount. Feeling extremely pleased with herself, she returned to her stall and made sandwiches ready for the midday rush.

By teatime, she had sold everything, even the large bunches of watercress supplied by George. Nora left her barrow and came over to give Hetty a hug, and to present her with a bag of cinder toffee from her own stall. 'Well done, ducks. You're a natural, I'd say. I've been keeping an eye on you and I can see that you've got your head screwed on right. We'll make a proper coster of you yet. You'll be sewing pearl buttons on your clothes afore the year is out.'

'Ta, Nora,' Hetty murmured, feeling the ready blush rising to her cheeks at such fulsome praise. 'And ta for the toffee. Me little brothers will go mad for it.'

'So they should. Nora Jackson is famous for her cinder toffee and raisin fudge.' She took a square of fudge from the capacious pocket of her apron and popped it into her mouth as if to prove her words. She returned to her barrow, chewing and chuckling.

Hetty began packing everything away, still elated by her success and by the friendliness of the other costermongers. She felt as though she had just joined a large and happy family, but then a shadow fell over her stall, and a shiver ran down her spine. Slowly, she turned her head.

'So here you are.' Cyrus Clench was standing so close to her that his rank odour of sweat and stale tobacco made her feel physically sick.

'I'm closed for the day,' Hetty said sharply.

'I see you got the can back from the canal,' Cyrus said, curling his lip in a snarl. 'I should have weighted it down with bigger bricks.'

'It was you,' Hetty gasped. 'Why? Why did you do that to me?'

'Because Cyrus Clench never forgets or forgives a wrong done to him in the past.' He leaned closer to her, baring his teeth. 'When your sainted grandpa caught me with me fingers in the till so to speak, and had me dismissed from my position at the bank without a character, he ruined my life.'

Hetty tried to back away from him but he had her pressed up against her stall. 'But it wasn't my fault,' she protested. 'It has nothing to do with me.'

'I vowed then to get even with your family, but it's taken me all these years to get a hold over you. I've watched and waited for me chance, and I've seen you grow into a tasty bit of skirt. Then you and your old hag of a grandmother humiliated me in front of me friend Jasper. And that bloke over there,' he jerked his head in George's direction, 'pitched me into the canal. I'll get him one of these days, and I'll get you too, lady. We've got unfinished business, you and me.'

Hetty opened her mouth to cry for help, but Cyrus skittered off, walking sideways like a malevolent crab as he left the market hall. Hetty leaned against her stall, clasping her hands to her chest in an effort to still her erratic heartbeats. She looked across at George, but he had his back to her and was busy serving a customer. She had only to call out and he would come running, but she did not want to draw him any further into her troubles. Gradually, and with a supreme effort, she regained her composure. Cyrus Clench was all hot air, like one of the big balloons she had once seen floating above Victoria Park. She would take great care never again to put herself in a position where he could attack or terrorise her. Dismissing his threats with a defiant shrug of her shoulders, Hetty turned away to resume packing the clean cups back in their box. She had done well today, and if her stall continued to prosper she would get another stall in a different site, and then another. She would rent a larger house where they could all be comfortable. The possibilities were endless.

'Daydreaming again, Hetty?'

George's voice broke into her reverie and she almost dropped a cup. 'You made me jump, George.'

'You done well today, girl. You couldn't have had a better start.' He kissed her on the cheek. 'I'll just pack up and then we'll wander off home together, if that's all right with you?'

She smiled and nodded. 'Ta, George. I'd like that.' Hetty stifled a sigh of relief as she watched him stroll back to his barrow. She would be more than glad to have his company on the way home. She had toyed with the idea of telling him what Clench had said, but then she decided that it would serve no useful purpose. She did not want him to go rushing off to fight her battles. Violence was not the answer, although for the life of her, Hetty couldn't think what to do about her tormentor. She finished packing up her stall, and she tried to put Clench and his threats out of her mind as she counted her takings. When she had counted the last farthing, she was feeling much more cheerful. She did a quick sum in her head and smiled. If she continued like this, by the end of the week she would have cleared a whole pound. It seemed like riches beyond her wildest dreams. She was now on her way up and no one, not even a brute like Clench, was going to stop her.

When she arrived home, hot and tired, but triumphant, Hetty found Tom sitting in the parlour with Granny and Jane. Sammy and Eddie were outside in the back yard, making a great deal of noise as they washed themselves at the pump, although from where Hetty was standing she could see through the window that they were having a water fight instead of doing their ablutions. She turned her back on them, hoping that Granny would not realise what was going on and put an end to what was just a harmless bit of fun. Hetty bent down to pick up Natalia and she kissed her chubby cheek. Talia was going to have time to play and enjoy her childhood. With a pound a week profit, there was no telling where they would end up.

'You look pleased with yourself,' Granny said, frowning as if this was a crime in itself.

'Did you have a good day, Hetty?' Jane said quickly. 'You'd gone by the time I woke up.'

'I done well,' Hetty acknowledged, smiling. 'If trade keeps going like it did today, I shan't complain.'

Tom rose to his feet. 'It's not what I want for you, ducks. Working long hours and out in all weathers. It ain't right.'

'She's got to earn money, young man,'

Granny snapped. 'If you can keep her in comfort, and take care of her brothers, not to mention Jane and her nipper, then you're welcome to take over. If not, then I'll thank you to hold your tongue.' She raised herself stiffly from her seat, scowling at Tom, who opened his mouth as if to retort, but Granny's attention had been deflected by the sounds emanating from the yard. Plumes of water were shooting skywards and hitting the windows like a sudden cloudburst. 'The little devils.' She rolled up her sleeves and hurried from the room.

Through the window, Hetty saw Granny erupting into the yard, which made Sammy drop the pump handle in fright. Even with the window closed, she could hear Granny's strident tones telling them to clean up the yard and then go to bed without any supper. Hetty sighed. She couldn't really blame Granny for being short-tempered sometimes. There were just too many of them cramped together in a small space with no indoor facilities, not even a stone sink. She had seen magazine illustrations of houses that boasted sculleries, kitchens and even bathrooms. One day, she thought dreamily, we'll have the lot.

'I kept your tea warm,' Jane said, getting up from her chair and taking a plate from beneath a saucepan lid on the top of the range.

'It's pie and mash. I thought you could do with something a bit more filling than bread and cheese.'

'When you've eaten, we could go for a walk,' Tom suggested tentatively. 'I know you must be tired, but I wanted to apologise for me behaviour the other day, and there's something I want to ask you.'

One look at Tom's eager face confirmed Hetty's worst suspicions and her appetite deserted her. 'I've been picking all day, so I'm not hungry, but ta for the thought, Jane.'

'Then you'll come for a walk with me?'

Tom held his hand out to her and Hetty saw that it trembled slightly. She could not bear the thought of hurting him, but she was tired to the point of exhaustion. She shook her head. 'Not now, Tom. I've got to boil eggs for the morning. Perhaps we could leave it until Sunday?'

'I don't want to wait, girl. I'd rather say what I got to say now.'

'I can take a hint,' Jane said, taking Natalia from Hetty. 'I'd best put baby to bed.'

Natalia began to howl dismally, holding her arms out to Hetty, but Jane ignored her small daughter's protests and carried her from the room.

'You ought to eat something,' Tom said anxiously. 'You're doing too much, Hetty. It's a man's work pushing a barrow all the way to Spitalfields, not the sort of thing for a girl to do on her own.'

'I can manage perfectly well. I know you mean it kindly, but really what I do is my business, not yours. I don't come round to the Gas Light and Coke Company and tell you what to do.'

His tense expression melted into a smile. 'I should think not. I can't imagine what the foreman would say if you did.'

'No, well, it's the same with me. I can make this work, I know I can.'

'You're always so busy that we never get a moment alone, Hetty. I can't go on without knowing your mind on a certain subject.'

She looked into his earnest eyes, and she knew she must be straight with him. Tom was her oldest and dearest friend, and she could not allow him to harbour false hopes. 'If it's what I think it is, then my answer must be no, Tom.'

He did not pretend to misunderstand her. 'But why? I love you, Hetty.'

'And I'm very fond of you too, but it's not the right time.'

He grasped both her hands, holding them close to his chest. 'That's just an excuse. If you go on like that it'll never be the right time. Please hear me out.'

She shook her head. 'Don't do this to me, Tom. Not now. I'm tired and I've got a lot to do before I go to bed.'

'And it kills me to see you working like a slave, Hetty. It was bad enough when you were spending twelve hours a day making matchboxes, but at least you were safe at home. Street trading is dangerous, especially for a girl. They've never caught the Ripper and those poor women were found not a stone's throw away from where you're trading.'

Hetty squeezed his fingers and she smiled. 'You mustn't worry about me. My pitch is in the market place alongside a hundred or more costermongers. Some of them are already like a family to me. George sees me home . . .'

He drew his hands away, scowling. 'Yes, and I know what his game is, Hetty. His sort preys on innocent girls. He's waiting his chance and you'll be just another of his conquests.'

'Stop it, Tom. Don't talk like that. You've got it all wrong.'

'Have I? I don't think so. Marry me, Hetty. I love you and I think I've always loved you. Marry me and I'll take care of you for the rest of me life.'

'It wouldn't work, Tom. I do love you, in

me own way, but I can't imagine belonging to any man, not even you. I got to prove meself and find me place in the world. Can't you understand that? Maybe one day . . .'

If she had slapped his face he could not have looked more stricken. 'One day ain't good enough, Hetty.'

'Tom, please.' Hetty reached out to touch his hand, but he drew away from her.

'I'm sick of being second best. I want a straight yes or no.'

A pain shafted through her heart, but she could not lie to him. 'Then it must be no. I'm sorry.'

'Goodbye then, Hetty. I won't trouble you no more.' Tom slammed out of the room and his booted footsteps echoed down the narrow passageway. Hetty heard the front door open and then close with a loud bang that rattled the windowpanes.

Jane stormed into the parlour. 'Hetty, you bloody fool. What have you done?'

Tiredly, Hetty picked up her teacup and sipped the rapidly cooling brew. 'I had to refuse him, Jane. It wouldn't have been fair to keep him dangling after me. We'd just end up fighting.'

'You are so selfish,' Jane cried, wringing her hands. 'How could you send him away? Are you mad? He would have taken care of all of us. How can you not love a man like Tom?'

Hetty stared at her in a moment of stunned silence. The truth had hit her like a punch in the stomach.

# Chapter Nine

Hetty stared at Jane in disbelief. 'You and Tom? You can't be – I mean, why didn't you tell me that you were in love with him?'

Jane rounded on her. 'He don't know how I feel, and now he never will, because you sent him away and I'll never see him again. You've done a bad thing today; a bad, wicked thing and I hate you for it.'

Dazed and feeling numb with shock, Hetty was lost for words. She could hear Granny berating the boys in the room overhead, followed by their loud protests that she was scraping all the skin off their backs with the towel. Jane was weeping openly now and pacing up and down like a caged tigress.

'I didn't know,' Hetty murmured. 'I thought you was still grieving for Nat.'

'I am. I mean, I was at the beginning. But it's well over a year since he died and I'm young. I've got a life ahead of me and I ain't a nun, Hetty. I always had a soft spot for Tom, but he was your fellow, so I never allowed meself to think about him in that way. But since you've been tied up with your hot taters and then your blooming coffee stall, Tom and me have spent a lot of time together and : . .' Jane's voice trailed off and she buried her face in her hands.

'Oh, Jane, I had no idea.'

'No, you wouldn't have,' Jane said bitterly, raising her head to glare at Hetty. 'You just go pushing ahead and never mind the rest of us what can't keep up with you. You are so single-minded that you didn't stop to think how poor Tom might feel. You didn't even care that he was jealous of George. You just took it all for granted and you led him on.'

'No!' Hetty cried, stung by this injustice. 'I never did that. I was always straight with him, and if I'd known that you cared for him, I would have finished with Tom long since.'

'Well, it's too late now. He's gone for good this time, and he'll never come back. You've ruined everything for all of us, Hetty. Why couldn't you be like an ordinary East End girl? Why do you have to be so different from the rest of us?'

Before Hetty could think of a suitable reply, Granny burst into the parlour and stood arms akimbo, eyes blazing. 'What's all this noise? You two sound like a couple of alley cats screeching at each other. What's it all about?'

'Ask her. It's all her fault.' Jane fled from the room in a flood of tears.

Granny turned the full force of her wrath on Hetty. 'If it isn't those young limbs up to some mischief, it's you two behaving like fish-wives.'

'It's something and nothing, Granny,' Hetty said wearily. 'I need to boil some eggs, if you don't mind.'

'I do mind, as it happens. I can't have all that steam wilting the stiffening in my bonnets. You'll have to use the copper outside to boil your eggs. That's if you can wade through the water in the back yard. I gave those boys a good piece of my mind.'

She eyed the untouched food on Hetty's plate. 'Good vittles cost money. I hope you're not going to leave that, my girl?'

Hetty picked up the plate, intending to sneak it upstairs to Sammy and Eddie who had been sent to bed with no supper. 'No, Granny. I'll eat it while I stoke the fire under the copper.'

'And I expect you to pay for the coal, miss.'

Hetty nodded her head in mute acknow-ledgement as she left the room, closing the door softly behind her. She tiptoed upstairs and gave the food to the boys, who fell on it like starving animals. Sammy glanced up from the plate, swallowing a mouthful of cold pie. 'Is everything all right, Hetty? Tom sounded cross and then we heard you and Jane shouting at each other.'

'I like Tom,' Eddie said, cramming cold mashed potato into his mouth.

'You mustn't worry,' Hetty said soothingly. 'All grown-ups have arguments every now and then.'

'He will come back, won't he?' Sammy asked. 'He will take us to the park on Sundays?'

'Maybe not this week, but you mustn't worry. It will all come right in the end. You won't remember it, but that's what Ma always used to say.'

Early next morning, when Hetty was loading up her barrow, Jane came out of the house, bleary-eyed with sleep and still wearing her nightgown. She shivered in the cool breeze, and she pulled her crocheted shawl a little closer around her body. 'Can I help?'

Hetty smiled and nodded her head. She knew that this was the nearest that Jane would ever get to an apology. 'You could pack the eggs in the wicker basket.'

Jane went into the outhouse to fetch the bowl of hard-boiled eggs and she began stacking them carefully in the straw-lined basket. 'I didn't mean what I said last night – about hating you. I don't, of course, but I am very cross with you, Hetty.'

'You should have told me how you felt about Tom. I really had no idea.'

'Well you know now, and it's too late.'

'I'm sure it isn't. Tom flies off the handle but he soon calms down. If you like, I'll go round to his house this evening and make my peace with him.'

Jane dropped an egg and it landed with a dull thud on the ground. The shell split and fragments of golden yolk spilled out onto the concrete. 'Damn! Sorry, Hetty. It slipped out of me fingers. But you mustn't say nothing to Tom about me. I'd feel like a fool, and it would only make things worse.'

'You could have any man you wanted, Jane. Don't throw yourself away on the first one who comes along.'

'I'm seventeen and I've got a baby. What man is going to take me on with another bloke's child?'

Hetty lifted the cardboard box containing the cups onto the barrow and she smiled. 'With your pretty face and winning ways, when you ain't pouting that is, blokes will be queuing up to step out with Miss Jane Huggins.'

'The trouble is, I don't want other fellows, Hetty. I got me heart set on Tom, but I can hardly go running after him, especially when he's hankering after you.'

Jane's lips were trembling and her eyes were

magnified by unshed tears. The breeze had whipped her chestnut curls into a halo around her head and she was shivering violently. Hetty shook her head. 'What am I going to do with you, Jane?' She gave her a gentle push towards the back door. 'Go inside. You won't get a chap at all if you catch your death of cold. Leave it to me, I'll think of something.'

Jane grasped her hand. 'Promise me you won't tell Tom what I said.'

'Don't talk soft, of course I won't. It's our secret.' Hetty cocked her ear to listen. 'Talia's crying.'

'I wish I hadn't given her that outlandish name,' Jane said crossly. 'And I still wish she had been a boy.'

Hetty let this pass. 'I've got to go now, or I'll miss the breakfast trade, but don't fret, Jane. I'll make things come right if it's the last thing I do.'

Pushing her barrow, Hetty trudged through streets crowded with people, many of them appearing to be only half awake, making their way to their workplaces in factories, timber yards and mills that clung to the river's edge. The soot-blackened brick buildings looked even darker and more forbidding in the brilliant spring sunshine, and an east wind brought with it the noxious stench of boiling bones from the glue factory. Hetty tried to imagine fields filled with daffodils and the scent of wild violets, but today the real world forced itself upon her. She had hurt the man she had always thought she would marry one day in the far distant future. Tom had been an anchor in her life; someone solid and dependable, whose affection was constant and unchanging. The realisation that she could never love him in the way he desired was almost as shocking and disturbing as the fact that Jane could. Hetty felt almost envious of her sister's ability to allow her heart to rule her head. First there had been Nat and now she had transferred her affections to Tom. Hetty simply could not imagine feeling like that about any man. Perhaps it was not in her nature? Maybe she would go through life without ever experiencing such strength of feeling?Perhaps she was destined to be a business woman and remain a spinster?

She quickened her pace. Dawdling and daydreaming would not make her fortune. By the time she had reached Commercial Street, she was already formulating plans for renting one of the permanent stalls in the market and expanding her business. With two stalls, she could afford to move her family to a larger house, perhaps in Hanbury Street or Wood Street. Since the terrible murders by the person they called the Leather Apron, or Jack the

Ripper, the cost of renting property had plummeted. The police had never caught him, but at least the dreadful carnage seemed to have stopped. Now would be the ideal time to take out a lease on one of the houses in that area. Hetty was only too well aware that they could not impose on Granny for very much longer, and she would soon need a proper kitchen in which to prepare food for her stall. There was such a lot to think about.

She did even better in the market that day, and putting her personal problems aside she revelled in the atmosphere of camaraderie amongst the costermongers. She felt that she was part of a large and boisterous family, and that she was safe in their company. In the bustling clamour of the market, she was able to put all thoughts of Clench out of her mind. It was hard work, but she was so busy that she had no time to worry about an aching back or sore feet. She did such a roaring trade that she put in an even larger order at the bakery, not only for more loaves of bread, but also for a batch of sticky buns and a large seed cake.

She was too exhausted to go looking for Tom after work, but on Sunday afternoon she took Jane, Sammy, Eddie and Natalia round to his home in Dye House Lane. Tom's surprised expression was almost comical as he opened the door and saw the whole family, with the exception of Granny who was at home having a nap, standing outside on the narrow pavement.

Hetty held out her hand. 'I've come to apologise, Tom. I shouldn't have said what I said, and I hope you'll find it in your heart to forgive me. We've been friends for too long to let a silly argument come between us.'

'I wouldn't call it a silly argument,' Tom said coldly. 'You made it clear that you wanted nothing to do with the likes of me.'

'That's not true,' Hetty said softly. 'I love you, Tom. But not in the way you want me to love you. I'm just not made that way, but I value your friendship more than anything else in the world.'

'We miss you,' Sammy cried, pushing Hetty aside and wrapping his arms around Tom's waist. 'We want you to come to the park with us, like you always do.'

'Please, Tom,' Eddie urged, seizing Tom's hand. 'It won't be any fun without you.'

Jane stood on tiptoe to kiss Tom's cheek. 'That goes for me too, Tom. You can't desert us now.' She held Natalia up to him. 'Baby misses you too.'

As if to confirm this bold statement, Natalia gave Tom a sunny smile and held her arms out to him. He took her from Jane, holding her as if she was a fragile blossom, which he might crush if he held her too tightly. 'Hello, little 'un. I missed you as well.' Tom's eyes glistened with tears as he rubbed his cheek against Natalia's soft baby curls. 'I missed all of you too.'

'Then you'll come with us?' Hetty asked, hardly daring to breathe. Tom was so much a part of their lives that she could not bear the thought of losing him.

He gave her a long, searching look and then a slow smile spread from his lips to his eyes. 'Well, I suppose I could manage to put up with the lot of you for an hour or so.'

'And we could have a penny lick from the hokey-pokey man,' Sammy said eagerly.

Tom handed Natalia back to Jane. 'We'll see. Just let me fetch me jacket and cap and we'll go for a stroll in the park.'

As he retreated into the dingy hallway, Hetty and Jane exchanged triumphant glances. 'Just be yourself, Jane,' Hetty whispered. 'He'll soon learn what a treasure you are.'

'Why is she a treasure?' Eddie demanded.

'Never you mind,' Hetty countered, playfully tweaking his ear. 'You'd better be good if you want some ice cream.'

Tom reappeared in the doorway, shrugging on his jacket. He put his cap on his head, and held his arms out to Natalia. 'Here, let me have her, Jane. She's getting too big for you to carry far.'

Jane fluttered her eyelashes and smiled as she handed her daughter into his arms. 'Ta, Tom. She's always good when you hold her. Baby knows what a splendid chap you are.'

'I'm glad someone does,' he said, hoisting Natalia onto his shoulders.

Hetty took Sammy and Eddie by the hand. 'Come on then, let's go for a walk in the park. I think we'd best avoid the rowing boats though.' She gave Tom a sideways glance and was relieved to see the amused gleam in his eyes. She knew now that he had forgiven her.

The afternoon passed off without incident. Tom's good nature soon overcame his initial awkwardness and Jane was on her best behaviour. Sammy and Eddie gambolled about on the damp grass like a couple of spring lambs, and Natalia crowed with delight as she watched them from the safety of Tom's arms. Hetty couldn't help thinking that he would make a wonderful father, and found herself hoping that one day he would look at Jane with the eyes of love, and not just see her as the little girl who used to tease and torment him. They strolled beneath the flowering cherry trees and listened to the band. Tom bought everyone a penny lick from the Italian hokey-pokey man, and as Hetty savoured the sweet, vanilla-flavoured confection she wondered if, one day, she could add ice cream to her bill of fare.

When they went into the refreshment room, Hetty was so busy comparing the quality of the food and the prices that she charged on her stall that Tom and Jane laughed at her and teased her about never being off duty. At that point, Hetty remembered that she had to go home to prepare her barrow for the next day, and, amidst protests from everyone, she got up from the table. 'You'll see them home, won't you, Tom?' she asked with a persuasive smile. 'Please.'

'Of course I will,' Tom said, chuckling. 'You go and see to that old stall of yours. That's where your heart really lies, isn't it, Hetty?'

As she walked home alone, she could not quite put Tom's words out of her head. They had been said in a jocular fashion, but, as in many a jest, there was truth in them. She had put profit before her own wants and needs, but what no one seemed to understand was that she alone bore the responsibility for the well-being of her family.

She had learned long ago that having money made the difference between living and simply existing. She would never allow her family to go hungry again, or to work for long hours sweating at the various trades from making matches, or shoes at fourpence a dozen, or finishing boots at twopence halfpenny a pair, or even boxes for expensive soap at one and six per gross. Such were the lives of most people who lived in these parts. There had to be a better life somewhere, and Hetty was determined to work until she had found this other place, where the streets were not knee deep in horse dung and rotting vegetable matter, where sewers did not overflow every time there was a rainstorm, where disease did not claim the lives of babies and small children, and where men and women were not withered into a premature old age by poverty and want. She lifted her chin and strode on towards Totty Street. She had eggs and a large piece of gammon to boil, ready for the morning. Monday was the start of a new week and it would be the beginning of a more prosperous future for them all.

It was raining. Steady, drenching rain was pouring from a leaden sky. With a piece of sacking draped over her head and shoulders, Hetty pushed her barrow along the Mile End Road, heading for Spitalfields. The wheels of passing horse-drawn vehicles threw up sprays of muddy water, soaking the hem of her skirt, and she could feel the damp seeping through the soles of her boots. It was not the best start to the week, and when Cyrus Clench fell into step beside her, she was barely surprised. 'Go away, Clench. I ain't in the mood to speak to the likes of you.'

His face had a greenish tinge to it as he huddled beneath a large black umbrella that had several broken spokes, giving it a curious humpbacked appearance. He bared his teeth in a rictus grin. 'That ain't very polite of you, Miss Hetty.'

'I've nothing to say to you, Clench. Leave me alone.'

'But you owes me money, missy. I'm a poor man and I can't write off the interest you owe me. I want it now.'

Hetty trudged onwards, ignoring his whining voice.

He quickened his pace to keep up with her. 'Acting stuck-up won't get you nowhere, Miss Hetty. I'm a patient man, and a good-natured fellow, or I'd have sent the bailiffs in to your grandma's house in Totty Street before now. She made a big mistake when she threw my mate Jasper out. A big mistake.'

Hetty came to a sudden halt. She turned to look at him and the malicious gleam in his beady eyes frightened her. 'What are you saying?'

'Just this, sweetheart. Either you pays up the accumulated interest on the loan, or you pays me in kind.'

A cold shiver ran down Hetty's spine and it was not just the rainwater trickling through the sodden sacking. 'I don't owe you any money. You know very well that my grandmother paid off the loan in full.'

'Can you prove it? Have you got it in writing?'

'You know that I haven't, but that doesn't make any difference. You were paid off.'

'It's my word against yours and Jasper will back me up. Who do you think the bailiffs will believe, dearie?'

'You're bluffing, Clench.'

'Pay up or pay me in kind. Meet me in the Ten Bells on the corner of Church Street at six o'clock this evening, or you'll be sorry.'

'You don't frighten me,' Hetty lied, clenching her teeth in order to stop them chattering.

He chuckled deep down in his throat. 'Ho! Don't I? I can see it in your eyes, missy. I want to see a different expression in them this evening when we meet up. I want to hear you say "Yes, Cyrus", in a loving tone mark you, and we'll go on from there. I reckon once or twice a week for a month or two will just about pay your debt to me.'

'Never!' Hetty almost choked on the bile that had risen to her throat. She knew exactly what Clench intended and the thought of it sickened her. She hurried on as fast as she could, but his hoarse laughter followed her along the street. Mercifully, he allowed her to go on her way, and a quick glance over her shoulder reassured her that he had moved off in the opposite direction. Hetty abandoned her barrow at the side of the road and she dashed into a side alley to vomit.

She was late arriving at the market and George was already busy on his stall. She received a cheery wave from Brush and she managed a weak smile in return, as she began to set up her stall.

'Hello, ducks. What's up?'

Nora's rasping tones made Hetty drop a cup and it shattered on the cobblestones. She knelt down to pick up the pieces. 'I'm sorry I was late. I got held up.'

'You look terrible. Are you poorly?'

'N-no, I'm fine, ta.' Hetty bit back a sob. Her hands shook and she yelped with pain as a shard of broken china cut her finger.

Nora helped her to her feet. 'Come over to me stall, love. I'll bind that up, and you can tell me what's got you in such a state.' She led Hetty over to her sweet stall where a ragged boy, who could not have been more than six or seven, was about to steal a handful of boiled sweets. 'Get away with you,' Nora screeched, cuffing him soundly round the head. He dropped the sweets and his small face, which was so blackened with grime that his features were indistinguishable, puckered as if he were about to howl. Nora popped a piece of fudge between his lips. 'That's enough of that, sonny. Pick up them sweets and take them away. I can't sell nothing what's been trodden underfoot. But if I catch you stealing again, I'll tan your hide.'

The boy scrambled about on the ground, picking up the sweets and stuffing them in the pockets of his torn, threadbare breeches before scuttling off into the street. Nora pulled up a stool. 'Sit there, Hetty, and you can tell me what's up while I see to that cut.' She bent her head to peer myopically at the wound. 'It's deep. I seen cuts like that turn green like rotten meat. You could lose your whole arm if the gangrene sets in.' On this cheerful note, she lifted her skirt and tore a strip off one of her voluminous petticoats.

Hetty had not told anyone about Clench and his continued threats, but it was a relief to blurt it all out to Nora, who listened intently while she set about cleaning and bandaging Hetty's injured hand. She showed neither shock nor surprise at Hetty's revelations. She tied a knot in the bandage and stood back, folding her arms across her ample bosom. 'Well, now. He's a blighter and no mistake. You needs to steer clear of that one, girl.'

Hetty stood up, swaying slightly as a wave of dizziness overtook her. 'Yes, I know.'

Nora pushed her back onto the stool. 'Sit tight. You need some vittles inside you and a nice hot cup of tea.'

'I – I haven't got the fire pot going yet,' Hetty said, half-heartedly attempting to rise.

'Leave it to me.' Nora thrust her money pouch into Hetty's hands. 'Watch me stall and don't let them young knaves steal me sweets. I'll see to the fire and I'll get one of the girls to start slicing bread and ham for you. Don't fret, ducks. You won't miss the breakfast rush, if you do as I say.' Nora bustled off, leaving Hetty feeling overwhelmed by such kindness and unaccountably wanting to cry.

Despite her great size, Nora was surprisingly quick and efficient. In a short space of time, she had the charcoal glowing in the fire pot beneath the can, and had co-opted a couple of girls from other stalls to start making the sandwiches. The stall was set up and Norah had served several customers before Hetty had had time to finish her cup of tea laced with sugar. Nora waddled back to her own stall, taking the money pouch from Hetty and tying it round her waist, which was a feat in itself. Hetty watched in fascination as the long strings were wound around Nora's corseted but still enormous middle.

'There, ducks,' Nora said, panting for breath from the effort. 'You look like you can take over without falling in a heap on the floor. And don't worry about that bugger Clench. I've eaten men like him for me dinner. When it comes to six o'clock, he'll find both you and me waiting for him in the pub. I can't wait to see his face.'

Hetty stood up slowly and was relieved to find that everything around her stayed in its rightful place. 'I can't thank you enough, Nora.'

'Nonsense, ducks. Us costers stick together, and I can see that you're a good girl, Hetty. You'll go far.'

Nora turned away to serve a customer and Hetty went back to her stall, thanking the girls who had helped her and giving them each a penny by way of payment. She was busily slicing the seed cake when George came striding up to her, his brow creased in worried lines. 'Are you sick or something, Hetty?'

'No, George. I cut me hand on a piece of broken china. Nora saw to it for me, but I'm fine now, ta.'

'Nora blooming Nightingale! Who'd have thought it? She must have taken to you, girl. Old Nora can be a bit of a one if she takes a dislike to a body.'

'Hey, George,' Ginger shouted from his stall

across the way. 'Stop spooning with Hetty. You got a customer waiting.'

'Take no notice of him, Hetty,' George said, chuckling. 'I'm just glad you ain't sick. Your face was the colour of skimmed milk when I first saw you. Are you sure there wasn't something else? Because if anyone upsets you, just tell me and I'll sort them out good and proper.'

Hetty laughed in spite of herself. 'Ta, George. I'll remember that.'

Business was booming and Hetty had no time to worry about her meeting with Clench, but as six o'clock approached she started to feel apprehensive. George was still busy selling, but Hetty could see that Nora had already packed up her stall and was ready to leave. They exchanged meaningful glances and Hetty pointed mutely to George. Nora nodded her head in response and Hetty went to his stall to tell him that she was leaving early and wouldn't be walking home with him. As luck would have it, he was too busy to question her motives. 'All right then, ducks. I'll see you in the morning. Mind how you go.'

Hetty pushed her barrow out of the market hall, and waited for a gap between the drays, carts and hansom cabs with Nora at her side.

'You can leave your barrow at my drum in Princelet Street,' Nora said as Hetty seized her chance to get into the flow of traffic. 'If you leave it outside the Ten Bells it'll be stripped of everything before you can blink.'

'Ta, Nora. I'd be finished if it happened again.'

'Again?' Nora cocked an eyebrow at her. 'Was it that Clench bloke?'

Hetty sighed. 'Yes. Like I said, he's had it in for me for ages. If he has his way we'll end up begging on the streets.'

'We'll see about that,' Nora said, bristling like a turkeycock. 'Turn right here, dearie.'

It was not far to walk and soon they were in the narrow street lined with late-seventeenth-century terraced houses. Hetty stared up at the three- and four-storey brick-fronted houses, which must have been the height of fashion when they were built for the wealthy French Huguenot silk weavers and mercers, but times had changed and they now housed a different class of tenant. Nora's house was unremarkable from the rest, but it boasted a large back yard reached by an alleyway at the rear of the terrace. It was here that Hetty left her barrow, and Nora took her into the scullery and out through a large kitchen into a long and narrow passageway. Hetty's first impression was of a once elegant townhouse that had fallen into a sad state of decay. The wallpaper was peeling off like blistered skin, the skirting boards were cracked, and the paintwork badly chipped. The pervading smell was of mouse droppings, dry rot and burnt sugar, but there was no time to loiter as Nora hurried her out through the front door.

'Do you own this house?' Hetty asked breathlessly.

'For me sins,' Nora wheezed. 'My old man and me bought it thirty years ago from a cove who was going bankrupt. We planned to fill it with nippers but we wasn't blessed in that way, and then my Eric ups and dies of a fever so I was left on me own.' Her eyes filled with tears which she brushed away with the back of her hand.

'I'm sorry,' Hetty murmured.

Nora stopped for a moment, leaning against the wall of a second-hand furniture shop in order to catch her breath. 'It's all right, ducks. It was a long time ago, but I can never think of my poor Eric without becoming a bit sentimental. Anyway, the old house is a bit of a white elephant really. I can't sell it and I doubt if I could give it away, so I lets out rooms, but business has been bad since the Ripper started his evil doings. They say the first two women were seen close to the Ten Bells pub just afore he killed them. Makes your hair stand on end, don't it? Anyway, it's a good few months since he got the Kelly woman, so hopefully he's gone far away from here.' She straightened up, took a deep breath and resumed a brisk pace. 'Come on, ducks. Don't loiter, or he'll think you're not coming. Just wait until I gets me hands on him, the old bastard.'

Even though Nora was built like a galleon in full sail, Hetty had quite a job to keep up with her and she was out of breath by the time they reached the corner of Church Street and the Ten Bells pub. Nora stopped and clutched her hands to her heaving bosom while she struggled to breathe. 'Well, ducks, this is it. You go in first. It won't do no good if he sees you're not alone. I'll be right behind you.'

# Chapter Ten

The smell of tobacco smoke mixed with the fumes of alcohol assailed Hetty's nostrils as she entered the taproom. Nora was just a step or two behind her and it was obvious from the cheery greetings she received that she was a regular customer and well liked. Hetty blinked as her eyes grew accustomed to the gloom, and a shiver ran down her spine as she saw Cyrus emerging from the shadows. He seized her by the arm and drew her into a corner. He pushed her down onto a high-backed oak settle. 'Let's talk business, girlie.' He was about to sit beside her when Nora grabbed him by the scruff of his neck. He struggled, but she caught him by the seat of his trousers and he dangled helplessly like a marionette in the hands of an expert puppeteer. Hetty clamped her hand over her mouth to stifle a hysterical giggle.

'What's all this?' Cyrus demanded, choking. 'P-put me down.'

Nora yanked his collar until his face turned purple. She leaned closer to him, placing her lips to his ear. 'Now see here, little man. I know your game, and you won't get away with it. Hetty's got friends and if you don't want to have your legs bent the wrong way, I suggest you leave her be.' Nora gave him a shake like a terrier with a dead rat and then she dropped him.

Cyrus collapsed on the settle, holding his throat and gasping for breath. 'Who d'you think you are, you ugly old bladder of lard?'

Hetty slithered away from him and went to stand behind Nora. 'You act respectful to Mrs Jackson,' she cried angrily. 'She's an important lady.'

'Lady!' Cyrus spat on the sawdust-covered floor. 'If she's a lady, then I'm a Chinaman.'

'Ching chong,' Nora said with a loud guffaw. She snatched a tankard of ale from the table in front of Cyrus and tipped its contents over his head. 'Now you're a drownded Chinaman. You don't frighten me, cully. And if I catches you anywhere near my friend Hetty, you'll wish you was in China or even further away.'

A loud burst of applause followed this, and Nora bowed to her appreciative audience. 'Keep your eyes on this one, boys. He's an evil bastard and no mistake.' She turned to Hetty with a triumphant smile. 'Come on, ducks. I don't think this vermin will bother you again.'

'Just you wait,' Clench hissed, as Hetty was about to follow Nora out of the taproom. 'You'll pay for this, Miss Hetty.'

The malevolent look in his eyes sent shivers down her spine. She might be safe for the moment, but she knew that Nora's well-meaning intervention had only made Clench even more determined to get even. Outside in the street, Nora paused to wipe the perspiration from her brow with a grubby hanky. 'He's a mean bastard, Hetty. I'd keep well out of his way if I was you.'

'I'll try, but he's not going to give up so easily.'

'Tell you what, young Hetty. Why don't you leave your barrow at my place tonight? You'd be quicker on your feet if you didn't have to lug that thing around, and you could pick it up in the morning.'

Hetty fell into step beside her as Nora headed off towards Princelet Street. It was a tempting proposition, but, having given it due consideration, she realised that it was not very practical. 'Ta, Nora. I appreciate the offer, but if I did that, I'd have to carry me sandwich makings all the way from Totty Street.'

'You live too far away from the market,' Nora said, gasping for every breath as she waddled along the pavement. When they reached her house, she took a large iron key from her pocket and unlocked the front door. 'Come in, Hetty. I've just had another idea.'

As Hetty followed her into the entrance hall, she paused to admire the fine, if slightly worm-eaten, wooden wall panelling and the elaborate joinery of the staircase that rose majestically to the upper floors. It must, she thought, have been a really grand house in its heyday. It had fallen into a sad state of disrepair, but even so it was like a palace compared to number one Autumn Road. Until now, she had always thought Granny's house in Totty Street was a desirable residence, but in her mind's eye she could see this old silk weaver's house restored to its former glory. One day she would own a house like this, only in a better part of London, away from the slums and industrial filth of the East End. She was so deep in thought that she was barely conscious of the sound of footsteps on the staircase.

'Well now, what have we here?'

Hetty looked up with a start. A nattily dressed young gentleman was strolling down the stairs. His well-cut jacket was unbuttoned, revealing a mustard-yellow waistcoat and matching check trousers. In his hand he carried a bowler hat and his blond hair flopped in an artistic manner over a high forehead. He smiled, revealing a row of perfect white teeth.

Hetty stared up at him transfixed. As he

paused, leaning against the dark and battered wooden panelling, he seemed to shine like a golden god of youth and vitality. For once in her life, Hetty was speechless.

He ran lightly down the remaining stairs. 'Hello there,' he said, with a friendly smile. 'Who are you? I don't believe we've met.'

'H-hello,' Hetty murmured, suddenly acutely conscious of her own shabby apparel.

At the sound of his voice, Nora stopped halfway down the passage and turned her head to give him a cursory glance. 'I don't usually see you at this time of day, Mr Wyndham.'

He flashed a charming smile in her direction. 'No ma'am, I guess not.'

Hetty swallowed hard, trying to think of something to say to this handsome gentleman who spoke with a strange accent, but whose good opinion she was suddenly quite desperate to obtain. Lost for words, she bobbed a curtsey.

'May I introduce myself, ma'am? Charles Wyndham the third, from Philadelphia, gentleman of the press, at your service.' He took her hand and raised it to his lips.

Hetty found herself looking into a pair of smoky blue eyes set slightly aslant. As his lips brushed the back of her hand she felt her skin tingle and her heart did a wild leap inside her chest. 'Hester,' she murmured shyly. 'Hester Huggins, but everyone calls me Hetty.'

'What a delightful name. I'm charmed to meet you, Miss Hetty Huggins.'

Nora bustled up to them. 'That's enough of your soft sawder, Mr Wyndham. Miss Hetty ain't used to your Yankee ways. She's a good East End girl, so don't go getting no ideas.'

'Nora!' Hetty said, feeling the ready blush rise to her cheeks. 'I'm sure Mr Wyndham never meant no such thing.'

'Certainly not,' Charles said amicably. 'Where I come from, Miss Hetty, we know how to treat a lady.'

She could not decide if he was serious or merely teasing her, and she snatched her hand away. 'I'm glad to hear it, sir. It was a pleasure meeting you.' Holding her head high, she left him standing at the foot of the stairs. Suppressing the urge to glance over her shoulder to see if he was watching her, Hetty followed Nora into the kitchen.

Nora went over to the huge cast-iron range and began to riddle the glowing embers of the fire. 'Don't get no fancy notions about him, ducks. He's just here for a short time. He's a reporter writing a story about the Ripper. Seems they got a notion in America that the killer could be one of them. Anyway, he's just lodging here to get the feeling of the place and he'll be up and gone afore you can say Leather Apron.'

Hetty felt quite weak at the knees. She had never met a toff before, let alone one from the United States of America. With his shining blond hair and expensive clothes, he might have stepped straight out of the pages of a magazine or even a story book. It was true that he didn't wear armour, but he could easily have been the Sir Galahad of the stories that Ma used to read them about the Knights of the Round Table. Ma had been fond of books, and occasionally, as a special treat, she had taken Hetty and Jane to the public library in London Street. These brief forays into the world of art and literature had been like journeying into a foreign land.

'Forget him,' Nora said, pointing the poker at Hetty. 'He's a real charmer is that one, but take my advice and stick to your own kind.'

'I dunno what you're talking about,' Hetty said, tossing her head. 'I only exchanged a couple of words with the bloke.'

'And if you've got any sense you'll keep it that way. Now then.' Nora suddenly became business-like, and she put the poker down with a clang. 'Let's be sensible, Hetty. You've got a problem with that worm Clench, and you can't keep pushing that heavy barrow all the way from Totty Street to Spitalfields and back again.

You say the old bugger has threatened to have your family thrown out of your granny's house.'

Hetty came back to earth with a bump. Reluctantly, she pushed the dashing image of Mr Charles Wyndham from Philadelphia out of her mind. 'Yes, that's true.'

'Well, I've been thinking. I got plenty of room here and I need a girl to help me keep the place clean and tidy, maybe to do a bit of cooking for me as well.'

'I don't see how I could help you out there, Nora. The coffee stall takes up all me time.'

Nora moved her bulk to a chair at the scrubbed deal table and she pushed a pile of dirty crockery aside to lean her elbows on its surface. 'I weren't thinking of you, silly girl. You got a future with your coffee stall. I meant that young sister of yours, the one you told me about that had the baby out of wedlock, after her man got killed.'

Hetty shook her head. 'Jane can't cook. She don't know how, and anyway she's got little Talia to look after.'

'And she needs to earn a living from what you told me. You can't support her and her nipper for ever, Hetty. As to cooking, I'm sure she could learn, and it don't take a genius to sweep floors.' Nora leaned towards Hetty, fixing her with a hard stare. 'I'd like to help you, ducks. And you could help me. I'll let you have a couple of rooms in return for a modest rent and a bit of help in the house from your sister.'

Hetty sank down on the nearest chair. 'I dunno, Nora. I can't speak for Jane, and there's me brothers to consider.'

'They can come too. I don't mind kids as long as they don't get in me way. I need someone I can trust, Hetty. The last girl I had stole things from my gentlemen lodgers and was a bit too fond of the drink, so I had to give her the sack. I know you work hard, and I expect your sister would do likewise. You'd be safe from Clench and you wouldn't have so far to go with the barrow.'

'It's a good offer, Nora. But I must talk it over with them at home.'

'Course you must. But let me be plain with you, girl. I can see that you're a goer. You got ambition, Hetty, and that's a good thing. I was like you once. Maybe I can see something of me in you, but I know as how you won't be satisfied with the one stall. When you make enough money you'll want to expand. This here is the ideal place for you to do that. I wouldn't charge you for the use of me kitchen. On the top floor there's a large room where the weavers used to work. You could use that too if needs be.'

'I'll have to think about it, Nora.'

'Yes, you will. But you won't get a better offer, and I've been looking for a suitable tenant for the top floor. You've got something about you, young Hetty. I think you'll go far.'

That evening, after supper, Hetty gathered everyone in the parlour and told them in plain terms of Clench's threats and Nora's offer. There was a moment of silence as she finished speaking, when everyone, even young Eddie, sat staring at her as they digested this startling information.

'Well?' Hetty said, glancing at their dumb-struck faces. 'What do you think?'

Natalia, apparently bored with sitting on her mother's lap, wriggled and squirmed until Jane set her down on the floor. She crawled over to Hetty and tugged at the hem of her skirt. Hetty scooped her up in her arms and she gave her sister a searching look. 'What do you say, Jane?'

'I can't cook, and I ain't no skivvy. How can you suggest such a thing?'

'Stop whimpering, girl,' Granny snapped, glaring at her with undisguised irritation. 'You should be grateful to Hetty for standing by you. It's time you did something for yourself instead of relying on others.'

Jane leapt to her feet. 'How can you be so

cruel, Granny? It ain't my fault that I can't go out to work.'

'And it isn't Hetty's fault that you couldn't say no to your young man, and allowed him to get you in the family way. Your sister's worked her fingers to the bone to keep you and the child, and don't you forget it.'

'How can I?' Jane wailed, covering her face with her hands. 'You won't let me. I made one slip, that's all, and I'm paying for it.'

'What did you do, Jane?' Sammy asked innocently.

'Nothing,' Hetty said quickly, seeing that the situation was about to escalate into a full-blown row. 'Jane, sit down, please. I'm not going to force you to do anything against your will, but I'm worried that Clench might know something we don't. He's thick as thieves with Mr Shipworthy, who as far as I know still works for Tipton's bank, and they own this house. Ain't that so, Granny?'

'It is so,' Granny said, nodding her head. 'When your grandpa died, the bank allowed me to stay on at a fixed rent for my lifetime.'

'You see, Hetty,' Jane said, wiping her eyes on her apron. 'You're panicking unnecessarily. We're safe as houses here with Granny.'

'You didn't see the look on Clench's face when Nora threw beer all over him,' Hetty murmured, shuddering at the memory. 'He's out to get me one way or the other. I never told you what he did to me under the railway bridge.'

'What did he do, Hetty?' Sammy demanded, jumping up and down with his hands fisted. 'If he hurts you, he'll have me to deal with.'

Eddie began to snivel and Natalia's mouth drooped at the corners as if she was about to join in. Hetty hugged her and leaned across to pat Eddie on the head. 'He was a bit nasty, that's all. Nothing to worry about, boys.'

Granny frowned. 'Seems to me that you're the one in danger, Hetty. I think you should accept this woman's offer. Not that I mind having you here, but you can't go on boiling your eggs in me copper, let alone walking all the way to the market with that barrow of yours. You're all skin and bone as it is and you'll wear yourself into the ground.'

'I'm stronger than I look, Granny. And I don't mind the hard work because I'm going to make a success of me stall, and open another one as soon as I've saved enough money.'

'Even so, I think that you and Jane would be better off in Princelet Street, but the boys will stay here with me.'

Sammy and Eddie stared at her in horror. 'No, Granny . . .' Sammy protested.

She held her hand up for silence. 'You boys are at a good school, and I don't want you mixing with the guttersnipes and young thieves that hang about Spitalfields and Whitechapel. You will stay here with me and that's that.'

Hetty bit her lip. The last thing she wanted was to abandon her little brothers, but she could see the sense in Granny's words. 'It would be for the best, boys. You're both doing well at school, and we could still meet up on Sundays and go for our walks in the park.'

'And what about me?' Jane stamped her foot. 'Don't I get a say in all this?'

'Of course you do,' Hetty said, rocking a sleepy Natalia in her arms. 'You must do what you think best for yourself and for Talia. She's your child when all is said and done.'

'You don't have to keep on reminding me of that. She's a millstone around me neck, that's what she is. If I was free I could get a job in one of them big stores up West. I could wear a black dress and sell perfume and soap that smells of flowers instead of carbolic. But you want me to scrub floors and peel taters. It's just not fair.'

Granny rose majestically to her feet. 'Life isn't fair, Jane Huggins. You got yourself in this pickle and you have to live with the consequences. I say you should go with Hetty.'

'Oh! You are so cruel,' Jane sobbed. 'I hate

you all.' She flung out of the room, slamming the door.

Eddie buried his head in his arms and began to sob. Sammy hooked his arm round his brother's shoulders. 'She don't mean it, Ed. You know how women are.'

Hetty swallowed a lump in her own throat. She did not want to be parted from them, but it was important for the boys to have a good education, something which was denied to her and Jane. She did not think that Clench would go so far as to pick on two small boys and an old woman. Reluctantly, she had to admit that it would be better for them to stay with Granny in Totty Street. She gave Sammy an encouraging smile. 'Good boy. I know you'll look after Eddie for me, and it won't be forever. When I get another stall going, I'll make lots of money. We'll all be together again soon, I promise you that.'

Sammy began to weep silently, which touched Hetty's heart even more than Eddie's abandoned sobbing, but Granny frowned at her, shaking her head. 'They'll get over it, don't you worry, girl. They'll be all right here with me. I'll look after them.' She took a pitcher of milk from the windowsill and poured some into a pan on the hob. 'A cup of warm milk will settle them, and they'll see things different in the morning. We all will.'

Hetty thought she might find Jane in their room, but when she went to put Natalia to bed she discovered that Jane's shawl and bonnet were missing from the peg behind the door. It was not hard to guess where she had gone, and Hetty's suspicions were confirmed when, an hour later, Jane returned to the house with Tom. By this time, Sammy and Eddie were tucked up in their bed, and Granny was busy stitching silk flowers onto a bonnet, squinting at the intricate work in the light of a single candle.

'I've told Tom what you want me to do,' Jane said with a defiant toss of her head. 'And he's come to sort things out.'

Hetty had been darning one of Sammy's socks and she looked up, raising her eyebrows at Tom in a mute question. He dragged off his cap and scratched his head. 'Jane's a bit upset.'

'Huh!' Granny muttered. 'She's always flying into a miff about something.'

Jane rounded on her. 'That's not fair, Granny.'

'Can I speak to you in private, Tom?' Hetty put the darning down on the table and she rose to her feet.

'You can say anything you have to say in front of me,' Jane stormed. 'I ain't a child, Hetty.'

'No, but you're behaving like one,' Hetty

snapped, losing patience. 'I only wanted to save you the grisly details, but if you insist, then I'll tell Tom right now, and you can both hear exactly why I need to get away from Clench. And it's not just me that he's got his eye on. If he can't get to me, then Jane will be his next victim. That man is mad and he's dangerous.'

Jane's lips trembled into a pout, but she took off her bonnet and slumped down on a chair by the fire. 'All right. Let's hear what you got to say.'

'Don't mind me,' Granny added, setting her work aside. 'At my age, there isn't much that will shock or surprise me.'

'Tom?' Hetty held out her hand to him. 'Sit down, please, and hear me out.'

He perched on the edge of the chair beside her, twisting his cap round between his fingers with an anxious expression on his face. 'Go on, Hetty.'

She took a deep breath. This was not going to be easy. 'I never told you the full story. For one thing, it's hard for me to put it into words, and for another I didn't want you going after Clench and getting yourself in bother with the coppers. But now I see I must tell all, and not spare the details.' Hetty launched into an account of Clench's behaviour from the time they lived in Autumn Road to the attempted rape under the railway bridge and his continued propositioning, including his veiled threats to her family. She could see the muscle tightening in Tom's jaw, and a vein throbbing at his temple. His fingers flexed as though he would like to wrap them round Clench's skinny neck and squeeze the life out of him: it was just this extreme reaction that Hetty had feared. She laid her hand on his arm, and she could feel the tension in his muscles. 'That's why I didn't tell you before, Tom. I feared that you would seek him out and beat him up. Not that he don't deserve it, but he's a crafty one and he would see you in Newgate before he'd admit he was to blame.'

'I'd kill him,' Tom said through gritted teeth. 'I'd make him pay for what he done to you, Hetty.'

Jane said nothing, but her fingers plucked nervously at her woollen shawl and her face had paled alarmingly.

Granny cleared her throat. 'Hetty's right. It won't do to take the law into your own hands, young man.' She turned her head to glare at Jane. 'And you, miss. What have you to say for yourself now?'

Jane's mouth worked for a few seconds before she managed to speak. 'I – I'll go with you, Hetty. But only if Tom promises he won't desert us. You wouldn't leave us alone and unprotected in Spitalfields, would you, Tom?'

'Of course not, ducks.' He leaned over to pat her hand. 'But will you be any safer there, Hetty? Clench is bound to find out where you're living.'

'I expect he will, but it's much nearer to the market, and I'll be able to walk home with Nora. With Jane and me out of the way, I hope he'll leave Granny and the boys alone. They're of no interest to a man like him.'

Tom nodded thoughtfully. 'It's a rough area and not the best place to live, but I daresay Clench is more of a danger to you than the Ripper, who only picks on women of a certain kind.'

'That's true,' Jane said, brightening. 'We'll give it a go, Hetty. But if that woman works me too hard, I'll come straight home to Granny.'

'No you won't, miss.' Granny glared at her over the top of her spectacles. 'You'll stick it out and help your sister. I don't hold with niminy-piminy little whiners. You'll do what the Jackson woman asks of you, and you'll do it well.'

They had to wait until Sunday, but it did not take much effort to move their few possessions to Princelet Street. Tom helped push the barrow with everything piled up on it, including Natalia's wooden cradle. Sammy and Eddie had insisted on accompanying them, treating it as a day out. It was overly warm for the beginning of May and by the time they reached Nora's back yard they were all hot and thirsty, and Natalia was decidedly crotchety. Hetty opened the gate but she came to a sudden halt at the sight of a partially clad Charles Wyndham standing at the pump and allowing the cool water to gush over his naked torso. Even as she stifled an involuntary gasp, he straightened up to shake droplets of water from his hair, and he reached for a towel. A smile of recognition dawned on his handsome features. 'Miss Hetty! I'm sorry, I wasn't expecting visitors. I must apologise that you find me in a state of undress.'

Hetty cast her eyes down. 'I – I didn't know you would be here, sir.'

'Charles, please.' He hooked the towel round his neck and strode across the yard to hold the door for her. 'Allow me, ma'am. Nora told me that you would be arriving today, but she failed to warn me that you would be early.'

Jane had followed Hetty into the yard and she was staring at Charles, open-mouthed. Even Natalia had stopped crying and she plugged her thumb into her mouth, gazing at him with wide eyes. Sammy and Eddie pushed past Tom, who was trying to manoeuvre the barrow through the narrow gateway. 'You talk funny. Who are you, mister?' Sammy demanded, eyeing Charles suspiciously.

Hetty laid her hand on Sammy's shoulder. 'Don't be rude, dear. This is Mr Charles Wyndham and he comes all the way from America.'

'Do you know Buffalo Bill?' Sammy asked, angling his head. 'I wanted to go to his Wild West Show but we didn't have the bus fare.'

'That's a great shame, young man,' Charles said sympathetically. 'I believe Mr Cody's show was a great hit when he brought it to your country for the Queen's Golden Jubilee.'

'But do you know him, mister?'

'Hush, Sammy,' Jane said, frowning. 'I'm sure that Mr Wyndham has more important things to do than to answer your questions.'

'Not at all, ma'am. I have four young cousins at home in Philadelphia, and two sisters.' Charles beamed at her. 'We haven't been introduced, but I guess you must be Miss Hetty's sister, and this little beauty must be your daughter.' He tickled Natalia under her chin and she chuckled, holding out her arms to him.

'Well, you certainly have a way with the women,' Tom said as he finally managed to manoeuvre the barrow into the yard. He held out his right hand. 'Tom Crewe, close friend of the family.'

'Pleased to make your acquaintance, Tom.' Charles shook his hand. 'Now if you'll excuse me, I'd better make myself presentable.' He strode over to where he had left his shirt and he shrugged it on, fastening the buttons and turning away from his fascinated audience to tuck the tail ends into his trousers.

To hide her embarrassment, Hetty made a pretence of checking the items on the barrow. The sight of a well-muscled male torso wet and glistening in the sunshine had unnerved her to the extent that the blood was pounding in her eardrums, and she felt quite dizzy as a hot wave of desire ripped through her whole being. She had never experienced anything like this before in her entire life. It was as thrilling as it was shocking. If she had believed in such things, she would have thought she had fallen head over heels in love with Charles. Seeing him like this had sent her all of a flutter like some silly schoolgirl. She managed to regain control of her wildly fluctuating emotions and she turned to Tom. 'I'd be ever so grateful if you'd carry the cradle into the house.'

He moved swiftly to heft the heavy wooden crib in his arms. 'Of course. Lead on, Hetty.'

'And you'd better bring Talia in out of the

sun, Jane,' Hetty said, tugging at her sister's arm. She could see that Jane was also falling under Charles Wyndham's spell, and that wouldn't do at all. Jane was too susceptible to men with looks and charm, and, if anything, Hetty felt a little jealous at the thought that Charles might prefer her sister. She adopted a brisk manner. 'Sammy, Eddie, you can carry things indoors too. Make yourselves useful.' She picked up her can and was about to take it into the house when Charles took it from her hands.

'Allow me, ma'am.'

She gazed up into his eyes. In this light they were the colour of woodsmoke drifting in a summer sky, and his smile was just a little crooked, which was endearing rather than detracting from his otherwise flawless good looks. 'Th-thank you, sir.'

'Charles,' he corrected, holding the can in one hand, as if it weighed no more than a pennyweight.

'Charles,' Hetty repeated, savouring the name as if it were one of Grandpa's pepper-mint creams. 'But I don't want to hold you up, if you've more important business to attend to.'

'Not at all. I am a lazy fellow really, and I never go out before midday. As this is Sunday, I will probably just write up my notes

255

to telegraph to my editor in Philadelphia in the morning.'

Tom came striding out of the scullery door and he stopped, scowling, as he saw Charles and Hetty standing by the barrow. 'There's no need to trouble yourself, mate,' he growled. 'I'll help the girls with their things. You can get off and do your prying into matters what don't really concern you Yankees.'

'Tom!' Hetty said in a low voice. 'For goodness' sake, stop being so – so petty.'

'I know his game, Hetty. What I want to know is, why is a gent like him stooping so low as to doss down in a house like this?'

Hetty drew him aside, speaking in a low voice. 'Stop embarrassing me, Tom. Mr Wyndham is a newsman and he's writing an article on the Ripper.'

Charles cleared his throat. 'What Miss Hetty says is true, Tom. I am here purely on business, and you insult me, sir, if you think I would not treat either of the young ladies with the greatest respect.'

'Well, I should hope so.' Tom had the grace to look slightly abashed. 'But Hetty and her sister are very important to me. If I hears of anything untoward I shall be back, fists flying, if you gets my meaning, cully?'

'Tom!' Hetty tugged at his arm. She could feel his muscles tensed as though he would like to land a punch there and then. 'Stop behaving like a playground bully. I won't have it, I tell you. You've humiliated me and I just won't have it.'

'Fine!' Tom said through clenched teeth. 'Suit yourself, Hetty. I know where I'm not wanted, but you watch out for him and his kind.' He strode towards the gate, but the barrow blocked his path and he had to squeeze past it. At that moment, Jane came running out into the yard. Hetty could tell by her face that she had heard Tom's last impassioned words.

'Tom!' Jane shrieked, hurrying to his side. 'Don't go like this. Please don't abandon us.'

# Chapter Eleven

Tom hesitated for a moment and then he shrugged his shoulders. 'Don't worry, Janey. You won't get rid of me so easily. I'll be back.' He strode out through the gate and left it swinging and groaning on its rusty hinges.

'Gee! I'm sorry if I upset your friend,' Charles said apologetically. 'It was not my intention.'

Hetty shot a warning glance at Jane. 'Of course not, Mr Wyndham – I mean, Charles. You'll have to excuse Tom, he's a bit quick-tempered, but he'll come round.'

'You'll say that once too often, Hetty,' Jane said, turning on her heel and stamping back into the scullery.

Hetty covered her embarrassment by re-arranging things on her stall and Charles wandered over to observe her efforts. 'This looks fascinating, Miss Hetty. You must tell me all about your work. Maybe I can include it in one of my articles.'

She looked up at him and she knew she was lost. The unthinkable really had happened – she had fallen in love.

In the days that followed Hetty's time was fully occupied with running her coffee stall and settling into the house in Princelet Street, but her thoughts turned constantly to Charles and their deepening friendship. Her life seemed to have taken on a new meaning, and nothing could mar the joy she felt when she was in his company. They were rarely alone together, and Charles never betrayed his innermost feelings, but Hetty was certain that he was not indifferent to her. She set about her daily routine with renewed hope and enthusiasm.

Nora had put the large attic room at her disposal and had given them two smaller rooms on the floor below. Jane and Natalia took the larger of the two, and Hetty, for the first time in her life, had a room all to herself. It was simply furnished with a cast-iron bedstead, a deal washstand and a chest of drawers, but it was spotlessly clean and free from bugs. Having use of the attic enabled Hetty to store greater quantities of tea, coffee, sugar and flour. With her eye on a second stall, she picked up oddments of china and cutlery in the market, and stored them in a tea chest under the eaves.

As the weeks went by, although she was careful to keep her expenditure down to the minimum, she added her own personal touches to her room with a patchwork coverlet and a multicoloured rag rug purchased from Petticoat Lane market. Her window overlooked Princelet Street, and, when she had time, she loved to look down on the bustling, polyglot crowds as they went about their daily business. At night, when the lamplighter had done his rounds, a totally different class of person sidled out of the shadows to be caught momentarily in the pools of yellow gaslight. Opium addicts sought oblivion in foul-smelling dens hidden away in narrow alleys and courts, and prostitutes still traded their favours, despite the lurking threat of the Ripper. Early in December, Rose Mylett's body had been found in Clarke's Yard and now neither Hetty nor Jane ever ventured out alone at night. They knew that they were safe enough in Nora's house, but in the hours of darkness this part of London belonged to the denizens of the criminal underworld.

Nora seemed to enjoy having young people living with her, and she taught Jane the rudiments of cooking. A surprisingly apt pupil, Jane showed unexpected enthusiasm for leaning the new skill. Hetty thought privately that this was largely because the gentlemen lodgers, who took meals in their rooms, were always very generous in their compliments when Jane managed to produce a roast that was not burnt beyond recognition, or a pie that did not require the use of an axe to break through its crust.

Nora allowed Hetty unlimited use of the kitchen, and it was a relief to be able to boil eggs and ham without anyone complaining about the smell. The black-leaded range was enormous compared to the small hob in Granny's parlour, and Hetty managed to persuade Jane to try her hand at baking currant cake for the stall. Her first efforts were a complete disaster and even the sparrows and pigeons could not dig their beaks into the brick-hard end product, but Jane persevered, with much encouragement from Charles, who took to sitting at the kitchen table to write up his notes in the evenings, watching them while they worked.

Natalia had taken an instant liking to him, and he would dandle her on his knee or rock her to sleep in her cradle while he edited his copious output. Hetty grew to love this part of the day, when she escaped from the hurly-burly of the marketplace to the relative peace and quiet of the old house. She and Jane worked in more or less perfect harmony, apart from the odd sisterly skirmish when things went wrong. In the glow of paraffin lamps which cast smoky shadows on the kitchen walls, and with Charles scribbling away at the table, Hetty felt almost absurdly content. Her coffee stall was prospering. If trade improved still further she would soon have saved enough money to rent a permanent stall in the market place, and this would enable her to find another pitch for her barrow. She would not stop there, since she intended to expand further and eventually to rent premises in a better location and open up her own coffee shop.

When work was done for the day, she would sit and discuss the seemingly endless possibilities with Charles, who was as enthusiastic about her prospects as if he were actively involved in her business. Even though he had never spoken to her of romance, she was convinced that he returned her love. Whether it was a shared moment of laughter, a meeting of eyes or the touch of a hand, she sensed that his feelings for her were growing deeper with every passing day. She knew that George suspected that she harboured a passion for Charles, and he often teased her mercilessly but without any hint of jealousy. Hetty was secure in the knowledge that she and George were the best of friends, with no shadow of physical desire to complicate matters.

Tom still called in to see them at least twice a week and sometimes more, if he was not doing overtime at the gasworks. Friendly relations were restored although Hetty realised that things would never be quite the same between them. It seemed that the silken thread which had bound them since childhood had been stretched to breaking point. She knew now that she had never felt anything other than sisterly affection for Tom. She had given her heart to Charles and if she could not have him, then she wanted no other. One day, in the foreseeable future, Charles would have to return to America, but somehow she managed to push that inescapable fact to the back of her mind. She lived in the here and now. The future was a distant place, and Hetty lived for the moment, savouring every minute she spent with Charles.

The months flew by, but in her blissful state of newly-found love Hetty barely noticed the passing of the seasons. Suddenly it was summer and the weather grew hot and humid with flies tormenting the working horses and pedestrians alike. The stench of putrefaction hung heavy in the still air, but Hetty was still living in paradise. She sang as she worked on her stall, and she was oblivious to the pain of sore feet or the burns on her fingers. Clench was a dim and distant memory and she knew she was safe in the market with George and the other costermongers watching over her like guard dogs. George had started walking out with Poppy, a girl who sold jellied eels, winkles and cockles. She was pretty, in a flamboyant way, but rather loud and vulgar. Her laugh was like the cackle of a goose, and she did not seem to know the meaning of the word modesty, but she kept George happy, or so it seemed.

Charles was still gathering material for his newspaper, although Hetty wondered sometimes at the generosity of his editor, who allowed him to stay on in London when danger from the Ripper appeared to be a thing of the past. Then, on 17 July, another body of a young woman was found in Castle Alley, Whitechapel, and it appeared that the Ripper was up to his old tricks again. Hetty was terribly sorry for Alice McKenzie, or Clay Pipe Alice as the victim was commonly known, but she was secretly overjoyed that another Whitechapel murder would make it necessary for Charles to extend his stay.

The following Sunday, Hetty was packing up a picnic luncheon to take to Victoria Park when Charles came into the kitchen. He was not normally an early riser and she stared at him in surprise.

'Hetty.' He paused in the doorway, clutching a straw boater in his hand and looking unusually serious. 'May I ask you something?'

She smiled as she wrapped up a parcel of ham sandwiches. 'Of course, Charles. What is it?'

'I know you and Jane take the children to Victoria Park every Sunday, but do you think you could make an exception just this once?'

Her heart made a strange movement inside her chest, as if it had flipped over and then stood still for a moment. Hetty was suddenly breathless. 'I might,' she said cautiously. 'What is it, Charles? Is there anything wrong?'

'I thought we might take an omnibus to Hyde Park and go for a stroll by the Serpentine. I believe it will be much cooler there, by the water . . .' He broke off, seeming to struggle for words.

A shaft of fear stabbed through Hetty's whole body and her hands were shaking as she automatically packed the sandwiches in her wicker basket. 'There's something wrong, I can tell. You don't have to take me all the way to Hyde Park to tell me that you're leaving.' The words tumbled from her lips before she could stop them, and when he did not correct her, her knees gave way beneath her and she sank down on the nearest chair. She had known that this moment would come, but not like this. She closed her eyes, gripping her hands to her breast. 'Say something, Charles.'

He strode across the room to grasp both her hands in his. 'Hetty, you're right in a way.

I wanted to take you somewhere pleasant to break the news, but it isn't quite like that.'

She raised her eyes to his face and her lips trembled. She would not cry. She must not cry. He had never promised her anything or even spoken words of love. 'What is it? Please tell me.'

He drew her to her feet, clasping her hands to his chest, and when she looked into his eyes she saw only a mirror image of herself. His lips were curved into a tender smile. 'I wanted you to sit on the grass beneath the trees, with birds singing overhead and the sunlight playing on your hair. I wanted to get you away from this stinking, crime-ridden part of London to a place where decent folks take their leisure. This isn't the proper setting for a girl like you, Hetty. I've wanted to tell you that for months – ever since I first set eyes on you, in fact.'

'I still don't understand what you're trying to say, Charles. Has your editor called you back to Philadelphia? Are you leaving me?'

He raised her hands to his lips and kissed them softly, first one and then the other. He looked deeply into her eyes. 'You must know how I feel about you, Hetty. But it's complicated. I . . .' He released his grip and turned away, running his hand through his hair in a gesture of desperation. 'I can't talk to you here. Come with me now. Let me explain things in

my own good time, in a better place than this.'
He turned back to her, holding out his hand.
'Will you trust me this once, Hetty? Please?'

There was a slight relief from the blistering
heat as they strolled by the Serpentine. A hint
of a breeze ruffled the glassy surface of the
lake, and the air smelt clean and fresh. The
grass was baked brown by long days of un-
interrupted sunshine, but there was a blissful
absence of the flies and wasps that plagued
the East End. The heady scent from the rose
garden was so delicious that Hetty could taste
the perfume. She pushed all thoughts of home
and family to the back of her mind, hoping
that Jane would find the hastily scribbled note
of apology she had left on the kitchen table,
and that the boys would not be too disappointed at missing their outing to Victoria
Park. It was sheer heaven to be alone with
Charles in this part of London, which was as
unfamiliar to her as a foreign country, and
Hetty was determined to make the most of
every single minute.

She tucked her hand in the crook of his arm,
gazing in awe at the middle-class merchants,
bank clerks and lawyers strolling with their
families, all of them done up to the nines in
their Sunday best. Then there were the toffee-
nosed upper-class gentlemen, impeccably

suited in black with silky top hats on their heads, escorting their ladies who wore gowns straight out of the pages of fashion magazines, and such hats – hats to die for, Hetty thought, sighing enviously. Even Granny would be impressed by those creations of flowers, fruit, feathers and even a dead bird or two. Hetty knew that her simple muslin gown, bought in a dolly shop near Farringdon Station, was not in the latest mode, but her straw bonnet was one of Granny's finest, even if it did pale into insignificance compared to those worn by the rich women. Glancing rather shyly up at Charles, she saw nothing but admiration in his smile and her heart swelled with happiness. Charles was a gentleman, even if he was an American, and he didn't seem to think she looked too bad. 'What was it you wanted to say to me, Charles?'

He guided her to a bench in the shade of a London plane tree. 'Let's sit for a while, Hetty. This isn't easy for me to say, but I'm afraid I have a confession to make.'

She sank down onto the hard wooden bench, shivering in spite of the heat. 'You're – married?'

He threw back his head and laughed, sending a host of sparrows twittering up into the leafy branches. 'No, honey. That's not the problem.'

Honey! Hetty savoured the word as if she were tasting the real thing. Charles had never used any term of endearment before; she wanted him to repeat it again and again. 'What is it then?' she asked breathlessly. 'Please tell me.'

He sat down beside her, taking her hand in his. 'For a start, Hetty, I've misled all of you, including Nora. I'm not a reporter. At least, I did come to London to write about the Ripper, and it's true that I sent some of the facts to a newspaper in Philadelphia, although I have no idea if they were accepted.' He paused, staring down at their entwined fingers. 'Hell, this is hard to explain. You'll think I'm a real mountebank.'

'I won't,' Hetty said earnestly. 'For one thing I don't know what that is.'

He looked up, a ready laugh springing to his lips. 'That's one thing I love about you, Hetty. You are so honest. You never pretend to be what you are not.'

'I know, I'm a common girl and you are a gent. There's no getting away from it.'

'Don't ever say that.' He raised her hand to his lips, kissing each of her fingers in turn. 'You are a wonderful girl, and I love you just as you are.'

Her breath hitched in her throat and she gazed into his eyes, trying to decide whether or not he was teasing her. 'Y-you love me?'

'From the first moment I saw you, Hetty. That's what makes this so hard for me to do. You see, honey, I've been living a lie all these months. I'm not a journalist but I am a writer, or maybe I should say an aspiring one. I have been writing about the Ripper, that is true, and I've been following up the idea that he might be an American quack doctor named Francis J. Tumblety.'

'I still don't understand. You're writing about the Ripper, so I don't see the difference.' Hetty felt a shiver run down her spine. Charles was not laughing now, in fact he looked deadly serious and she knew that there was worse to come.

'I'm not a published author, honey. I'm the no-good son of a wealthy Philadelphia banker. My father sends me an allowance every month, hoping that I will "find myself" as he calls it while I am here in London. He sent me to the best schools and on to Harvard, where I failed to shine at anything except having a good time. Now he's grown impatient with me and he's threatened to cut off my allowance unless I return home straight away and take a job in his bank.'

'Oh, Charles. How dreadful! Couldn't you explain that you really are working hard on your book? You might get it published after all.'

'Honey, I've just got pages and pages of

scribbled notes. I've no more idea of putting a story together than I have of flying. I've just been procrastinating all this time, pretending to work so that I could stay close to you. There never will be a book by Charles James Wyndham the third: he's a phoney and a fraud.'

Hetty snatched her hand free and she jumped to her feet. 'I don't care about any of that, Charles. I love you with all my heart. I wouldn't care if you was a costermonger or a chimney sweep, I'd still think you was the best of men and the most dear to me.'

'Oh, my darling girl.' Charles rose to his feet, taking her in his arms in one fluid movement.

His kiss robbed her of what little breath was left in her body, and she slid her arms around his neck, responding with all the emotion that she had suppressed for so many months. When they finally drew apart she laid her head against his shoulder, closing her eyes and inhaling the scent of the man she adored. 'Don't leave me, Charles. Don't go back to America.'

Her bonnet had fallen off and her hair had tumbled free of its pins during their passionate embrace. Charles smoothed it back from her forehead, smiling tenderly. 'This is why I couldn't break the news to you in Princelet Street, honey. I had to get you away from there, if only for an hour or two. I have to return to Philadelphia, and I can't put it off any longer. I wasn't raised to earn a living. I wouldn't know where to begin, let alone how to keep a wife and family.'

Hetty drew away from him as anger replaced despair. 'I ain't asking you to keep me, Charles. I never thought of marriage, not to a toff like you.'

'And I never thought of anything else, my darling. I'm going home, but only in order to do what my father has wanted me to do all along. I'll take a junior position in his bank, and I'll work my way up as quickly as the devil knows how, so that I can send for you. Will you wait for me, Hetty? Will you promise to come to me when I am able to do the honourable thing and ask you to be my wife?'

'I will,' Hetty breathed. 'I'll swim across the ocean if I have to.'

Charles brushed her lips with a tender kiss. 'I guess that won't be necessary, sugar. I think we can scrape the fare together – first class, of course.'

'Now you're teasing me.'

'No, my darling, I've never been more serious in my life. Will you trust me, Hetty? I give you my word that I will do everything in my power to make myself worthy of you.'

She rubbed his hand against her cheek,

barely able to speak. She did not know whether to laugh or cry. She was so happy she could burst, but at the same time she was distraught at the thought of being separated from her love. Smiling up at him, she nodded her head. 'I trust you, Charles.'

He raised her hand to his lips and kissed it again, and then he frowned. 'Could you – I mean, would you consider being unofficially engaged to me, honey? Just until I can square things with my father, and propose to you properly with champagne and roses and a symphony orchestra playing in the background?' His eyes pleaded with her, and, for the first time since she had met him, Hetty saw Charles looking humble and unsure of himself.

'You want a secret engagement?' Hetty could hardly believe her ears. Such things never happened in Autumn Road or Dye House Lane. This was the stuff of penny novelettes.

'Just for the time being, but, damn it, I can't afford to buy you a ring.' His brow lightened and he pulled a heavy gold signet ring from his little finger. 'This will have to do until I can buy you a diamond as big as a rock. Hold out your hand, honey.'

In a daze of happiness, Hetty held out her left hand and Charles slipped the ring on her finger. 'I plight you my troth, or whatever they say on these occasions, Hetty. And I promise to send for you as soon as ever I can. Will you come to me, my love? Will you be mine?'

'I will, Charles,' Hetty said with feeling. 'Oh, yes. I will.'

He slipped her hand through his arm. 'This calls for a glass of champagne. I think my pocket will run to that, but it's just as well Papa sent me the ticket home, otherwise I would have been tempted to spend the whole lot on you.'

The sun had gone behind a large grey cloud, and Hetty's heart missed a beat. 'He's sent you the ticket? When are you leaving?'

'I'm sorry, honey. That is the worst of my bad news. I'm sailing from Liverpool tomorrow. I have to catch the boat train tonight.'

It had all happened so quickly. One moment she was deliriously happy, secretly engaged and drinking champagne in a private room at the Café Royal, and within hours she was standing alone and totally bereft on Euston Station, watching the last carriage of the train disappearing into the distance. Charles had begged her not to accompany him to the station, but every last second they spent together was precious to her and Hetty had insisted. Now she wished that she had listened to him.

She had never felt so alone or so miserable. Until she met Charles, she had been a girl with no heart. Or, at least, that was what she had always thought. She had never been able to empathise with Jane's emotional involvement with Nat and then Tom, until now. Blinded by tears, Hetty made her way towards the bus stop and the long trek back to Princelet Street. She barely knew what she was doing or where she was going, but somehow she managed to get home. She went straight to her room and locked herself in.

Next morning, Hetty was up and out of the house before anyone else had risen. She had taken off the ring that Charles had given her and now it hung on a ribbon round her neck. It nestled in the warm valley between her breasts and close to her heart, where it would stay until she was reunited with her love. She set off for the market, walking quickly with a determined out thrust of her chin, and she was one of the first to set up her stall. George arrived a bit later and he came straight over to her, his brow furrowed into lines of concern. 'What's up, Hetty? You look as though you lost a tanner and found a farthing.'

'Not now, George.' Hetty turned away to butter the bread that she had sliced ready to make the sandwiches.

'Have I done something to upset you, ducks?'

The genuine concern in his voice brought tears to her eyes and Hetty sniffed, shaking her head, quite unable to speak. He hooked his arm around her shoulders. 'Come on, love. You can tell old George anything, you know that.'

Suddenly she had to tell someone. She couldn't talk about it to Jane or Nora, but George was somehow different. She leaned her head against his shoulder, inhaling the familiar smell of leafy green vegetables, apples and damp earth that always hung about him in an aura, bringing a breath of the country to the stinking heat of the city. 'H-he's gone, G-George.'

He did not pretend to misunderstand. 'I'm sorry, love. That's a bugger and no mistake. But then it was bound to happen sooner or later. I suppose he's scarpered back to America?'

Hetty wiped her eyes on his coarse hessian apron, nodding her head.

'Still, it seems odd him sloping off like that when there's been another murder,' George continued thoughtfully. 'You'd think he'd want to send the story back to his editor in Philadelphia or wherever it was he comes from.'

'He isn't a reporter, George. Charles said he was writing a book about the Ripper, but now his father has threatened to cut off his allowance if he doesn't go home straight away.' It all came out in a rush, followed by a gulping sob.

'His old man must be a wealthy geezer, but Charlie's a big boy. Surely he could tell his dad where to get off?'

'His pa owns a bank and Charles was raised like a gent. He's never had to earn his living.'

George frowned. 'Well, in my opinion, it's time he got down to it like the rest of us.'

'That's just it, though. Charles isn't like us. He's sensitive and artistic, and working in his pa's bank will kill him.'

'I don't think so, Hetty. Maybe his old man is right and young Charlie needs to buckle down and work. But, if you ask me, I think you're better off without him. You stick to your own kind.'

She looked up, seeing him through a mist of tears, and she managed a watery smile. Dear old George, he was always so down to earth, saying just what he thought, and he was usually right. 'I suppose you mean like you, George?'

He grinned, pinching her cheek. 'Of course. You know I love you, Hetty. I'm your most devoted admirer and loyal friend.'

Despite everything, this blatant lie drew a chuckle from her. 'Me and a hundred others, tell the truth now.'

He let her go, clutching his hand to his heart and pulling a mock tragic face. 'I'm deeply wounded, Miss Huggins. You know my heart belongs to you.'

'You'd better not tell Poppy that.'

'Ah, yes. Poppy got a bit fed up with me and she's found herself a big, burly meat porter from Smithfield market. Can't say I admire her taste, but I suppose a free sausage beats a couple of spuds and a cabbage any day.'

Hetty reached up and kissed his cheek. 'George, you're a scoundrel.'

'Will you be all right now? I could mind your stall if you wanted to go home for a while and have a kip. You look like you could do with a rest.'

'I didn't sleep much last night,' Hetty admitted, sighing. 'But I'll manage. Ta all the same, George. Besides which,' she added, taking his soil-stained hand and turning it palm upwards, 'I don't think my customers would appreciate dirty fingerprints on their sandwiches.'

'Well, the offer's still there, Hetty. If it gets too much for you, I'm sure I could find one of me old flames to give you a hand.'

'You'd best be careful of old flames,' Hetty

retorted with a hint of her old spirit. 'They can burn your fingers.' She picked up the knife and began to scrape butter onto the thinly sliced bread.

'He's a bloody fool,' George muttered as he strode back towards his barrow. 'If it was me I'd sweep horse muck off the streets or pick oakum rather than leave the girl I loved in a foreign country.'

'He'll send for me,' Hetty whispered to his retreating back. 'Charles will send for me soon. He promised.' She felt the reassuring weight of his gold signet ring nestling between her breasts on its length of satin ribbon. To wear such a valuable article on her finger was asking for trouble. There were muggers who would cut a person's hand off in order to steal a piece of jewellery such as this. She closed her eyes, conjuring up his face: his laughing, smoky blue eyes and his tender lips. She could still taste his kiss and feel the gentle touch of his hands, which were as smooth-skinned as a lady's.

She sighed as she placed a slice of ham on the buttered bread; Charles was a gentleman, unused to hard work, or work of any kind come to that. She knew he would try to make a go of his position in his father's bank, but she had a nagging suspicion that if she wanted Charles badly enough, it would be up to her to raise the passage money for

America. Her beloved was a thinker; a dreamer of grand and impossible dreams. If she married Charles, and she had every intention of doing so, she would either have to win his father round or make enough money herself to set them up in style. Spreading mustard thinly on the ham, Hetty came to a decision. She would not sit back and wait for Charles to send for her. She was doing well with the one stall and she had been thinking about expanding the business. Now was the time to turn her plans into deeds, so that when she went to meet her prospective in-laws in Philadelphia she was not a mere costermonger from Spitalfields, but a successful businesswoman who could hold her head high in any society.

'A ham sandwich, please, love. And a mug of split pea, with plenty of sugar.' Brush Barber grinned down at her. 'And a slice of that currant cake would go down well.'

'Certainly,' Hetty said, giving him her brightest smile. 'Anything else?'

'That'll do for now, Hetty. You make the best sandwiches in London, so I reckon.'

'I do, and I'm not going to stop at this one stall, Brush. D'you know anyone who could rent me a permanent one in the market?'

'Well now, I do as it happens. Throw in a couple of hard-boiled eggs and a bunch of cress and I'll wheel him over to meet you at dinner time.'

'Done,' Hetty said, handing him his food. 'I got a feeling this will be the start of the Hetty Huggins string of coffee stalls.'

'Don't forget the "and Co.",' George shouted above the din in the market place. 'I got a stake in this too, Hetty.'

'Yes, you have, I hadn't forgotten, George. We'll talk about it in the pub after we finish up here.'

In the dark, smoky atmosphere of the Ten Bells, George sat beside Hetty with his pint of ale untouched in front of him. Hetty sipped a glass of port and lemon, feeling more optimistic with every mouthful. 'I've spoken to the market inspector, George, and he's willing to let me rent the stall that belonged to the old fruit and veg bloke who dropped down dead last week. I've got enough saved to start up, but it would mean that I can't afford to pay you back what I owe for a while yet.'

'But I don't want you to, Hetty. I'm the "and Co.", and I want it to stay that way.'

Hetty laid her hand on his as it rested on the table. 'Ta, George. You're a toff.'

'I dunno about that, but I can spot a good business proposition when I see one. You've got brains as well as beauty, and now you're fired up and wanting to follow that fellow of yours, I know you'll make a go of anything you sets your heart on.'

'Do you? Do you really, George?'

He lifted his tankard to his lips and swallowed a draught of ale. He did not look at her, and his fingers toyed with the pewter handle. 'You really love this bloke, don't you?'

'What's that got to do with it?'

He looked up, and for once his expression was serious. 'Answer me, Hetty. I need to know.'

'Yes, I do. I love everything about him. He's far above me, but I know I can make him happy, just given the chance.'

George dropped his gaze. 'I see. Well, I hope he don't break your heart, that's all. I care about you, Hetty. And if anyone plays you false or harms you in any way, he'll have me to answer to.'

Taken aback, Hetty stared at him. She had never seen him in this sort of mood before. 'Ta, George, but I know what I'm doing.'

He opened his mouth to reply, but before he could utter a word, Jane burst in through the pub door, still wearing her apron and her face streaked with flour as if she had come straight from the kitchen. Her eyes were enormous in her pale face and she uttered a shriek when she spotted them. 'Thank God I've found you.'

Hetty leapt to her feet and ran to put her arm round her sister, who was trembling and close to hysterics. 'What's happened to put you in such a state?'

'I ran all the way to the market,' Jane paused, struggling for breath. 'They said you'd packed up early, and then someone told me to try here. You got to come home quick, Hetty.'

'Why? What's up? What's got you in this state?'

'It's him – he's in the house – he crept up behind me and grabbed me round me waist. I fought and kicked but he was swearing and going on at me, muttering something about getting even with you. He put his filthy hand over me mouth and I bit it. He let me go cussing something horrible and then he snatched Talia from her cradle. Clench has got my baby. Come now, for pity's sake.'

# Chapter Twelve

Hetty burst into the kitchen, coming to an abrupt halt when she saw Clench dandling Natalia on his knee. 'Put her down.' The words came out in a shriek, and not in the way she had intended. Fear had made her voice shrill and sent diplomacy flying out of the window. Jane was close behind her, leaning on George's arm and oddly silent now after her hysterical outburst.

'What's all the fuss about?' Clench demanded, bouncing Natalia up and down and making her chuckle. 'I ain't hurting her. See, she likes it.' He bounced her higher and higher.

Hetty struggled to control rising panic and she forced herself to move slowly towards him, holding out her arms. 'Please give her to me, Mr Clench.'

Natalia seemed to sense the tension in the room and her chuckles turned into a frightened whimper. She turned her head to gaze appealingly at Hetty, and tears welled up in her blue eyes. Clench rose to his feet, thrusting Natalia into Hetty's arms. 'Oh, take the brat.

I can't be doing with all this female fuss and bother.'

'What's all this about, mate?' George demanded, helping Jane to a chair. 'What d'you think you're doing by scaring the women out of their wits?'

Clench sidled past him, making for the door. 'No need to get aggressive, cully. I came to see Miss Hetty on private business.'

'I've got nothing to say to you, Mr Clench,' Hetty said, cuddling Natalia, who had stopped crying and was all smiles again.

'You heard the lady,' George said, advancing on Clench with his hands fisted. 'She don't want nothing to do with you.'

Clench paused in the doorway. 'She'll want to hear what I got to say about her granny and the nippers.'

Cold fingers of fear gripped Hetty's heart, and her breathing was suddenly ragged. 'What have you done to them, you evil man?'

'Sticks and stones, Miss Hetty!'

There was something both malevolent and triumphant in Clench's smile, and, despite the heat in the kitchen, Hetty shivered. Setting Natalia down on Jane's lap, she faced up to Clench. 'If you've harmed my brothers or granny I'll . . .'

'You'll what?'

She recoiled at the all too familiar, foetid

smell of his breath, but she did not back away. 'Never you mind. Just say what you came to say and then leave.'

He stuck his fingers in his waistcoat pockets, eyeing her with contempt. 'Put it this way. From first thing tomorrow morning, your granny will be looking for lodgings elsewhere.'

'I don't believe you. That house in Totty Street is hers for life.'

'Now that is where you're wrong, missy. After old man Huggins died, his widow was allowed to live there on a peppercorn rent, but, just recently, the governors of the bank discovered that Mrs Huggins has been running a business from the house, which ain't allowed, according to the terms of the lease. In other words, the old girl forfeits her right to remain in said premises.' Clench leered into Hetty's face. 'Someone must have split on her.'

'You!'

'It weren't me, as it happens.'

George moved to Hetty's side. 'D'you want me to throw him out, Hetty?'

'No, not yet, George. I want to know who did this wicked thing to a defenceless old woman, and why.'

'I'm not the only one with a grudge against the Huggins family,' Clench said with a malicious grin. 'There was only one person who stuck by me when your granddad had me dismissed from the bank, and that was my friend Jasper Shipworthy.'

'Yes, we know all that,' Hetty cried impatiently. 'I don't see what Mr Shipworthy has to do with this. Get to the point, if you have one.'

'Number ten Totty Street was always kept for the head clerk at Tipton's. Jasper should have had the house when he received his promotion, but your granny refused to leave, so Jasper took lodgings there while he bided his time. Then he just happened to find a copy of the tenancy agreement filed away in the bank vaults, and he knew he'd found a way to get rid of the old woman. He'll be moving in as soon as she moves out.'

'Well shame on you,' Hetty cried. 'Shame on you both for treating a poor widow woman in such a shabby way. How could you do such a thing?'

'Very easily, my dear, and there's still a matter of the interest you owe me on your loan. Don't think I've forgotten. I'll be back to collect it when you've got your second stall up and running.'

Hetty stared at him in disbelief. 'How did you know about that?'

Clench tapped the side of his nose with his forefinger. 'I got spies everywhere. I know what you're doing, where you're going and who you're seeing, like that American reporter fellow, who's been sticking his beak into things what don't concern him.'

Hetty couldn't speak. She couldn't find words to express her alarm, disgust and dismay at what she had just heard.

'Get out of here, you villain,' George roared, grabbing Cyrus by the collar. 'I'm sorry, Hetty, but I've had enough of this snivelling little bastard.'

'That's right, George,' Jane cried, clapping her hands. 'Toss him out in the dirt where he belongs.'

Before Hetty had a chance to gather her scattered wits, George had frogmarched Clench down the passage and she heard the front door open and then slam shut. George returned with a triumphant smile on his face. 'That's got rid of him, for now at least. If I see him round here again I swear I'll wring his scraggy neck.'

'Forget him for now,' Hetty said, snatching her bonnet off the hook behind the door. 'I've got more important things to worry about at the moment. I'm going to Totty Street to bring Granny and the boys back here.'

'But, Hetty,' Jane protested. 'Shouldn't you ask Nora first? I mean, her letting rooms are all full.'

'There's the room that Charles had.' Hetty's breath hitched on a sob, but somehow she managed to keep a tight rein on her emotions. Granny and the boys needed her help and she was not going to fail them. 'I don't mind sleeping in the attic. We'll cope, and Nora will welcome the extra rent.'

'How will we manage though, Hetty?' Jane asked, setting a wriggling Natalia down on the floor, where she made a beeline for Hetty. 'How will we find food and rent for all of us, let alone pay for the boys' schooling?'

George hooked his arm around Hetty's shoulders. 'I can help if needs be, Hetty. Don't forget I am the "and Co."'

'I won't ever forget that, George. Ta all the same, but we'll manage. The boys can go to the ragged school and Jane can manage my stall in the market.'

'What?' Jane shrieked. 'Me run a coffee stall? I don't know how. And, anyway, I got to do the cooking and look after baby.'

'You'll soon learn,' Hetty said, smiling. 'I did. And with two stalls we'll double our income.' She bent down to scoop Natalia up in her arms. 'Granny will stay at home and look after Talia, won't she, my little pet?'

As if in answer, Natalia made cooing noises and gave Hetty a rather wet kiss on the cheek.

Jane threw up her hands in despair. 'You know that Granny doesn't like babies. She won't do it.'

Hetty met George's amused gaze with a determined lift of her chin. 'Oh yes she will. If we're to make money, everyone will have to do their bit. The boys can help on the stalls when they've finished their lessons and Granny can learn to bake cakes. One day I'll get you all out of here into a house of our own. You see if I don't.'

George gave her shoulders an encouraging squeeze. 'I don't doubt you for a minute, girl. My barrow is outside. I'll come with you to Totty Street and we can start shifting your granny's things here.'

'You're not leaving me to face Nora on me own,' Jane declared, jumping up and reaching for her shawl. 'I'll put baby in her perambulator and we'll come too. I'm sure Tom would give us a hand, if we asked him nicely.'

Hetty nodded in agreement. 'Yes, I'm sure he would. You go on ahead and ask him, Jane. He won't be able to refuse you.' Despite her agitation, Hetty couldn't help smiling at Jane's eagerness to include Tom. Perhaps one day he would see beneath her youthful flightiness, and realise that Jane was a kind and loving person, who would make him a wonderful wife. With her own heart bursting with love for Charles, and safe in the knowledge that he returned her affection, Hetty wanted everyone in the world to experience the joy she was feeling. Even the thought of Clench and his hateful crony Shipworthy could not completely dampen her spirits. Besides, it would be good to have the whole family together again under one roof. She had missed her brothers, even if they were little imps at times, and she had even missed Granny with her caustic tongue and strict rules. She might have the very devil of a temper when roused, but at least you knew where you stood with Granny Huggins.

'No! No! No! I ain't budging from this house, and that's my final word.' Granny sat bolt upright in her chair by the fire, gripping the armrests as though she was afraid that someone might attempt to remove her bodily. 'You can all go back where you came from and leave me here to defend what's mine.' She scowled ominously at Tom and George who stood, caps in hands, filling the small room with their large presence.

'Please, Granny,' Hetty said softly. 'You must come with us. They'll send the bailiffs in if you insist on staying put.'

'I don't care. It would take more than that to make me leave my home. I've lived in this house since I was a young bride. For forty years or more I've cleaned and scrubbed, polished and kept this place as neat as a new pin. Your grandfather earned the right to have this house for his lifetime and mine. I won't be turned out of it now.'

Jane gave a nervous cough. 'But Granny . . .'

'Don't you try your wheedling ways on me, girl. I'm staying put and I'm not budging for anyone.' Granny turned her attention to George, wagging her finger at him. 'I don't know what you're doing here, young man. This is a family matter.'

Hetty cast him an apologetic glance. 'He is almost family, Granny. George has helped me out no end of times, and you know it.'

'He's a costermonger. A street trader! You could do better for yourself, Hetty. Don't forget that your grandpa was a respectable head clerk. He wouldn't have allowed you to go walking out with a common coster.'

'Granny!' Hetty knew she was blushing and she cast an anxious glance at George, but he seemed to be genuinely amused.

'You mustn't worry, Mrs Huggins,' he said, chuckling. 'Hetty is not stepping out with me. She has better taste. I'm just a friend and business partner, and I've come to help you move your belongings to the house in Princelet Street.'

'Have you now? Well, you've had a wasted journey, young man. I ain't going.'

Jane nudged Tom in the ribs. 'Say something, Tom. She likes you.'

'I heard that, Jane Huggins,' Granny said, scowling. 'I'm not deaf and I'm not senile. I can make my own mind up, and I tell you, I won't leave my home.'

Sammy and Eddie had been sitting quietly on the floor with Natalia, who was crawling all over them, but at this moment Sammy scrambled to his feet. He clutched Hetty's hand. 'I'll come with you. I've missed you, Hetty. And I don't mind leaving school to help you on the stall. I could be part of the "and Co." with George.'

'Me too,' Eddie cried, attempting to get up from the floor, but Natalia was sitting on him and chuckling as if this was all part of a game. 'Get her off me, Jane. She's got a wet bum.'

Tut-tutting, Jane picked up Natalia and took her, protesting loudly, out of the room.

'Maybe she needs a hand,' Tom murmured, hurrying after her.

'Go on,' Granny said, waving her hand at Hetty and George. 'You go too. I don't need any of you. I can look after myself.'

'Oh, Granny. Must you be so stubborn?' Hetty demanded, sighing. 'Why won't you come with us?'

'Because this is my home. I've lived here for most of my life and I'll die here. You can take the boys if you must, but I'm staying. I've got my business to run, and neither Shipworthy nor all the governors of Tipton's Bank are going to force me to move out.'

Hetty's patience was being stretched to its limit. Granny was a stubborn old woman, and, although she admired her spirit, Hetty was not going to stand by and allow her to be ejected forcibly or humiliated in the eyes of her neighbours. She nudged George in the ribs. 'Leave this to me. I'd like a few words with Granny in private.'

'Call me if you need me,' he said, beckoning to the boys. 'We'll wait outside.'

Hetty waited until the door closed behind them and then she turned to her grandmother. 'Well?'

'I'm not going.'

'Yes you are, Granny. You either come with us now, keeping a bit of dignity, or I'll go away and leave it to the bailiffs to throw you out on the street in front of all your neighbours.' Folding her arms across her chest, Hetty stood squarely in front of her. 'It's your decision, but I'd think about it carefully if I was you.'

'Don't you try to browbeat me, girl.'

Hetty was quick to hear the tremulous note in her grandmother's voice, and, for the first time, she saw a hint of fear in the faded blue eyes, which must once have been almost the same deep shade as her own. She realised suddenly that they were alike, she and Granny

Huggins: strong, determined women with wills of their own. But for all her bold words, Granny was growing old, and the world was a harsh place for the elderly and unprotected. Hetty knelt down in front of her, taking the thin, veined hands in hers. 'Granny, you took us in when we was destitute. You never asked us to come here and you didn't want us, but you still fed us and gave us a roof over our heads. You saw off Clench and Shipworthy with all guns blazing. They might have won for now, but I promise you I'll make them both sorry they ever had it in for the Huggins family.'

'You and whose army?' Granny demanded, sniffing.

Hetty chuckled. 'You'll see one day that I'm a chip off the old block. Come with us now, please. We need you in Princelet Street, honest we do.'

Granny drew her hands away and she fumbled in her pocket, bringing out a handkerchief and blowing her nose. 'You and your wheedling ways, Hetty Huggins. You get that from your grandpa. He could talk his way out of anything.'

'Then you'll come with us?'

'I suppose someone has got to keep an eye on you all, but I want every last stick of furniture moved out of this house. I won't leave anything for those blackguards, not a thing.'

It took Tom and George several trips with the barrow, but eventually they managed to empty the house before midnight. Hetty sent Granny, Jane and Natalia home in a hackney carriage while she pushed the perambulator filled with Granny's best china and silver-plated spoons, and Sammy and Eddie trudged beside her with their few possessions bundled into two sacks.

By the time they reached Princelet Street, Jane had explained everything to Nora who, as usual, had taken it all in her stride and was bustling about organising the rooms. She greeted Hetty with a cheerful smile. 'No need to say nothing, girl. We look after our own in the East End, and Nora Jackson has never turned away a soul in distress.' She drew Hetty aside, nodding her head in Granny's direction as she sat in the rocking chair by the fire. 'She's fair wore out, ducks. She might be spunky, but she's old and tired. You done right in bringing her here, Hetty. I'll put the word round the market. If that bloke Clench sets foot in there again, he'll be sorry.'

If Hetty had had any doubts about how Granny and Nora would rub along together, she was surprised and delighted to find that she had worried needlessly. Despite Granny's notion that people fell into two basic categories, those with brains and breeding and those without, she and Nora hit it off from the start. Granny appeared to recover quickly from the shock of being evicted from her home, but Hetty sensed that the hurt went far deeper than she was prepared to admit. Her altered circumstances might have chastened her abrasive spirit just a little, but Granny Huggins was not one to give in to despair. She accepted her new role with resignation, if not with good grace, and she took over the cooking with more enthusiasm than Hetty would have thought possible. Perhaps it had something to do with the huge kitchen range, which had two ovens and a large water boiler creating an endless supply of hot, strong tea. Nora was not stingy when it came to housekeeping, and, although their diet was plain, there was plenty to go round and no one went to bed hungry.

Granny was a reluctant nursemaid, but she tolerated Natalia now that she had grown past the helpless baby stage and was attempting to walk, pulling herself up on her chubby legs and clambering round the furniture with the inevitable tumbles. Sammy and Eddie were sent to the ragged school, coming home with the occasional black eye and an impressive selection of bruises from playground fights, but Granny's advice was unchanging. 'You've got to stand up for yourselves in this world.

If they're the same size as you, hit them back. If they're smaller than you, tell them that Spring-heeled Jack will get them. If they're bigger than you, kick the little blighters in the shins and run for it.'

Having left Jane in charge of the market stall, Hetty took her newly equipped barrow to a pitch outside Liverpool Street station. At first she had to jostle for a place, competing with other street traders, but she had learnt to be tough, and was not as easily scared as she had been when she had first tried to sell hot potatoes in Bethnal Green. In a matter of weeks she had attracted a regular stream of customers, and she had added cocoa to her menu, as well as tea and coffee. She knew that some stall-holders adulterated their coffee with chicory but Hetty bought freshly roasted coffee beans and ground them herself. She used only the prime cuts of gammon, and bread fresh from the bakery each day which she spread with butter and not margarine. She might have made more profit by what she considered to be cheating, but she soon earned the reputation for the finest coffee and the tastiest sandwiches in the East End. Hetty took pride in providing only the best.

To everyone's surprise, Jane had taken to working on the market stall with enthusiasm, and she was proving to be a great success. Her naturally vivacious and flirtatious nature attracted customers both male and female, and she was soon the darling of the costermongers. She even began collecting pearl buttons and spent her evenings sewing them on her clothes under the guidance of Nora, whose festive costume was so heavily embellished with mother-of-pearl that it would almost stand up by itself. Both Tom and George were regular callers at the house, although, as Granny remarked with acerbity, 'it's hard to say which one of you girls attracts them the most.'

Hetty hoped that Tom was coming to see Jane, but he seemed to be as happy when he was amusing Natalia or the boys as he was when chatting to either Jane or herself.

When Hetty had finished work for the day, she would drag her tired limbs up four flights of stairs to the attic room where she slept amongst the items saved from Granny's house. It was like living in a furniture repository, but Hetty ignored the discomfort. In the flickering light of a single candle she would read and reread the letters from Charles which arrived with unfailing regularity every week. In these rare quiet moments she would write in reply, struggling with her grammar and spellings and the occasional ink blot made even larger by the tears that sprang to her eyes when she realised how much she loved and missed him. He was, he said, now working in his father's bank and was the most junior of all the clerks. He was at everyone's beck and call, but he wrote, underlining the words in bold strokes, that he did not mind this at all if it brought their reunion a little nearer. His pay was so low that it was an insult, but his father was adamant that Charles was not to be given any privileges above the rest of the staff. He was going to learn the banking business if it killed him. With a hint of humour, Charles said that he was so far at the bottom of the heap that he could go no further without tunnelling into the vaults.

When Hetty wrote back she was careful only to tell him about the positive aspects of running a coffee stall outside one of the busiest railway stations in London. She did not recount the incidents when certain cabbies refused to pay, threatening her with a beating if she called a copper, or the insults she had to bear from other stallholders who resented a woman working in a male-dominated trade. She failed to mention the pilfering of food by half-starved street urchins, to which she turned a blind eye, reasoning that in different circumstances it could have been Sammy or Eddie who were driven to such depths of despair.

In the silence of the attic room Hetty felt so close to Charles that she could almost reach out and touch him. She would hold the ever increasing bundle of letters to her breast, closing her eyes and conjuring up a vision of his face. She recalled the way his hair would suddenly flop down over his eyes, causing him the thrust it back with an impatient hand. She could mentally trace the firm outline of his cheekbones and the slightly lopsided curve of his lips when he smiled, and his eyes that changed from smoky blue to misty grey when he was sad. Every look and every word he had ever addressed to her was imprinted on her memory to be remembered with delight and a great deal of heartache. Even the paper on which he had written in elegant copperplate held a faint trace of his own familiar scent: expensive cologne and sandalwood soap with just a hint of a fine Havana cigar. She could still feel the tender touch of his lips when he had kissed her in the park, that hot and steamy Sunday in July. Her longing for him was a physical pain, but the memory of it put steel in her soul and made her even more determined to make a go of her business. If Charles did not send for her within a year, Hetty had made up her mind to go to Philadelphia and seek him out.

On the hot summer nights, when she was too exhausted to write any more, she would lie down on her narrow iron bed and stare through the grimy panes of the roof window, peering at the diamond pinpoints of stars twinkling in the black velvet sky. Was Charles looking up at them and thinking of her? She would eventually drift off to sleep and dream that he had come for her, but harsh reality would return with the dawn, and each new day brought the prospect of long hours, sore feet and blistered hands. Hetty suffered it all without complaint. As long as she could put away a little money each week in a leather pouch which she hid beneath a loose floorboard in the attic, she was satisfied that she was on her way to a blissful reunion with the only man she had ever truly loved.

The blistering heat of August eased gradually into the mellow month of September. The days grew shorter and the mornings chillier in October, and November brought the return of the dreaded pea-souper fog that wrapped itself around London in an evil-smelling, suffocating blanket, blotting out sight and sound, and making trade impossible. When the fog lifted, the pot-bellied clouds brought torrential rain to the streets, and workers who might have stopped for a cup of something hot or a bite to eat before embarking on their bus or train journeys to the suburbs hurried past Hetty's stall intent on getting home as fast as possible.

Late one afternoon towards the end of November, a sudden thunderstorm had forced Hetty to pack up her barrow earlier than she would normally have done. She was soaked to the skin before she reached Spital Square, and the sore throat which had started that morning had now developed into a racking cough. She trudged homewards, pushing the heavy barrow with her booted feet slipping and sliding on the wet cobblestones. Someone hailed her as she was about to pass the north entrance to Spitalfields market, and she stopped to wipe the rainwater from her eyes. George came hurrying out of the market with a piece of sacking held over his head and a look of concern on his face. 'Hetty, you looked like a drownded rat, girl. Come inside and dry off a bit before you catch your death of cold.'

Seized with a fit of coughing, Hetty shook her head. 'Got to get home,' she wheezed.

George took the handles of the barrow and pushed it inside the entrance, tucking it against a wall close to Jane's stall. 'Keep an eye on Hetty's barrow, ducks. I'm just taking her to the pub to get a brandy inside her.'

Jane hurried over to them. 'She ought to be in bed by the look of her. Take her straight home, George.'

Hetty raised a wet hand. 'I can speak for

meself, ta.' Another fit of coughing rendered her speechless.

'I'll take her home, but first she's going to have a tot of something stronger than ginger beer. I won't be long, Jane.' George took Hetty by the arm and guided her out of the market to a pub on the opposite side of the road. He found her a seat close to the fire where he helped her off with her sodden jacket, which he hung on the back of her chair. Steam billowed from her wet skirts as she warmed her chilled limbs by the fire while he went off to fetch their drinks.

He returned, handing her a glass of brandy. 'Here, drink this and no argument.'

Hetty sipped it and coughed as the spirit hit the back of her throat.

'All of it,' George said firmly. He sat watching her as she struggled to get the alcohol down her sore throat, nodding in approval when she drained the glass. 'Why didn't you take shelter? What was you thinking of, Hetty Huggins?'

'M-money,' Hetty murmured with a slightly tipsy smile. 'I c-can't afford to lose a day's earnings, G-George.'

'You'll lose more than that if you go down with the lung fever, girl.' He sat back in his chair, taking a swig of his ale. 'You can't keep on working like this in the winter, Hetty. For one thing, trade drops off when the weather is bad, and for another, you ain't fit enough to stand on street corners in rain, sleet and snow, to say nothing of the London particulars.'

Warmed by the brandy, Hetty grimaced as the feeling came back to her extremities, making them tingle painfully. Her chilblains began to throb and her chest was so sore that every rattling breath hurt. She didn't want to admit it, but she knew that what George said was true. The coffee stall trade was largely dependent on the weather. If she could have done the night shift she might have been able to earn more, but with the possible resurgence of the Ripper the streets were dangerous after dark and the risk too great for a young, unprotected female. She nodded her head, sighing. 'I know you're right, George.'

'Thank the Lord for that. I thought you'd put up a fight. You must be feeling off colour.'

She managed a weary smile. 'Just a bit, but I'll be fine in the morning.'

'You'll be a corpse if you go on like this, Hetty. I'm sick of standing by while you flog yourself to death on that stall.' George leaned over and clasped her hands, looking deeply into her eyes. 'You mean a lot to me, Hetty. I mean, we're business partners, ain't we? And as such, I've got a proposition to make.'

His earnest face was moving in and out of

focus as the heat from the fire and the alcohol began to take effect. Hetty blinked hard, forcing herself to concentrate on his words, which seemed to make little sense. 'Go on, George. Say what you got to say, because I don't feel so good.'

'It's this, Hetty. I have to say it now because I never get a chance to speak to you on your own in that madhouse of Nora's. What I want to say is that I've got a little nest egg saved up, and I want to invest it in our business venture, all proper and above board.'

'Y-you do?'

'I've been doing a bit of snooping round and I think I've found the ideal premises for you to open up a coffee shop.'

'A coffee shop?'

He squeezed her fingers, and his mouth curved in a grin. 'That's right, girl. It's close to Liverpool Street station, not far from Petticoat Lane. I know you've been saving up for just this event, and if I put my money in we could sign the lease in the morning and be ready to open for business before Christmas. What do you say?'

# Chapter Thirteen

Hetty could never remember what her reply had been to George's startling proposition; in fact she lost several days completely as she lay in her bed racked with fever. Jane told her afterwards that they had feared for her life, and Granny had even gone so far as to send for the doctor, paying his fee out of her own purse. The crusty old physician had made them strip the cotton sheets off the bed so that Hetty was lying between thick woollen blankets. 'She must sweat it out. Give her some drops of laudanum in water if she becomes too restless,' he had said, shaking his head. 'I can do no more. The rest is in the hands of the Lord.'

Jane giggled at this point and said that Hetty would have died laughing if she had seen Granny's face when she saw the bed piled high with blankets and rugs. Granny had swooped on the covers like an avenging angel and stripped off everything, replacing the cotton sheets and calling the doctor all manner of names. She had insisted on bathing Hetty with cool water to bring her temperature down, ignoring Jane and Nora's protests that it would probably kill rather than cure her. Granny had condemned the doctor as a charlatan and not worth the half-crown he had charged for the visit. It was scandalous taking money from poor folks on false pretences. Jane did a pretty fair imitation of Granny in one of her sniffy moods, placing her hands on her hips and rolling her eyes. 'Anyone knows that if you have a pot boiling over you take it off the heat, you don't pile more coal on the fire. It's the same with a fever, any fool can see that.' Jane emphasised each word with a toss of her head, in just the way that Granny did when she was annoyed or offended.

Hetty couldn't help laughing, but this made her cough and she had to sip some water from the cup that Jane held to her lips. 'I was terrified that she was going to do you more harm than good,' Jane continued, wiping Hetty's mouth with a corner of the sheet. 'But then, just like a miracle, the fever broke, and you opened your eyes and spoke to me, quite like your old self.' Jane's voice quavered, and, as if embarrassed by this show of emotion, she plumped up the pillows behind Hetty's head. 'Now all you got to do is sip this broth that Nora made for you, and get your strength back.'

Obediently, Hetty took a little of the beef

broth from the spoon that Jane held to her lips. 'How long have I been like this, and what's happened to my stall?'

Jane chuckled, dipping the spoon into the cup and waiting until Hetty had swallowed another mouthful. 'Trust you to put the stall first.'

Hetty attempted to sit up. 'I must get up. I'm better . . .' Her voice tailed off as a spell of dizziness forced her to sink back against the pillows.

'Yes, it looks like it.' Jane put the cup down on a box beside the bed. 'You're not to worry about anything, Hetty. I've been working your barrow outside the station, and the boys helped Granny to keep the stall in the market ticking along nicely.'

If Jane had said that the Archangel Gabriel had descended from heaven to work the stall in Spitalfields market, Hetty would not have been more astonished. 'Granny and the boys! You're joking.'

'I am not, I swear it. George kept an eye on them, of course, and Nora took care of baby. Although most of the time Natalia was being passed around the market women like a little doll. She's been spoilt to death by everyone.'

Tears spilled from Hetty's eyes. She had never felt so weak and helpless, or so grateful to her family. 'I dunno what to say.'

Jane smoothed the coverlet with a practised hand. 'You didn't think we'd let you down, did you? We may have our differences at times, Hetty, but you're my sister and I love you. We all do, and Tom's called round every evening to see how you are, and George has done all the buying for both stalls. He's been a real brick.'

'I must see him, Jane. I can't remember much about what he said in the pub, but I think he offered to set me up in a proper coffee shop, although maybe I dreamt it.'

'You didn't dream it, Hetty. George told me all about it and you can see him tomorrow, but only if you take a little more of this broth.'

When Jane had gone downstairs, Hetty lay in her bed staring up at the windowpanes where sleety rain traced patterns in the coating of city grime. Her mind was filled with visions of her coffee shop. It would be warm and welcoming, with spotlessly clean floral-patterned tablecloths and comfortable chairs. She would attract the better class of customer, especially the young lady type-writers, clerks and secretaries who now worked in the city offices. The coffee shop would be a place where they could spend their midday break, meet their friends and maybe even flirt a little with the gentlemen who also worked in offices. She would serve behind a glass-fronted counter and there would be luxury items like chocolate cake and pastries, as well as ham sandwiches and perhaps even salmon and cucumber in season, or cheese and pickle. Gentleman liked cheese and pickle; sausage rolls, too. Hetty closed her eyes and she could see it all. A waitress in a black uniform with a starched white cap and apron was scurrying in between the tables, serving the customers with their orders. Outside her imaginary coffee shop the rain was sheeting down, but the well-dressed clientele were chatting and laughing as they lunched off freshly prepared sandwiches and pastries. Hetty could smell the coffee and taste the rich, dark chocolate cake. It would all be wonderful and she would soon make enough money to pay her fare to America. Hetty smiled as she slipped into a deep and dreamless sleep.

As promised, George came round after he had packed up his stall the following evening. Hetty had been allowed downstairs for an hour and she sat by the fire with a shawl wrapped around her shoulders, and everyone fussing around her. She realised just how ill she had been when George presented her with a bunch of hothouse grapes. 'How are you, girl?' He pulled up a stool to sit beside her. 'Are you feeling well enough to talk?'

'I'm much better now, ta.' Hetty glanced over

his shoulder. Sammy and Eddie were eyeing the grapes and she could tell by the expressions on their faces that they were longing to taste them. She beckoned to Sammy. 'I'm sure that George won't mind if you and Eddie have a few of my grapes. Leave a couple for me, though.'

Sammy's eager hand shot out to take the fruit. 'Ta, Hetty. I'm glad you didn't die.'

'So am I, Sammy,' Hetty said, chuckling. 'So am I.'

George took her hand in his. 'You mustn't overtire yourself. I just wanted you to know that I meant what I said before you was took sick. Just give me the nod and I'll go ahead and sign the lease on the shop in Artillery Lane. Then, when you've got your strength back, we can see about fitting it out as a proper coffee shop.'

'As easy as that,' Hetty said, smiling at his boundless optimism. 'Haven't you forgotten something, George?'

'What's that, Hetty?'

'I haven't seen this place and it might not be what I had in mind. And then there's the small matter of money, George. What I want to do will cost a lot.'

'I told you that I've got a bit put by, and I'm more than willing to invest it in the business. This is just the start, Hetty. I reckon we could have a whole string of coffee shops in a few years' time.'

He looked so much like an eager schoolboy that Hetty had not the heart to pour cold water on his scheme, but, even so, she had to be practical. Her memories of living in poverty were all too vivid and she had no intention of allowing her family to fall back into that particular trap. She covered his hand with hers. 'We got to work it all out, George. There's tables and chairs to be bought or hired, and crockery, glassware, cutlery, tablecloths . . .'

'Stop, you're making my head spin.'

'I want to do it properly, George. There are plenty of places for working men to get their food and drink, but I want to cater for young women office workers, and mothers with children who can afford to take them out for a glass of lemonade and maybe an ice cream in the summer.'

Jane bustled over to them, wiping her hands on her apron. 'That's enough excitement for today, Hetty. You need to rest or you'll get sick again.'

'Yes, of course.' George rose to his feet. 'As soon as you're well enough I'll take you to see the place.'

She raised her hand to pluck at his sleeve. 'Tomorrow you're taking me to look at the premises and then if I like it we'll sign the lease. We'll go to the bank if we have to, and ask for a business loan.'

He bent down to kiss her on the forehead. 'We'll talk about this some more tomorrow. Now you get a good night's sleep and I'll see you in the morning.'

'I hope you know what you're doing,' Granny said gloomily as the door closed on George. 'If you're not careful, Hetty, you'll end up in Queer Street.'

'Don't talk like that, Granny,' Jane protested. 'Hetty knows what she's about.'

'Yes, Mattie, leave the girl be.' Nora heaved her bulk up from the chair at the table. 'If anyone can do it, my money is on Hetty. Now let's have some supper, I'm bleeding starving.'

Jane hefted a black cast-iron saucepan off the range and set it down on the table. 'Go and wash your hands, boys, while I serve up the mutton stew.'

Sammy and Eddie needed no second bidding, and as they went out into the yard Tom came in through the scullery. He sniffed the air appreciatively. 'Boiled mutton, my favourite.'

Jane waved the ladle at him. 'It's funny how you always turn up just as I'm about to serve supper.'

He grinned ruefully. 'It's a happy coincidence, that's all. Your cooking would tempt

314

anyone.' Dragging off his cap, he went over to Hetty. 'It's good to see you up and about again, love. How are you?'

'Well enough, Tom. No, better than that. I'm much better and I got good reason to get well quickly.'

He sent a questioning look to Jane, but she smiled and shook her head. 'Come and sit down at the table, Tom. There's plenty to go round.'

'I will in a minute.' He perched on the stool recently vacated by George. 'What's going on, Hetty?'

Unable to contain her excitement, she told him about her plan to go into business with George, but if she was expecting Tom to be impressed, she was sadly disappointed. He ran his fingers through his hair, causing it to stand on end. 'It's a big risk, Hetty. You could lose everything you've worked so hard for.'

'Or I could make our fortunes, given time.'

'I dunno, ducks. I do me week's work and I collect me wages at the end of it, but at least I know where I stand. As to going into business with George, I'm sorry, Hetty, but I've never trusted that fellow. He's all talk if you ask me. If I was a bank manager, I don't think I'd trust him with other people's money.'

The bank managers were obviously of the same opinion as Tom. A week later, Hetty and

George had been turned down by all the banks in the area; the only one they had not tried so far was the Bishopsgate headquarters of Tipton's Bank. Hetty had been reluctant to try there, fearing that news of her request might filter back to Jasper Shipworthy at the Bethnal Green branch, or, even worse, that Cyrus Clench might get wind of her plans. She had not seen him since the day he came to tell them that Granny was about to be evicted from her house, but that did not mean that he had given up. He had a habit of melting into the shadows and popping up at unexpected moments. When George suggested that they try Tipton's, Hetty was doubtful, but also desperate. She had carefully calculated how much they would need to equip their new premises and George's nest egg, even when combined with her savings, would not cover the initial outlay. Reluctantly she agreed that they ought to make an appointment to see the manager.

Henry Maitland, the manager of Tipton's Bank in Bishopsgate, took off his spectacles and polished them on a white cotton hand-kerchief. He replaced them on his nose and shuffled the sheaf of papers on the desk in front of him. Hetty couldn't help observing that his fat white fingers looked like uncooked veal sausages with smooth, shiny skins. There was something furtive in Maitland's manner and from the start he had not looked her directly in the eye. She held her breath. George had put forward their proposals very well, or so she thought, but the sudden silence was unnerving. A glance in George's direction confirmed that he too was feeling the strain. Beads of perspiration stood out on his top lip and he held his cap in clenched hands, his knuckles showing through the skin like white marbles.

Mr Maitland looked at them over the top of his spectacles. 'I've listened to your business proposition, Mr Cooper, but if I were to consider such a loan I would need some collateral.'

Hetty bit her lip. She had been dreading this and she cast an anxious glance at George. She could tell by the way he ran his finger round the inside of his collar and cleared his throat that he too was nervous. 'Well, sir, there's my stall in Spitalfields Market and Miss Huggins has two coffee stalls . . .'

'That's not exactly what I had in mind, Mr Cooper. I cannot risk my investors' money without some form of security, and I'm afraid a couple of handcarts will not be adequate. Have you any property, stocks and shares, or gilt-edged securities?'

'Well, er, no, sir.'

Mr Maitland turned his attention to Hetty.

'And you, Miss Huggins. What have you to offer?'

'Hard work and the will to do well, mister.' Hetty was trembling with emotion, and she had to clasp her hands together to stop them shaking. 'My grandfather spent all his working life at your branch in Bethnal Green. He gave his all to Tipton's Bank and if he was here now he would vouch for me. I'm going to make a success of my coffee shop and I won't stop with just one. Given time I'll have a whole string of coffee shops from Bishopsgate to Marble Arch, you see if I don't.'

George laid his hand on hers, giving her an encouraging smile. 'Well said, girl.'

Mr Maitland rose to his feet. 'Your enthusiasm does you credit, Miss Huggins, but it's hardly a solid financial basis on which I can grant you a loan.'

'You're turning us down?' Hetty leapt to her feet. 'Oh, please, won't you give us a chance? We're not asking for a fortune.'

Maitland reached behind his desk and tugged on a bell pull. 'I'm sorry, Miss Huggins, but I've made my decision. My clerk will show you out.'

'This is so unfair,' Hetty protested. 'You haven't given us a proper hearing.'

Maitland looked over her shoulder as the door opened and someone entered. 'Mr Clench, will you show these young people out, please. Our business is concluded.'

George uttered a muffled oath, and Hetty spun round, coming face to face with Cyrus Clench.

'Certainly, sir.' Clench's features were set in a deadpan expression but his eyes blazed with malice as they met Hetty's startled gaze. He held the door open. 'This way, please.'

Hetty hurried past him but she stopped in the corridor outside the manager's office, her anger inflamed by disappointment. 'You! What are you doing here?'

'I work here. As luck would have it, my mate Jasper received his well-deserved promotion and a transfer to this branch of Tipton's Bank. He is now assistant manager here and he was kind enough to put in a good word for me. I'm a respectable bank clerk again, no thanks to you and yours, Miss Hetty Huggins.' He leaned closer to her so that his lips were against her ear. 'You still owe me. I'll have me twopenn'orth one way or another, dearie.'

'I dunno what you just said, cully,' George snarled, grabbing Clench by the collar, 'but whatever it was, I'm betting that it was no way to speak to a lady.'

Clench made a gobbling sound in his throat like a turkey about to have its neck wrung, but before he could shout for help George had marched him out through the main concourse of the bank into Bishopsgate. 'You deserve to be strung up for the way you've treated Hetty and her family, and for two pins I'd be the man to do it, but you ain't worth swinging for, Clench.'

'Let me go or I'll call a copper,' Clench hissed. 'I'll have her thrown in jail for debt.'

'Don't bother with him, George,' Hetty said, uncomfortably aware that they were attracting the attention of passers-by and that a police-man was strolling along the street towards them. 'Let him go. He's not important.'

Reluctantly, George released Clench. 'I'm warning you, mate. Keep away from Hetty or it'll be the worse for you.'

'Not until I gets me one pound ten shillings,' Clench muttered. 'And the interest goes up every week.'

'You made that up,' Hetty exclaimed hotly. 'I don't owe you anything.'

He curled his lip. 'Like I said, you can always pay me in kind.'

George flexed his fingers. 'Shall I kill him now, Hetty?'

'Leave him, George. He's a nasty little weasel but he's all hot air and bluster.'

George thrust his hand in his pocket and pulled out a handful of coins. He selected a sovereign and four half-crowns. 'Here's your blood money, Clench.' But instead of giving it to him, he caught hold of Clench by the wrist. 'You'll have the cash, mate, but not until I get a signed receipt.' George marched him back into the bank with Hetty following close behind them. She watched in awe as George manhandled Clench to the counter and made him write out the receipt. After checking it, George handed it to Hetty. 'Keep it safe and if this sewer rat comes near you again, you can have him arrested and thrown in clink.'

At that moment, Mr Maitland came out of his office. He stopped short when he saw them. 'Mr Clench, I thought I told you to see these people off the premises.'

'Yes, sir,' Clench said, fawning and wringing his hands. 'I tried to make them but they refused to leave.'

Hetty waved the piece of paper in front of his face. 'Would you care to explain this to your boss, Mr Clench?'

'It's nothing, sir,' Clench said, cringing visibly. 'Just some street directions I was giving the young person.'

Maitland frowned. 'Get back to work, Mr Clench. And the next time I give you an order, I expect it to be obeyed instantly and to the letter, or I might reconsider my decision to employ you.'

As soon as they were outside in the street,

Hetty flung her arms around George's neck and kissed him on the cheek. 'You were wonderful, George. Thank you so much, but that was your own money you gave to Clench and we need it more than he does.' She shivered as large flakes of snow began to tumble from a pewter sky.

George rammed his cap on his head. 'It'll be worth every penny if it gets rid of him, and if it doesn't – let's just say I've got contacts and Clench might meet with a nasty accident if he's not careful.'

'No violence, George. Heaven knows I hate the man, but I won't stoop to his level.' She huddled against him, squinting as the snowflakes swirled in a merry dance around her head. 'We'd best get home before we freeze to death.'

'Another half an hour won't make any difference. The shop is just round the corner and I've got the keys. We can shelter in there until the worst is over.' Without waiting for an answer, George guided her along the slippery pavements to Artillery Lane. He produced a key from his coat pocket and unlocked the door.

Hetty wrinkled her nose as she entered the dilapidated premises. 'I didn't notice it before, but what's that awful stench, George? It smells as though something died in here.'

Shaking the snow off his cap, George chuckled. 'I wasn't going to mention it unless you asked, but the last occupant was a bloke who stuffed dead animals and birds for a living.' He prodded a pile of suspicious-looking material with the toe of his boot.

'That's horrible,' Hetty said, shuddering. 'I hope he didn't leave any dead bodies in the cupboards.'

'A few feathers and bits of fur maybe.' George caught her by the hand as she was about to make for the street door. 'Just joking, Hetty. There's nothing here that can't be fixed by soap and water and a bit of elbow grease.'

She glanced around at the cracked and crazed plaster on the walls and the peeling paintwork. 'It didn't look so bad when I saw it for the first time, but I wasn't quite myself then and I didn't realise just how much needs doing.' She walked about the room, peering into empty cupboards and brushing aside long trails of spiders' webs. 'I hate to say it, but I think we might have to let this place go. Maybe in the spring . . .'

'That's not like you, Hetty. Where's your fighting spirit, girl?'

She smiled, shaking her head. 'I'm just being sensible, George. If we'd got the money from the bank . . .'

'We've got better than that. We've got friends.'

He took her by the shoulders, looking deeply into her eyes. 'Do you want this coffee shop or not, Hetty?'

'You know I do, George.'

'Then leave it to me.' His eyes darkened and the smile left his face. 'I know what you think of me, Hetty. Good old George, always acting the clown, carrying on with women and never doing a stroke of work if he can get away with it. But I'll surprise you one day, and you'll find out there's more to George Cooper than you thought.'

'You're the best friend a girl could have. Don't ever change, George. I love you just as you are.'

He released her abruptly, turning away to peer out through the dirt encrusted window-panes. 'It's easing up a bit. I'd better get you home before you go down with another chill.'

'Ta, George, but I'm perfectly capable of going by myself. You've lost enough time on your stall because of me.'

He turned to her with a shadow of his old smile. 'You're forgetting that we're partners now, Hetty. I'm not just the "and Co." any more - it's Huggins and Cooper now, and I'm going to pull my weight. There'll be no more larking around with the market girls. From now on I'm going to be a reformed character.'

It was Hetty's turn to gurgle with laughter. 'That'll be the day.'

Hetty went home to Princelet Street determined to sit down and work out a revised budget for her coffee shop. She had no intention of giving up, but she was not going to rely on George. Bless him! He meant well, but he would only have to see a pretty face or spot a well-turned ankle and he would forget all about mundane things like earning a living. He would be off like a shot and everything else would fly out of his mind. If it wasn't a girl, then it might be a game of cards or a day at the races. Hetty knew that George enjoyed a flutter every now and again, although he was not a serious gambler. He just liked to have a good time, and if he was unreliable he made up for it with his generous heart and kindly nature. No one, she thought, could possibly dislike George.

She sat up late into the night with a pencil and a sheet of paper, only this time she was not writing a love letter to Charles, she was making lists of the most basic needs for starting up her new business. Perhaps the awful weather was a godsend in disguise as people were more intent on staying indoors and keeping warm than on standing around the freezing street corners while they ate their food or drank rapidly cooling coffee, tea or cocoa. There were three weeks left before Christmas, and Hetty made up her mind to enlist Jane's help next day. Working together with mops, brooms and scrubbing brushes, they would make a start on clearing up the shop premises. She might even be able to persuade Fred Dixon to sell her some distemper at a cut price, and Brush Barber might have a couple of paintbrushes that he wanted to sell off cheap. Hetty had never painted anything in her life, but surely it couldn't be too difficult? Sammy and Eddie might lend a hand too – it would be a real family effort.

She huddled beneath her shawl. It was too cold in the attic to even consider taking off her top clothes and she slipped under the covers fully dressed. She lay down on her bed and blew out the candle. Surprisingly, even with all her plans buzzing round inside her head, Hetty fell into a deep and dreamless sleep.

When she awakened next morning, the sound of distant church bells made Hetty snap upright in her bed. She had forgotten that today was Sunday and the market would be closed. This sent all her plans awry, but at least it seemed to have stopped snowing. The roof window was covered in a thick white blanket of snow but pale strands of sunlight filtered through it, sending coloured prisms dancing on the bare floorboards. Swinging her legs over the side of the bed, she pulled on her boots and gathered up the scattered scraps of paper on which she had written her lists. She was almost overwhelmed by a sudden surge of optimism and enthusiasm for her new venture, and she made her way downstairs with a feeling that today was going to be special.

As she entered the kitchen Hetty could smell porridge simmering away on the range. Nora and Granny were nowhere to be seen but Jane was cutting slices off a loaf of bread, while Natalia sat at the table attempting to spoon bread and milk into her mouth. Most of it seemed to have found its way down her front, but what she could not get into her mouth with the spoon she ate using her fingers. She managed a sticky smile of pleasure when she saw Hetty, but she continued eating as though her life depended on it.

Hetty went over to her and dropped a kiss on Natalia's dark curls. She glanced at Jane and was quick to note the dark smudges beneath her eyes. 'You're up early. Couldn't you sleep?'

'Don't think I wouldn't give my right arm for an hour longer in bed,' Jane replied, sighing. 'But young missy here was up with the lark and so were Sammy and Eddie.

They're outside now, supposed to be fetching water, but I expect they're messing around in the snow.'

'They're just nippers. At least they can play like normal kids now, and they don't have to spend twelve hours a day making matchboxes.'

'That seems like a lifetime ago,' Jane said, scraping butter on a slice of bread. 'It's still hard work, but we've got a decent enough life here, even if it ain't exactly living in the height of luxury.'

'And it'll get better, Jane. When I've got my coffee shop up and running there'll be no more standing around in the cold selling sandwiches in the street. There's just one thing, though . . .'

Jane sighed. 'All right, out with it, Hetty. What do you want me to do?'

An hour later, they set off for Artillery Lane armed with mops, buckets and a couple of sweeping brushes. Sammy and Eddie had been bribed with the promise of earning a penny each if they helped to clear the rubbish from the shop, and Natalia was wrapped warmly against the cold, sitting in her perambulator surrounded by cleaning cloths and scrubbing brushes. The snow had settled several inches deep on the pavements and cobblestones, but the thaw was beginning to set in and they had to trudge ankle deep through slush.

'This ain't exactly my idea of a splendid Sunday morning,' Jane grumbled.

'Nor mine, but at least we can make a start,' Hetty said, hoping that she sounded more positive than she was feeling.

Sammy and Eddie had gone on ahead, running and then sliding on the slippery surface with loud shrieks of glee. They reached the shop first, and disappeared through the open door. 'Oh, my God!' Hetty cried. 'I know George locked up when we left yesterday.'

'Perhaps it's burglars,' Jane whispered. 'We'd better find a constable, Hetty.'

'The boys might be in danger.' Hetty dropped the mops and brooms she had been carrying and she ran. She slid to a halt in the doorway, and she leaned against the doorpost in stunned amazement. Inside was a hive of activity. The floor had been swept and Floppy Flora, the flower lady, was on her hands and knees scrubbing the boards until they gleamed palely in the dim light. Brush was slapping distemper on the walls and Fred was sanding down the woodwork. There was a great deal of chatter as people raised their voices to make themselves heard over the sound of Joe Jenkins sawing up lengths of wood. The air was redolent with the mixed smells of sawdust, carbolic soap and wet paint.

George was standing in the middle of the

room with a pencil held between his teeth as he studied some kind of plan drawn on a sheet of paper. They were all so fully occupied that no one seemed to notice Hetty's presence. Sammy bounded up to George and tugged at his sleeve. 'May I help you?'

'Me too,' Eddie said, jumping up and down and receiving a slap round the legs with a wet floor cloth from Flora.

'Keep off me clean floor, you young scoundrel.'

Hetty hurried over to George. 'How – I mean – why?'

He turned to look at her and a grin split his face from ear to ear. 'Great, isn't it, Hetty? I told you, ducks. We've got something far more precious than money.' With an expansive sweep of his hand, he encompassed everyone in the room. 'I told you they would rally round in our time of need, and they have.'

Joe stopped sawing the wood for a moment to wipe the sweat from his eyes. 'Where d'you want your counter exactly, Hetty? I need to know before I start putting this lot together.'

Jane pushed the perambulator into the shop, and she uttered a strangled cry of surprise. 'Oh, my Lord. What's going on here?'

Hetty clutched George's arm, and she reached up to kiss him on the cheek. 'It's a miracle, that's what it is. I can't thank you all enough. I just don't know what to say.'

There was a sudden silence and everyone stopped what they were doing. Hetty turned her head to follow their gaze and saw two police constables standing in the doorway. She walked towards them, angling her head. 'Good morning, officers. Can I help you?'

The more senior of the two cleared his throat. 'Yes, ma'am. You can tell me what you and all these people are doing here. This is private property.'

George stepped forward. 'Excuse me, officer, but we've rented this shop. I've got the papers all legal and above board.'

'That may be, sir, but have you got the owner's permission to make alterations to the said premises?'

Hetty's heart hitched in her throat as she turned to George. 'Have we, George?'

A dull flush rose from his open shirt collar to his cheeks. 'I – er – well, not exactly, but I understood . . .'

'I don't think you did, sir.' The constable took a notebook from his pocket and flipped it open. 'At least, according to my information, the owner made it clear that no alterations were to be made to the premises without their permission.'

'But the agent never mentioned anything of the sort,' George protested.

'Who told you all this?' Hetty demanded.

'Apparently the said party was driving past in his carriage this morning, on his way to church, when he saw unlawful activity being carried out on the premises. I must ask you to accompany me to the station, sir and madam. In the meantime, all work must cease.'

An angry murmur greeted this but George held up his hand for silence. 'Just a minute, constable. Who is this person? I'd like to see him so that we can sort it out between us.'

'You'll find out soon enough, sir. The gentleman in question is waiting at the police station, where he will decide whether or not to make formal charges against you and the young woman. Now, I hope you will come quietly. We don't want to make a fuss on the Lord's Day, now do we, sir?'

# Chapter Fourteen

Hetty remained tight-lipped on the way to the police station. Everything had been going so well and now it seemed that there was something badly amiss. Why was nothing ever simple? She stole a glance at George's profile and she could tell by his clenched jaw and lowered brows that he was simmering with rage. There must have been a mistake, or at least that was what she kept telling herself, but she had a nagging suspicion that there were outside forces at work here. It seemed that Clench's shadow was still hanging over them, and her worst fears were confirmed as they entered the police station and she came face to face with Henry Maitland. She would not have been surprised to see Clench and Shipworthy lurking in the shadows, but it was just Maitland who paced the floor, wearing an angry expression that did not sit well with his Sunday best clothes, and the white carnation which he sported in his buttonhole. 'So, I might have guessed that you would be involved in this heinous act,' Maitland said, emphasising his words by slapping his silver-headed cane on the palm of his gloved hand. 'Arrest these people, officer. They are nothing better than common vandals.'

'Now hold on a moment, mate,' George said, taking a step towards him. 'I've got a legal document to prove that Miss Huggins and me are the lessees of the premises in Artillery Lane.'

Maitland glowered at him. 'I think you'll find, if you take the trouble to read the small print, that no alterations are to be made to the internal structure of the building without the consent of the owner.'

Hetty pushed past George; she could see that anger and outraged innocence were not going to get them very far. She managed a tight little smile. 'Mr Maitland, I intend to turn the premises into a coffee shop, and this means that I need a counter, but that is all. We wasn't knocking holes in the walls or anything.'

The senior constable cleared his throat. 'Do you wish to make formal charges, sir? If not, I suggest you continue this discussion else-where.'

For a moment Maitland looked unsure of himself. 'I – well, I need to consult the owner of the premises.'

'Did you plan all this with that snivelling

little bastard Clench?' George demanded in a voice that throbbed with suppressed anger.

Maitland backed away from him. 'Certainly not! Mr Clench is a junior member of staff, although he did impart some interesting information which convinced me that my decision to reject your request for a bank loan was the correct one.'

'You might have said that you knew about the shop in Artillery Lane,' Hetty protested. 'I call that underhand, mister.'

The constable cleared his throat noisily. 'Now then, that's enough of that talk, miss.'

'I am acting on behalf of a client.' Maitland said stiffly. 'You will hear from their solicitors, but in the meantime you must cease work on the premises.' He made for the door, but George was quicker on his feet and he barred the way.

'Then tell us who that person is and we'll go and speak to him direct. We've invested time and money in this project, Mr Maitland, and Miss Huggins and me ain't going to give up so easily.'

The constable stepped in between them. 'If I may make a suggestion, Mr Maitland? Perhaps it would serve best if you were to allow the owner of the premises to speak for himself?'

'Yes,' Hetty said eagerly. 'You've been fed a lot of lies about me and George, mister. Let me speak to the cove who owns the shop. I'm sure I can talk him round.'

Maitland frowned. 'Very well then. I'm late for church as it is, but if you want to waste your time you are welcome to try to see the owner, although I must warn you that it is highly unlikely. Miss Tryphena Heathcote is a recluse, and she does not welcome visitors.' Maitland took a silver case from his pocket, and taking out a calling card he scribbled something on the back and gave it to Hetty. 'The matter is out of my hands now. I want nothing more to do with either of you.' He stalked out of the police station, and stepped into his waiting carriage. Through its window, Hetty caught sight of a pale-faced woman wearing a feathered hat and an angry expression. That must be Maitland's wife; no doubt she would make his life a misery for keeping her waiting. Serve the old bugger right!

'There, now I hope that's the last we'll see of you too,' the constable said, holding the door open. 'But you'd best see the owner of the shop and get her permission to continue, or I'll be forced to arrest you both.'

Outside on the pavement, standing ankle deep in mud and slush, Hetty stared at Maitland's spidery scrawl. 'Berkeley Square, George. That's up West where the toffs live, isn't it?'

George hailed a passing hansom cab. 'Berkeley Square, please, cabby.'

'We can't afford this,' Hetty whispered as George helped her into the cab.

'We can't afford not to, ducks. Just you watch the old charmer at work. I'll soon have the lady in question eating out of my hand.'

'I'm sorry, sir, but Miss Heathcote is not at home to anyone today.' The butler looked down his long pointed nose at George and Hetty as they stood on the steps beneath the portico of Miss Heathcote's impressive mansion in Berkeley Square. He was about to close the door, but Hetty moved quickly to put her foot over the doorsill.

'Please, mister. This is a matter of life and death. Mr Maitland, the manager of Tipton's Bank, sent us. He said that the lady was very gracious and if we asked nicely she might give us a couple of minutes of her time.'

A flicker of something akin to amusement crossed the butler's well-schooled features. 'Miss Heathcote sees no one, miss.'

Hetty was not going to give in so easily. 'Be so good as to tell Miss Heathcote that Miss Hester Huggins of Princelet Street, Spitalfields, begs a few minutes of her time. Tell the lady that it will be very much to her advantage. And I ain't budging from this doorway until you let me in, so there.'

For a moment she thought that he was going to refuse, call for a constable, or even slam the door on her foot, but he did none of these things. After a moment's consideration he nodded his head. 'Very well, miss. I'll pass the message on, but only if you will remove your foot and allow me to close the door.'

'Not on your life, mate. Do you think I come down in the last shower of rain?'

'Perhaps it would be better if you waited in the vestibule, miss.' He opened the door just far enough for Hetty to step inside. 'And you, sir, can wait outside. Miss Heathcote does not like gentlemen.'

Hetty was not going to argue. She stepped into the marble-tiled vestibule, which opened out into an entrance hall that was big enough to house most of the stalls in Spitalfields Market. Hetty gazed round in awe. Everything, from the tall columns that supported the high ceiling to the tiled floor and grand staircase, was carved out of pink and white marble. It was, Hetty thought, just like standing on a huge iced cake. Gilded cherubs carrying lyres and cornucopias overflowing with fruit smiled down at her from the intricate plaster cornices. Others plucked at stringed instruments with such lifelike fingers that Hetty could imagine the strains of heavenly music floating down to them from heaven above. The staircase rose from the centre of all this grandeur and silver-scrolled banisters curved out into galleries on several floors until they ended in a glass-roofed cupola. It was just as Hetty had imagined the interior of St Paul's Cathedral might look, although she had only seen that building from the outside. She had to suppress a sudden urge to call out, just to hear her voice echoing back to her in this beautiful but ice-cold palace.

'Wait here, miss.' The butler made a stately progress up the stairs, his black patent-leather shoes making tip-tapping sounds on the marble treads and fading out altogether as he reached the first landing. Hetty held her breath. She could hardly believe that one lady owned all this. She couldn't imagine that the Queen herself lived in more regal surroundings. After what seemed like an eternity, the butler re-appeared at the top of the staircase. 'Miss Heathcote will see you, miss. Step this way, please.'

Walking as if she were in a trance, Hetty negotiated the stairs and followed him along a high-ceilinged passage, her feet sinking into the thick pile of the carpet. Hothouse flowers spilled out of porcelain vases set on spindly side tables, their brilliant blooms reflecting in gilt-framed wall mirrors on either side of the wide corridor. The heady scent of the blooms filled the air, and as Hetty breathed in their intoxicating fragrance she felt as though she had entered another world.

The butler ushered her into a large room, elegantly furnished with Regency style sofas and chairs upholstered in blue and silver damask. Windows reaching from floor to ceiling allowed in the cold white light that came just before a fresh fall of snow. An involuntary shiver ran down Hetty's spine; it was almost as chilly inside as outside, even though a coal fire blazed up the chimney. Seated in a wingback chair by the fire, Hetty could just make out a tiny figure, huddled beneath a fur rug.

'You may leave us, Hicks.' A surprisingly strident voice emanated from the frail personage seated in the chair, and a tiny, childlike hand beckoned to Hetty. 'Come here, girl. I can't see you clearly from that distance.'

Hicks bowed to his mistress and left the room, closing the door behind him. Hetty swallowed hard, feeling suddenly nervous and wishing that George were here to charm this irate person, who did not look to be a very friendly lady. 'Well?' Miss Heathcote glared suspiciously at Hetty. 'What do you want? Did Maitland send you?'

As she drew closer Hetty couldn't take her eyes off Miss Heathcote's face. She was not as

elderly as Hetty had at first thought. Despite
her silver-white hair, Miss Heathcote could
have been any age from forty to sixty. She was
glaring at Hetty with eyes that were such a
pale shade of grey they were almost colour-
less, and this odd appearance was emphasised
by a frosting of silver eyelashes. Hetty dropped
her gaze. 'Er, not exactly, ma'am.'

Miss Heathcote's thin fingers fluttered to pat
her hair, which was scraped back from her face
and confined by a snood. 'Speak up, girl. I hate
people who mumble. And for heaven's sake
sit down. Looking up at you is making my
neck ache.'

Hetty looked around for a chair, but they
were all placed in intimate groups around
small tables, as if unseen guests had been
sitting and chatting amicably over afternoon
tea. Hetty did not like to disturb them and she
knelt on the carpet in front of Miss Heathcote.
'If you please, miss.'

'Oh, get on with it. Say what you have to
say and then leave me alone. My head is beginning to throb with pain.'

Hetty's patience was at an end, and she
was overcome with nervous frustration. Her
future now depended on the caprice of a
spoilt old woman who obviously had more
money than sense. Keeping her back very
straight and holding her head high, she met

the old lady's pale eyes, stare for stare. 'All right, Miss Heathcote. I'll say what I come to say straight out. My partner Mr George Cooper and me have rented a property in Artillery Lane that belongs to you. Even though the premises ain't fit for a pig to live in at present, I want to do it up nice, so that I can run a respectable coffee shop there.'

'What does this have to do with me? I pay people to look after my business interests. Take the matter up with them.'

Hetty sat back on her haunches. 'Is that all you got to say to me, when it cost me an arm and a leg to come all the way from the East End in a hansom cab especially to see you?'

A glimmer of what might have been interest lit Miss Heathcote's eyes. 'So why did you make this long and expensive trek to see me?'

'Because your Mr Maitland, the manager of Tipton's Bank in Bishopsgate, had us arrested and accused of doing things to the building against the terms of the lease. I come to speak to the organ grinder, not the monkey.'

'So, I'm the organ grinder, am I?' Miss Heathcote said with a hint of a smile. 'I've never been called that before.'

'This might be a laughing matter to you, miss, but it ain't funny to me. This is my life and the lives of me family that you're playing with. I don't suppose you've ever been poor or hungry, but we've known want and we've had to struggle hard to get where we are now. I ain't about to be put off by a spoilt old woman who shuts herself away in an ice palace like she was an exhibit in a museum.' Hetty stopped, clamping her hand over her mouth. She had gone too far and she knew it. Now she would never get permission to renovate the rotten shop. She waited for Miss Heathcote's wrath to explode about her head.

'You have passion, young woman,' Miss Heathcote said, leaning forward and fixing Hetty with a piercing stare. 'All this for a mere coffee shop?'

Hetty scrambled to her feet. 'I used to make matchboxes twelve hours a day with me sister and little brothers. The strike put an end to that and I started working the streets selling hot taters. Then I got a barrow and sold ham sandwiches and coffee. I done well enough to rent a market stall, and now I want to open a coffee shop where respectable folk, like young lady office workers, can go and have their dinner in a clean and pleasant place. And I don't intend to stop there neither. When I'm finished I'll have a coffee shop in all the main thoroughfares of the East End and up West too. And if you won't alter the terms of the lease, then I'll blooming well find another shop to rent. Nothing and no one is going to stop me.' Hetty clasped her hands to her chest as she struggled for breath. The words had tumbled from her lips and she had heard her voice break with emotion, but she had said her piece. When Miss Heathcote remained silent, Hetty took this as her dismissal and she made a move towards the door. 'Well, I'm sorry if I've given offence, miss. I'll go now and I won't trouble you again.'

'Stop! I haven't finished with you yet.'

Hetty glanced over her shoulder. 'I've said I'm sorry for any offence caused. What more do you want?'

Miss Heathcote flung off the fur robe and rose slowly to her feet. Hetty couldn't help staring at her tiny misshapen figure. A pair of crutches rested at the far side of her chair and Miss Heathcote picked them up, leaning her weight on them as she limped towards Hetty. 'So you see me now as I am – a pitiful hunch-back – a figure of fun from the Punch and Judy shows that so delight the ignorant masses. I was born to great wealth but it couldn't buy me a straight back or make my weak limbs strong.'

Hetty swallowed hard. 'As to that, miss. I can't say, never having had much money, but I would have thought you might have managed to be a bit more cheerful in the circumstances, even if you are a bit on the lame side.' For a moment it seemed that she had really gone too far this time, as Miss Heathcote's wizened features twisted into a grimace.

'Would you indeed, Miss Huggins? So you think I ought to ignore my wretched, crippled body and enjoy life, do you?'

'I daresay you could have a good try, miss. I mean, I seen far worse off than you in Bow and Bethnal Green. I seen men and women who have to shuffle along the ground on their bums so that they can sit on street corners and beg for money just to keep body and soul together. I seen blind children scavenging in the gutters for scraps of food and little girls sold to bad men by their own parents in order to keep the rest of the family from starving to death. At least you don't have to do that.'

'No, I don't have to beg for my food, that is true.' Miss Heathcote made her way awkwardly back to her chair by the fire and lowered herself down onto the seat. 'But my life is just as blighted as that of those poor creatures you mention.'

'Then I'm very sorry for you, miss. Can I go now?'

'No. Come over here and tell me exactly what you plan for this coffee shop of yours.'

Hetty hesitated. 'My partner, Mr Cooper, is standing outside your house in the snow, miss. Would you allow him to come inside?'

'Ring for Hicks. Your friend may wait in the vestibule, but I don't like men, Miss Huggins. I never have and I never will. They are a beastly breed and not to be trusted. You would do better to manage your business on your own, but that is just my opinion. I doubt if a pretty young woman like you will take any notice of a sour old spinster like me. Now, pull up a chair and tell me exactly what a coffee shop is, for I have never been in one.'

When Hetty and George alighted from the hansom cab outside the shop in Artillery Lane, they were surrounded by their friends clamouring to know what had happened.

'We thought they must have locked you up in jail,' Brush said, slapping George on the back. 'We was getting really worried, mate.'

Jane pushed past him to give Hetty a hug. 'What happened? Why have you been so long?'

It was snowing in earnest now. Large flakes settled quickly on their hair and clothes and everyone hurried back into the comparative warmth of the shop. Sammy and Eddie jumped up from the floor where they had been amusing Natalia by building off-cuts of wood into piles and then knocking them down. 'Have you been in prison, Hetty?' Sammy asked, clinging to her hand. 'Jane was certain something bad had happened to you.'

'No, we're all right,' Hetty said, gently caressing his cheek with the tips of her fingers. 'In fact, we're back in business, everybody. It's a long story, but we've got permission from the owner to do whatever is necessary to the inside of the shop, and what's more, as it's improving her property, she's going to pay for materials.'

'Let's get back to work,' George said, shrugging off his jacket. 'There's a pint in it for everyone if we can get this finished today.'

Floppy Flora raised her considerable bulk from the one and only stool in the room. 'Ta, George. Make that a hot rum punch and I'll clean the windows inside and out.'

'You're on.' George hooked his arm around Hetty's shoulders. 'It looks like you'll soon be in business, girl.'

Hetty shook her head. 'The shop will be ready, and we can get the tables and chairs from a second-hand shop in Brushfield Street, but there's still the crockery to be bought, not to mention cutlery and tablecloths. I've got some stuff I bought cheap stored in Nora's attic room, but there won't be enough.'

Ginger Turner cleared his throat. 'Er, I couldn't help overhearing, Hetty. I can let you have the tablecloths at cost, and I got a mate down Wapping way who might be able to do you a good deal on china and spoons. He owes me a favour or two.'

'Would you, Ginger? I'd be ever so grateful,' Hetty said, smiling.

George slapped Ginger on the back. 'Ta, cully. I won't forget this.'

'You been good to me in the past, George,' Ginger replied, blushing to the roots of his copper-coloured hair. 'I ain't forgotten how you give me and the missis free fruit and vegetables for a month when I was laid up with a broken ankle.' He cleared his throat noisily and sniffed. 'Must get on. Standing about chatting won't get the walls painted.'

Hetty slipped her hand through George's arm. 'It looks as though we'll be able to open up for business before Christmas after all.'

'You can bet on it, ducks.' George covered her hand with his, giving her fingers a gentle squeeze. 'We'll go far, you and me, Hetty Huggins.'

'Huggins and Cooper's Coffee Shops. I like the sound of that, George.'

He brushed her forehead with the lightest of kisses. 'So do I, love. So do I.'

With Granny working the stall in the market and Jane minding the barrow at Liverpool Street station, there was enough money coming in to keep them going while Hetty concentrated on the coffee shop. She bought tablecloths from Ginger and extra crockery and cutlery from his mate in Wapping. George insisted on accompanying her on this trip, as he said the bloke might try to get one over on a young female. Hetty was quite sure that she could stand up for herself, but she had used George's hard-earned money and she did not want to dent his male pride by appearing too independent. Joe worked on his market stall by day, and in the evenings he went to Artillery Lane to finish off the counter. Granny and Jane washed and stacked the china ready for use, and Sammy and Eddie polished up the cutlery. Natalia toddled around the room, putting sticky fingerprints on the newly polished furniture, but Hetty just laughed. She was too elated to allow anything to spoil her pleasure in her new establishment. She spread the floral-patterned cloths over the tables and hung matching curtains at the windows. Festoons of holly intertwined with ivy were hung on the walls, adding a festive touch. With just over a week to go until Christmas, Hetty was ready to open for business. She allowed Sammy and Eddie to have the day off school so that they could parade up and down the streets carrying cardboard placards advertising the coffee shop, and Hetty was there first thing in the morning to get the charcoal burning in the fire pots beneath her new cans, one each for tea, coffee and cocoa. She had been up until late the previous evening helping Jane and Granny bake cakes, and the fragrance of warm currants, chocolate and gingerbread permeated the room.

Trade was slow at first and by midday Hetty was beginning to panic. What if no one came? What if they came and did not approve of her efforts? What if— The door opened and a group of young women entered the shop, bringing with them a gust of cold air and the sound of cheerful chatter. Soon all the tables were filled with office workers, male and female, eating sandwiches, drinking coffee, and above all they seemed to be enjoying the experience. A warm fuggy atmosphere had developed and the windows were steamed up on the inside. Hetty was rushed off her feet, serving customers, making fresh sandwiches to order and pouring countless cups of tea and coffee. Trade slackened off a little after the lunchtime rush ended, giving her time to have a well-earned cup of tea and a slice of currant cake. With renewed energy, she cleared the tables and washed the dishes in the tiny scullery. Having substituted clean cloths for those which were stained, she was ready to begin again. She started to get busy at about four o'clock and kept up a steady trade until six-thirty, when the workers hurried homewards. She was just putting the *CLOSED* sign on the door when Sammy and Eddie came bursting in demanding food. 'We come to eat up the leftovers,' Sammy said, rushing to the counter. 'There's nothing here, Hetty. It's all gone.'

Eddie's mouth turned down at the corners. 'I'm starving, Hetty.'

Hetty sat down on the nearest chair and she pulled him onto her lap. 'D'you know, Eddie, I think I must have sold out, but I've been so busy that I haven't had time to take stock.'

Sammy dived round the counter and came back with a single crust of bread which he broke in two, handing one piece to Eddie and sinking his teeth into what Hetty noticed was the slightly larger portion. 'Looks like we're back to bread and scrape.'

Sliding Eddie off her lap, Hetty chuckled. 'I think we can run to a better supper than that tonight, boys. What'll it be, fish and chips or pie and mash?'

'Pie, mash and pease pudding,' Sammy said, swallowing a mouthful of dry crust.

'Fish and chips, please.' Eddie rammed his cap back on his head. 'Can we go now?'

Rising to her feet, Hetty went to the till behind the counter and she took out a handful of small change. 'Here, you two go and get the supper while I tidy everything away and lock up. Then I'll come straight home. Best get some pie and mash for George and Tom too; I expect they'll drop in after work.' As usual, she thought smiling, as the boys let themselves out into the dark and snowy street. George and Tom spent so much time at Nora's house that they might as well rent rooms there. Hetty emptied the till and put the money in a leather pouch, intending to count her takings later, but now she must make sure that the fire pots were all extinguished, the last crumb swept away and the door to the back yard firmly locked. She did not want intruders, the two-legged human kind or four-legged vermin, invading her shop during the night.

When she was satisfied that everything was safe and secure, she put on her bonnet and shawl and went out into Artillery Lane, locking the door behind her. The moon had emerged from the clouds and its silvery beams turned the snowy streets into a white fairyland, far removed from sordid reality. The yellow and blue flames of the gaslights flickered in their glass prisons, and in the distance, floating on the still night air, Hetty could hear children's voices singing a Christmas carol. She was tired to the point of exhaustion as she trudged through the snow, but she was also elated by the success of her first day's trading. She couldn't wait to tell George how well it had gone, and, more important, she would have a lot to write about when she reached the peace and quiet of her attic room. She always told Charles everything – well, almost everything.

That evening, after supper when Natalia had been put to bed and Tom and George had left for their respective homes, Hetty and Jane had to roll up their sleeves and start the baking process all over again. Their homemade cakes had been such a success that they had sold out in the shop and the two coffee stalls. Even with Granny and Nora helping with the preparation they did not finish baking until well after midnight, and by that time Hetty was too tired to do anything but lie down on her bed and fall fast asleep.

On Christmas Eve Hetty was at the coffee shop even earlier than usual. She had added mince pies to her menu and these were flying off the counter almost as fast as she could put them out. Trade had continued to be brisk and she knew that if things went on like this she would have to take on help. Tom had said that his youngest sister, Sally, was still working at Bryant and May and she would be the ideal person to help in the coffee shop. Hetty promised that Sally would be the first to know if she decided to go ahead and hire someone, but she was reluctant to do anything until after

Christmas as the brisk trade might just be seasonal.

In the middle of the lunchtime rush, Hetty was taken by surprise when Tom's sister walked into the shop. Hetty had always thought of Sally as a small, skinny child with burnished brown hair scraped into pigtails and a scattering of freckles over her snub nose. Of the three Crewe sisters, Sally was the one who most resembled Tom, and in spite of having worked at the match factory since she was ten, she did not seem to have suffered any of the ailments and diseases that went hand in hand with the work. Her grin was so reminiscent of Tom's that Hetty had to smile, even though she was in the middle of serving several customers.

'Tom said I should come,' Sally said, leaning against the counter. 'He said you needed help and I've had enough of that bloody factory.'

'Hush,' Hetty said, glancing nervously at a rather prim-looking lady clerk who was trying to decide which type of cake to choose. 'Come back later, Sally. I'm busy.'

Sally took off her bonnet and shawl and skittered round behind the counter. 'Here, let me take those to the customer. Who ordered ham sandwiches and watercress?'

'I'm not sure about that,' Hetty began, but a meaningful cough from a man sitting at a table near the window changed her mind. 'All right, Sally. Take that to the man over there, the one with leather patches on the sleeves of his jacket.' Hetty went back to serving the indecisive lady, who opted in the end for a mince pie. Sally returned with an empty tray and a big smile on her face, and it seemed foolish not to use a willing helper.

By mid-afternoon, things had quietened down and Sally was in the scullery washing dishes while Hetty cleared the tables and set them up for the next wave of customers, when she saw a carriage drawn by a magnificent pair of matched bay horses pull up in the street outside. At first Hetty thought that there must be some mistake. It was obviously a private carriage and not a mere hackney. In fact it looked so out of place in this part of London that a small crowd had already gathered to stare at the coachman who leapt from the driver's seat and came striding into the coffee shop.

He tipped his top hat. 'Good afternoon, ma'am. Am I addressing Miss Huggins?'

'Yes, that's me.'

'Miss Heathcote requests the pleasure of your company, Miss Huggins.'

Hetty stared at him dumbfounded. 'She wants to see me?'

'Yes, miss. I'm to take you to her now.'

'I'm very sorry, but that's impossible. I can't

close up just like that. I've got a business to run.'

'Miss Heathcote expects you, miss.'

'Well, you'll just have to tell her that I'll come another day. I am truly sorry, but that's how it is.'

'I – I can't tell her that, miss. I'll lose my job.'

He looked so downcast that Hetty felt sorry for him. 'What is your name?'

'Milton, miss.'

'Well, Mr Milton, I dunno what Miss Heathcote wants with me, but I ain't in business for the fun of it, and she should understand that since this shop belongs to her. If I don't sell coffee and sandwiches I won't be able to pay my rent, and she'll be the loser.'

'I don't think losing the rent from one shop would worry Miss Heathcote unduly. She owns this whole street and more besides. Please, miss, come with me now, just for half an hour or so. I promise to get you back as quickly as possible.'

Hetty shook her head. 'I'm really, really sorry, Mr Milton, and I hope the old lady don't sack you, although I'm sure she wouldn't be so unreasonable, but I can't and won't shut up shop just because she's got a bee in her bonnet about wanting to see me. You go back to Berkeley Square, and tell her that I'd be more than pleased to come and call on a Sunday, which is me only day free, if she still wants to see me.'

'I'll pass the message on, but I don't know how she'll take it. You don't know her, miss. If she gets into one of her states, she'll scream and shout and cry like one of them wailing banshees that Irish Paddy the boot boy is always going on about. Fair turns your stomach it does, and the doctor has to be sent for to calm her down. I'll tell her, but she won't like it. No one goes against Miss Tryphena Heathcote.'

'Well,' Hetty said, folding her arms across her chest, 'then it's time someone stood up to her, that's all I can say. I wouldn't even let little Talia get away with that sort of behaviour and she's just a baby.'

Milton acknowledged this with a nod of his head and he stomped out of the coffee shop with a dispirited hunch of his shoulders.

'What was all that about?' Sally demanded, coming out of the scullery and wiping her hands on her apron.

'Nothing to worry about,' Hetty said, shaking her head. 'There's some folks in this world who have got so much money they think they can make others dance to their tune just by snapping their fingers. Miss Tryphena Heathcote may be rich and she might own this whole row of shops, but she don't own me.'

It was almost seven o'clock by the time Hetty put the *CLOSED* sign on the door. She had sent Sally home earlier, with the promise of a job starting straight after Christmas. Hetty emptied the till and was delighted to see that her takings were up on the previous day. It would be wonderful if they could continue like this after Christmas, but she knew that nothing was certain. The worst of the winter was to come and money was short when people had to buy extra food and fuel to keep out the cold. She checked that the back door was locked, blew out the candles and the oil lamp behind the counter and was just putting on her coat when she heard the sound of horses' hooves on the cobblestones and the rumble of carriage wheels, which came to a grinding halt outside her shop. Hetty let herself out of the premises, locking the door behind her. She was so keen to get home that she had paid little or no attention to the carriage, but as she was about to walk past it the door opened and a shrill voice pierced the night like a scream.

# Chapter Fifteen

'Get in the carriage; I want to speak to you.' A pale face peered at her from the dark depths of the landau. 'If you won't come to me then I have no alternative but to come to you.' Miss Heathcote's voice sounded petulant and tremulous, as if she were about to cry.

'I told your man that I couldn't come today,' Hetty said, torn between anger and pity. 'It's Christmas Eve and I want to go home to my family.'

'You at least have a family. I have no one.'

'No one?'

'All dead.' Miss Heathcote shuffled along the seat, making room for Hetty. She patted the luxurious leather squabs. 'Come. I'm sure you can spare me a half-hour of your valuable time, and I don't have to remind you who it is who owns your shop.'

'Are you threatening me, miss?'

'I am used to getting my own way, Miss Huggins. Now get inside, please. I am unused to being out in the cold night air and I have a delicate constitution. Do you want to be responsible for my early demise?'

'That's not fair, miss.'

'Life isn't fair, Hetty. Look at me. Do you think I wanted to come into the world half formed? Now do as I say or I will have one of my turns, which I can assure you are not pleasant to behold. Get in the carriage now and I promise to send you home in it when I have done with you.'

With the utmost reluctance, Hetty climbed into the landau and Miss Heathcote ordered the coachman to drive on. Hetty leaned back against the soft, padded leather squabs but she was far from relaxed. Miss Heathcote subsided beneath a fur travelling rug and lapsed into silence. The roads were remarkably clear of traffic and it seemed to Hetty that everyone in London had hurried home to be with their families, except perhaps for those unfortunates who huddled in shop doorways sheltering against the bitter cold. These destitute souls might slip away from this world painlessly in their sleep. Those who awakened next morning would begin yet another day in their battle of survival against the twin ogres of disease and poverty. She experienced a wave of pity as she saw three children, clad in rags, huddled together in a shop doorway and clinging to each other like the survivors of a shipwreck.

Hetty could stand it no longer and she rapped on the roof of the carriage. 'Stop. Oh, stop please, coachman.'

Miss Heathcote's head popped up from her furs, looking like a startled owlet. 'What are you doing?'

Hetty opened the door and beckoned. 'You, child, come here.'

The eldest of the three, a girl who could have been no older than eleven or twelve, scrambled to her feet and approached the carriage, her pinched features assuming a smile that was so eager to please that it cut Hetty to the heart. She loosened the strings of her reticule and took out a shilling. 'Here, this will pay for a night or two in a lodging house for you and the nippers. Spend the rest on food.'

A small hand shot out to snatch the coin and the girl backed away as if expecting someone to take the money from her. 'Ta, miss.'

'What is your name, child?'

'Dorrie, miss, and these are me brothers, Wilfred and Stanley.'

'Isn't there anyone who would take care of you, Dorrie?'

'Close the carriage door,' Miss Heathcote snapped. 'I'm freezing to death.'

Hetty turned on her angrily. 'These poor children are more likely to suffer that fate. Have you no pity?' She leaned out of the door, addressing herself to Dorrie. 'Come to the back of number three Artillery Lane on Thursday, Dorrie. Bring your brothers and you will be given a meal.'

'Ta, miss. Merry Christmas.' Dorrie limped back to her small brothers and dragged them to their feet.

'She'll probably spend it on gin,' Miss Heathcote said, scowling ominously. 'There are plenty of institutions for children like those.'

Hetty waved to the coachman. 'Drive on, please, Mr Milton.' She closed the carriage door and leaned back against the squabs, shivering. She could see that Miss Heathcote was angry but she was not going to apologise.

'I am sure I have caught a chill,' Miss Heathcote said, making a big show of wrapping her furs closer around her body. 'And you had no right to give orders to my coachman.'

'I'm sorry, miss. I thought you wanted to get home quick.'

Miss Heathcote eyed her speculatively. 'What extraordinary behaviour, to be sure. You are a strange girl, Hetty. Why do you care what happens to those filthy little children? There are urchins and beggars all over London; it's an undeniable fact of life.'

'And now there are three who will survive this night,' Hetty replied calmly. 'I have brothers who are similar in age, and I wouldn't want to see them in such dire circumstances.'

Miss Heathcote's mouth turned down at the corners. 'You are wasting your time and money. Their sort are all alike: idle, shiftless and ignorant. You may help them today but tomorrow they will be in just the same state. You merely protract their miserable existence.'

'What would a lady like you know about how the poor struggle to exist?' Hetty demanded angrily. 'You live in your ice palace, pampered and cosseted, with servants running round after you. You wouldn't be able to imagine what it's like to be so hungry that you faint from lack of vittles, or so cold that you lose the feeling in your limbs.'

'Stop, stop.' Miss Heathcote held up a tiny, gloved hand. 'If I want a lecture on social reform I'll join the Fabian Society.' She peered out of the window. 'Thank heavens for that. We're almost there.'

'I think I should go straight home,' Hetty said nervously. 'I don't think there's much for us to talk about, miss.'

'Nonsense, girl. I'll tell you when I've done with you, and for heaven's sake stop calling me miss. You address me as ma'am or Miss Heathcote.'

'Yes, m-ma'am.' Hetty subsided into silence as the coach drew to a halt and the groom opened the carriage door to let the steps down. He leaned in and lifted Miss Heathcote in his arms as easily as if she had weighed no more than a child, and he carried her up the steps to the house. Hetty had little choice but to follow them but she was still uneasy, and she knew that her family would be worried if she did not return home soon.

As they entered the mansion, a liveried footman hurried on ahead of them to throw open double doors that led into an anteroom off the main entrance hall. With a flick of a switch the room was ablaze with light and Hetty gasped out loud. She stood in the doorway marvelling at the miracle of electricity that turned night into day. She had heard of it, of course, but only very wealthy toffs could afford such a luxury. The groom carried Miss Heathcote over to a chair by the fire, where he set her gently down amongst a pile of velvet cushions. Hetty could only gaze in awe at the hand-painted wallpaper, ornately carved rosewood furniture and gilded light fittings sparkling with new-fangled light bulbs. The footman placed a stool beneath Miss Heathcote's feet, and a maidservant bustled into the room with a cashmere shawl draped over her arm. 'That will be all, Henry,' Miss Heathcote said, dismissing him with an imperious gesture. She beckoned to the maid.

'Minnie! Help me off with my mantle, and take Miss Hetty's shawl. She will be staying for supper. Tell Cook.'

'Yes'm.' Minnie bobbed a curtsey, and, having helped Miss Heathcote to take off her fur-lined mantle, she wrapped the shawl around her thin shoulders. She turned to Hetty holding out her hand. Somewhat reluctantly, Hetty took off her bonnet and shawl and handed them over. Even though the maid's face remained a mask of polite indifference, Hetty was certain that she saw a flicker of disdain in her eyes as she took the shabby garments.

'Don't hover in the doorway, girl,' Miss Heathcote said, beckoning to Hetty. 'Come over here and sit down.'

Hetty was in no position to argue. She crossed the floor to perch on the edge of a chair opposite Miss Heathcote. 'Why was it necessary to bring me here, ma'am?'

'You're direct. I like that in a person, Hetty. And you aren't afraid of me as are the fools who are in my employ.'

'I am not, ma'am. But you still haven't told me why you wanted to see me so urgently.'

'I don't socialise, and I have very few friends. When you have nothing but money it is almost impossible to distinguish between those who want you for yourself and those who are merely using you to further their own selfish cause.'

Hetty did not know how to respond to this, and she remained silent.

'You are so young and full of vitality,' Miss Heathcote continued, not seeming to require a response to her previous remarks. 'You had the courage to come here and demand to see me, which I admire. Had I been born with a body like yours, I might have been just such a bold young woman. Had I looked like you, my father might have paid more attention to me, instead of shutting me out of his life with a succession of governesses and paid companions. I was a huge disappointment to him. He wanted a son to carry on his business empire, and all he got was me. My poor mother died giving birth to me, and my father held me responsible for that also. I hated him and I did not mourn him when he died.'

'That is so sad, ma'am,' Hetty murmured. 'I am sorry.'

'No you are not. Why would you be sorry? You think I am a spoilt creature who deserves to be all alone at Christmas. Isn't that so?' Miss Heathcote leaned towards Hetty, her pale grey eyes reflecting the orange flames of the fire, which gave her a strange, unearthly appearance.

'Yes,' Hetty said truthfully. 'It is so, and I don't think my being here is going to help you.

I'm a poor girl from a humble background. I can't talk the same as what you do.'

'No, but you have ambition, Hetty. I admire that, even if you are a little bit too honest for your own good. You have the will to succeed but neither the experience nor the wherewithal. I have both and I think I could mould you into a successful businesswoman. I may have a crippled body, but there is nothing wrong with my mind. The management of my business interests was never given to me. My father put men in charge of every aspect of my inheritance and I am never consulted. You and I have to struggle in a world dominated by men, Hetty. You have the youth, health and burning ambition, I can see that. I think, with my help, you will go far.'

'But what would you get out of it, miss?'

'Satisfaction and a purpose in life, that's what I would achieve. My father's contemporaries have never taken me seriously. They only see a frail cripple and a woman at that – they have never given me credit for having a brain or a mind of my own. If I am to help you it would have to be our secret. If my part was known you would attract opposition from male competitors. I doubt if they would pay much attention to a girl from Spitalfields opening up a few coffee shops with no one to back her.'

Hetty was still struggling to come to terms with this unexpected proposition, but she could see a flaw in Miss Heathcote's plan. 'George,' she murmured. 'George is me partner, ma'am. He wouldn't take kindly to the idea.'

'George is my partner,' Miss Heathcote corrected with a humourless smile. 'You see, Hetty, you will need to polish up your grammar if you are to succeed in the world of business. You will need to know how to behave in public and how to deal with men who think themselves superior in every way. As to your friend George, I'm certain he will see sense when he knows that there is money involved.'

Hetty rose to her feet. 'I should be getting home now, ma'am. I need a bit of time to think this over, and to speak to George about it too.'

'Absolute nonsense! You've got a mind of your own, haven't you?'

Hetty hesitated, torn between wanting to escape from the oppressive splendour of Miss Heathcote's mansion and the temptation to hear more. She nodded silently.

Miss Heathcote pointed a bony finger at her. 'Do you want to spend the rest of your days grubbing around in Artillery Lane, serving behind the counter of a poky little coffee shop?' She shook her head vehemently. 'No, of course you do not. The answer lies in expansion, and business acumen, my girl. Hard work is all very well, but it is something one makes other people do. You will have to learn to delegate and give orders.' She reached out to tug on a bell pull. 'We will have supper now, and Milton will drive you back to the East End when we have eaten.'

'But, ma'am . . .'

'Perhaps you would rather set off now and walk through the snow? I can assure you that it would take longer than if you obliged me by staying for supper.'

Before Hetty could say anything, Hicks entered the room to announce that dinner was served. He picked up a pair of crutches and helped Miss Heathcote to her feet, steadying her until she had gained her balance and was able to walk.

'Thank you, Hicks.' Leaning heavily on her crutches, Miss Heathcote limped past Hetty. 'I only have a light repast at this time in the evening. As with everything else, my digestion is delicate. Follow me, Hetty, and do stop worrying about your wretched family. I'm sure they can manage without you for another hour.'

Hicks held the door for them and Hetty followed Miss Heathcote's slow progress to the dining room, where once again she had to bite back a gasp of awe. Silver candelabra marched down the vast expanse of the mahogany dining table. In the middle was an epergne over-flowing with hothouse fruit and scented flowers, the like of which Hetty had never seen in all her life. There must have been at least twenty chairs set around this magnificent table. Hetty felt very small and insignificant as she took her place beside Miss Heathcote. When Hicks approached them holding a tureen of soup, Hetty watched carefully as Miss Heathcote took the ladle and helped herself to a small portion. Hetty dutifully copied her, but she had no idea which of the cutlery to use. Again she watched Miss Heathcote, who picked up a spoon from the right hand side of the place setting. Hetty did the same.

'Very good, my dear,' Miss Heathcote said, smiling. 'You learn quickly. That is excellent. You will have to learn how to mix with all types of people, and nothing betrays a person's background as much as their table manners. Take this as your first lesson in etiquette.'

Hetty might have walked out there and then, but she had missed breakfast and had been too busy to eat at midday and she was starving. The soup proved to be delicious and she was not going to allow good food to go to waste. She decided that she would finish it and then take her leave, but she was soon to discover that Miss Heathcote's idea of a light repast featured several courses. A fish dish in a delicate dill sauce was followed by medallions of lamb served with vegetables that Hetty had never seen before, let alone tasted. She wondered what George would make of this exotic fare, and she was assailed with feelings of guilt. Here she was eating like a queen and the family at home would be making do with boiled beef and carrots. She was about to ask if the carriage could be sent for when a footman placed a dessert on the table made out of ice cream and meringue drizzled with chocolate sauce and studded with brandied cherries. Hetty decided that another few minutes would make no difference now. She might as well make a complete pig of herself. After all, it was Christmas.

When the meal was over and Miss Heathcote rang the bell for Hicks, Hetty rose to her feet. 'Ta for the dinner, ma'am. But I really must be going now.'

Miss Heathcote frowned. 'It's thank you, not ta. Only babies say ta.'

Hetty bobbed a curtsey. 'Yes, Miss Heathcote.'

'That's better. Sit down and wait for Hicks to send for the carriage. I want to see you again tomorrow. We have a lot to discuss.'

'Not tomorrow. It's Christmas Day.'

'Christmas Day! It's just another day on the calendar. I don't know why people make such a fuss about it.'

Hetty was determined not to give in. This Christmas was going to be special. In fact, it was going to be the first proper Christmas that the boys and Talia had ever enjoyed, and she was not going to spoil it for anyone. She clenched her jaw, ready to argue the point, but then her throat contracted with emotion as a sudden vivid memory of her mother flashed into her mind's eye. She could see Ma's smiling face and hear her soft voice teasing her when she had rebelled against something that she had considered to be unjust. Ma had called it 'Hetty's stubborn mule face', and had joked about her wayward streak, telling her that she was just like her father and Granny Huggins – once they had made their minds up to something, there was no shifting them. Well, she thought, I am not going to be shifted now. She met Miss Heathcote's gaze and saw it waver.

'Maybe not tomorrow,' Miss Heathcote conceded. 'But I will expect you the next day, and don't tell me that it's Boxing Day, for I'm very well aware of it. You won't be opening your coffee shop, so there is no excuse for your not attending here at ten o'clock sharp.'

Hetty nodded her head. 'Very well, miss – I mean, Miss Heathcote. Can I go now?'

When the coachman assisted Hetty to alight from the carriage outside the house in Princelet

Street, she was even more aware of the contrast between Spitalfields and the elegant mansion in Berkeley Square. For the first time in her life she felt embarrassed to admit that this was home. Despite the frosting of snow, the pavements were littered with rubbish, and the cobblestones carpeted in horse dung and excrement, both animal and human, she suspected. The cold night air was crisp but it could not disguise the odour rising from the drains and the choking fumes of burning soot. Hetty glanced nervously at Milton but his face was a mask of well-schooled indifference, and whatever thoughts he might have about this part of London, he kept them to himself.

She had her own key now and Hetty let herself into the house. She hesitated for a moment in the dimly lit entrance hall. When Nora had first taken them in, this once fine house had seemed like a palace to her. It might be sadly in need of repair and refurbishment but it had given them shelter in their time of need. Even so, she could not help making an unfavourable comparison between this place and the magnificent dwelling in Berkeley Square. She took a deep breath, forcing the image of Miss Heathcote's grand mansion out of her mind; after all, living like a queen had not brought that lady much happiness.

Ashamed of her unworthy thoughts, Hetty

braced her shoulders and headed for the kitchen, where she found the family busily preparing the Christmas feast. The floor might be rough flagstones and the ceiling blackened with smoke and soot from the range, but the room was fuggy with the heat of cooking and fragrant with the scent of herbs and spices. The air was filled with the excited babble of voices and laughter. Hetty did not know whether to be pleased or disappointed that her late homecoming had gone virtually un- noticed. If she had expected everyone to fuss around her demanding to know where she had been until this hour, she was sadly dis- appointed. Granny was seated by the range, plucking a large goose, and Nora sat opposite her, peeling potatoes. Tom was sitting at the table dandling Natalia on his knee.

Jane glanced up from peeling the skin off blanched almonds and smiled. 'Good. You're just in time to stir the pudding and have your wish, Hetty.'

Tom was sneaking plump raisins from the mixing bowl and popping them into Natalia's open mouth. Jane spotted him and slapped the back of his hand. 'Oy, you! Those raisins cost money, Tom Crewe.' She spoke crossly but the tender look in her eyes betrayed her true feel- ings to Hetty at least.

Tom grinned sheepishly. 'The pudding won't

lack for a couple of raisins, girl. And young Talia here just loves them, don't you, poppet?' He chucked Natalia under the chin, making her giggle and curl up in his arms like a playful kitten. 'She's a real treasure, ain't she, Hetty?'

Hetty's heart swelled with pride and she could have kissed Tom for loving the little girl almost as much as she did. Jane was not a bad mother – she looked after Natalia's physical needs and Hetty knew that she would protect her child like a tigress if danger threatened – but she still seemed to find it difficult to show affection to her daughter.

Hetty took off her bonnet and shawl and laid them on the back of a chair. 'Don't you want to know why I was so late home?'

With her hands covered in feathers, Granny looked up from the half-plucked carcass of the goose. 'Whatever it was you've missed most of the hard work. Nora's been peeling taters and she made the stuffing. Jane's made the pudding all by herself, which should have been made months ago, if we'd had the time and money to buy the makings. I got the worst job of all, plucking and drawing this here goose. You've come just in time to stir the pudding mixture and have a wish. I call it crafty.'

'Have a heart, Mattie,' Nora wheezed, dropping a pared potato into a pan of cold water. 'The girl's been out working all day.'

'We've all done a day's work,' Granny shot back at her. 'And people our age ought to be sitting by the fireside taking things easy.'

Nora's deep bosom heaved as a chuckle escaped her lips. 'Your age maybe, Mattie. You could give me ten years or more. I ain't ready to turn up me toes just yet, nor sit by the fire with a lace cap on me head. In fact, when we've finished here, I suggest we all go to the pub for a glass of buttered rum punch. There's not much more we can do until morning.'

'I don't hold with public houses,' Granny said, sniffing. 'Evil places they are, leading men and women into bad habits, drunkenness and worse.'

Hetty went over to her, holding out her hands. 'Here, let me finish that off, Granny. And if you'll stop grumbling for a minute or two, I'll tell you what happened to keep me out so late.'

Granny assumed a martyred expression. 'No, I started it and I'll finish the job. I don't trust you to do it properly, Hetty. And I don't want to get a mouthful of feathers in my Christmas dinner. Heaven knows it's taken long enough to save up for this feast, so it's got to be just right.'

At that moment, the scullery door burst open and a wave of merriment heralded Sammy,

Eddie and George as they dragged a huge Christmas tree into the kitchen.

'Look at this tree,' Sammy cried gleefully. 'Have you ever seen anything like it in your life, Hetty?'

'It's bigger than George,' Eddie said, dragging off his cap and staring at the fir tree in awe as George held it upright.

'We haven't had a tree since Pa died,' Jane said, wiping her floury hands on her apron. 'It's a corker, George, but we haven't got anything to hang on it.'

Hetty looked round at their happy faces. How could she have compared their way of life unfavourably with the lonely existence of a spoilt and unhappy rich woman? Everyone had been saving up to make this a special celebration and it would certainly be a Christmas to remember. Her news could wait.

George gave the tree to Sammy to hold while he went out into the yard to fetch a suitable container, which turned out to be half a beer barrel filled with soil. When the tree was safely planted, George stood back and everyone clapped their hands. Hetty hurried across the floor to kiss him on the cheek. 'Thank you, George. It's a beautiful tree, and it smells wonderful. I just have to close my eyes and I can imagine myself walking in a pine forest on a cold, snowy day.'

He hooked his arm around her shoulders. 'Is there anyone with you in this pine forest, Hetty?'

The intimate tone of his voice brought her back to reality with a start, and she drew away from him rather more abruptly than she had meant to. 'No, and I'm never likely to see a pine forest let alone go tramping through one.' She turned away from him and beckoned to the boys. 'Let's see what we can find to decorate the tree.'

'I've thought of that,' George said, putting his hand in the capacious pocket of his topcoat and pulling out a handful of small candles. 'Here, we can fix these on the branches.'

'And I've got some scraps of ribbon,' Granny said, entering into the spirit of things with surprising enthusiasm. 'You girls can make them into bows and tie them on the tree. We always had one just like this when my Harold was alive. We had some glass balls too, but they all broke.'

'It's a topping tree,' Sammy cried enthusiastically. 'It's the best tree in the whole of London.'

'It's the best tree in the whole world,' Eddie added, not to be outdone.

Jane gave the contents of the basin a final stir. 'There, I've had my wish. It's your turn, boys, and then it's bedtime for you two and

Natalia, who should have been tucked up in her cot an hour ago.'

Sammy and Eddie took it in turns to stir the pudding. Hetty smiled as she watched them surreptitiously lick the spoon while Jane was busy with Natalia, who objected to being prised off Tom's lap.

'I called in earlier, Hetty, but you weren't home,' George said in a low voice. 'What kept you?'

'It's not important, George. I'll tell you later.' Hetty took the spoon from Eddie. 'My turn now.'

'Close your eyes and wish,' Sammy said, running his finger round the rim of the bowl and licking it. 'And you mustn't tell anyone or the wish won't come true.'

Hetty closed her eyes and thought of Charles. She could see his loving expression and hear his voice telling her that he adored her. It was so clear that she raised her face ready to receive his kiss. Her eyes flew open as she felt the soft touch of someone's lips on hers, but it was George's smiling face hovering so close to her own. It was not her beloved Charles. She pushed him away angrily. 'George, don't be such a fool.'

A dark shadow clouded his eyes. 'It was just a little kiss, Hetty. A Christmas kiss.'

She knew she had hurt him, and she

regretted her abrupt tone, but he had caught her unawares and shattered her dream of Charles. She shook her head. 'It's not Christmas yet, George.'

An irrepressible dimple deepened at the corner of his generous mouth. 'Then can I have another kiss tomorrow?'

'You should have brought some mistletoe, George,' Jane said eagerly. 'We must have some mistletoe.'

Tom put his arm around Jane's waist and planted a smacking kiss on her lips. 'Who needs mistletoe?' He released her and moved towards Hetty, pushing George out of the way. 'What about you, Hetty? Have you got a kiss for your oldest friend?'

She couldn't help smiling. 'Yes, why not?'

Granny sniffed. 'What a to-do. All this kissing isn't seemly.'

Nora raised herself from her chair. 'Don't be an old killjoy, Mattie. You can kiss me, boys. I ain't too old to enjoy a little bit of a kiss and a cuddle, even if you are both young enough to be me sons.'

Hetty bent down to kiss Sammy and Eddie, and they both wiped their cheeks on their sleeves, pulling faces which were obviously intended to demonstrate their disgust as they giggled self-consciously. Natalia held her arms out to Hetty and she took her from Jane, burying her face in Talia's curls. This was what was important in life, being with her family and her dear friends. If only Charles were here too, then it would be the happiest Christmas of her entire life, but that would come. That was why she would go and see Miss Heathcote on Boxing Day and why she would accept her terms for their business partnership. Money was not important in itself, but financial success would enable her to go to Philadelphia and hold her head high amongst Charles' wealthy friends and relations.

'Hetty, you haven't been listening to a word I'm saying,' Jane said crossly. 'You were miles away.'

'Sorry,' Hetty murmured, kissing Talia on the tip of her tiny nose and making her giggle. 'What did you say then?'

Jane reached for her bonnet and shawl. 'I said, since I've done all the hard work, it's only fair that you should put the nippers to bed so that I can go to the pub with Tom and Nora.'

'I'm coming too,' Granny said, taking off her apron. 'Put the goose in the larder when you've done, Hetty.'

'Go along with you,' Hetty said, smiling. 'I'm tired anyway and I'll be glad of an early night.'

Jane linked her hand through Tom's arm. 'Come on. What are we waiting for?'

'Are you sure you don't want to come,

Hetty?' Tom cast an anxious glance in her direction. 'I'm sure that good old George would stay and mind the nippers.'

'I haven't seen the kids all day,' Hetty replied, shifting Natalia's weight to her hip. 'I'll stay and see them to bed. You go and enjoy yourselves.'

George moved to her side. 'And good old George will be happy to stay and keep Hetty company.'

Nora put on her feathered hat and secured it with a hatpin. She wrapped a thick woollen shawl round her shoulders and headed for the door. 'Come on. I'm so parched I'm spitting feathers.'

'You're so vulgar, Nora,' Granny muttered. 'If you start singing, I'm coming straight home.'

Jane seized Tom's cap and placed it at an angle on his head, smiling up into his face. 'Let's go, Tom.'

When the kitchen door closed on them, Hetty turned to the boys. 'Are your hands and faces clean?' They nodded, holding up their hands. 'All right, Sammy, lead on.'

'If they don't do as they're told, just give me a call,' George said cheerfully. 'I'll sort them out.'

'Oh yeah?' Sammy said, dancing about on his toes and playfully fisting his hands. 'You and whose army, George?'

Before Sammy could run away, George had swooped on him, hefting him over his shoulder. 'Cheeky little blighter,' he said, chuckling. 'I'm bigger than you, young Samuel, and don't you forget it.'

With Natalia's sleepy head resting on her shoulder, Hetty stopped in the doorway, and she couldn't help smiling as Eddie threw himself at George, who clamped him securely under his free arm, lifting him off his feet. 'Lead on, Hetty. I've got these two under control.'

'And Father Christmas doesn't come to bad boys,' Hetty said, tapping the side of her nose. 'Just remember that, you two.'

They stopped struggling immediately and there were no more protests about going to bed. Having settled the children for the night, Hetty smiled happily. This really would be a Christmas to remember. Even though she had been busy with work, she had found time in the past few weeks to search the market stalls in Petticoat Lane for toys to put in their stockings. It would be the first Christmas when they had had more than just an apple and a few boiled sweets. George had provided some oranges and a bag of walnuts, almonds and Kentish cobnuts, and Nora had been generous with slabs of toffee, liquorice and even some bars of chocolate. Hetty left a nightlight burning on the mantelshelf in their room, and then she followed George downstairs to the kitchen.

'Come and sit down, love,' he said, taking a seat by the fire. 'You'll wear yourself to a shadow.'

She picked up the goose on its platter and carried it into the larder, setting it down on a marble slab. 'I'm nearly done.'

He caught her by the hand as she went to pass him. 'Sit down and tell me what kept you so late. I know you wasn't at the coffee shop because I went by that way intending to walk you home and found it closed.'

She gave his fingers a squeeze and subsided onto the chair beside him. She began, a little haltingly at first, to tell him what had happened earlier that evening. George listened without interruption until she had finished. 'So you're going to let this woman talk you into some wild business venture.' He rose to his feet and began to pace the floor.

'I'm thinking about it. Yes.'

'And have you told the others about this crazy scheme?'

'Not yet. I wanted to talk it over with you first.'

'That's noble of you. I thought the old woman didn't approve of men.'

'What's the matter, George? Why are you so cross?'

He stopped to stare down at her with a frown creasing his brow. 'You don't know anything about this person, Hetty. She might be completely nuts for all you know.'

Hetty leapt to her feet. She was tired and now she was angry. 'She's not mad. She's an educated woman but she hasn't been allowed to have control over her own affairs.'

George curled his lip. 'I wonder why that is? Could it be because the lady is completely off her chump? Why else would she pick a girl from the stews of Spitalfields as a business partner?'

'You're insulting her and me. She could see that I got sense and I'm a hard worker. You're just put out because she wouldn't speak to you.'

With uncharacteristic roughness, he seized her by the shoulders. His strong fingers cut into her soft flesh and his eyes darkened. 'You mustn't allow yourself to be taken in by a complete stranger, even if she does live in a mansion up West. She's just amusing herself, Hetty. She's playing games at your expense and when she gets bored with you she'll drop you like a hot potato, and you'll have lost everything.'

Hetty wrenched herself free of his grasp. 'It's not like that. She's going to put up the money. She's not going to run the coffee shops.'

'Shops!' George rolled his eyes in disgust. 'You've only just opened up one, girl. You've got to learn to walk afore you can run.'

She clamped her hands over her ears. There might be a grain of truth in what George was saying, but there was no need for him to shout at her. She had wanted his help and advice, not a lecture. 'Shut up! Shut up!'

'Is that all you can say? What about me? What about Huggins and Cooper? We were supposed to be partners, Hetty. You can't just go ahead without consulting me.'

She was too angry now to be reasonable. 'Can't I? Well, let me tell you something, George Cooper. I don't need you. If you don't like what I'm doing then you can sling your hook, mister.'

George's expression hardened. 'If that's the way you want it, then I'll leave you to it.'

'Good!' Hetty cried passionately. 'Go away and leave me alone. That's what you men always do.'

Without saying another word, George slammed out of the kitchen. Hetty sank down onto the chair. The silence was deafening. She was alone.

# Chapter Sixteen

Hetty climbed the stairs leading up to the attic room and she crawled into her bed beneath the roof window, huddling up under the coverlet in an effort to get warm. She tried to comfort herself by rereading the letters she had received from Charles. She had been vaguely aware that they did not arrive as frequently these days, but she had been so preoccupied with work that she had pushed the niggling worry to the back of her mind. His letters used to arrive promptly once a week, sometimes more often, but now two weeks could pass without hearing from him, and when she looked at the date on the last missive she realised that it had been written in the middle of November. As she read and reread it in the flickering light of a single candle, she smiled at the amusing references to his place of work and his clever, but sometimes cruel, caricatures of his colleagues in the bank. She skimmed through the rest of the closely written pages with a cold feeling in the pit of her stomach. How could she have missed the undeniable fact that there were fewer terms of endearment now than there used to be? And there was no mention at all as to when he might send for her, or if he was planning to return to London.

Hetty wrapped her shawl a little tighter around her shoulders. She shivered as she peered into the shadows where Granny's old furniture loomed out of the darkness, seeming to move as the candle flame flickered in the draughty room. The whole area was alive with the sound of tiny feet scampering under the floorboards and beneath the eaves. She was used to bats zooming through gaps in the roof tiles, but tonight they had taken on sinister and threatening shapes, and Hetty was suddenly afraid. She could still hear George's angry voice railing at her, and the cold, hard look in his eyes was indelibly printed in her memory. In the distance, she could hear the peal of church bells calling people to midnight mass, and she realised that it was the beginning of Christmas Day. She felt beneath her nightgown for the gold ring that she wore around her neck at all times like a talisman against evil and a pledge of Charles's undying affection. Tears rolled down her cheeks. 'M-merry Christmas, H-Hetty,' she whispered as she blew out the candle and lay down to sleep, still clutching his signet ring.

What should have been the best Christmas

morning of her life was overshadowed by her bitter parting with George. She made excuses for his absence, although they sounded feeble even to her own ears. He was missed, of course, but no one seemed to doubt Hetty's word that he had gone to visit a sick relative in Shadwell. They all seemed to think it was just like George to put others first, and this made Hetty feel even worse. She had been tempted to walk to his lodgings in Cottage Green and offer him an apology, but it was not only pride that had prevented her: she was still angry with him for his unreasonable behaviour. If he had given her half a chance she would have reassured him that their partnership still stood, no matter what Miss Heathcote might offer in the way of terms and conditions. She had meant to ask him to accompany her to the mansion in Berkeley Square on Boxing Day, and she had intended to tell Miss Heathcote that there was no deal unless it included her friend and colleague. But George had ruined it all, and now she was not even sure if she wanted him to be her partner. He had acted like a spoilt child last night, and to make matters worse, Charles had not even bothered to send her a Christmas card or a token of his love and respect. Perhaps Miss Heathcote was right when she said that all men were unreliable and untrustworthy.

Hetty hid her heartache beneath a bright smile and did her best to enter into the Christmas spirit; after all, it was the children's day when all was said and done, and she must not spoil it for them. The boys were bubbling over with excitement and delight on finding their stockings filled with small gifts. Natalia did not seem entirely sure what was going on, but she loved the rag doll that Hetty had found in the market and refused to be parted from it, even when tempted by her breakfast bread and milk. Nora had hung the tree with sugar candy canes and boiled sweets wrapped in coloured paper. There was an exciting-looking pile of presents wrapped in brown paper and tied with string lying beneath its pine-scented branches.

Tom arrived in the middle of the morning and from the deep pockets of his overcoat he produced two bottles of claret as his contribution to their feast. The kitchen was redolent with the aroma of goose roasting in the oven, apple sauce, cinnamon, cloves and the zest of orange and lemon peel as Tom mulled the wine with a hot poker. There was bustle and not a little confusion as they set chairs and stools around the table and the boys squabbled about where they would sit. Nora lifted the goose from the oven and began to carve while Granny served the potatoes and Jane was left stirring the gravy. Having sorted out the boys' seating, Hetty took the saucepan of cabbage into the scullery where she drained the water into the stone sink. The room was filling with steam when the back door opened and a gust of cold air preceded George, who came in holding a huge bunch of mistletoe. Closing the door with his foot, he took the saucepan from Hetty's hand and put it down on the wooden draining board. Holding the mistletoe over her head, he drew her to him and kissed her soundly on the lips. 'Merry Christmas, Hetty.'

It was all the apology she needed and she sighed with relief. 'Merry Christmas to you too, George.'

Sammy burst into the scullery and threw his arms around George's waist. 'I knew you'd come. Is your grandpa better?'

'I told them about your sick relative,' Hetty said hastily. 'He must have made a miraculous recovery.'

George met her eyes and he grinned. 'Us Coopers are hard to put down, Hetty. We come bouncing back, no matter what.'

She caressed his cheek with the tips of her fingers. 'I'm glad, George. I wouldn't want to lose a good friend like you.'

'What are you talking about?' Sammy demanded, grabbing George by the hand. 'Come on, George, dinner's on the table and I'm starving.'

'I'm not sure I'm invited,' George said, holding Hetty's gaze with a question in his eyes.

'Don't talk soft. You know you're always welcome.' Picking up the saucepan she hurried into the kitchen. 'Look who's come, everyone. George managed to get here in time for Christmas dinner. Isn't that splendid?'

It was a noisy meal and the pitch of their voices rose as a result of generous libations of mulled wine. Sammy and Eddie ate so much that Hetty was afraid they would make themselves sick, but they were having a good time, and after everything they had suffered in the past it was wonderful to see them having fun. The long days spent making matchboxes seemed to have been in another lifetime, and seeing everyone so relaxed, happy and well fed only hardened Hetty's resolve to make a secure future for her family.

Jane's Christmas pudding was a triumph and when the last scrap had been eaten and the dishes cleared away, Granny announced that it was time to open their presents. They were only small gifts but each one was opened and shown round with exclamations of delight. Afterwards, while Granny and Nora dozed by the fire, Sammy and Eddie sat on the floor with Tom showing them how to line up their lead soldiers in battle formation. Jane had taken Natalia upstairs for her afternoon nap, and George sat at the table smoking the cigar that was Hetty's Christmas present to him. She smiled as she went to sit beside him. 'I like the smell of cigars.'

He took another puff and blew a cloud of smoke up to the ceiling. 'It's a fine cigar, Hetty.'

'I'm glad you came, George.'

'Maybe I was a bit hasty yesterday.'

'You were a bit.'

He lowered his voice. 'Have you told them yet?'

Hetty glanced anxiously round the room, but no one was listening, and she shook her head. 'No. I wanted it to be settled before I said anything.'

'Very wise. It certainly needs thinking through.'

'I'm going to see her tomorrow, George. Will you come with me?'

'I most certainly will. I want to see the old dragon face to face and hear what she has to say for herself.'

'Miss Heathcote will see you now, miss.' Hicks motioned Hetty to follow him.

Hetty stood up, brushing the creases out of her Sunday best skirt. 'What about Mr Cooper? I ain't, I mean, I'm not leaving him sitting here like a beetle on a birthday cake.'

'Thanks, Hetty,' George said, chuckling. 'I've been called a lot of things but never a beetle.'

She ignored this remark, keeping her gaze fixed on Hicks's stern face. 'Well, Mr Hicks, what did she say?'

'I'm sorry, but Miss Heathcote made it clear that she is not at home to your friend.'

'We'll see about that,' Hetty said, picking up her skirts and making for the staircase. 'Wait there, George. I won't be long.' She did not wait for his reply and she ran lightly up the stairs with Hicks following her at a more sedate pace. She glanced over her shoulder as she reached the first landing. 'It's all right, Mr Hicks. I know the way.'

'Maybe, miss. But I have my duty to perform.' He quickened his pace and he managed to get to the door just ahead of her. 'Miss Huggins to see you, ma'am.'

'What a palaver,' Hetty said as she hurried past him. 'I can open doors on me own, Mr Hicks. I ain't a cripple.' Realising what she had said, she clapped her hands over her mouth in dismay, but fortunately Miss Heathcote was seated at the far end of the vast room and she did not seem to have heard.

'Stop dithering in the doorway, Hetty. Come here where I can see you.'

Hetty advanced slowly, choosing her words carefully. 'Miss Heathcote, ma'am. I have brought my friend and business partner, Mr George Cooper, with me. If you don't mind, I would like him to be present.'

Miss Heathcote raised an eyebrow. 'This is not a board meeting, Hetty. It was supposed to be an informal chat.'

'Nevertheless, I want George to be included. He's helped me right from the beginning when I started with a handcart and a tin can to keep the taters hot. I wouldn't be here today if it wasn't for George.'

'I always knew you had spirit, Hetty. It remains to be seen if you have enough backbone and determination to succeed.' Miss Heathcote leaned forward and pointed to a silver-backed mirror and hairbrush on a side table. 'Pass me my brush and mirror.'

Hetty did as she was asked. 'Does that mean you'll meet George?'

'No.'

'No? You mean you won't even give him a chance to speak for hisself?'

'Himself, Hetty, not hisself.' Miss Heathcote stared at her reflection in the mirror and then hurled it at the wall. 'I hate what I see. I would give my soul to have a face and body like yours, but I am trapped in this hideous, twisted shell.'

'No, don't say that.' Hetty leapt to her feet and went to retrieve the mirror, but the glass was shattered and the silver backing dented beyond repair. 'Look what you done. This must be worth a small fortune.'

'The cost is immaterial.' Miss Heathcote made an impatient gesture with her hand. 'Sit down for goodness' sake; you make me feel tired just watching you.'

Hetty stood before her with her hands clasped tightly behind her back. 'Why won't you see George? What has he ever done to you?'

'Nothing. I don't know him and I don't wish to. He's a man – that says it all.'

'But Miss Heathcote, they ain't all bad. Some of them can be rotters, and who knows that better than me, but George is kind and decent and we're in this together.'

'Then beware, little Hetty Huggins.' Miss Heathcote's eyes glittered as she leaned towards Hetty, wagging her finger. 'That's when they are at their most dangerous. I'm telling you that you cannot trust men. I speak from experience.'

'You do?' Her curiosity aroused, Hetty forgot to be angry and she sank down on the stool by Miss Heathcote's side. 'What happened?'

'The details aren't important. Let's just say that once, many years ago, a young man showed an interest in me. He brought me flowers and small gifts and he made me feel as though I was a whole person and desirable. He wanted to marry me, but my father said he was merely after my fortune. I wouldn't believe him, but Papa said he would disinherit me if I accepted my suitor's offer of marriage.'

'And you refused the gentleman?'

'I never saw him again. He sent a note expressing his deepest regrets, but he had been offered a position abroad and he would be gone for a year or maybe two. It was not fair, he said, to expect me to wait for him.' Miss Heathcote uttered a hollow laugh. 'He was an adventurer, just as Papa had said. I tell you, Hetty, all men are the same. They either want to rule you or to own you.'

Hetty shook her head. 'George isn't like that.'

'Do you want me to help you with your business or not? It's a simple question.'

'I think I do, but George . . .'

Miss Heathcote held up her hand. 'Is not my problem. My business dealings will be with you and no one else.'

'What exactly do you want of me, Miss Heathcote?'

'Let's put it another way, Hetty. How do you see the future of your coffee shop? Are you content to slave away in Artillery Lane, making cups of tea and coffee for penny-pinching clerks and type-writers? Or do you have more ambition?'

'I've got this far and I want to make money. I've had enough of being poor and watching my family suffer. I want to be a successful businesswoman with a whole string of coffee shops.'

Miss Heathcote clapped her hands like an excited child. 'Exactly so. I visited your little shop yesterday. I had the spare set of keys from Maitland, although he wasn't very happy about being disturbed on Christmas Day, but I always get what I want. Anyway, I had a look inside your premises and I liked what I saw. With very little outlay, you have created a warm and welcoming atmosphere aimed at an up and coming middle-class clientele.'

'I never thought about it like that. All I wanted was somewhere clean and decent where women wouldn't feel out of place if they was on their own.'

'And you have done just that. You have a talent for design and an eye for the small details that transform a simple café into a smart venue. I would want you to choose suitable locations, design the interiors, set the menus and the standard for the catering. I saw from your bill of fare at the coffee shop that everything is homemade, and that is a good selling point. Our motto should be honest homemade food at affordable prices. What do you think?'

'I think you're going too fast for me, miss – I

mean, Miss Heathcote. I've only just got me shop up and running. I haven't got the experience to handle more just yet.'

Miss Heathcote threw up her hands. 'You wouldn't have to work in them, you silly girl. No one makes money by slaving away in a kitchen or waiting on tables. You pay other people to do that. You would delegate, my dear.'

'I ain't sure what that means, and anyway, without George . . .'

'Stop! Don't mention that fellow's name again in my presence. We will do this together, Hetty. We will find suppliers of everything from tables and chairs to currant buns. You will tell me what we need, based on your experience in Artillery Lane, and we will start from there.'

Hetty was still unsure. 'But . . .'

'No buts, Hetty. You want to be a success, don't you?'

'Of course.'

'Then put yourself in my hands. You cannot lose. I will put up the money and find the properties through one of my agents, incognito of course. It will be so exciting to pit my wits against men. I want to prove that I can beat them at their own game.'

'The business wouldn't be mine, though,' Hetty said slowly. 'It would be your success and your money, not mine.'

'Nonsense. I'm not interested in the money. I have more than I could ever spend in one lifetime. I need to prove that I am not a useless cripple. You can repay the capital expenditure if you must, but you can have the profits for yourself. Share them with your gentleman friend if you like, but allow me the thrill of being involved in a project where I can use the intelligence that God gave me. I cannot do it without you, and you need my money in order to start your catering empire.'

'Put like that, it don't sound half bad,' Hetty said slowly.

'Wonderful. You've seen sense at last.'

'There's just one question I have to ask you.'

'What is that, Hetty?'

'Why pick on me? With your money you could get someone far more experienced and clever than me.'

Miss Heathcote laid her hand on Hetty's sleeve. 'I hadn't even thought of doing something like this until you came barging into my life. You started with nothing and you now own a coffee shop, which has been an initial success solely due to the ambience which you created and the good food you provide. If you can do all this in such a short space of time, then I know I have the right person to further my interests and your own. Does that satisfy you, Hetty?'

Rising slowly from the stool, Hetty nodded. 'Yes, ma'am. If you put it like that then let's have a go. I can do it, I know I can.'

'I knew that you would see sense.' Miss Heathcote suddenly became businesslike, folding her hands in her lap and looking Hetty in the eye with a determined expression on her thin features. 'Now, I want you to come here tomorrow morning at the same time. I will give the matter a great deal of thought and tomorrow I will tell you my plans and how you are to set about them. Do you understand me, Hetty?'

'I do, but I have to open up my coffee shop first thing in the morning. I can't afford to lose a day's trading.'

Miss Heathcote frowned and then a slow smile curved her thin lips. 'Good. I see that you are a true businesswoman at heart. Very well, then, you will come here when you close down for the day. I will send my carriage to collect you. Now you must leave me. I'm tired and I must rest.' She leaned back against the cushions and closed her eyes.

Summarily dismissed, Hetty left the room and went running down the great staircase to tell George her news. He came to meet her with a worried puckering of his brow. 'What's been going on? You've been ages.'

She linked her hand through his arm. 'I

know I have, George. I wanted you to be there but she wouldn't have it. She don't like men very much and I can't say I blame her.' Seeing the downturn of his mouth, Hetty chuckled. 'I don't mean you, silly. But she's had bad luck with men and it's made her bitter.'

'Ahem.'

A polite cough from Hicks made them both turn to look at him.

'Excuse me, miss, but will you be leaving now?'

'Yes, Mr Hicks,' Hetty said, smiling. 'We're going right away.'

'It's just Hicks, ma'am.'

Hetty angled her head, eyeing him doubtfully. 'It seems a bit disrespectful to a bloke of your age, but I suppose you know what you're talking about.'

'Yes, miss.' Hicks bit his lip as if he was suppressing a grin, and he signalled to the footman. 'Miss Heathcote's guests will be leaving now, Henry.'

'Come on, Hetty,' George said, taking her by the arm. 'Let's get out of here.'

The footman stood to attention by the open door and Hetty paused as they were about to walk past him. 'Ta-ta, Henry. I expect I shall be seeing you again soon.'

'Good day, miss. Good day, sir.' A crimson

flush rose from above Henry's collar to stain his cheeks, but he maintained a stony expression.

Hetty was certain that he winked at her, or perhaps he had something in his eye. She could not be sure, but she decided that they were a rum lot in Berkeley Square. She was glad to be going home, even if the roads were ankle deep in slush and she could tell by his set expression that George was far from happy. She shot him a glance beneath her eyelashes. 'Shall we take a cab, and hang the expense?'

He looked down at her and his expression softened. 'Yes. It's too far to walk on a day like this. We'll stand a better chance of getting one in Piccadilly.' He patted her hand as it lay in the crook of his arm. 'You can tell me what the old dragon said to you on the way.'

As they set off at a brisk pace down Berkeley Street, Hetty recounted the details of her conversation with Miss Heathcote. George listened in silence but she could feel the muscles in his arm contract when she mentioned Miss Heathcote's intransigent attitude towards him and men in general. 'She can't help it, George,' Hetty said hastily. 'It's nothing personal.'

'If you ask me, it's very personal. She hasn't given me a chance to speak for myself and I resent that. You and me are partners, Hetty, and the sooner she gets that into her head the better.'

'There's a cab, George,' Hetty cried, pointing at a hansom cab that had just dropped off a fare. She hurried across the street, waving frantically to attract the cabby's attention, leaving George little alternative but to follow her.

'Where to, mister?'

'Princelet Street, Spitalfields, please, mate.' George held out his hand to help Hetty up the high step, but she hesitated.

'No, George. First I want to check on the coffee shop, just in case Miss Heathcote forgot to lock the door or something dreadful.' She raised her voice, addressing the cabby. 'Artillery Lane first, and then Princelet Street.'

'Right you are, lady.'

'What's the matter, Hetty? Are you afraid the old girl's a bit doolally and can't be trusted to do a simple thing like locking a door?' George said, handing her into the cab and climbing in to sit beside her.

'Don't be horrible. She's a cripple and she's not used to doing things for herself. For all I know she might have walked out and left the place wide open, or knocked over a candle and set the building on fire.'

'If that's so then I don't think you should be going into business with her.' He moderated his tone. 'Come on, Hetty. Think about it, girl. It's a harsh world out there. How can two women manage without a bloke to stand up for them?'

'You'd be surprised.'

'If I could just get in to speak to the old girl, I know I could make her see sense.'

Hetty smiled. 'I think you would have met your match with Miss Tryphena Heathcote.'

'Rubbish. There ain't a woman in London who wouldn't succumb to my charms, if I was so inclined.'

'Well, there's one here who has your measure.' Hetty took his hand and she smiled. 'You're one of the best, George. I couldn't wish for a better friend.'

'One of the best?' He squeezed her fingers with a reluctant grin. 'I am the best, Hetty, and don't you forget it.'

'I won't, but you must let me do this my way.'

'I know, but I still think you're making a big mistake.'

Hetty subsided into silence, huddling in the corner of the cab. She was not going to argue. George would come round. He always did.

They continued their journey in silence, and when they arrived in Artillery Lane it seemed unnaturally quiet with all the business premises closed for the day. As the cab drew to a halt Hetty leaned out to gaze anxiously at the shop front and to her relief the door was firmly closed, but huddled together on the doorstep she saw three small bodies. She leapt out of the cab, barely waiting for it to come to a halt, and she raced across the pavement. Her breath caught in her throat when she saw their bare, blue feet sticking out from beneath their ragged clothes, and for a dreadful moment she thought that they were all dead. 'Dorrie,' Hetty whispered, giving her a gentle shake.

Dorrie opened her eyes and they were blurry with sleep. 'Is that you, miss?'

'Yes, and it's lucky for you that I happened along. I told you to come tomorrow, not today.' Hetty stared anxiously at the two boys, who had not stirred. 'Are they . . .'

Dorrie nudged each of them in the ribs and received a grunt in reply. 'They ain't dead, they're just worn out.'

'What's going on?' George called impatiently. 'Check the door, Hetty, and let's be on our way.'

She glanced over her shoulder and saw him standing by the cab, stamping his feet and blowing on his hands. She beckoned to him. 'Come and help me. These poor children are half frozen to death.'

He strode over to her. 'Please don't tell me that you want to take them home with you.'

Hetty helped Dorrie to her feet. 'Of course

I'm taking them home. Would you have me leave them here to freeze to death? No, of course you wouldn't. You'll have to carry the little ones, George. I'll get Dorrie into the cab.'

'What about the coffee shop? Have you forgotten about that already?'

Hetty laid her hand on the doorknob and gave it a twist. She peered through the window. 'It's locked and everything looks just as we left it. The children are more important now. They need food and warmth.'

'I hope you know what you're doing, Hetty,' George said, scooping the sleeping boys into his arms.

Hetty climbed into the cab. 'Pass the little ones to me, George,' she said, holding out her hand to help Dorrie scramble onto the seat beside her.

Shaking his head, he lifted them into her arms. 'For all we know they've got a father and a mother out looking for them, or, worse still, hiding round the corner waiting to accuse us of stealing their nippers.'

'I doubt it very much. Get in the cab, George, and stop grumbling. I know what I'm doing.'

'Do you? I'm beginning to wonder, Hetty.' He leapt nimbly into the cab, taking care not to squash Dorrie. 'Drive on, cabby.'

It was past midday by the time they arrived back in Princelet Street. With Stanley hooked over his shoulder, still fast asleep, George paid off the cabby and followed Hetty as she led Dorrie and Wilfred into the house. The familiar homely smell of baking bread and soup simmering on the hob assailed Hetty's nostrils and she realised that she was hungry, but that only served to remind her that her little strays had eaten very little in the past twenty-four hours, if at all. From outside the kitchen door she could hear the cheerful babble of voices, but as she opened it and led Dorrie and Wilfred into the room there was a sudden silence. Hetty had been so intent on rescuing them that she had given little thought to the reception they might receive.

Granny was the first to recover. She came towards them wiping her hands on her apron. 'What the devil is this, Hetty? What have you been and gone and done now?' Her expression hardened when George came into the room with Stanley in his arms. 'I hope you don't expect us to take them street kids in. Haven't we got enough mouths to feed already?'

'It's just temporary,' Hetty explained hastily. 'I found them in the shop doorway. I couldn't leave them to perish from cold and hunger, now could I?'

Nora raised herself from her chair by the fire. 'We can spare them a bite to eat, dearie, but Mattie is right, we can't take in every waif that lands on our doorstep.'

Sammy and Eddie had been building a tower of wooden bricks but they abandoned it, scrambling to their feet and advancing ...ily on Wilfred as if they expected him to break th... Natalia knocked the bricks to break th... ...ful gurgle and that seemed ...one started talking at once. Jane dropped the wooden spoon into the cake mixture and swooped on Natalia, picking her up and scolding her. Nora bustled over to the table and began cutting slices off a loaf and buttering them. Granny took Wilfred by the ear and peered down at his matted hair. 'This one is running with head lice and fleas. Take them all out into the scullery, Hetty, until we've filled the bathtub with hot water. I ain't having parasites brought into the house. Next thing you know we'll all be itching and scratching.'

'Don't let them near Talia,' Jane said, backing away from Dorrie and Wilfred as if they were carrying the plague. 'It's typical of you, Hetty. You don't think things through.'

The sound of raised voices had awakened Stanley. He began to whimper and George set him down on the floor. Stanley ran to his sister and clung to her, hiding his face in her skirt.

'Now steady on, everyone,' George said,

hooking his arm around Hetty's shoulders. 'Hetty only did what she thought best. There's nothing wrong with these nippers that some carbolic soap and hot water won't cure.'

Hetty shot him a grateful smile. 'Thank you, George.'

'I'm just being fair, which is more than you've been with me.'

Hetty was uncomfort... and Jane were listening to every word and that they were not in the mood to be generous. 'I thought you were on my side, George.'

'I am, more than you know, but there's one matter on which we don't see eye to eye and you know what that is.'

'Hetty, I'll scream if you don't tell us what's going on,' Jane cried, stamping her foot.

George gave Hetty a gentle nudge. 'Go on, girl. You've got to tell them sometime, but quite frankly I wouldn't want to be in your shoes when you tell them what you've been and gone and done.'

# Chapter Seventeen

'What's all this, Hetty?' Granny released Wilfred, who had begun to snivel, and she wiped her hands on her apron. 'I knew something was up.'

Nora made her way to the table and picked up a pitcher of milk. She beckoned to Dorrie. 'Bring your little brothers over here, dearie,' she said, pouring a small amount into the cups.

Dorrie glanced up at Hetty and she gave her an encouraging smile. 'Go on. Don't be frightened; you're with friends.'

'That's right,' Nora said with a nod of approval as the children rushed to the table. She set a plate of bread and butter in front of them. 'Eat up. There's plenty more where that came from.'

Jane stood arms akimbo, glaring at Hetty. 'You take a lot on yourself, Hetty. But then you always did. And what's this George says? What have you done?'

'Yes,' Granny added. 'You'd best come out with it, miss.'

'I was going to tell you when the moment

was right,' Hetty said, casting a reproachful glance at George.

He shrugged his shoulders. 'I think it's time you told your family about the mad old woman who lives in Berkeley Square, and your grand plans for the future. Or don't they include them either?'

'That is just not fair,' Hetty replied hotly. 'It's not my fault that Miss Heathcote doesn't like men. As far as I'm concerned you are still my partner and always will be. I still need you to keep an eye on the shop in Artillery Lane.'

'I'm sorry, but you've got the wrong bloke. I'm either a full business partner or I'm not. You can't have it all ways, Hetty. You'd best give this matter a good deal of thought before you go ahead.' George was not smiling now. He made a move towards the door. 'I've got to go now, but we'll talk about this again.'

Hetty made to follow him but Jane reached out and caught her by the wrist. 'What's all this? What's been going on, and where have you been today? You've got some explaining to do, Hetty Huggins.'

Hetty licked her dry lips and launched into a detailed account of her dealings with Miss Heathcote. Her voice trailed off at the sight of their hostile expressions. Jane was the first to speak. 'So where do we fit in with all this?'

'I – I thought you could run the shop in

Artillery Lane. You'd like to be manageress, wouldn't you, Jane?'

'And if I wouldn't? What would you say to that?'

'I just thought . . .'

'No, you never. You never gave any of us a thought. You got carried away listening to this crazy old woman who shuts herself up in her big mansion surrounded by servants. What does she know about business? Has she ever run a stall in Spitalfields market? No, of course she ain't. She's having you on, Hetty. You've been took in by her big talk.'

'No, it's not like that,' Hetty protested. She turned to her grandmother. 'Granny, you're a businesswoman. What do you think?'

Granny frowned, shaking her head. 'I think we all gave up a lot to help you get started, Hetty. I don't have time to make bonnets nowadays because I'm helping out on your coffee stall – so what do I do now you don't need me? Have you given up on me as well as on George?'

Nora sat down on her chair by the fire, fanning her face with her apron. 'I think you're being a bit hard on the girl, Mattie. This could be her big chance in life.'

Granny rounded on her. 'And it could be her downfall. "Stick to what you know" has always been my motto. Hetty don't know a thing about dealing with people above her station in life. They'll eat her for their dinner.'

'Yes,' Jane added bitterly. 'And she's landed us with three more mouths to feed. I don't call that clever.'

'I know this has come as a shock,' Hetty said, making an effort to keep calm. 'I would have broken it more gently if it hadn't been for George and his big trap.'

Granny chortled with laughter. 'That's fine talk coming from someone who wants to be a lady.'

That hurt and Hetty's eyes filled with tears. She could be a lady if she tried. She would be a lady when she married Charles. They were not being fair to her. All she was trying to do was to make a better life for everyone. She held her head high. 'I can be ladylike if I want to be, but that's not the point. I'm doing this for all of us. With Miss Heathcote's backing I can start a chain of coffee shops and make real money. Then you, Jane, won't need to wear yourself out with cooking and working on the stall. Granny will be able to sit by the fire and take things easy. The boys can go back to their old school, and we will be able to have a home of our own again, with no fear of Clench or anyone else for that matter.'

'And if it fails?' Granny said, narrowing her eyes. 'What then, Hetty?'

'We'll still have the shop in Artillery Lane, and the coffee stall. But I won't fail. I'm determined to make a success of my life.'

'I hope you won't move out too soon,' Nora wheezed. 'I like having you all here. I love having the nippers around and the old house filled with noise and the smell of baking. I should miss you all if you got rich and moved away.'

Hetty opened her mouth to tell Nora that she was a wonderful friend and they would never desert her, but at that moment Tom breezed into the kitchen. 'Hello,' he said cheerily. His expression changed to one of puzzlement. 'Why the glum faces? What's up?'

Jane rushed over to him and flung her arms around his neck. 'Oh, Tom. You've come just in time. Hetty's gone and done something really stupid. Perhaps you can talk sense into her.'

Dorrie and her brothers had been sitting silently at the table, stuffing their mouths with bread and butter and gulping down cupfuls of milk, but at this point Dorrie slid off her stool and bobbed a curtsey to Nora. 'Ta for the vittles, missis. But I think it's time we was on our way.'

Hetty had almost forgotten about them and a wave of guilt swept over her. 'But where will you go, Dorrie? Have you any family who would look after you?'

'We're orphans, but I can take care of Wilf and Stan. We ain't going to the workhouse and that's that.'

'It's started snowing again,' Tom said, taking off his cap and muffler and tossing them onto a chair. 'It ain't fit for man nor beast out there.'

Nora rose to her feet. 'That settles it. Dorrie, you and the boys are staying here for the time being. Tom, be so good as to bring the tin tub from the scullery, and you big boys, Sammy and Eddie, can fetch water from the pump.'

Dorrie seized Wilfred and Stanley by the hand and she backed towards the doorway. 'We've never had a bath. It ain't healthy, missis. We'll catch our deaths of cold.'

Granny moved swiftly to bar the door. 'No you don't. If Nora says you've got to be clean, then clean you will be. There's no place for fleas and lice in this house.' She looked over their heads to meet Hetty's anxious gaze. 'We'll talk about your plans again later, when the children are in bed.'

There followed a very wet session of bathing three incredibly dirty children who did not want to get into a tub of hot water, let alone have their hair washed with carbolic soap, rinsed with vinegar and then combed through to rid them of lice. Sammy and Eddie seemed to think it was a huge joke to see the newcomers suffering the torment of an energetic scrubbing and delousing, but a sharp word from Granny silenced them and they were sent to pick up their bricks and put them back in the box. Unseen by her mother, Natalia attempted to climb into the tub with Wilfred and Stanley and fell in head first. Hetty rescued her before she could receive a smack from Jane, who had paled with fright at the sight of her child submerged beneath the scummy water, but Natalia recovered quickly and would have dived off Hetty's lap into the water had she not been firmly wrapped in a towel. Hetty stripped off Natalia's wet clothes, and when she was dry she pulled a nightgown over her fluffy curls. In spite of everything Hetty couldn't help chuckling at her small niece's irrepressible good humour and determination to get her own way.

'You spoil her,' Jane said crossly. 'She did a stupid thing and she should be punished.'

Tom had been sitting quietly in the chimney corner, smoking his pipe and keeping well away from the water as it splashed from the tub, but he spoke up now, frowning at Jane. 'Have a heart, ducks.'

'Didn't you ever do a stupid thing, Jane?' Hetty demanded angrily.

'That's not the point,' Jane said, rubbing soap into Wilfred's scalp until he protested. 'Sit still, boy. I'm not done with you yet. Your hair is still running with lice.'

'Poor little sod,' Tom said with feeling.

Jane turned her head to glower at him. 'You could give us a hand instead of making stupid comments.'

Clenching the stem of his pipe between his teeth, Tom grinned and threw up his hands. 'Not me, girl. That's women's work.'

'Men!' Granny muttered, wringing water from her wet apron. 'Maybe that Miss Heathcote ain't so far wrong.'

Nora tipped water from a steaming kettle into the tub, taking care not to scald either of the boys. 'Go on, Mattie. You don't mean that, I'm sure.'

'I suppose they have their uses,' Granny acknowledged grudgingly. 'Let's get this over and done with. My back is aching something chronic.'

When Wilfred and Stanley were finally deemed clean enough to towel dry, they were lifted from the bath, and Dorrie was next to undergo the discomfort of being scrubbed from head to toe. She bore it bravely, but Hetty's heart went out to the child when she saw her bottom lip quivering as Granny dragged the fine-tooth comb through her straggly hair. Hetty dressed the boys in nightshirts that had been outgrown by Sammy and Eddie, and

Dorrie sat primly on the edge of a chair by the fire, wrapped in a towel, while Jane cut one of Hetty's nightgowns down to size. The finished garment swamped Dorrie's small body, and without the thick layer of grime she looked very young and vulnerable. Her tow-coloured hair formed a halo around her pinched features, giving her the appearance of a world-weary angel. Hetty was almost unbearably touched by this child who had somehow managed to survive on the streets whilst caring for her two small brothers. She gave her a hug. 'How old are you, Dorrie?'

'Eleven or twelve, I don't know exactly, but Wilf is six and Stan is four. I remember when he was born, because that's when our mum died and our dad took to the drink.'

'Dear me,' Nora said, sniffing. 'And how long have you been living like this, dearie?'

'I dunno, missis.' Dorrie frowned thoughtfully. 'A long time.'

'Never mind that now. It doesn't matter.' Hetty took Dorrie by the shoulders and led her to the table where the boys and Natalia were polishing off bowls of warm bread and milk. 'Have your supper and then it's time for bed.'

'We'll go first thing in the morning,' Dorrie said with an anxious glance at Granny. 'We don't want to be no trouble.'

Hetty glanced at Granny over the top of Dorrie's head, raising her eyebrows in a mute question. She had the satisfaction of seeing her grandmother look slightly ashamed. 'Well, er, we'll talk about that tomorrow,' Granny murmured. 'Eat your food before it gets cold.'

'Where will they sleep?' Jane demanded. 'I'm not having them in with me. It's bad enough having Sammy and Eddy snoring away in my room.'

Nora put her head on one side as if giving the matter due consideration. 'Well, there's only old Mr Dobson in at the moment. I'm not expecting any of my regulars in until Sunday evening. The nippers can share the big front room for tonight. We'll sort something better out tomorrow.'

'The top floor is huge. I don't mind sharing and I can keep them in order.' Hetty winked at Sammy who had opened his mouth to protest, and he grinned in response.

'You can have Natalia up there too,' Jane said. 'I haven't had a good night's sleep since she was born. You're welcome to them all, Hetty. Although I should have thought you'd be too grand now to share with the nippers.'

Hetty shook her head. 'Never, Jane. My family will always come first. I only want to make a success in business so that I can share it with all of you.'

When the children were settled in their beds and all was quiet, Hetty sat at the kitchen table with Nora, Granny, Jane and Tom. They waited expectantly for her to say something. Sensing the importance of the occasion, she rose to her feet. 'I know this has come as a bit of a shock to you all,' she said humbly. 'I just want to make a better life for us, but if you are dead against my going into business with Miss Heathcote, then I'll go and see her in the morning and tell her I won't be going ahead. It's up to you. You're my family and I love you all and I wouldn't do anything to hurt you.'

'And what about George?' Jane demanded. 'You seem to have put his nose out of joint all right.'

'George is a sensible bloke. He'll come round.'

'I think Hetty should have her chance,' Tom said stoutly. 'It's really none of my business, other than the fact that I've always considered meself one of the family, and me and Jane are stepping out together.'

Jane stared at him wide-eyed. 'We are? You never said.'

'I didn't think I had to, ducks. I thought we had an understanding.'

Jane's pretty face flooded with colour. 'Oh, Tom!'

'Oh, for goodness' sake!' Granny exclaimed,

slamming her hand down on the table. 'Keep the sweet talk for later.'

Tom slipped his arm around Jane's shoulders. 'Don't worry, Granny. We will.'

'That's the spirit,' Nora said, chuckling. 'But you haven't given Hetty an answer. She's put it to you all nice and fair. I think she deserves a bit of consideration.'

Jane cuddled up to Tom and a beatific smile lit her face. 'I think Hetty should do what she thinks is right.'

'That's my girl,' Tom said, giving her a hug.

Hetty turned her head to give Granny a questioning look. 'Granny?'

'Suit yourself. You always do.'

'But I need you all on my side.'

'And where do you think I would be, you silly girl? Haven't I always stood up for you children?'

This made Hetty smile. 'Not always. I can remember a time . . .'

Granny rose majestically to her feet. 'Nonsense. I've always done my duty by you all. You do what you want, Hetty. I'll not stand in your way, but now I'm tired and I'm going to my bed.' She picked up a candle. 'I'll say goodnight then.'

As she left the room, Tom stood up and helped Jane to her feet. 'I'd best be going too. It's work for me in the morning.'

'I'll see you out, dear,' Jane said, smiling dreamily into his face. In response, Tom kissed her on the tip of her nose, and they left the room arm in arm.

'There'll be another baby on the way soon, you mark my words,' Nora said, with her great gusty laugh.

'Oh, no. Surely not.' Even as the words left her lips, Hetty knew that what Nora said was probably true. Jane's heart would always rule her head. We are so unalike, Hetty thought with a tinge of sadness. I am the exact opposite of Jane. My head rules my heart – but someone in the family has to be practical and sensible.

Next day, Hetty left the house laden with two baskets filled with Jane's slab cake and rock buns for the coffee shop. She was just unlocking the door when Sally came hurrying down the street with her shawl flapping and her bonnet strings flying out behind her. 'So you decided to come back,' Hetty said, smiling.

'It's me job, ain't it?' Sally replied with a cheeky grin. 'I done well on Christmas Eve, didn't I?'

'That you did,' Hetty agreed. 'And I'm glad to see you, Sally. Come in. I've got a lot to tell you.' She opened the door and went inside. The room was stuffy and filled with the over-powering smell of stale tea, fresh paint and carbolic soap. Despite the cold outside, Hetty opened the windows and left the door ajar in order to air the room. She lit the fire pots beneath the boilers and sent Sally into the scullery to fetch a broom and a mop. As they worked, she explained the situation to her. 'I'll work here all day, but as soon as we close I have to go and see Miss Heathcote and give her my answer.'

Sally leaned on the broom handle. 'What are you going to tell her?'

'I don't know,' Hetty replied, shaking her head. 'I just don't know.'

'I couldn't manage on me own just yet, Hetty. Maybe I could later on, when I've had a bit more practice, but I'd get muddled with the money and I'd panic if there was a queue waiting to be served.'

'Don't look so worried, love. I wouldn't expect you to cope by yourself. Jane would be here to run things.'

Sally pulled a face. 'Oh, well. I suppose I'll have to get used to having her around anyway, seeing as how Tom is sweet on her.'

'You knew?'

'Of course I knew. Hasn't he been spending more time round your place than his own home? We hardly ever see him nowadays.'

Hetty turned away to lay a clean cloth on one of the tables. It was silly to feel piqued and she knew it, but once, not so long ago, it had been she whom Tom had courted, and now he was as good as engaged to her sister. Charles had not written for weeks. Perhaps all men really were as fickle and untrustworthy as Miss Heathcote had said.

'Penny for 'em?' Sally said, chuckling.

'I was wondering what was keeping the baker's boy. We should have had the bread and rolls delivered by now. Will you go to the bakery round the corner, please, Sal? Find out what's keeping him.'

Sally grabbed her shawl from the peg and wrapped it around her shoulders. 'I'll go right away.'

'And you might call in at the grocer's shop and remind him I ordered boiled ham, a truckle of cheddar cheese and two pounds of butter.'

'Right you are.'

As the shop door closed behind Sally, Hetty lit the gas mantles so that a warm glow filled the room. The fizzing and popping of the gas made companionable sounds, and outside the city street was coming to life with horse-drawn traffic and pedestrians hurrying on their way to work. The water in the boilers was starting to bubble and the room was feeling a little warmer now. Soon, Hetty hoped, they might have the first customers of the day: men who had just come off night shift and wanted a cup of something hot to help them on their way, or perhaps clerical workers who had arrived on an early train and had not had time to eat breakfast before leaving the suburbs. It was still very early days and she was unsure as to the exact nature of her clientele. She could only hope and pray that trade continued to be as good as it had been at the start.

It was still dark outside and the snow had turned to a steady drizzle. While she waited for Sally's return, Hetty went behind the counter to arrange the cakes on plates beneath glass domes. She was intent on her task when the door opened and the bell jangled on its spring. She looked up expecting to see Sally or at least one of the delivery boys, but it was George who came in carrying a wicker basket filled with watercress. 'Hello, Hetty. I was passing the door so I thought I'd drop this in for you.'

She knew him well enough to realise that this was his way of apologising and she smothered a sigh of relief. 'Liar! It's well out of your way.'

His lips twisted into a wry smile. 'That's not the way to speak to your ex-partner, Miss Huggins.'

She moved slowly round the counter, holding out her hands to take the basket from him. 'I hoped we were still partners.'

'It'll be Huggins and Cooper in name only from now on, girl. You deserve your chance and you've got to grab it with both hands. I ain't one to stand in your way.'

There was a note of finality in his voice that made her blood run cold. 'But I still need you, George.'

He reached out to caress her cheek with the tips of his fingers. 'You go ahead and do what you think right, and I'll keep my doubts to myself.'

'Oh, George!' Choked by tears, Hetty dropped the basket on the floor and she flung her arms around his neck. The coarse woollen material of his jacket was pearled with raindrops and the smell of wet wool mingled with the scent of apples and damp earth. She stood on tiptoe and kissed him on the cheek. 'Huggins and Cooper it will always be. Never mind what Miss Heathcote says.'

'You tell the old besom that, girl. If it don't work out then you know where to find me, but I think it's best if we don't see too much of each other for the time being.'

'I don't understand.' Hetty unclasped her hands and stepped away from him. 'Why can't things be like they always were?'

'You're moving up in the world, Hetty.'

'But that's silly. It won't make any difference to us.' She met his gaze with a sinking heart. 'You will still come round to Princelet Street, won't you?'

'I don't think that would be good for either of us.'

'But you're my best friend and I still want you as my business partner.'

'Best friend, of course; business partner in name only. You know that's the way it must be.'

'It's not so very different, George. Nothing has changed between us.'

The smile faded from his eyes. 'No, and that's the trouble.'

Hetty stared at him, nonplussed. 'I really don't understand why you're being like this.'

'Don't you, girl? Then there's no point in me telling you.'

She opened her mouth to argue, but he laid his finger on her lips. 'Tell me one thing honestly. Are you still hankering after that damn Yankee Doodle fellow?'

'I – well, yes. I do miss Charles, but what has that to do with you and me?'

'First it was Tom you was sweet on and then along comes the Yankee. There never was a time when you looked on me as anything other than a pal, and now you've taken up with Miss Heathcote. Soon you won't want to know old George, the costermonger from Spitalfields market. I know when I'm beaten, Hetty.'

'You're so wrong. I care about you a lot and I'll always be your friend.'

'That's the pity of it,' he said with a rueful smile. 'I'll be around if you should need me, but I can't stand seeing you slip away from me inch by inch. Goodbye, Hetty.' He left the shop and the bell was still tinkling long after he had disappeared into the gloom.

Hetty bit her lip as tears welled up into her eyes. This was a situation that she could never have foreseen. She loved Charles with all her might but George was an important part of her life. She could not imagine going on without him. Why couldn't they just be friends? Why did he have to spoil everything by being so difficult?

She tried to carry on where she had left off, but her vision was blurred with unshed tears, and she went to make a pot of tea, which was Granny's answer to every situation imaginable. It was only when the tea was brewing that she realised there was no milk and she had forgotten to tell Sally to fetch some from the dairy. Hetty found herself sobbing because there was no milk for her tea. She was not crying because George had abandoned her. If he was being pig-headed and stupid, that was his business. She sniffed and wiped her eyes on her apron. George wouldn't stay away for long, and by next week he would probably have fallen in love with a pretty redhead or a blowsy blonde. Somehow that thought made her feel better – it was easier to brand him as a hopeless flirt than to accept that his feelings for her were genuine. He would return, she knew he would, and things would be the same as they ever were.

She had calmed down by the time Sally returned with the baker's boy, closely followed by the lad from the grocer's shop with the ham, cheese and butter. Hetty sent Sally out again to buy the milk, and soon the first customers of the day began to come through the door. Hetty was too busy then to dwell on her personal problems.

At the end of a long and profitable day, she said goodbye to Sally and she was just locking up when Milton brought Miss Heathcote's carriage to a halt outside the shop.

'Huggins and Cooper!' Miss Heathcote spat the words out as if they had a bad taste. 'No such thing. That man has nothing to do with our business venture.'

Hetty stood with her hands clasped tightly behind her back. 'No, but I think it sounds better than just Huggins alone and it was George who helped me to get started. If I am to come in with you, my only condition is that we keep that name.'

Miss Heathcote's silver eyebrows drew together in a knot over her pointed nose and her eyes narrowed to slits. 'Do you defy me, Hetty?'

'In this, I do. I am willing to work with you, Miss Heathcote, but you said that the business would be mine and that you only wanted to prove a point to your board of directors.'

Miss Heathcote seemed to subside into a small heap in her chair and her lips trembled. 'Don't bully me, Hetty. I am a poor cripple . . .'

'You might have a twisted spine, Miss Heathcote, but you don't fool me. You are as wayward and self-willed as I am, and I think that is why you chose me. I will go along with you in everything you say except in the matter of the name above the door. It will be Huggins and Cooper, Coffee Shops, or nothing.'

Miss Heathcote's face puckered as if she were about to scream or cry, and Hetty braced herself for the outburst, but nothing came. Miss Heathcote glared at her for a moment and then a reluctant smile lit her pale eyes. 'All right. I grant you that Huggins on its own does not have a ring to it, and Huggins and Heathcote, which does sound quite impressive, gives the game away, so I will concede this point to you. You may keep your name and his above the door, but that is as far as that man gets. I won't have him interfering in our business. Do you understand me?'

'Perfectly, Miss Heathcote. When do we start?'

'Tomorrow morning, first thing.' Miss Heathcote reached for a silver-bound note-book, pen and ink. 'I assume that you can read and write?'

Hetty took the writing implements from her. 'I may not speak like a toff, Miss Heathcote, but I ain't ignorant.'

'I am not ignorant,' Miss Heathcote said automatically. 'Very well then, write down the things that you must do, starting tomorrow morning. I have a list of premises in the East End that Mr Maitland has drawn up for me which I think might be suitable for further coffee shops.'

'Mr Maitland!' Hetty's heart sank. 'Why him?'

'Are you questioning my wisdom?'

'No, ma'am, it's just that . . .'

Miss Heathcote raised a thin hand. 'Never mind your petty prejudices, my girl. Henry Maitland has handled my finances for twenty years and I trust him implicitly. If we are to get on together, Hetty, you must not question everything I say or do. Your part in all this is quite straightforward. You will visit the premises listed and use your own judgement as to which is the most suitable. We will begin with four coffee shops, concentrating on the heart of the City. If these prove successful, we will move into the Strand and finally into the West End. At every stage you will report back to me and I will give you further directions.'

Hetty frowned. 'It doesn't sound as if I have much choice at all.'

'You will have your chance to prove just how bright and clever you are, Hetty. But you must never underestimate me. I have a good brain in my head and a mind as sharp as any man. You will act as my eyes and ears and your healthy young body will take you to places where I may not go. To all intents and purposes the coffee shops will belong to you, but the real power behind the throne will be mine. Accept this for what it is, or else walk out of that door and never come back. The choice is yours, my dear.'

# Chapter Eighteen

Hetty had made her choice and her life seemed to change overnight. Before Miss Heathcote would allow her to venture into the world of commerce, Hetty had to have a whole new wardrobe made for her. She underwent rigorous lessons in elocution and Miss Heathcote drilled her like a sergeant major in matters of etiquette. Her table manners were scrutinised, criticised and picked apart until she felt like throwing her dinner plate at her mentor's head, and there were tedious sessions where she had to walk round the room with books balanced on her head in order to improve her deportment.

It was fortunate that Miss Heathcote was not an early riser, as this gave Hetty an hour or two in the morning before Milton arrived to collect her in the carriage. It allowed her time in which to balance the books in the coffee shop, to check the stock and to make certain that Jane was coping with her new responsibilities. It was something of a relief to discover that Jane and Sally were getting along well together, and Granny was managing the stall in Spitalfields market as if she had spent her whole life as a costermonger. Dorrie helped out when needed, and she also kept an eye on Natalia. Wilfred and Stanley attended the ragged school with Sammy and Eddy, although Wilfred had been caught playing truant a couple of times and had received a sound telling off from George and the threat of a caning from Granny, which had apparently been enough to convince him that it was in his best interests to have at least a smattering of education.

Hetty was glad that George had not abandoned them entirely, although he rarely visited the house in Princelet Street when she was at home. She was hurt by this and she missed his company more than she would have thought possible, but she had made her choice. She knew that she must either abide by her decision or abandon the whole project, and that would be to admit defeat. She was never going to give in; she had made her mind up to that. She would prosper and she would make herself into someone whom Charles would not be ashamed to introduce to his family.

On a particularly wet day at the beginning of February Hetty was summoned to Miss Heathcote's drawing room. She found her huddled beneath a fur rug in her usual chair by a blazing fire. 'I am not well today, Hetty,' Miss Heathcote murmured. 'I hate the winter and the constant damp and cold makes my back ache dreadfully.'

'I'm sorry, ma'am.'

'Well, yes, I suppose you are, but how could a healthy young woman like you understand the torments that I have to suffer?' Miss Heathcote waved a bony hand at her. 'Sit down, please. You know that I hate people towering over me.'

Hetty pulled up a footstool and sat down. 'What did you want me for, Miss Heathcote?'

'I called you here to tell you that the time has come for you to go out into the City and select suitable properties from those on my list. We've knocked the rough edges off you, although I doubt if you will ever lose that dreadful cockney accent entirely.'

'I'm not sure I want to. I won't pretend to be something I'm not.'

'And you won't get far in business if people think you have just crawled out of the gutter.' Miss Heathcote lay back against the cushions and closed her eyes. 'Let us not argue about trifles. The fact is that I have purchased a Victoria phaeton to take you round London, as I don't want anyone to recognise my carriage. You will have your own coachman, and, for the sake of propriety, I think you ought to have a lady's maid to accompany you. Do you know a person whom you could trust implicitly? We don't want a gossiping, tittle-tattling maidservant who would tell the world our secret.'

'A maid? I dunno about that.'

'Grammar, Hetty.'

'I'm sorry, but I wouldn't know how to treat a maidservant.'

'Then you must learn. Surely there is some young girl of your acquaintance whom you could trust?'

Hetty smiled. 'There's Dorrie, but she's only a child.'

'It doesn't matter. Just so long as you have a chaperone of some sort. It is only for the sake of appearances.' Miss Heathcote pointed to a purse lying on a table near Hetty. 'There is enough money there to outfit the girl. Milton will take you to a suitable emporium this after-noon. Tomorrow you will go to the first address on my list, and so we will begin.'

Taking Dorrie to be her maid proved more difficult than Hetty had thought possible. Granny was adamant that she could not manage the coffee stall and keep an eye on a toddler, and Jane was reluctant to take Talia to the coffee shop. In the end it was Tom who provided the solution. He arrived at the house that evening just after Hetty and Dorrie returned from their shopping expedition, and he walked in during the middle of a fierce argument between Hetty and Jane.

'You just think about yourself,' Jane cried angrily.

'That's not true,' Hetty protested. 'Talia is your child. You should take care of her.'

'Well, you make such a fuss of her anyone would think she was yours.' Jane sat down at the table, pouting. 'I work me fingers to the bone in the shop. I'm on me feet all day long making sandwiches and pouring cups of tea and coffee. Sally and me haven't had a minute to ourselves all day.'

'What's wrong?' Tom demanded, picking up Natalia, who had begun to cry at the sound of raised voices. 'What's all the fuss about?'

Granny thumped the teapot down on the kitchen table and the teacups rattled on their saucers. 'It's Hetty. She's gone all grand on us and wants to take young Dorrie for a lady's maid, of all things. I can't look after the child as well as working in the market. At my age I should be sitting by the fire with my feet up all day, not slaving away on a coffee stall.'

Tom shot a questioning glance at Hetty. 'What's all this, Hetty?'

'I'm to start looking for suitable premises tomorrow, Tom. Miss Heathcote says I've got to look respectable. I'll be dealing with businessmen and she says I ought to have a maid to chaperone me. It seems a bit of a palaver to me, but I expect she's right.'

For a moment Hetty was afraid that he was going to side with Jane and Granny. He thought for a moment and then he nodded his head. 'I think the old girl is right. You shouldn't go round the City on your own. We all know what Clench tried to do to you and there's plenty more ruffians like him.'

'But, Tom,' Jane protested, her eyes brimming with tears. 'I can't manage the coffee shop and look after baby, especially now she's started toddling.'

He put his arm around her shoulders and kissed her on the tip of her nose. 'Of course you can't, poppet. But it just so happens that my sister Marie has had a tiff with her boss in the pub over Wapping way, and she's come home to live. Apparently the fellow had wandering hands and he tried to take advantage of her, so she slapped his face and walked out.'

'Good for her,' Hetty said with feeling.

Tom grinned. 'Well, the Crewe girls are a spunky lot and she won't stand for any old nonsense. What I suggest is that Marie helps Jane in the coffee shop, since she's had experience working in the pub, and Sally can look after

Talia. She's a born mother is that one and she'd be happy to play nursemaid.'

'That sounds good to me,' Hetty said, turning to Jane. 'What do you think?'

Jane shrugged her shoulders. 'Do I have a choice? It seems you two can manage things perfectly well without me.'

'Stop being a moody little mare,' Granny scolded. 'Tom offers a perfectly good suggestion and you show him a sulky face. Serve you right if he changed his mind and found himself another girl.'

Nora was sitting in her usual seat by the fire with a cup of tea in her hand. She nodded wisely, saying nothing.

With a throaty chuckle, Tom patted Granny on the shoulder. 'If I was twenty years older, you would be the one for me, Granny, but Jane's my girl and I love her, even if she is a bit grumpy sometimes.'

Jane pushed him away half-heartedly. 'Oh, get on with you, Tom.'

He ignored the rebuff and slid his arm around her waist. 'You like Marie, don't you, Janey?'

'Yes, I like her well enough. But she has to know that I'm in charge,' Jane said pouting.

Hetty sighed with relief. 'Thank goodness. That's settled then. Tomorrow, Dorrie and me will go out together and conquer London.'

'Boastful talk,' Granny muttered. 'Don't get too big for your boots, miss.'

Sammy had been listening to all this with his head on one side, his round steel-rimmed spectacles giving him an owlish look. 'Will your feet really grow bigger when you conquer London, Hetty?'

She ruffled his hair and smiled down into his serious face. 'No, Sammy. It's just a manner of speaking. I'll always be the same Hetty as I was when we lived in Autumn Road and we made matchboxes for a living.'

'We won't have to do that again, will we?' Sammy asked anxiously.

'No, love. Never again.' Hetty squeezed his hand. 'Why don't you go and play with the boys until supper is ready?'

He hesitated. 'When you've got your string of coffee shops, can I leave school and come and help you?'

'When you're older, of course you can.'

'You get book learning, boy,' Granny said, pursing her lips and frowning. 'You work hard at school and make something of yourself. You aim to be a professional man, never mind being in trade.'

Hetty suppressed a smile. 'But that's just what we are, Granny. We're in trade, like it or not, and I'm going to make a fortune or die in the attempt.'

Next day, Hetty dressed with extra care in a gown of fine merino trimmed with braid in a military style, which set off her slim figure to its best advantage. The deep shade of blue brought out the violet hue of her eyes, or so the shop assistant had said, and Hetty had been pleased to believe her. Her blue mantle was trimmed with Persian lamb, and a matching hat sat at a jaunty angle on top of the elaborate coiffure executed by Dorrie's nimble fingers. Hetty was not particularly vain, but when she saw her reflection in one of the wall mirrors in Miss Heathcote's grand entrance hall she hardly recognised herself, and she wished with all her heart that Charles could see her now.

With Dorrie seated beside her, looking very pleased with herself in her smart new clothes, Hetty set off to look at the first property on the list. The spanking Victoria was driven by a coachman who had been elevated from the position of under groom in Miss Heathcote's stables, and had been given strict instructions to look after the young ladies.

When they stopped at the first premises Hetty was greeted by an obsequious middle-aged gentleman with a balding pate and a pinstripe suit which smelt strongly of mothballs. He showed her around the empty shop, extolling the virtues of being so close to Liverpool Street station. Hetty decided that it was a good deal too close to the station. For one thing the floor-boards vibrated every time a train ground to a halt at the buffers, and when the engine let off steam the piercing shriek of the whistle echoed throughout the building. The smell of hot cinders and smoke pervaded the atmosphere in a choking fog which would put anyone off their meal. She listened politely to the agent's sales pitch, made notes in the leather-bound book that Miss Heathcote had given her for the purpose, and she assured him that she would give the premises her full consideration. She explained that she had other places to inspect but she would send him word when she had made her final decision.

'A definite no,' she told Dorrie as they climbed back into the Victoria. 'Drive on, Peters.'

At the end of the day Hetty had visited no less than six of the places on Miss Heathcote's list. She had written copious notes and had made sketches of the interiors which she intended to turn into scale drawings, together with ideas for their design and refurbishment. For the rest of the week, Hetty and Dorrie continued their search, travelling as far north as King's Cross and as far west as the Strand. Hetty spent all of Saturday and Sunday working on the plans for the premises which she considered to be most suitable, and on Monday morning she took them to Miss Heathcote for her consideration. By the end of the afternoon, when the light had faded and the curtains were drawn against the winter dusk, they had finally agreed on three properties.

'I think we should celebrate,' Miss Heathcote said, reaching for the bell pull. 'Would you like tea or something a little stronger, Hetty?'

Hetty's throat was parched and her head was aching after their long discussion, and she was tired. 'A cup of tea would be lovely, but I should be getting home.'

Miss Heathcote frowned. 'You must stay for dinner, Hetty. There is more to discuss.'

'I have to get home. They're expecting me and they'll worry if I'm late.'

'Nonsense, you must have a life of your own. You need to escape from the stranglehold that those people have on you.'

Hetty could see that Miss Heathcote was going to be difficult and she rose to her feet. 'They are my family, Miss Heathcote. I want to go home.'

'You want to leave me to eat alone, yet again. You don't care what happens to me. I am just a convenient source of funds to you.'

Hetty moderated her tone. 'You know that isn't true. We are business partners, but that doesn't mean I have to neglect my family or treat them badly.'

'And yet you treat me badly. I want you to stay for dinner. No, actually I insist that you stay to dinner.' A smart rap on the door halted this anguished tirade and Miss Heathcote took a deep breath. 'Enter.'

The door opened and Minnie hurried into the room, closely followed by Dorrie, who shot an enquiring look at Hetty. 'Yes, we will be leaving shortly,' Hetty said in answer to the unspoken question.

'No!' Miss Heathcote screamed, slamming her hand down on the arm of her chair. 'You will not be leaving shortly; you will be staying for supper. And then we will talk about your moving into this house. I cannot have you living in that slum or keep sending the Victoria for you every day. It is quite ridiculous.'

Minnie gave a nervous cough. 'You wanted something, ma'am.'

'Yes. Tell Cook there will be two of us for supper this evening.'

'No, Minnie,' Hetty said firmly. 'I am afraid that I cannot stay. Please send word to the stables for Peters to bring the Victoria round to the front entrance.'

'What?' Miss Heathcote shrieked. 'Are you giving orders to my staff in my house? How dare you?'

Hetty packed the papers away into a folder and she stood her ground. 'I beg your pardon, ma'am, but if you will not listen to me, then I must speak out.'

'Supper for two in the dining room, Minnie.' Miss Heathcote dismissed her with an imperious wave of her hand and Minnie fled from the room.

Dorrie was left standing in the doorway, staring open-mouthed at Miss Heathcote, who had half risen from her chair and was visibly shaking with rage. 'You will do as I tell you, Hetty. Send the girl away and sit down.'

'Miss Heathcote, I will not,' Hetty replied, forcing herself to appear calm although she felt far from comfortable. She could see that Miss Heathcote was working herself up into one of her tantrums, but she was not going to give in. 'Calm yourself, please, ma'am. You will only make yourself ill.'

'You will do as I say. Everyone does as I say or I will make myself sick. I will be obeyed.' Miss Heathcote opened her mouth and began to scream.

Dorrie ran the length of the room, and before Hetty could stop her she slapped Miss Heathcote hard across the cheek. Hetty gasped in horror as Miss Heathcote swayed on her feet and fell back against the cushions clutching her face. Her eyes were wide and staring and her mouth open as if she was still screaming, but no sound came from her throat.

Unrepentant, Dorrie took her by the shoulders and gave her a good shake. 'What sort of behaviour is that for a grown woman? I wouldn't let me little brothers act up like that and you're a grown woman who ought to know better.'

Hetty rushed forward to lay a restraining hand on Dorrie's shoulder. 'That's enough. Let her be.'

Dorrie stepped away from the chair, shaking her head. 'She's all right. She just needed to be brought to her senses. I'll get her a drop of brandy, that'll put the colour back in her cheeks.' She hurried across the room to select a decanter from a side table, and she poured a measure into a cut-crystal glass.

Hetty knelt down in front of Miss Heathcote, more alarmed by her silence than by her hysterical outburst. She clasped her cold, claw-like hands and chafed them. 'Miss Heathcote, are you all right? Please say something. Dorrie didn't mean to strike you. She's just a child.'

Miss Heathcote's eyes slowly focused on Hetty's face. 'She hit me.'

'Yes, and it was wrong of her.'

'Leave me alone,' Miss Heathcote said, pulling her hands away from Hetty's grasp.

'Girl, Dorrie, whatever your name is. Come here.'

Dorrie approached her holding out the glass. 'Brandy. Take a sip; it'll make you feel better.'

Hetty was about to snatch the glass from Dorrie, but Miss Heathcote's hand shot out and she seized it, took a large mouthful and swallowed the brandy with a sigh. 'Quite right. I needed that for shock. I could have you arrested for common assault, my girl.'

'I had to do it,' Dorrie said calmly. 'You would have suffered a spasm if I hadn't slapped you round the chops. I'm sorry, miss, but you can't say it didn't work.'

Hetty held her breath. She was certain that Miss Heathcote would call a constable and have Dorrie arrested, but to her considerable surprise Miss Heathcote's face crumpled into a grimace and she cackled with laughter. 'Oh, you little witch. You're quite right, of course, but no one has ever dared to strike me before. The only person who has stood up to me is Hetty, and now you.' Tears were running down her hollow cheeks and Hetty took the empty glass from her hands and thrust it at Dorrie.

'Best get her another drop to calm her nerves.'

Dorrie shook her head. 'No, miss. I seen the effects of strong liquor on me dad before he took sick and died. A little drop of brandy is like medicine, a lot of brandy is like poison. That's what he done – poisoned hisself with strong drink and dropped dead. We don't want the same thing to happen to her, now do we?'

'I think I can take another small measure,' Miss Heathcote said, wiping her eyes on a lace handkerchief. 'Get me another drink and then sit down, child. I want to hear about your father. Perhaps we have more in common than I thought possible.'

'No, miss,' Dorrie said firmly. 'Another time maybe, but we got to get home. There's always tomorrow.'

'Yes,' Miss Heathcote said slowly. 'There's always tomorrow. I want you to consider removing to this address, Hetty. The child can come too. I find her interesting.'

Hetty was not about to argue and cause another emotional outburst. She attempted a smile. 'We'll talk about it tomorrow, Miss Heathcote. But now I think you ought to rest. You've worked hard today and so have I.'

'Yes, we have worked hard, but tomorrow we will work even harder. You will visit warehouses in order to select the fixtures and fittings for the new premises, and we will have to find wholesalers and suppliers of fresh produce for the coffee shops. You won't have time to worry about that family of yours, Hetty.'

Miss Heathcote's words proved to be prophetic. In the weeks that followed, Hetty and Dorrie were kept fully occupied with the business of setting up the coffee shops. They became a familiar sight driving round the streets of East London in the Victoria with Peters standing guard over them when they did business in the warehouses around the docks. Hetty still kept an eye on the premises in Artillery Lane and often had to sort out the bitter quarrels that sprang up between Jane and Marie, as they seemed to disagree about everything and both wanted to be in charge. In the end Hetty had to ask Tom to intervene but he declined, saying that he would rather be flung into a lion's den than face two angry women, particularly if one of them was his intended and the other his elder sister. In the end it was Granny who came up with the solution, and Hetty put Marie in charge of the newly opened coffee shop in London Wall. The business in Artillery Lane was making enough profit for them to hire a girl from the Foundling Hospital, who was well trained in matters domestic, to look after Natalia, which left Sally free to help Jane. Hetty was beginning to realise that handling staff was going to be one of the most challenging aspects of her new venture.

In May, two more coffee shops were ready to open for business, one in Broad Street and the other in Fenchurch Street. The shop in London Wall was already doing a brisk trade and Miss Heathcote was so delighted with their progress that she instructed Hetty to find three more suitable premises. By now Hetty had established a good working relationship with the managers of the various furniture and fabric warehouses, and as each coffee shop was fitted out in exactly the same style all she had to do was to put in a repeat order. Miss Heathcote's prompt settlement of their invoices made them all the more eager to give good service. Hetty now had a team of artisans who could do the necessary alterations, repairs and decoration in the minimum amount of time. She spent her days going from one coffee shop to the next, inspecting the books, checking on sales and sorting out the inevitable problems with staff. As she became more experienced, she grew more adept in selecting the girls and women who were to work for her, and was able to spot troublemakers at an early stage. This often meant giving them their marching orders but she always tried to be fair, giving them a second chance and only resorting to sacking a person if she did not mend her ways. This was Hetty's least favourite part of the job, but for the most part she enjoyed using her wits to make the company a success, and it seemed that her endeavours were paying off when, at the end of the first six months' trading, Miss Heathcote announced that they had made a healthy profit.

Although Hetty had resisted Miss Heathcote's suggestion that she and Dorrie should move into the house in Berkeley Square, she had allowed herself to be persuaded to set up an office in the ground-floor room that Miss Heathcote's late father had used as a study. It was relatively small compared with the rest of the reception rooms, but it was cosy and the walls were lined with shelves crammed with books on every subject imaginable. Hetty had no time to read anything other than business letters and account books, but she liked the cosy feeling of being surrounded by leather-bound volumes. There was a certain musty odour from the bindings and the dusty smell of old paper, which was oddly homely and reminded her a little of the attic room in Princelet Street.

Despite the fact that she was now earning good money, Hetty spent very little on herself and she still slept in the attic room, but now she shared it with Sammy, Eddie, Wilfred and

Stanley. She gave Nora a generous sum for their keep but the rest of her money was safely tucked away in the leather pouch beneath the loose floorboard under her mattress. Hetty's experiences with Clench and Henry Maitland had led her to distrust banks, and it worried her that Miss Heathcote still entrusted much of her business to Maitland. When Hetty had again tried to warn her against him, Miss Heathcote had grown angry and declared that she had known Henry Maitland all her life and that he had always handled her affairs to her complete satisfaction. Hetty was not happy about this but all her efforts to persuade Miss Heathcote to transfer some of their money to another bank fell on deaf ears.

Despite the family's initial misgivings about Hetty's business venture, she had so far proved them to be unfounded. They were all doing well and she took great satisfaction in the knowledge that everyone had enough food to eat and footwear that fitted properly. They had new clothes and did not have to search the local dolly shops for other people's cast-offs. The boys attended school regularly and Tom had given Jane an engagement ring which she flaunted proudly, refusing to take it off even when she was working in the coffee shop. Natalia had celebrated her second birthday in August, and was now a lively and mischievous toddler, who ran into Hetty's arms when she arrived home and covered her face with kisses.

Tom had been promoted to foreman at the gas works and he and Jane planned to get married at Christmas. They were looking round for a rented property not too far from Artillery Lane, even though Nora had assured them that they could have one of her rooms at a nominal rent. Jane wanted her own front door, she said, and her own back yard where she could hang out the washing, especially now that there was another baby on the way, which would be born in early spring. Granny was tight-lipped with disapproval at this announcement, and even though she said very little, she made her feelings perfectly plain. Nice girls did not behave in that way. Hetty took the news in her stride. She was not surprised, nor was she shocked. She had never given herself to a man, but she knew that if Charles had stayed on in London things might have been different. She was not sure whether she would have been strong enough to resist temptation, and Jane's news made her yearn for him even more. His letters were becoming sporadic, and Hetty couldn't help worrying that he might be forgetting her. When he did put pen to paper he still addressed her fondly, but he seemed to be slipping further and further away from her. Sometimes she wondered if she would ever see him again, but she quickly put all such thoughts out of her mind. They were meant for each other, of that she was certain.

She had seen very little of George in the busy months when she was setting up the coffee shops. He still came round to Princelet Street to see the children, and he had given Natalia a beautiful doll for her birthday, from which she refused to be parted. Dolly went everywhere with her and Talia could not sleep unless her favourite toy was tucked up in bed beside her. George had also gone to the enormous expense of buying one of Richter's Anchor Stone building boxes for Sammy's birthday. The composite stone bricks had kept all four boys occupied for hours building castles, houses and forts. Hetty knew that the children loved George dearly and he had become almost a father figure to them, which she thought was ironic since he was most definitely not the marrying kind.

'You spoil them, George,' Hetty said when he turned up unexpectedly one Sunday with a bag of violet creams, boiled sweets and sugared almonds for the children. He gave her one of his unfathomable looks and a wry smile. 'Well, since I will be unlikely to have any children of my own, I might as well spoil these ones who are very close to my heart.'

'If you stopped chasing after everything in a skirt and settled down with one girl, you could have a family of your own,' Hetty said with more acerbity than she had intended. Her mind was on Charles and his failure to reply to her last letter. She shot George a sideways glance beneath her lashes. 'I'm sorry. I didn't mean it to sound like that.'

He laid his hand on his heart and rolled his eyes. 'You know there's only ever been one girl for me, Hetty, and she is standing not a million miles from here.'

Sammy and Eddie curled up with laughter at his antics and Hetty smiled. 'You are such a clown, George. Can you wonder that no one takes you seriously?' She gathered up the ledgers that she had been attempting to study at the kitchen table, and she took them up to her room. She tried to settle down to do the books but she could not concentrate. In the end she abandoned her work and began to pace the floor. What was the use of being successful in business if the man you loved was thousands of miles away? The fear that she had been pushing to the back of her mind was rapidly turning to panic. The long separation from Charles was working its destructive evil – he was forgetting her. If she did nothing then all was lost. Her heart would be broken and all the money in the world would not make things right. If he would not come to her, then she must go to him. It was as simple as that.

# Chapter Nineteen

'What?' Miss Heathcote cried with her eyes almost popping out of her head. 'You want to go to America?'

'Yes, Miss Heathcote. I've worked very hard for you since February and in a few weeks' time it will be Christmas. I want to go now. I must go now.'

'You want to run halfway across the world after a man?' Miss Heathcote's voice rose to a bat squeak. 'You must be out of your mind.'

Hetty acknowledged this barb with an attempt at a smile. 'I think I must be a little crazy, but I have to see him face to face. I must find out if he still feels the same way about me.'

'This is outrageous behaviour. I won't let you go. I need you here.'

'It would only be for a few weeks, Miss Heathcote.'

'A few days would be acceptable, but a few weeks – no, no, no.' Miss Heathcote clasped her hands to her chest. 'My heart is racing. I think I'm having one of my seizures.'

Hetty had witnessed this display too often to be moved. 'You are quite well, ma'am. Breathe slowly and please listen to what I have to say.'

Miss Heathcote glared at Hetty and her face had paled to the colour of parchment. 'Go on.'

Hetty knelt at her feet. 'Miss Heathcote, I love a wonderful man but his father has forced him to take up a position in the family banking business and will not allow Charles to return to England. I must go to him, can't you see that?'

'No,' Miss Heathcote said, scowling. 'No, I cannot.'

'But I love him, ma'am. I have saved every penny I could so that I have my fare to Philadelphia. All I ask is that you grant me leave for a month or two so that I can travel to America and see him.'

Miss Heathcote's mouth worked soundlessly for a moment and when her voice came it was just a whisper. 'You will not go. You cannot abandon me.'

'I am not abandoning you, ma'am. I will return, I promise.'

'You will not. You will marry your lover and he will persuade you to stay in America. I cannot run the business on my own, I simply cannot.'

Hetty took Miss Heathcote's cold hands in

hers and squeezed them gently. 'If you say that then the men have won. You will have proved nothing to them other than that a female cannot manage without a man's help.'

'I will be totally humiliated.'

'No, ma'am, you will not. You will manage magnificently. Dorrie can run errands for you. Peters will take her to the coffee shops and she can collect the books and bring them back to you here. The manageresses are all capable of running the day to day business and no one need know that I am away. If they ask her, Dorrie can tell them that I am occupied elsewhere. You know as much, or even more, than I do about profit and loss, and I assure you that it will be just for a few weeks. I will come back with Charles or without him, but I will return.'

'Do you promise?'

Hetty rose to her feet and made the sign of a cross on her chest. 'Cross my heart and hope to die!'

Miss Heathcote was silent for a moment and then, very slowly, she nodded her head. 'I can see that your mind is made up, and that nothing I can say or do will turn you from your chosen course.'

'I'm afraid not.'

'I know that you would not desert that wretched family of yours. You turned down my offer of accommodation because you would not leave them, and, based on that, I believe you when you say you will return. But if you let me down, Hetty . . .'

'I will not, ma'am. Everything I have worked for is here in London. My family are here and I know that if Charles really loves me he won't make me choose between him and them. He is a fine man, Miss Heathcote. I am sure when you meet him . . .'

'Enough. I will never meet this creature who threatens to take you away from me. Bring him back to London if you will, but don't expect me to have anything to do with him. You know how I feel about men, Hetty. You may go to America but I want you back here in as short a time as possible. Do you understand me?'

'I do, ma'am, and thank you.'

'Don't thank me, you silly girl. He'll break your heart as that wretch broke mine all those years ago. I know exactly how that feels so don't come crying to me when it happens. Now go away and make your arrangements. Send Dorrie to me. I have a headache and she knows how to massage my head to take the pain away.'

Having persuaded Miss Heathcote, Hetty braced herself to break the news at home. As she had expected, Granny was downright angry. 'You can't put your faith in toffs, Hetty,' she said, frowning. 'Especially them as comes from foreign countries. He's back at home now and he'll have other fish to fry.'

Nora nodded her head emphatically. 'Charles was a real charmer but he's been gone a long time, girl. He's back with his own kind now.'

Sammy ran to Hetty and threw his arms around her waist, clinging to her with desperation written all over his small face. 'Don't go away, Hetty. You mustn't leave us. Please don't go.'

That started Eddie off and he too threw himself at his sister, sobbing and begging her not to go away. Wilfred and Stanley also began to cry and that set Natalia off, although Hetty realised that she was too small to understand what exactly was going on and was merely taking her cue from the older children.

'I think you're all being very unfair to Hetty,' Jane cried, hurrying to her side. 'Hasn't she worked her fingers to the bone for us? When our ma died, Hetty became mother and father to the boys and me. She never gave a thought to herself and she suffered cruelly at the hands of old Clench, but she never gave in. She's a proper businesswoman now and we've all benefited from her hard work. I say, if she really loves Charles, she should have the chance to go and find him. I wish I had her nerve, I really do.'

'Well said, love.' The sound of Tom's voice made everyone turn round to look at him as he entered the room.

Jane greeted him with a hug. 'I knew you'd see it my way, Tom dear.'

He lifted her off her feet and kissed her long and hard.

'Oy, you. Put her down. There's nippers present,' Granny said crossly. 'I dunno what young people are coming to these days.'

Nora dug her in the ribs. 'Aw, c'mon, Mattie. You was young once. I'll bet you and your Harold acted just the same.'

'We did not,' Granny retorted hotly. 'At least, not in public.'

Nora gave her great wheezing chuckle and Hetty felt the tension lessen. She smiled re-assuringly at Sammy and Eddie. 'Now listen to me, all of you. I am going to Philadelphia but I won't be there for long and I will be coming home as soon as I can.'

'Will you bring Charles back with you?' Sammy asked, pushing his spectacles a little higher on the bridge of his snub nose.

'I hope so, Sammy, love. I really do.'

A fever seemed to be running through Hetty's blood. Her desire to see Charles again surmounted everything, and she went ahead with her plans with the same single-minded determination that had set her on the road to success in business. She did the rounds of the shipping company offices in the City and eventually managed to get a passage on the *Ohio*, sailing from Liverpool on 7 November for Queenstown and then on to Philadelphia. This was no luxury cruise liner, although there were first class berths, but Hetty could not afford one of these and she settled for steerage. The journey, she was told, would take about two weeks, although in fair weather the voyage could take as little as nine days. Hetty was not optimistic about crossing the Atlantic in the late autumn, but she was not going to be put off by the thought of sea sickness or stormy waters.

Tom and Jane insisted on seeing her off at Euston. Hetty would have preferred to get the tearful goodbyes over at home, but they were adamant that she should not go alone and Hetty had not the heart to disappoint them. She had meant to tell George about her plans, but she kept putting it off. Then there was so much to do and so little time in which to complete the necessary arrangements that somehow it slipped her mind. Miss Heathcote had to be primed as to any problems that might arise in any one of the coffee shops so that she

464

was ready to deal with them, and Dorrie had been given explicit instructions as to what to say when she visited them on her own. Peters, the strong taciturn coachman who protected them both like a snarling bulldog whenever danger threatened, had been told to guard Dorrie as if she were his own child, and Hetty was confident that he would not let her down. All the same, she worried about leaving everyone to cope without her. If her desire to see Charles had not been so great, she might have changed her mind.

'Don't wait,' she said to Jane, who was leaning on Tom's arm and looking rather pale. This pregnancy was not going quite so easily as her first and Hetty knew that she was suffering badly from morning sickness and fatigue.

'I want to see you off,' Jane insisted.

'Are you sure you're all right, ducks?' Tom asked anxiously.

'Yes, silly. It's just the usual. I expect it will pass in a minute.'

'You're doing too much at that shop,' Tom grumbled. 'You should leave more to young Sal. She's a capable girl.'

'Don't nag me, Tom. We ain't married yet.'

'No, but we will be at Christmas.'

Jane clutched Hetty's gloved hands. 'You will be home in time for our wedding, won't you, Hetty?' Her brown eyes were swimming with tears and her lips trembled.

Hetty gave her a hug. 'Of course I will, stupid. Would I miss my own sister's wedding to my best friend?'

'I thought I was your best friend, Hetty.'

She released Jane with a start and spun round to see George standing on the platform behind her. He was smiling, but there was a hint of reserve in his eyes. 'George!'

'That's me. You didn't think I would let you go off to America without saying goodbye, did you?'

'Well, I – I'm sorry I didn't tell you, George.'

Tom linked his hand through Jane's arm. 'Come on, ducks. Let's get you home.'

'But I want to see Hetty off on the train.'

He patted her hand. 'Give George a chance, girl.'

Jane hesitated. 'Hetty?'

'You go home, dear. Tom's right, you should try to get more rest.' Hetty gave her a searching look, and was assailed by feelings of guilt. Perhaps she was expecting too much from her sister. 'When I come back we'll see about getting more help in Artillery Lane. You'll have your hands full when the baby comes, and Natalia needs you too.' Realising that Jane was about to protest, Hetty chuckled. 'Don't give me that stubborn mule look, Jane. I'm not the only member of the Huggins family who is obstinate.'

George put his arm around Hetty's shoulders. 'I'll take care of her, Jane. I'll see her safely on board the ship.'

For the first time Hetty noticed that he was carrying a carpet bag and she shot him a questioning look. 'You're coming to Liverpool with me? That's silly. I can manage perfectly well on my own.'

George grinned at Tom over both sisters' heads. 'Stubborn mules the pair of them, eh, Tom?'

Tom nodded with mock seriousness. 'It'll be a brave man who takes on either of these two.'

Jane slapped his hand but she was smiling and a little colour had returned to her cheeks. 'All right, you win. I'll go home and leave these two to sort things out between them.' She reached out to pat Hetty on the cheek. 'Take good care of yourself, Hetty, and come back soon. I want you to be at my wedding.'

Hetty felt tears well up in her eyes and she swallowed hard. 'I will. With or without Charles, I'll be home for Christmas.'

'Look after her, mate,' Tom said, slapping George on the back. He turned to give Hetty a brotherly hug. 'Bye for now, ducks. Come back soon.'

Hetty smiled through her tears but her reply

was lost in the rumbling, grinding sound of the great steam engine arriving at the platform. Tom and Jane were enveloped in a cloud of steam, and by the time it cleared they had disappeared through the barrier. Hetty was left clutching the bandbox that held her precious new hat; one of Granny's best creations.

George picked up the suitcase which she had packed so carefully with the bare necessities for the journey, and her best gown in which she planned to dazzle Charles. 'Come on then, girl. Let's get on the train and find a couple of seats.'

Without waiting for her reply he strode off along the platform, and Hetty had to run to keep up with him. 'You don't have to do this, George,' she cried breathlessly. 'I'm quite capable of travelling to Liverpool on my own.'

He glanced over his shoulder and smiled. 'I'm sure you are, but I need to get away from London for a couple of days. There's a certain young lady who told her father that I'd popped the question. Outrageous lie, of course, but it might be wise for me to absent myself until he calms down, and, by the time I get back, I daresay she'll have set her sights on some other chap.'

This made Hetty giggle and the tears dried on her cheeks. 'You are such a cynic, George, and a terrible flirt. One day you'll meet your match.'

He put down one of the cases so that he could open the door to one of the third class compartments. 'I met my match some time ago, but she doesn't return my affection.'

Hetty lifted her skirts and put her foot on the step, but she hesitated, turning to give him a straight look. 'I'm going to Philadelphia to find Charles, and, if he'll have me, I'll marry him.'

'I know that, Hetty. He's a bloody fool if he doesn't see what he's got.'

'I don't want us to fall out, but if you're going to try to change my mind . . .'

'I know your mind is made up. Believe me, darling girl, I'm just here for selfish reasons. As I said, you'll be doing me a favour if you allow me to travel as far from London as this train goes.'

Hetty couldn't resist the twinkle in his eyes. 'All right, George. But one word against Charles and I'll never speak to you again.'

'Understood, but I think we'd better get on board. There's a grumpy old man with a flag and a whistle who is giving us dirty looks.'

Although she wouldn't have admitted it for the world, Hetty was secretly pleased that George had decided to accompany her to Liverpool. The train was crowded and after an hour or two the slatted wooden seats seemed to grow even more uncomfortable. Their compartment was filled with cigarette smoke and the smell of pickled onions as the family opposite them ate their lunch, crunching the pickles and munching hunks of bread which they washed down with draughts of ale from brown glass bottles. Small children ran up and down between the rows of seats and infants howled until their mothers put them to the breast. If she had not been saving every penny, Hetty might have paid the extra to go second class, but it was George who made the long and tiring journey bearable by diverting her attention with racy anecdotes or pointing out landmarks of interest as the train sped through the English countryside. He had an easy way with people and soon had their fellow travellers joining in the conversation, even offering to share their beer with him. He declined politely, producing a couple of bottles from a poacher's pocket inside his greatcoat, one of which he handed to the fellow who had by now drunk all his ale and the other he shared with Hetty. Opening his carpet bag, George took out two brown paper packets of sandwiches. 'Here, made fresh this morning by your own sister. The finest ham sandwiches in London, so I say.'

Hetty accepted gratefully. She had not had time for breakfast, and now she was starving. 'You are amazing, George,' she mumbled through a mouthful of sandwich.

He raised the bottle to her in a salute. 'Here's to you making the right choice, Hetty.' He took a swig, wiped the lip of the bottle with a surprisingly clean handkerchief, and passed it to her.

'Don't worry, I will.' She took a sip and pulled a face at the bitter taste. She didn't much like beer but she was thirsty.

It took almost six hours to reach their destination and Hetty had hoped to go straight on board the ship, but there had been some unexplained delay and she was told to come back first thing in the morning. Not for the first time, she was glad that George was with her. It was a rough area, heaving with sailors of all nationalities bent on having a good time, prostitutes, pimps and pickpockets, but he steered her through the crowds and eventually found them a hotel reasonably near the Huskisson dock. The hotel was cheap and clean, but there were some very shady characters hanging about in the public bar. George booked two rooms for the night and paid the landlord for the use of a private parlour. An overworked and surly maidservant informed them that a fire would cost extra, and they would have to wait for their dinner since she was rushed off her feet. Left to her own devices, Hetty would have accepted this without an argument, but George gave the girl a brilliant smile and encouraged her to talk about herself. He listened sympathetically to her tale of woe, and when she began to cry he patted her on the shoulder and told her that she was a brave girl. A generous tip made her smile and she hurried off to fetch kindling and a full coal scuttle. Hetty watched in silence and it occurred to her then that part of George's undeniable charm lay in his genuine concern for other people. The servant girl could not do enough to make them comfortable; within minutes they had a fire blazing up the chimney, and a jug of hot toddy to keep out the cold. They dined off the best cuts of roast beef from the kitchen together with a dish of freshly cooked vegetables and piping hot gravy, followed by treacle tart in a pool of thick yellow custard.

When they had finished their supper Hetty sat by the fire drinking a cup of coffee and George relaxed in the chair opposite her, smoking a cigar. The fragrant smoke wafted up the chimney and Hetty warmed her toes on the fender. She felt comfortable in his company, with no need to make small talk. She gazed into the fire, watching as the soot on the fireback was set alight, sparking and shifting like a miniature firework display. Jane called them glow fairies but Ma had always said it was people coming out of church.

'A penny for 'em,' George said, puffing a hazy blue stream of cigar smoke into the atmosphere.

Hetty looked up and smiled. 'I'm glad you came with me, George.'

'Are you really?'

'I am. I would have felt very strange staying in a hotel on my own.'

'Oh, well, then we're all happy,' he said lightly. 'I've escaped a possible breach of promise suit and you will have a safe and comfortable night.' He tossed the cigar butt into the fire and rose to his feet. 'I think I'll turn in, Hetty. We've got an early start in the morning.'

It seemed to Hetty that the spell was broken. They were no longer at ease together and she couldn't think what she had said that had altered things so radically. She stood up, smoothing the rumpled folds of her travelling gown. 'Yes, you're right. I am tired.'

He moved to the door and held it open. 'Goodnight, Hetty.'

His tone was oddly formal and he avoided her anxious gaze. Hetty walked past him and she shivered. She felt suddenly cold and very much alone. 'Goodnight, George.'

A chill wind whipped across the water as Hetty and George stood on the quayside early next morning. It was several hours until dawn and the masthead lamps bobbed up and down, sending jagged shards of light reflecting across the dark water. The ship tugged at its moorings as if restless to be on its way across the Atlantic. All around them there was hustle, bustle and noise. The raised voices of the crew and the stevedores competed with the sound of barrels being rolled across cobblestones, the metallic screech of cranes lifting heavy objects, the clank of anchor chains and the throb of the engines purring away below decks. Passengers were arriving both by coach and on foot and their luggage was piled high in readiness to be loaded onto the vessel.

Hetty had to hold on to her bonnet to prevent its being blown off, and she glanced up at George. He had been unusually silent during their hasty breakfast of bread rolls and coffee, and he seemed preoccupied as he stared up at the ship. He turned his head to look at her. 'They're boarding now. Perhaps you ought to go and stake your claim to a berth.'

His tone was offhand and Hetty was unaccountably hurt by his indifference. 'Anyone would think you were trying to get rid of me, George.'

'Sending you off into the arms of another man is not easy. For God's sake, Hetty, just go.'

She stared at him, shocked by his harsh tone. 'George. What's the matter with you?'

He ran his hand through his hair, which was damp with spray and looked almost black in the dim light. 'I can't do this, Hetty. I can't stand on the quayside and wave you off as if you were going away on the grand tour. I thought I could let you go to that fellow because I wanted above all things for you to be happy, but I just can't do it. I'm sorry, girl.' Ramming his bowler hat on his head, he strode off towards the hotel, leaving her standing alone and staring after him.

'George,' she cried. 'Don't go. Don't leave me like this.' She had witnessed all his moods, so she had thought, but she had never seen him so emotionally unbalanced. She had always thought of George as a good-natured clown who breezed through life without thinking or feeling deeply, but in these last hours together she knew that she had caught a glimpse of the man beneath the boyish devil-may-care façade George Cooper presented to the world. Anger roiled in her stomach. How could he be so cruel as to abandon her just when she was embarking on the most important journey of her life? Then, as she watched him disappear into the crowd, anger was replaced by a feeling of desolation and loneliness. Despite the coolness that had entered their relationship recently, she had always known that George was somewhere in the background. She had come to rely on him and had taken his friendship and loyalty for granted. Now she might have lost him forever and the thought sent a shaft of pain through her heart. She loved George like a brother and had always thought that he loved her in the same way. The truth slapped her in the face like the cold wind off the River Mersey. There could only be one cause for a man to act so unreasonably. George was jealous of Charles. If he was jealous, that meant . . .

'Move along, lady. You're blocking the gangway.'

The impatient tone of a man's voice startled Hetty out of her trance-like state. She craned her neck looking for George but he had gone. She bit back tears as she tried to imagine his feelings. It was only now that she realised he had been trying to tell her that he loved her on so many occasions and she had laughed it off, treating it as a joke. How that must have hurt him. She could not bear the thought of giving pain to her true friend. If only she could turn back time she would tell George how important he was to her and how much she cared for him. The last call went out for passengers to board the ship.

Someone jabbed her in the back. 'Are you

deaf, woman? Move on or do I have to carry you?'

Hetty mumbled an apology and hurried up the gangway. Once on deck she entered a scene of complete chaos. Emigrants laden with bedding rolls from which hung cooking utensils and all manner of objects, which were undoubtedly precious to them but looked like tinkers' cheap wares, stumbled about between the freight and baggage piled up on the deck. Children were crying and stewards were shouting instructions. Some of the passengers clung to the railings waving frantic goodbyes to their loved ones on shore and others huddled together looking lost and disorientated.

Clutching her ticket for berth number 34, Hetty followed a group of people who had been directed towards steerage. The scene below decks was even more confusing and disorderly than it had been above them. Passengers pushed and shoved their way along narrow, dimly lit passages and made their way down steep flights of stairs to the airless region above the hold. There was very little space in between the tiers of wooden bunks and the air was thick with fumes from oil lamps. Hetty was carried along on a wave of bodies until she managed to find a harassed steward who told her where to find her berth.

She was in an area reserved for women and girls. Men had separate quarters, as had families with young children. The bunks were three to a tier and Hetty was relieved to find that hers was at the top. She hefted her case onto the bunk, clambering after it with her bandbox clutched in her hand. Occupying the bunk below her was a thin, fraught-looking woman from Birmingham who was travelling with her four daughters. The youngest took the bottom bunk and her three sisters were in the next tier. From listening to their conversation, Hetty gathered that the father and two elder brothers were in the men's section. She watched the mother busying herself unpacking items that they would need for the journey and laying things out neatly in an effort to make their surroundings more homely.

It was only now that Hetty realised that steerage passengers were expected to provide their own bedding, and she had none. She was marooned on her burlap mattress stuffed with straw which crunched every time she moved, and, most depressingly, her lifejacket which apparently doubled as a pillow. It was going to be a cold and uncomfortable crossing for which she was ill prepared. The throbbing of the engines seemed to vibrate through her whole body, and all around her women were shouting at each other in an attempt to make themselves heard above the din. Her head ached and the smell of sweat, unwashed bodies and damp clothing was making her feel sick. Hetty drew her knees up to her chest, wrapping her arms around them and burying her face in the folds of her travelling gown.

Someone was tugging at her skirt and Hetty raised her head to peer down into the face of the older woman. 'Are you all right, lass?' The woman's face was creased with concern and Hetty felt a lump in her throat. This person had her hands more than full with her own family and yet she was showing compassion for a complete stranger. Hetty managed a wobbly smile. 'I – I'm all right, ta. It's just so noisy and I came so ill prepared. I didn't know we had to provide our own bedding.'

'There's nothing to cry about, love. I daresay we can spare you a blanket. Are you travelling on your own?'

Hetty nodded. Suddenly, in the midst of a hundred or more souls, she felt utterly alone. 'I'm going to Philadelphia to join my intended.'

'What's your name?'

'Hetty Huggins.' Hetty held out her hand. 'And you are . . .?'

'Bertha Shakeshaft, and these are my girls – Emily, Doris, Olive and Violet. My hubby, Ernest, is in the men's section with our boys, Ted and Jim. We're heading for a new life in

America.' While she was talking, Bertha was unpacking a blanket which she handed up to Hetty. 'There you are, love. It's a bit thin but it's better than nothing.'

'You're very kind,' Hetty murmured, wiping her eyes on the back of her hand. If Miss Heathcote could see her now she would have one of her seizures. The thought brought a reluctant smile to her face.

'There,' Bertha said with a satisfied grin. 'Things aren't so bad after all.'

'Mam, I'm hungry.' The youngest girl tugged at her mother's sleeve.

'You'll have to wait until I've unpacked all our things, Vi.' Bertha turned to the eldest girl who had bagged the top bunk and was sitting on it, swinging her legs. 'Make yourself useful, Emily. Go and find your dad and see how he's getting on. I'll feel happier when I know where he is and the lads too. Take your sisters with you, and if you see a steward, ask him what time we get our food. We're all bloody starving.' She shooed the girls off, flapping her apron as if they were a flock of geese, and she grinned up at Hetty. 'They're good girls really. This is a big adventure to them, although I can't say it's my idea of fun.'

Hetty nodded in agreement. She couldn't help wondering how she was going to survive for the next twelve or thirteen days. A sudden lurch of the ship almost toppled her off her bunk, and the engines began to roar as they built up enough steam to get the vessel under weigh. For the first time, she doubted the wisdom of her actions. Perhaps she should have stayed in London and waited for Charles to come for her. What if she arrived at his home and found that she was not welcome? Why had she not run after George and begged him to take her home? Dear George, who loved her and had always tried to look after her. She had treated him so badly and she would miss him very much. She lay back on the mattress and closed her eyes. Bertha had said this voyage was not going to be fun – in Hetty's opinion it was going to be sheer hell.

# Chapter Twenty

As if matters were not bad enough in the safe haven of the docks, things did not improve when the *Ohio* reached the choppy waters of the Irish Sea. Within hours half the women were suffering from seasickness and Bertha's girls were no exception. Hetty forgot all about her own discomfort as she held young Violet's head over a bucket while she vomited, and when the spasm passed, she lifted her onto the bottom bunk and bathed her forehead with the brackish water which was supplied for their personal needs. No sooner had Violet drifted into a sleep of sheer exhaustion than Olive began to feel queasy, and Hetty looked after her while Bertha attended to Emily and Doris. All round them girls and women moaned, and those who were not afflicted went up on deck to get some fresh air.

After an uncomfortable and disturbed night when sleep had evaded her, Hetty was glad to slither down from her bunk and take a turn on deck while others slept. It was still dark but there was a hint of light in the east and the huge vessel sliced through the Irish Sea like a hot knife through butter. Hetty breathed in the fresh salty air, and she leaned over the rail to watch the bow waves foaming and creaming on the surface of the inky water. The crew were going about their duties with quiet efficiency, and after a while a few early risers came up on deck to stretch their cramped limbs. A steward hurried past her carrying a can filled with steaming coffee, and as the fragrant aroma reached her nostrils Hetty realised that she was both hungry and thirsty. She went below to breakfast off hot rolls and several cups of strong, sweet coffee.

Later that day the *Ohio* arrived at Queenstown. Hetty had thought the ship was crowded when they left the Huskisson dock, but she was unprepared for the influx of Irish migrants who clambered on board bowed beneath the weight of all their worldly possessions, which were pathetically few. Some of them seemed determinedly cheerful at the prospect of a new life in the Americas, but others were silent and many were in tears as they left the country of their birth, most likely never to see it again. Hetty's heart went out to them and she felt quite ashamed of herself for inwardly bemoaning the discomforts of the voyage. This was just an interim in her life. She had a reason for going to America and was not driven from her home by poverty or lack of hope. She, Hetty Huggins, had known what it was like to face near starvation; she had been homeless and she had suffered at the hands of others, but that was all in the past. She had dragged her family from the gutter and they were never going to suffer in that way again – not while she had a breath left in her body. For her there was more than hope: there was certainty. Charles would greet her with open arms. She imagined the tender scene as she lay in her bunk at night listening to the alternate snores, sobs, moans and occasional bouts of sickness from her fellow travellers. This was a necessary journey, but it had forced her to remember her roots and to realise just how far she had travelled and how much she had achieved in a short space of time.

In the ensuing twelve days the capricious weather tumbled them into storms which lashed the ship, making it pitch and toss so that walking about the decks was virtually impossible. When there was a lull and the sun sparkled off the ultramarine waters Hetty made a concerted effort to be cheerful and to repay Bertha's kindness by taking the two younger girls on deck for some exercise. She listened patiently to the grumbles of sixteen-year-old Emily, who had left a boyfriend behind in Birmingham, and fifteen-year-old

Doris, who had been apprenticed to a dress-maker and whose ambition it was to own a dress shop. But these interludes were short and infrequent. For the most part they were all crammed together in the foul-smelling confines of the lower deck with the constant and deafening roar of the engines, and the slapping, crashing sound of the waves against the hull. These shared experiences made the women draw close together. People who would never normally have spoken to each other on the street suddenly became the best of friends. Occasional squabbles broke out but these were quickly settled and peace restored.

In the stifling heat of closely packed bodies, there were only the most basic facilities for personal hygiene, and the worst part of the trip for Hetty was feeling permanently dirty and dishevelled. Her clothes were grubby and she longed to wash her hair and take a bath. She missed her family and friends more than she would have thought possible, and it was only the thought of being reunited with Charles that kept her from despair in the long, dark nights when sleep eluded her.

The days were equally long and tedious with nothing to look forward to other than meal-times. Their diet now consisted mainly of bread and soup which was thick with vegetables and fairly tasteless. After the first few days, when the weather had calmed and most of the women had found their sea legs, the main topic of conversation had turned to food. They spoke longingly of cow heel, pigs' trotters, jellied brawn and faggots with gravy and mashed potato, of suet pudding thick with treacle and all kinds of cake and buns, but the treat they missed most of all was undoubtedly chocolate. Hetty decided there and then that, on her return to London, chocolate was to feature largely in her coffee shops. There would be chocolate cake, of course, and hot chocolate to drink, but also boxes of chocolates which might be expensive but would make ideal gifts. Gentlemen who were out to impress their lady loves would purchase them without giving a second thought to their cost. Hetty could not wait to share her hopes and dreams with Charles. With him by her side there would be no stopping her.

On the morning of the twelfth day out of Queenstown, the *Ohio* made landfall in America. They had arrived in Philadelphia and Hetty had to say farewell to her newfound friends. There were hugs and tears and promises to keep in touch, although Hetty knew that these would be broken the moment the women set foot on shore to begin a new life. Once the landing formalities had been completed, Hetty stood alone in the middle of the busy port, and for a moment her courage almost deserted her as she realised the enormity of what she had done. She was thousands of miles from home in a strange land, with just an address written on a scrap of paper which she had copied from one of Charles' letters. She glanced over her shoulder at the looming shape and the tall funnels of the *Ohio*, which suddenly seemed like a welcome refuge, and she was tempted to run back on board to the stark familiarity of her berth in steerage. She had to remind herself why she had braved the Atlantic. She had come this far and this was her beloved's home town. Soon it would not seem strange at all; everything would be all right once she was reunited with Charles.

She sought out a man in uniform with brightly polished brass buttons on his navy-blue jacket, and she asked directions to the nearest cabstand. Behind his steel-rimmed spectacles the man's eyes were a warm brown and there was something in his kindly smile that reminded her of George. He tipped his peaked cap and pointed the way out of the docks to the main street where he assured her she would find a cab. Her first encounter with an American had made her feel a little less of a foreigner, and Hetty took heart. She found the cab rank and gave the cabby the address in Washington Square.

As the vehicle tooled along the historic streets, she felt a surge of anticipation and a flutter of nerves. The buildings in this part of the town were not so different from those in the West End of London, but when they arrived in the square with its tree-filled garden and elegant townhouses, Hetty's courage failed her. She glanced down at her travel-stained clothing and she knew that she could not turn up on the Wyndhams' doorstep looking like a drudge and smelling far from fragrant. She swallowed her pride and instructed the cabby to take her to a cheap but respectable hotel that was not too far away from Washington Square. With a flick of his whip he urged his horse into a trot.

The modest hotel was in Walnut Street and Hetty judged it to be in reasonable walking distance of Charles' home. Having booked a room for the night, she followed the porter up several flights of stairs to her room. He placed her bandbox and suitcase on the bed, and he stood looking at her with an expectant expression on his face. Somewhat reluctantly, she took out her purse and gave him a tip. She had changed her English money for American dollars at a bank in London, but she was confused as to the value of the nickels, dimes and cents, and she knew she had over-tipped him when the porter gave her a beaming smile and left the room whistling a merry tune. She put her purse back in her reticule with a sigh. Her money would not last long at this rate; she must be extra prudent when it came to spending.

As the door closed on the porter, Hetty took stock of her new surroundings. The room was square, with a high ceiling and gas mantles on the walls, which were painted a rather sombre shade of cream. The brass bedstead was draped in a patchwork quilt and the tall window, framed with drab green curtains, looked out at rows of back yards and brick walls. Several slightly threadbare rugs were laid at strategic places on top of worn pink linoleum which had definitely seen better days. She glanced in the fly-spotted mirror on the dressing table and was shocked to see a bedraggled, pale-faced young woman staring back at her. The clock on the mantelshelf above the empty grate showed her that it was past midday. If she wanted to seek out Charles she must stop dawdling and get on with the matter in hand.

Hetty unpacked her suitcase, laying out a change of clothes on the bed, and she hung the rest of her garments in the chifforobe, hoping that the creases would drop out. Taking her soap and towel and clean clothes, she went in search of the bathroom and was relieved to find it unoccupied. She put the brass plug in the sarcophagus-like tub and turned on the taps. For the next half an hour she luxuriated in hot water and she washed her hair. One day she would have a house with just such a bathroom as this. There would be no more tin tubs set in front of the fire and filled laboriously with pans of hot water from the kitchen range. Hot and cold running water must be the ultimate luxury. Reluctantly, she got out of the bath to dry herself and dress in her clean clothes. Returning to her room, she towel-dried her hair and knotted it into a chignon at the nape of her neck. She put on her new bonnet and tied the violet-blue ribbons in a bow beneath her chin. She angled her head as she looked at her reflection in the mirror, and she pinched her pale cheeks in order to bring a little colour to them. When she was satisfied that she could do no more to improve on nature, Hetty shrugged on her cape. She picked up her reticule and left the room, locking the door behind her.

In the hotel lobby, the desk clerk took her key and placed it on a hook in front of a pigeonhole. 'Will you be requiring dinner this evening, ma'am?'

Hetty hesitated. 'I – I'm not sure.'

'No matter. Dinner is served prompt at seven; perhaps you could let me know later?'

'Yes, I'll do that. Thank you.' Hetty hurried out of the building and down the steep flight of steps to the pavement. The Wyndhams must invite her to dine with them, mustn't they? Of course they would, she told herself with a determined lift of her chin as she set off along the street in the direction of Washington Square. But once again her courage began to fail her as she approached the house with its elegant red-brick façade and imposing front door beneath a bracketed pediment. With its fluted pilasters, small-paned sash windows and white-painted shutters, the house looked to be even grander than Miss Heathcote's mansion in Mayfair. Hetty stood on the pavement gazing up at the windows, vaguely hoping that she might see Charles looking down at her, but they remained glassily blank and cold. A frisky breeze sent dry leaves tumbling down from the trees in a shower of red and gold, and they crunched beneath her booted feet as she took her first nervous steps towards the front door. She rang the bell and waited. She was finding it difficult to breathe, and her mouth was so dry that she had to lick her lips before she could answer the prim maidservant who opened the door and enquired as to her business. 'I've come to see Mr Charles Wyndham,' Hetty said, hoping that she sounded more confident than she was feeling at this moment.

'Mr Charles is not at home, ma'am.'

Hetty had not expected this. For some reason she had thought that Charles would be in the house waiting for her, almost as if he had known that she would be coming. She swallowed hard. 'Can you tell me when you expect him to return?'

'I cannot say for sure, ma'am.'

'But do you know where I might find him?'

'Why, he'll be at the bank, of course.'

Hetty was not going to be outfaced by a foreign maid and she gave her back look for look. 'Then I will call again later.'

The maid's impassive expression did not waver. 'Who shall I say called, ma'am?'

'You won't,' Hetty said, tossing her head. 'I wish to surprise him.' She turned and walked down the steps, forcing herself to go slowly and not to break into a run. She wrapped her cape more tightly around her shoulders and she crossed the road to the gardens. She found a bench situated in a position where she could sit and watch the house and wait for Charles to return from work. She had no idea of the time, and she ventured to stop and ask an elderly gentleman who was walking a rather large and hairy dog. He took a gold watch from his waistcoat pocket and he peered at the face through the thick lenses of his spectacles. 'It is three o'clock, ma'am.

Good day to you.' He gave her a half-smile and walked on.

Three o'clock. Hetty shivered. The sun had gone behind a solid bank of cloud and the heaps of golden leaves on the grass had turned to bronze. She stood up and began to walk about in an attempt to keep warm. She would have liked to explore a little, but she was afraid to leave the square in case Charles returned home early. When she grew tired of walking, she sat down again on the bench with the view of the Wyndhams' front door, and when that palled she rose to her feet and took another turn around the square. During her tedious vigil, several carriages drew up outside the house, but the fashionably dressed people who alighted and were admitted by the same prim servant were patently just visiting.

By the end of the afternoon Hetty was beginning to despair of seeing Charles. She toyed with the notion of calling at the house again, and this time asking to see his mother, but the thought of facing a stern American matron who might not know of her existence was daunting and Hetty abandoned the idea. She was tired, hungry and emotionally drained after her long wait. She had almost decided to give up for the day and return to the hotel, when a carriage pulled up outside the house and the liveried groom leapt down to open the door. Hetty rose to her feet. Her hand flew to her throat as a gentleman alighted from the coach, but although he was tall and fair-haired, she could see that he was a much older man. The likeness to Charles was striking and she could only assume that this must be his father. She hesitated, taking a step towards the road and then stopping. It would be no easier to introduce herself to him than it would have been to his wife. A sudden gust of wind whirled the leaves into bright eddies around her feet and for a brief moment the setting sun showed itself from behind a bank of cumulus.

Just as Hetty was about to leave the square, she heard the sound of a horse's hooves approaching at a brisk trot. She glanced up and saw Charles driving himself in a smart gig with yellow wheels. He was hatless, and the dying rays of the sun turned his fair hair into a golden halo. He looked, she thought, like a Roman emperor driving his chariot to the Colosseum. She had remembered him as being very good-looking, but dressed in his impeccably tailored suit he was even more handsome. He brought the spirited animal to a halt in front of his house, and, as if from nowhere, a groom appeared to take the reins. Charles leapt down from the driver's seat and was about to mount the steps when Hetty called out to him. She picked up her skirts and raced across the road. 'Charles. Oh, Charles. I had almost given up hope of seeing you today.'

He seemed to freeze, turning his head very slowly to stare at her with an incredulous expression. 'Hetty? Hetty, is it really you?'

She flung herself into his arms, laughing and crying at the same time. 'It is me. I am here, Charles. I am here.'

'By God, so you are.' He held her at arm's length, staring into her eyes with disbelief. 'But how? Why didn't you let me know you were coming? Hetty, what the heck do you think you're doing here?'

It was not the welcome she had been expecting or the one she had hoped for. In a shattering instant, Hetty's dream of an ecstatic reunion with hugs, tears and kisses, was smashed into a million tiny shards. She felt her lips trembling as she tried to hold back tears of disappointment. 'I – I came to see you, Charles. You haven't written for ages and I came to find out . . .' She broke off, unable to continue beneath his stern gaze.

'You came all this way on your own? What were you thinking of, Hetty?'

'Of you, Charles. I had to know if you still feel the same way about me.'

'Don't cry, honey.' His expression softened and he placed his arm around her shoulders.

'You caught me by surprise. Of course I'm pleased to see you.'

Hetty fished a rather grubby handkerchief from her reticule and blew her nose. 'You don't look very happy.'

He glanced up at the house as if expecting to see a row of faces peering out of the windows. 'Where are you staying, Hetty? I mean, I assume you have booked into a hotel.'

'O'Malley's Hotel in Walnut Street. I didn't want to impose on your family, Charles. At least, not until you have introduced us.'

'You've changed, Hetty.' Charles gazed at her as if seeing her for the first time. 'You've lost some of that cute cockney accent and you – you just seem different.'

There was a note of awe in his voice and Hetty took heart. She reached up impulsively and brushed his lips with a kiss. 'I've come up in the world, Charles. I wrote to you about Miss Heathcote and the coffee shops. Didn't you read my letters?'

'Of course, honey,' Charles said absently, but his attention had been diverted by an approaching carriage and he took Hetty by the arm, hurrying her back across the street into the gardens.

'Charles, what is going on?' Hetty demanded.

'Sorry, honey, but that carriage belongs to

my cousin Eugenie and she is the nosiest girl this side of the Mason-Dixon Line.'

'Don't you want me to meet your family?'

He stared at her with a perplexed look on his face. 'Sure I do, but there's a time and place for everything.' He took her by the arm and started walking at a brisk pace. 'I'll walk you back to your hotel, dear. We'll have dinner later and then we can talk.'

Hetty jerked her hand free and she stopped dead in the middle of the path. 'If you've changed your mind about us I would rather you told me now, Charles. If I've mistaken your feelings for me, I'll get the next ship home, even if I have to work my passage.'

A reluctant smile chased away his frown. 'Don't be so theatrical, honey. Of course I'm pleased to see you – it was just a shock to find you standing on the sidewalk outside my home.' He slipped her hand through the crook of his arm. 'We'll sort it out later, but I'm afraid I'm in a bit of a hurry now. My mother is entertaining this evening and I will be expected to put in an appearance, but I'll get away as soon as I can and we can talk over dinner.'

There was little that Hetty could say or do other than allow him to escort her back to her hotel, but her heart was heavy and all her instincts were warning her that the signs were not good. It was getting dark now and a chill wind was making her shiver. Light pooled on the paving stones beneath the gas lamps and the leaves that remained on the branches fluttered in the breeze, making a kaleidoscope of patterns on the path in front of them. Walnut Street was congested with horse-drawn vehicles and pedestrians alike. Charles guided her through the crowds and Hetty was quick to notice that people stepped aside to allow them to pass. She stole a sideways glance at him, realising for the first time that here in his native city Charles Wyndham the third was a man of some standing. It was not just his black silk top hat, or the expensive tailored suit, handmade shoes and silk cravat which made him stand out amongst the crowd; Charles had an air of authority and confidence born of good breeding and an expensive education. The carefree, easy-going young fellow she had known in London seemed like another person. When he escorted her up the steps into the hotel lobby and gave her a peck on the cheek, she felt cold fingers of fear clutching at her heart. As she watched him leave she had the uncomfortable feeling that he could not get away fast enough. Hetty collected her key from the desk clerk and climbed the stairs to her room on the third floor with a sinking feeling in her stomach.

For a long time, she sat on the edge of her

bed staring into space. This was not how it was meant to be. Charles had been almost like a stranger to her. Had she been imagining their mutual passion all this time? If his feelings had changed, hers had not. The pain in her heart was real and she wrapped her arms around her middle, rocking to and fro in silent agony.

How long she sat like this she could not tell, but when the clock on the mantelshelf struck seven she came to her senses with a start. Charles had not given her a specific time, but she must be ready for him when he called. Tonight would be the most pivotal moment of her life, she knew that very well. They would talk honestly and earnestly over dinner and she would draw the truth out of him even if it hurt. Hetty rose from the bed and went to the washstand where a china pitcher decorated with painted pansies and roses had been left standing in the matching wash basin, ready for her use. The water was cold but refreshing, and she washed her hands and face and dried them on the coarse huckaback towel. Then she stripped off her smart walking dress and changed into her newest and best gown, which Miss Heathcote's own dressmaker had made for her, copying a fashion plate in *The Young Ladies' Journal*. It had taken fifteen yards of silk and five yards of skirt lining, all purchased from Debenham's departmental store at a prohibitive cost, or so Hetty had thought at the time, but if the shimmering gown in a delicate shade of lavender-blue had the desired effect upon Charles, then it would be worth every penny she had spent. It was still sadly creased but she hoped he would not notice.

She dressed herself with care and put her hair up in sleek coils into which she pinned artificial cream roses. She could only catch glimpses of her attire in the small mirror, but as she pulled on her long cream satin evening gloves she had the satisfaction of knowing that she had done her best. She paced the floor, waiting for the bellboy to announce Charles' arrival. The minutes ticked on relentlessly and her stomach rumbled with hunger. She had not eaten since a breakfast of rolls and coffee on the ship that morning. Her appetite had deserted her at midday and she had not thought about food until she realised that she felt quite faint from hunger. When eight o'clock came and there was still no sign of Charles, she began to think that he was not coming. She continued to walk up and down the piece of drugget that lay between the bed and the chifforobe, and her heart was racing. Just when she was about to give up, a rap on the door brought her to a sudden halt. 'Yes, who is it?'

'Bellboy, ma'am. Mr Wyndham presents his

compliments and he is waiting for you in the lobby.'

'Th-thank you,' Hetty murmured, reaching for her cape. 'I'll be down directly.' She waited for a few moments, not wanting to appear too eager, and then she made her way slowly down the three flights of stairs to the lobby.

Charles came towards her, looking resplendent in his white tie and tails. He held an opera hat in his hand and he looked so dashing that it took Hetty's breath away. She recalled the first time she had seen him coming down the stairs at Nora's house in Spitalfields. He had made her breath catch then and it was no different now. She extended her hand and he raised it to his lips, brushing it with a kiss. 'My, Hetty, you look quite breathtaking.'

There was admiration in his eyes and her spirits soared. She felt herself blushing and she lowered her gaze, controlling her voice with difficulty. It was hard to maintain a calm exterior when she wanted to shout for joy, but after his initial cool reception she had no intention of making a fool of herself. 'So you managed to get away from your mother's social evening then, Charles?' she said lightly.

'Of course, honey. I wouldn't miss the opportunity to dine with a beautiful woman.' He proffered his arm and he was smiling, but his flippant words sent a shiver down Hetty's spine. She bit back an angry retort and allowed him to lead her out of the hotel. Above their heads the stars were shining and the moon hung over the city like a silver crescent stuck onto black velvet, but there was a chill in the air as they walked the two blocks to a small Italian restaurant which Charles informed her was one of his favourite places to dine. Hetty couldn't help wondering how many young women he had brought to this place, and her suspicions were intensified by the obsequious manner in which the head waiter treated him. In fact, everyone from the proprietor to the boy who took their coats seemed to know Charles very well indeed. They were shown to a candlelit table set discreetly behind a wrought-iron screen.

Hetty had never tasted Italian food but Charles ordered for both of them. After the waiter had filled their glasses with ruby-red wine, Charles leaned across the table to hold her hand and he was smiling. 'Now, honey, tell me everything that has been going on in old London town since I left.'

It was not the most flattering start to their evening together, nor the most encouraging. Charles listened intently enough, and his smooth fingers caressed her hand while she talked, but his interest seemed to lie mainly in her business exploits and the building of what he laughingly called her 'coffee shop empire'. In between sips of the rich, heady wine and mouthfuls of delicious pasta, Hetty told him about the events that had led up to her meeting with Miss Heathcote and how she had selected the sites for the coffee shops.

'So,' Charles said, refilling her glass with wine. 'You have proved yourself to be clever as well as beautiful, Hetty. I am impressed.'

'It was luck that brought me into contact with Miss Heathcote. It would have taken me years to get this far without her backing.'

'And you say that she is colossally wealthy, and a spinster too?'

Hetty was disturbed by the flash of avarice in his eyes. 'Yes, Charles, and she is likely to remain so. Miss Heathcote hates men.'

'Perhaps she has not met the right one?' Charles leaned back in his seat, eyeing Hetty over the rim of his glass.

She forced her lips into a tight little smile. 'Miss Heathcote was crossed in love and will have nothing to do with men. The poor lady is a hunchback and she is quite old.'

'You paint a most unattractive picture of your benefactor, honey.'

'I am just telling you the truth, and she is only backing me so that she can prove her business capabilities to the men who were put in charge of her affairs by her father. She is a clever woman, Charles, but a sad and lonely one also.'

'And yet you left her to her own devices while you crossed the Atlantic to find me. I call that . . .' Charles hesitated, frowning for a moment, and then he threw back his head and laughed. 'I call that brave, Hetty.' He raised his glass. 'Here's a toast to my courageous Hetty, the woman who risked all for love.'

She did not appreciate the levity in his tone, nor the sentiments that he expressed. He made it sound as though she was chasing after him like a silly, lovelorn girl. She had expected better of him.

'What's the matter, honey?' Charles demanded. 'Cat got your tongue?'

He was drunk, she decided. His eyes were suspiciously bright, his smile slightly crooked and his words a little slurred. She pulled her hand away as he reached out to grasp it. 'I'm tired, Charles. I'd like to go back to my hotel.'

'But the night is still young. I thought we might go dancing.'

'Dancing?' Hetty drained her wine glass and set it down on the table. She rose to her feet. 'I've travelled thousands of miles to see you, and you want to take me dancing like a common street girl? This isn't what I expected of you, Charles. In London you told me that you loved me and wanted me to be your wife.'

Charles stood up a little unsteadily and the jocular expression faded from his eyes. 'Hetty, for the love of God, don't make a scene in public.'

She was past caring. She was exhausted both mentally and physically and she was desperate to know his true feelings for her. 'I am not making a scene, but I want to know – I must know what your intentions are towards me. If you don't love me any more just say so, Charles, and I'll leave on the next ship bound for England.'

# Chapter Twenty-One

Charles signalled to the waiter. 'I'll have the check now.'

'I'm waiting,' Hetty said impatiently. 'I must know how I stand.'

He came swiftly round the table, placing his hand beneath her arm and guiding her towards the street door. 'Not here, Hetty.' He turned to the waiter who had reappeared with the bill, and Charles produced a handful of coins which he dropped onto the silver tray.

The proprietor advanced on them with an anxious look on his face. 'I trust that everything was satisfactory, Mr Wyndham.'

'Perfectly, thank you,' Charles said, snatching his cloak and top hat from the boy who was hovering tactfully in the background.

Hetty smiled her thanks as the proprietor stepped forward to assist her into her cape, but Charles barely waited for her to fasten it before hurrying her out of the restaurant. 'That was uncalled for,' he said between clenched teeth. 'You made a show of yourself in there, Hetty.'

'No, I won't have that. You're drunk and if anyone made a fool of themselves it was you, Charles.' She marched off in the direction of the hotel, too angry and hurt to continue the conversation. Commonsense was telling her that his actions were not those of a man deeply in love, but part of her still desperately wanted to believe in him. She could hear his footsteps growing closer, and she began to run.

'Hetty, stop.'

Ignoring him, she dodged in and out between couples strolling arm in arm, and narrowly missed being run down by a man on horseback as she raced across a side street. Charles caught up with her just as she reached the hotel steps. 'Honey, I'm sorry. You've got it all wrong. Just listen to me for a moment.'

Hetty paused with her foot on the bottom step and her hand clutching the railing. 'I don't think so. It was my mistake in thinking that you were sincere when you said you loved me. I can see now that it was all a game to you, Charles.'

'No, indeed it was not. I mean, it is not a game. I do care for you very deeply, Hetty. It's . . . it's just . . . look, can we go inside? I can't explain out here on the sidewalk. Someone might see us together and it would get back to my father.'

'And that would be a disaster, I suppose?'

'You don't understand my circumstances.'

'No, obviously not, but I'm tired and you're drunk. I think you'd better go home.'

'For the love of God, Hetty, let me come to your room and I'll explain everything.'

'That wouldn't be the done thing even in Spitalfields, Charles,' Hetty said, shaking her head. 'Go home. If you want to see me tomorrow, you know where to find me.'

He caught her by the hand as she was about to mount the steps, and taking off his top hat he clutched it to his chest with a slightly tipsy but genuinely apologetic smile. 'No, I can't leave you like this. We will speak further, but you're right, I am not in a fit state to talk sensibly. If you will do me the honour of calling on me at home tomorrow morning I will explain everything.'

Hetty looked down at his slim, pale fingers as they curled around her own small hand, and her heart beat just a little faster as she saw a glimmer of hope. Perhaps he had acted this way because she had caught him by surprise? Maybe he still harboured tender feelings for her? Why else would he invite her to visit his home? She gazed into his troubled eyes and she nodded her head. 'All right, I will.'

Once again, he raised her hand to his lips. 'Tomorrow morning then, at ten o'clock.'

'I'll be there. Goodnight, Charles.' Hetty

turned away from him to walk slowly up the steps. She did not look back as she entered the hotel lobby.

In spite of everything, she slept well that night and in the morning she was up early and was first down to breakfast. The waitress was frankly curious and obviously fascinated by Hetty's English accent, and every time she passed the table she stopped to refill her cup with coffee or to enquire if Hetty wanted more toast or butter. Gradually the dining room filled up with people, most of them businessmen, but there were a few couples who cast curious glances at a young woman sitting on her own. Hetty finished her meal and was glad to escape to the privacy of her room, where she waited until it was time to leave for Washington Square. She was both nervous and excited, but at the back of her mind there was the nagging suspicion that Charles had not been entirely honest with her. He seemed so different now from the carefree, fun-loving young man who had stolen her heart in London. She took his ring from the ribbon that she always wore around her neck, and she slipped it on her engagement finger. It was much too large, but she hoped it would soon be replaced by something more suitable.

She dressed with care in a grey watered-silk morning gown trimmed with black braid, which was the only other garment that she had been able to fit into her suitcase. Lastly, she opened the bandbox and took her new hat from its cocoon of tissue paper. Granny had spent many hours making it especially for her and it was a truly delightful confection. Fashioned from fine straw, iridescent feathers, satin bows and tulle, it perched on her head creating just the fashionable effect that Hetty desired. A quick glance in the mirror above the mantelshelf boosted her confidence. She was out to impress the women in Charles' family, and to win back his love for her, if indeed it had waned during their long separation. At a quarter to ten, she set off with high hopes, pulses racing and the sensation of a million butterflies fluttering about in her stomach.

A pale butter-yellow sun shone through the partially denuded branches of the trees in the gardens of Washington Square. Uniformed nannies pushed their small charges in perambulators. Well-dressed women walked pampered canines, with their maidservants in attendance ready to take the leash if their mistresses became fatigued by so much effort. Hetty braced her shoulders, took a deep breath and crossed the street to mount the steps of the Wyndham mansion with a show of confidence that she was far from feeling.

This time the maidservant admitted her to the entrance hall without any argument, and Hetty, although she was used to the grandeur of Miss Heathcote's Mayfair mansion, could not help but be impressed by the splendour and understated elegance of the Wyndhams' residence. A cantilevered staircase carpeted with an oriental runner rose majestically from the highly polished parquetry floor. The walls were hand-painted with a delicate tracery of foliage, and huge urns were filled with hothouse lilies and orange blossom emitting an almost overpowering fragrance. Hetty was vaguely aware of the ornate plaster cornices and corbels above her head, but her heart was hammering against her ribcage and her palms were damp. She felt quite breathless, and she wished that she had not laced her stays quite so tightly, even if they did reduce her already small waist to a hand's span.

She followed the maid through double doors into a parlour that was the size of Miss Heathcote's drawing room but much brighter. Daylight spilled in through four floor-to-ceiling sash windows, illuminating the panels of Chinese Garden wallpaper, where exotic birds with colourful plumage perched on stylised branches entwined with flowers. Crystal and gilt chandeliers hung from the ceiling, their facets glinting in the sunlight and reflecting in coloured prisms on the ceiling. The Empire-style chairs and sofas looked too delicate to hold the weight of anyone heavier than a small child. Hetty was dazzled, slightly overawed and more than relieved to see Charles standing with his back to the Adam-style fireplace where a welcoming blaze roared up the chimney.

He came towards her with his hands held out and a genuine smile of pleasure on his handsome features. Her heart leapt inside her breast and she would have walked straight into his arms, but he took her gloved hands in his, holding her away from him as his gaze travelled from her perky little hat to her high-button boots. 'My dear, you look splendid. You're quite a lady now, Hetty. Indeed you are.'

Her hopes of a passionate embrace were dashed but she revelled in the open admiration of his gaze. 'I am still the same girl you knew in London, Charles.'

He released her hands, shaking his head. 'No, honey, you've changed almost beyond recognition. I fell in love with a slip of a girl who was out to conquer the world. Now I guess you've done that, Hetty.'

'No, you're wrong. I am making my way in business, it's true, and I may have learnt how to dress and how to behave in company, but my feelings are just the same. I still love you, Charles.'

He turned away to stare into the fire, shoving his hands deep in his pockets. 'I guess you do, although I can't see why.' He shot her a brief glance over his shoulder. 'I am not the fellow you think I am, Hetty.'

'But you are, Charles. At least, you are not quite the person I thought you were at first, although you explained all that to me when we went to Hyde Park. Do you remember that day, when you kissed me by the lake and you told me that you loved me and wanted me to be your wife?' She dragged off her gloves, holding up her left hand so that the firelight glinted on his gold signet ring.

'I remember,' Charles murmured, keeping his face averted. 'I should not have said those things to you.'

Hetty's blood seemed to freeze in her veins and her heart missed a beat. 'Are you telling me that it was all lies? Don't you have any feelings for me at all, Charles?'

He turned slowly and his face was a mask of regret. 'My dear girl, of course I meant it then, and I guess I do still love you in my way, but . . .' His voice tailed off and he stared over her shoulder as the door opened. 'Mother!'

Hetty spun round to see a tall, slender middle-aged woman with fair hair and smoky blue eyes that were so similar to those of her son, it was impossible to mistake her for anyone other than Charles' mother. Standing just behind her were two young women, also blonde and blue-eyed, who were staring at Hetty as though she were an exhibit in a freak show. Charles took a step forward, clearing his throat. 'Mother, may I introduce Miss Hester Huggins, from London, England.'

Mrs Wyndham inclined her head, unsmiling. 'How do you do, Miss Huggins?'

Hetty bobbed a curtsey. 'How do you do, ma'am?'

'And these are my sisters.' Charles embraced them both with a vague wave of his hand. 'Cecilia and Isabella.'

The sisters nodded to Hetty but Cecilia's expression was calculating rather than friendly and Isabella's pretty face was alive with curiosity. Hetty felt as though Cecilia was evaluating the cost and style of her outfit and finding it sadly lacking. She nodded to them both, clasping her hands tightly behind her back so that they would not see the gold ring that hung loosely from the third finger of her left hand. Mrs Wyndham glided across the Aubusson carpet to alight on one of the spindly, damask-covered sofas. 'I understand from my son that you are on vacation in Philadelphia. Is it the custom in England for young women to travel abroad without a chaperone? I am afraid we are not so broad-minded or so careless of our daughters' reputations here.'

'Mother,' Charles protested mildly. 'That is not quite fair. Hetty and I became acquainted during my stay in London, and she is now a successful businesswoman in her own right. I believe that English girls are more emancipated than the daughters of Philadelphia society.'

'It would not do for me,' Cecilia said with a prim smile. 'I've never been anywhere without a chaperone.'

'Well, personally speaking, I would love to go out and about on my own,' Isabella said with an impish smile that dimpled her cheeks. 'I think you are most fortunate, Hetty.'

'Thank you, Isabella,' Mrs Wyndham said in a cutting tone. 'I don't think anyone asked your opinion.'

Isabella tossed her blonde ringlets and flounced over to the window seat where she collapsed in a flurry of starched petticoats and frilled tarlatan.

Charles shot his sister a grateful smile. 'I agree with Bella, mother. I think young women ought to be treated more like adults than irresponsible children. I admire Hetty for what she has achieved and for her courage in travelling across the Atlantic on her own.'

'Yes, if you say so, Charles.' Mrs Wyndham turned to Hetty and her expression was one of polite indifference. 'And do you have business here in Philadelphia, Miss Huggins? Is it true that you are in trade?'

Cecilia smothered a snigger and Charles placed his arm around Hetty's shoulders in a protective gesture that went straight to her heart. 'Hetty has built up a chain of coffee shops in London. It is an extraordinary achievement; don't you think so, Mother?'

'Extraordinary,' Mrs Wyndham agreed, but it seemed to Hetty that this was not meant to be a compliment.

'And how long do you propose to stay in Philadelphia?' Cecilia demanded. 'Or do you intend to open up more coffee shops here?'

'No, I do not,' Hetty said, struggling to control her rising temper. What right had these snooty women to cross-examine her and to look down on her? 'I came to Philadelphia because I had unfinished business with Charles.'

'Indeed?' Cecilia said scornfully. 'I can't imagine what that could be, unless you hoped to find yourself a rich husband. I think Eugenie might have something to say about that, don't you, Charles?'

'Hush, Cecilia.' Mrs Wyndham frowned. 'That's enough.'

516

Isabella had been peering out of the window and she turned to them with an irrepressible chuckle. 'Well, now is your chance to find out exactly what Eugenie will say. Your fiancée is just getting out of her carriage as we speak, Charles.'

The shock of her words was so great that for a moment Hetty was stunned into silence. She felt Charles stiffen and his fingers tightened as they grasped her shoulder. She pulled away from him, staring into his face, waiting for his denial or for him to laugh and tell her that it was his sister's idea of a joke. He had paled alarmingly and he avoided her gaze. As if struck by lightning, Hetty knew that Isabella's casually spoken words had been nothing but the truth. 'Charles?' His name was wrenched from her lips in a cry of anguish.

He held out his hand and then let it fall to his side. 'Honey, I was going to tell you . . .'

'Charles, it seems that you have been leading this poor creature on.' Mrs Wyndham rose from her seat, shaking out her silken skirts. 'That is not the sort of behaviour I would expect from a Wyndham.'

'Mother, you don't understand. It wasn't like that,' Charles protested. He turned to Hetty with an imploring look. 'Hetty, honey, you've got to believe me. I meant everything I said to you in London.'

'That would be the first time you ever did,' Cecilia said with a contemptuous snort. 'You always were a liar, Charles. Even as a child you would do or say anything to get your own way.'

Mrs Wyndham raised her hand in an imperious gesture. 'Be silent, Cecilia. It would appear that your brother behaved less than chivalrously when he was away from home, but that is by the by.' She turned to Hetty with a superior smile. 'My dear young woman, I am sorry if my son's behaviour has given you false hopes, but the truth is that there was an understanding between Charles and Eugenie long before he went to London.'

Hetty was stung into retaliation by Mrs Wyndham's patronising manner. 'It cannot have been a serious attachment if he was prepared to spend so long away from her, and people change. I believe that Charles was sincere in his feelings for me. Nothing will convince me otherwise.'

'Eugenie's maid has just rung the doorbell,' Isabella said conversationally. 'This should be interesting.'

'Be quiet, Bella,' Mrs Wyndham snapped. 'If you cannot say anything sensible you should hold your tongue.'

'You had better make up your mind, dear brother,' Cecilia said, slanting a triumphant glance at Hetty. 'Will it be the coffee-shop queen from London, or your beautiful cousin and heiress to a considerable fortune, who will be coming through that door any second now?'

Hetty slipped the ring off her finger and threw it at Charles. 'I won't stay here and be humiliated. I hate you, Charles. You are a . . . a . . .'

'Casanova,' Isabella suggested helpfully. 'A Lothario perhaps? Charles, I didn't know you had it in you.'

'Isabella!' Mrs Wyndham's voice rose to a pitch that made the crystals hanging from the chandeliers tinkle.

'I'm going,' Hetty cried angrily, but before she could get to the door it was flung open, and a young woman rushed into the room.

'Aunt Elvira, I had to come right over and tell you the silliest piece of gossip that I've ever heard.' She came to a halt as she almost collided with Hetty and the laughter died from her eyes. 'Oh, I'm sorry; I didn't know you were entertaining.'

'Get yourself out of this one, Charles,' Cecilia sneered.

Isabella leapt up from the window seat and hurried over to take Hetty by the hand. 'Hetty, may I introduce our second cousin Eugenie Inman. Eugenie, this is one of Charles' friends,

Miss Hetty Huggins, who has come all the way from England to visit.'

'Miss Huggins was just leaving,' Mrs Wyndham said with a meaningful glance in Hetty's direction. 'Charles, will you be kind enough to show her out.'

Flushed and looking for all the world as if he wanted the floor to open up and swallow him, Charles laid his hand on Hetty's arm.

'Thank you, I can see myself out.' She broke away from him as hurt, anger and despair roiled in her stomach. She didn't know whether she wanted to scratch Eugenie's beautiful brown eyes out or to slap Charles' handsome face. Admittedly he was looking ashamed and close to tears, but that did not excuse his execrable behaviour. She met Eugenie's innocent, confused gaze and Hetty knew that she held this young woman's heart in her own hands – she could break it or she could walk away and leave that privilege to Charles. She saw him now for what he undoubtedly was, a selfish, spoilt mother's boy and a would-be philanderer. There was so much she could say, so many bitter words on the tip of her tongue. She could feel the tension in the room. Cecilia had a smug smile on her face; Isabella was patently anxious and Charles looked as though he was about to be sick. Hetty shrugged her shoulders and walked out of the room. As she left the house in Washington Square, she knew that she was walking out of Charles Wyndham the third's life forever.

The time between leaving the Wyndhams' mansion and her arrival back in her hotel room was always to be a blank to Hetty. She was in a daze; totally numb. For a long time she lay on her bed, staring up at the ceiling. When she closed her eyes she saw the Wyndhams' faces and she could hear Cecilia's scornful words, coupled with those of her mother. Together they had done their best to make her feel like a common adventuress, and Charles had done little to defend her. Hetty's emotions were ragged as she attempted to come to terms with the way in which he had toyed with her affections. If only he had been honest with her. If he had confessed, even by letter, she would not have lived on false hopes for so many long months; she would not have crossed the Atlantic to find him, nor would she have exposed herself to the humiliating scene in Washington Square. Even in her more lucid moments, she could not think why he had invited her to his home when he must have known that the truth would out. Or perhaps that was the reason in itself. He must have realised that his mother and sisters would expose his duplicity. He was obviously too much of a coward to admit that he was engaged to someone else, and that they had an understanding even while he was making protestations of love to her and had gone so far as to make an offer of marriage. What a fool he must have thought her. What a simple, trusting little idiot she had been, taken in by a handsome face and sweet words.

It was growing dark by the time Hetty roused herself from her stupor. She sat up and swung her legs over the side of the bed. The sudden movement made her feel dizzy and she had to take a moment before she could stand and go to the washbowl to splash cool water on her hot cheeks. As she dried her hands and face on the towel, she knew that her dream of a life with Charles was irrevocably over. She must return home as quickly as possible. She chided herself silently for wasting so much time lying around when she ought to have gone straight to the shipping office and booked her passage to England. Perhaps it was not too late now? A quick look at the clock told her that it was half past four in the afternoon. If she hurried she could get to the docks before the office closed. Her hands were shaking as she put on her bonnet and cape, but she was desperate to get as far away as possible from Charles and all that he stood for.

She made her way downstairs to the lobby

and handed her key to the desk clerk. She was about to walk away when he called her back. 'Excuse me, ma'am. Someone left this for you just minutes ago.' With an ingratiating smile, he handed her a white vellum envelope.

'Thank you.' Hetty took the envelope, instantly recognising Charles' copperplate handwriting. Her first instinct was to tear it into shreds and toss it into a wastepaper basket, but curiosity got the better of her. She went straight to the hotel lounge where she could open the letter without fear of the desk clerk peering over her shoulder. It had been delivered by hand, and perhaps that explained the clerk's changed attitude towards her. Not that Charles would have dared to come himself; he had probably sent one of the servants, but in a modest hotel such as this, Hetty guessed that this would have been enough to arouse the curiosity of the staff. The parlour was empty apart from an elderly couple who were poring over a street map and took little notice of her. Hetty went to sit beneath one of the gas mantles and her pulses raced as she tore open the envelope. Perhaps Charles had written to apologise?

However, it was not a letter that fell out onto her lap, but a first class ticket for the return trip to Liverpool on the same ship that had brought her to Philadelphia just a couple of days previously. There was no accompanying note, and Hetty held the ticket between her fingers, staring at it incredulously. She was tempted to send it straight back to Charles, but she must be practical. She had very little money left, just enough to settle the hotel bill and to pay for a cab to the docks and her train fare from Liverpool to London. She realised now just what a risk she had taken by purchasing a single ticket on the assumption that Charles would be overjoyed to see her again. She had been convinced that his family would take her to their bosom, and that she would return to England officially engaged, or even married. It had simply not occurred to her that things would turn out this way. She had come to the painful conclusion that allowing her heart to rule her head was a serious mistake.

On reading the small print, Hetty saw that the ship was due to sail at midnight. The sooner the better in her opinion – false pride had no place here. If this was Charles' attempt at an apology, she would accept it with good grace. She tucked the ticket into her reticule and rose to her feet. There was no time to lose. She would ask the desk clerk to make up her bill and send the bellboy to her room to collect her case. She could be packed within minutes and ready to leave. She would go home where she belonged and forget all about Charles Wyndham the third.

The first class stateroom exceeded all Hetty's expectations. It was both luxurious and comfortable, and, best of all, she would not have to share it with anyone. She could not quite bring herself to be grateful to Charles for this extravagant gesture, but it did go a little way to ease the pain of his callous deception. She settled down to make the best of this unexpected treat, although her limited wardrobe and single status made it difficult for her to mingle with the type of people who could afford to travel first class. However, her own personal steward brought her meals to the stateroom, and was on call twenty-four hours a day to fulfil her slightest whim. The weather for late November was reasonably good, or so the steward told her, and Hetty took advantage of the fact to go out on deck as much as possible. The turbulent blue-green waters of the Atlantic and the vast vistas of ocean and sky acted as a balm to her troubled soul. Walking alone on the deck and breathing in the cold, salty air brought colour to her cheeks and a sense of calm. She was determined to put the past behind her and concentrate on the future. Perhaps Miss Heathcote had been right about all men being deceivers and cheats?

On the fifth day out, Hetty was on deck taking the air. Resting her arms on the taffrail she watched the ship's wake as it roiled and foamed, sending up a mist of spray and eventually fanning out as it vanished into the horizon. She was impatient to reach home now. She had missed her family more than she had thought possible, and she wondered how Miss Heathcote was coping with the day-to-day problems that cropped up in running the coffee shops. She thought almost constantly of George, and their bitter parting on the docks. She had taken him so much for granted and ignored his warnings about Charles. What a fool she had been, and how she must have hurt him when she brushed aside his attempts to tell her that he loved her. One of the first things she would do on her return to London would be to seek him out and apologise for the way in which she had treated him. She tried to comfort herself with the thought that he would probably have found a new lady-love by now. One day he would meet the right girl and he would get married and have a family of his own. The thought was oddly disturbing and Hetty shivered. She turned her back on the turbulent waves and walked briskly back to her stateroom.

That evening Hetty could not face the thought of yet another supper eaten in lonely splendour, and she changed into the gown she had worn on the fateful evening when Charles took her out to dinner. She did her hair in the same style, but this time she plucked fresh white camellias from the basket of flowers that had been waiting for her when she arrived in her cabin. There had been no note with the fragrant blooms, but she suspected that these also were a peace offering from Charles, or just another way in which to salve his guilty conscience. She took one last look in the mirror, and, satisfied that she could do no more to improve her appearance, she left the safe haven of her stateroom.

A steward met her at the entrance of the first class dining room and he led her to a table close to the orchestra, which was playing a Viennese waltz. The gentlemen present stood as she took her seat and she smiled, inclining her head with a confidence that she did not feel. She was very aware of covert glances from some of the older matrons at the table, although without exception her fellow diners greeted her politely and then resumed their conversations. The temptation to get up and hurry back to her cabin was almost over-powering, but just when Hetty thought she could bear it no longer, the empty seat next to her was claimed by a gentleman who was also apparently on his own.

He turned to her with a charming smile. 'As there is no one to introduce us formally, ma'am, may I be bold enough to ignore convention and introduce myself?'

Hetty was taken aback but also flattered. 'I don't see why not, sir.'

'Maynard Kingsley. I am returning from a business trip to Philadelphia and I live in London.'

'Hetty Huggins. I am a Londoner too.' Hetty found herself returning his smile and her initial shyness evaporated beneath his admiring gaze. He was, she judged, probably in his mid-forties and powerfully built, although by no means corpulent. He was not exactly good-looking as his features were somewhat heavy, and his dark hair and eyes gave him a slightly foreign look, but he was undoubtedly the most attractive man at the table.

'I am delighted to make your acquaintance, Miss Huggins. But why have we not met before? We have been out of Philadelphia for five days and this is the first time you have graced our table. Why have you denied us your company for so long?'

Hetty glanced over his shoulder and saw that the snooty matrons were straining their ears in order to listen to their conversation. She lowered her voice. 'I was unwell, Mr Kingsley.'

'Unwell or merely out of sorts, Miss Huggins?' He leaned towards her. 'I have seen you on deck, staring out to sea. I was tempted to speak to you, but I did not wish to impose on your obvious wish to be left alone.'

She was saved from replying by the arrival of waiters bearing the soup course and silver baskets filled with hot bread rolls. She took one and broke it into pieces, keeping her eyes averted although she could feel his gaze upon her.

'May I pass you the butter, Miss Huggins?'

This made her look up, and her lips quivered in response to the mischievous gleam in Maynard's dark eyes as he placed the dish on the table in front of her. 'Thank you, Mr Kingsley.'

'Maynard, please. If we are to become better acquainted then I think we are entitled to a degree of informality.'

'Are we?' Hetty could not help but be amused by his boldness and the fact that he did not seem at all bothered by the undisguised disapproval of their fellow diners.

He laid his hand over hers as it rested on the table. 'Oh, yes, my dear Hetty. I have a feeling that you and I are going to become very much better acquainted before we make landfall in Liverpool.'

# Chapter Twenty-Two

At first Hetty had put Maynard Kingsley down as a middle-aged roué, the sort of man who took advantage of vulnerable young women, but she soon discovered that this was not at all the case. Maynard was a charmer, of that there was no doubt, but he was certainly not a philanderer. After dinner, when they took coffee in the ship's lounge, he informed her that he had been happily married for twenty years, and had three daughters whom he loved dearly. He said that he would not have wanted them to find themselves in the difficult situation in which Hetty had been placed at table, and this was why he had flouted the unwritten rules of polite society and effected an introduction. Hetty was still slightly wary, since her dealings with toffs had been limited to her relationship with Charles, and look how that had turned out. At the end of a most enjoyable evening, she allowed Maynard to escort her back to her stateroom, and was reassured by the fact that he left her at the door, wishing her goodnight with an avuncular smile.

The next morning he joined her on the wet and windy deck where she had gone for her customary walk. The sea and sky were painted in shades of grey and a lowering cumulus cloud formation hovered over the horizon. The deck heaved beneath their feet, but Hetty was untroubled by seasickness and Maynard also appeared to be a good sailor. There were only a few intrepid souls who had ventured out to brave the weather, and as the wind increased and the ship pitched and tossed, Maynard offered Hetty his arm.

'You don't have to look after me,' Hetty said, accepting his assistance with a smile. 'I am not helpless, you know.'

'Of course not. From what you told me last night I know that you are a most redoubtable young woman, which is why you interest me so much.'

She held on to his arm as the ship plunged into a trough and then took the crest like a racehorse leaping over the sticks. The spume from a huge wave showered them with foam, and Maynard grasped the handrail in order to save them from sliding helplessly towards the stern. Hetty glanced up and laughed at the sight of his dark hair, eyebrows and moustache glistening with tiny bubbles of foam. 'You look like Father Christmas.'

'I feel more like King Canute,' he replied,

chuckling. 'But the ocean is not going to pay any more attention to me than it did to that poor fellow. I suggest we go into the saloon before we are washed overboard and drowned.'

Hetty's reply was lost in the thunderous sound of the wind, the waves and the ship's engines as they struggled to maintain speed against the gathering storm. They made their way slowly back to the relative calm of the saloon, which was empty of all but the hardiest passengers. Maynard helped Hetty off with her cape and a steward came hurrying up to relieve them of their damp outer garments. 'May I bring you anything, sir?'

Maynard shot an enquiring glance at Hetty. 'What would you like, my dear?'

'Coffee, please. And some of those little pastries with nuts and cherries on top that we had for dessert last evening.'

'Certainly, madam. And for you, sir?'

'The same for me,' Maynard said with an easy smile.

The steward left them, negotiating his way between the chairs and tables with the ease of long practice.

Hetty sat down rather more quickly than she had meant to as the ship yawed, and Maynard took a seat opposite her. He plucked a red silk handkerchief from his pocket and mopped the salt water from his face. 'You are truly remarkable, Hetty. I can imagine my daughters being terrified by the storm, but you seem unperturbed. Does nothing frighten you?'

'I'm not a well-brought-up young lady like your girls, Maynard. I was raised in Bow and I've had to fight for everything I've achieved. I've had to deal with chancers, bullies and downright villains. I'm no hothouse flower.' She met his eyes and she giggled. 'In fact I'd say I was more a dandelion growing up through the cracks in the pavement than a blooming orchid.'

He threw back his head and laughed. 'You are a breath of fresh air, if I may say so, and that young idiot Charles should have his head examined. If I was twenty years younger and had not met my dear Margaret, I wouldn't allow a pearl like you to get away.'

'You're very kind, but I'm afraid that I wasn't good enough for Charles. His mother certainly didn't think I was.'

'Then she was a fool also. America's loss is London's gain, Hetty. I hope that you will be able to put this whole sorry affair behind you.'

'I have already. I'm going home to concentrate on the business. I don't think that marriage is for me. In fact, I'm off men forever.'

Maynard's lips twitched but he said nothing as the steward approached bearing a tray of coffee and pastries, which he set down on the table in front of them. Having poured the steaming liquid into tiny cups with consummate skill, he hurried off to answer the summons of a choleric gentleman who was holding up an empty glass.

'Tell me more about your enterprise,' Maynard said, leaning back in his seat.

'I'm sure it can't be very interesting to a bloke like you.' Hetty bit into a pastry, savouring its sweetness. These would go down well in the City coffee shops, she thought, dabbing her lips with a starched linen napkin. She looked up and realised that he was regarding her thoughtfully. 'I mean what me and Miss Heathcote are doing is going to seem trivial to a bloke like you.'

'On the contrary, my dear. I know of Miss Heathcote by repute only, but I met her father once at a trade exhibition. He was a formidable character and a brilliant businessman. If his daughter has inherited a fraction of his brains she will be a woman to reckon with, and she obviously thinks very highly of you or she would not have put her trust in one so young.'

'I just came along at the right moment. The poor lady was lonely and desperate to have something to occupy her mind.'

'Then tell me about it from the beginning.

I believe you said you started by selling hot potatoes and then graduated to a coffee stall in Spitalfields market. It's a gallant tale. No wonder Miss Heathcote was impressed by you.'

Hetty hesitated for a moment, wary of confiding in a man of Maynard's standing who was old enough to be her father. She could not think why he was interested in such a sordid tale of struggle against the odds, and of treachery from men like Cyrus Clench and Jasper Shipworthy. But Maynard's dark eyes were intent upon her face and he angled his head with an encouraging smile. 'Go on, my dear. I can assure you that there is a purpose behind my apparent nosiness.'

In the encapsulated world of the ship's lounge, with the storm raging around the vessel and tossing it about like a child's toy, Hetty began at first haltingly to describe the horrors of life as a matchgirl, and her subsequent struggle to survive in the tough world of the East End streets. She told him about her mother's painful and tragic death, and how Granny had reluctantly taken them into her home. Hetty talked until her voice was hoarse and her throat sore. She left nothing out. She admitted her mistakes and she was matter-of-fact about her triumphs. Maynard listened in silence until she came to an end, finishing on her painful parting with Charles.

'I'm so sorry, my dear. I know it won't be of much comfort now, but I think you are well rid of that young man.'

'I know, and George warned me about him, but I wouldn't listen.'

'It sounds as though you have a very good friend there,' Maynard said, leaning across the table to pat Hetty's hand.

She nodded, blinking back tears. 'He is the best, but he wants to be more than just a friend.'

Maynard smiled. 'I can't say I blame him, and you obviously care very deeply for him too.'

'I do, but I love Charles. I mean I did love Charles, and look where that got me.' Hetty rose unsteadily to her feet as the ship pitched on its beam ends. 'I won't let that happen to me again, Maynard. I will never allow emotion to cloud my judgement. From now on I am going to concentrate on making my coffee shops a success.' She righted herself by clutching the back of her chair. 'One day I am going to be rich, like you and Miss Heathcote.'

Maynard stood up, swaying slightly on his feet in time with the motion of the vessel. 'Don't forget who you are, Hetty. And don't turn away from those who love you.'

'If by that you are referring to George, then you are sadly mistaken. He might have cared for me once, but I've treated him very badly

and I doubt if he will forgive me this time.'
Without giving Maynard a chance to argue the
point, Hetty made her way back to her stateroom and locked the door.

She was not ill, but her spirit was troubled.
Speaking about her past had brought back
demons to haunt her. She was still racked with
guilt for the way she had treated George since
she became involved with Charles and then
Miss Heathcote. She remembered how he had
joked about being the "and Co." when they
had painted her name on the cart in Granny's
back yard. They were still Huggins and Cooper,
as displayed on the signs above the doors of
seven coffee shops, but it was only now that
Hetty realised just how much she owed him.
He had stood by her throughout and even
though they had quarrelled he had still come
back to help her open the shop in Artillery Lane.
She valued his friendship above all others, and
yet she had sent him away because he had tried
to make her see sense. It was hard to admit
that he had been right all along and that she
had been infatuated with Charles, endowing
him with virtues that he did not possess. He
had toyed with her affections and she doubted
whether he had ever seriously intended to
return to London or to send for her. He was
an idler who was prepared to marry for money,
or maybe he really did love his beautiful and

extremely wealthy cousin. Hetty did not know, but her bright hopes of love and marriage to Charles had been dashed, and now she must face reality.

She sat down at the elegant little escritoire and began to list all the things she must do on her return to London. She did not go down to dinner that evening, choosing to eat alone in her cabin. It was not that she was afraid to face Maynard again, but she needed time to think. She had made a complete fool of herself over Charles and now she must go home and pick up the threads of her old life. It was not going to be easy but the thought of seeing her family again cheered her immensely, and at least she would be back in time for Jane and Tom's wedding. Hetty decided that they would have the biggest and best party that she could afford. She would invite all her old friends from the market – Brush Barber, Joe the butcher, Ginger, Fred, Floppy Flora, and, if he was still speaking to her, George. There was so much she wanted to say to him, and a great many things for which she needed to apologise. If only they could turn the clock back and be as they were when they first met – the best of friends – that would be enough. Wouldn't it?

The storm abated during the night and next morning, after breakfasting in her cabin, Hetty donned her bonnet and cape and went out on deck. The sun shone from a cloudless sky, and apart from a slight swell the sea was calm. Resting her arms on the ship's rail Hetty gazed at the thin purple line where the sea met the sky. In three days' time she would be back on English soil. She would soon be home.

'Are you avoiding me, Hetty?'

Maynard's deep voice startled her out of her reverie. She turned her head and greeted him with a smile. 'No, of course not.'

'But you didn't come down to dinner or to breakfast.'

'I needed time on my own. You made me think long and hard about my life and I am grateful to you for that.'

He stood a little apart from her, staring out to sea. 'And may I ask what conclusion you came to?'

'From now on I'm just going to be myself – plain Hetty Huggins from Bow. And I'm never going to fall in love again. From now on I'm going to concentrate on my business interests. Miss Heathcote and I will show the world of men exactly what two determined women can accomplish.'

He frowned. 'I don't think I said that exactly, my dear.'

'No, maybe not in those words, but that is my decision, Maynard.'

'Well, in that case perhaps you will join me for dinner this evening and we will toast your epiphany in champagne.'

Hetty shot him a suspicious glance. 'What's an epiphany when it's at home?'

'A sudden and great revelation or realisation, Hetty.'

'Well, I dunno about that, but I think I'd rather stay in my cabin, if it's all the same to you.'

'And I thought that you and I were friends. May I ask why you don't want to dine with me?'

Hetty bit her lip. 'If you must know, I can't face those old tabby-cats staring at me all the time I'm eating. For one thing they seem to think that you and I are . . .' She hesitated, aware that she was blushing, and she turned her head away. 'You know what I mean, and anyway I've only got one fashionable gown with me. I don't want them looking down their snooty noses at me. It's as if they knew I'd travelled out steerage.'

'And I thought you were determined to be yourself!' Maynard's serious expression was offset by the twinkle in his eyes. 'It is a very becoming gown, Hetty. Wear it and be damned to them, I say.'

This elicited a reluctant gurgle of laughter from her and Hetty laid her hand on his arm.

'You're right, of course. I would love to dine with you tonight and let them think what they will.'

They dined together that evening and the next. Hetty knew that they were the subject of much speculation and that their every move was followed with great interest, but she did not care. In all likelihood she would never set eyes on any of the toffee-nosed ladies and gentlemen again. Let them think what they may; there was nothing untoward going on between her and Maynard. If those censorious snobs had been party to their conversations, they would have known that Maynard spoke fondly of his family and had told her a little of his history. His father was an Armenian Jew, a trader in cloth who had migrated to London half a century ago to set up business in Whitechapel. Over the ensuing years he had risen from poverty to relative wealth, building up a successful importing company, which Maynard had entered as a boy and had eventually taken over on the death of his father. He now owned several warehouses in Wapping as well as a manufactory turning out good quality gentlemen's clothing. His recent acquisitions were retail outlets in all the major cities in England and Wales, where working men could purchase smart clothing at affordable prices.

Hetty found herself fascinated by his disclosures and she listened avidly. When he saw that he had roused her interest, Maynard went out of his way to pass on the knowledge that he had gained over the years. In the last few days of their voyage, Hetty learned more about business practice than she would have thought possible. Miss Heathcote's ideas were based on theory, but Maynard's knowledge was gained from years of experience in trading. When the ship docked in Liverpool, Hetty was genuinely sad on parting with her new friend. As they prepared to disembark, and regardless of the inquisitive stares of their fellow passengers, she threw her arms around his neck and hugged him. 'I am so glad we met, and so sorry to say goodbye,' she told him tearfully. 'You saved me from wallowing in self-pity and you have restored my will to succeed. I can never thank you enough.'

Maynard held her at arm's length, smiling and gently squeezing her hands. 'No, my dear, I was just the catalyst. You would have come to the same conclusion with or without me.'

'I wish you'd stop using those big words,' Hetty said, torn between tears and laughter. 'But I will miss our chats, Maynard.'

He released her hands to take a small shagreen case from his breast pocket. He took out a gilt-edged calling card and gave it to her.

'This is the address of my office in Wapping. If you need help or advice in the future you know where to find me.'

She tucked it safely away in her reticule. 'It's such a pity you have business in Liverpool. We could have travelled back to London together. I would have enjoyed that.'

His reply was lost in the general confusion as passengers eager to disembark surged towards the gangway. Maynard took Hetty by the arm and she couldn't help noticing how even the most forceful characters moved aside to let them pass. He insisted on seeing her safely to the railway station, and, ignoring her protests, he purchased a first class ticket for her. 'I wouldn't have my daughters travel anything other than first class and you must humour an old man's whim, my dear.' He summoned a porter to carry Hetty's suitcase and proffered his arm. 'Allow me.'

She smiled as she linked her hand through his arm. 'Your daughters are very lucky to have you for their father. If mine had lived he would have been as kind, but not so blooming rich.'

Maynard's laughter caused heads to turn as people hurried past them on their way to the platforms. Some people smiled and others looked slightly shocked at the sight of a middle-aged man with a young woman who might or might not be his daughter. 'We seem to attract the attention of others wherever we go,' he said, coming to a halt at the barrier. 'But then people are always ready to believe the worst.'

'Let them. I don't care.' Hetty stamped her foot, and meeting his amused gaze she giggled. 'Don't care was made to care, don't care was hung, don't care was put in the pot and boiled till he was done – that's what Granny would say.'

'I would like to meet that lady one day; she sounds a lot like my own formidable grandmother. You and I have more in common than you know, Hetty. Goodbye, my dear.'

The porter cleared his throat. 'Best hurry, ma'am. The London train is due to leave in two minutes.'

'Goodbye, Maynard. Thank you so much for everything.' She tried to smile but unaccountably there were tears in her eyes and her lips trembled. She had only known him for such a brief time, and yet he seemed to have come to represent the father whom she had loved so dearly and lost. A tactful cough from the porter reminded her that the train was about to depart, and she hurried through the barrier without a backward glance.

It was early evening when Hetty arrived back in Princelet Street, and it was raining. The wet cobblestones glistened in the lamplight, and the air was heavy with chimney smoke. People were drifting in and out of the pub on the corner, and every time the door opened a waft of beer and spirit fumes belched into the street. Nothing had changed since Hetty's departure less than a month ago and it seemed as though she had never left Spitalfields. Her time in Philadelphia was rapidly fading from her memory like a bad dream. She paid the cabby and, picking up her case and bandbox, she stood for a moment, looking up at the façade of Nora's house. It might not be as grand as the Wyndhams' mansion in Washington Square, or as elegant as Miss Heathcote's house in Mayfair, but it was her home, and she was glad to be back. She did not have her key and so she knocked on the door. The sharp rat-a-tat echoed throughout the house, followed moments later by the sound of footsteps pitter-pattering on the bare boards. 'Who's there?' Jane's voice was muffled by the thickness of the oak door but it occurred to Hetty that she sounded nervous.

'Jane, it's me.'

The door opened slowly and Jane peered out. She stared at Hetty as if she couldn't believe her eyes, and then she let out a shriek and flinging the door wide open, she threw her arms around her, laughing and crying at the same time. 'Oh, Hetty, thank God you've come.'

Stunned by this unexpectedly enthusiastic welcome, Hetty followed Jane down the narrow passage and into the kitchen. 'Granny, Nora, look who's here,' Jane cried. 'It's Hetty, she's come home.'

Granny dropped the ladle she was holding and it fell into the pan causing the liquid to spill over, hissing and bubbling as it hit the hot coals. Nora rose from her seat in the chimney breast and waddled towards Hetty with her arms outstretched. 'You've come back just in time, girl.'

Abandoning their reading primers, Sammy and Eddie leapt up and ran to Hetty with shrieks of delight. Natalia dropped her bread and jam and it fell to the floor. 'Hetty, Hetty,' she cried, struggling to get down from the chair where she was secured by the strings of an apron.

'Well, this is a welcome and a half,' Hetty said, dropping her luggage on the flagstone floor. 'I should go away more often.'

'You won't say that when you hear what's been going on in your absence,' Granny muttered darkly. 'Gallivanting off across the ocean after a man. I never heard of such a thing.' She stood arms akimbo, glaring at Hetty. 'And it looks like you've come home without him. Turned you down, did he?'

Jane hurried to Hetty's side. 'Don't be

unkind, Granny. Hetty's home and that's all that matters. Everything will be all right now.'

'Did you bring us a present?' Eddie demanded, tugging at Hetty's sleeve.

'Be quiet, stupid,' Sammy said crossly. 'You don't ask questions like that. It ain't polite.'

Hetty bent down to give them both a hug. 'I didn't have time to go shopping, boys. But I'll make it up to you, I promise. If you're very good I'll take you to Lowther Arcade and you can choose something extra special.'

'You spoil them,' Granny muttered, turning back to the pan and retrieving the ladle. 'And you didn't answer my question. Where is he, then? That fancy man of yours?'

'Leave her be, Mattie,' Nora wheezed as she bent over to release Natalia from the chair. 'Hetty will tell us in her own time.' She set Natalia down on the floor. 'There you are, ducks. You show your auntie how well you can walk now.'

'Hetty,' Natalia cried, holding out her chubby arms and toddling towards her.

Hetty picked her up and kissed her jammy cheek. 'Hello, poppet. I've really missed you.'

'Put her down,' Jane said impatiently. 'It's time she was in bed anyway, and I've got something to tell you that won't wait.'

'No bed.' Natalia wrapped her arms around Hetty's neck, holding on for dear life and eyeing her mother with such a mutinous expression that Hetty couldn't help smiling. This little scrap of a girl was going to be quite a handful when she grew up, but she was totally adorable. Hetty felt her heart swell with love and happiness to be home with her family. She turned to Jane with a placating smile. 'I'm sure it will keep for another five minutes or so. Let me put her to bed, and then we'll talk.'

'Hurry up then,' Jane said crossly. 'You'll be laughing on the other side of your face when you find out what's been going on.'

Hetty chuckled as Natalia planted a wet and sticky kiss on her cheek. It was good to be home and Jane was probably being over-dramatic as usual. She hitched Natalia onto her hip. 'I'll be as quick as I can and then you can tell me everything, Jane.'

'I will, don't worry,' Jane said with an ominous frown. 'And you boys can go to bed too. You've got school in the morning.'

'Not me,' Sammy protested. 'I ain't a baby.'

'You'll do as you're told,' Granny said, advancing on him with a purposeful step.

'All right, I'm going.' Sammy snatched up an oil lamp and backed towards the door. 'I'll carry the lamp for you, Hetty. Talia don't like the dark.'

Eddie followed Hetty as she carried Natalia

out of the steamy kitchen and he clutched her free hand. 'There might be bogeymen upstairs.'

Hetty smiled down at him. 'There's no such thing, Eddie.'

'Granny says there is,' Eddie countered. 'She says they'll come and get us if we're naughty.'

Hetty gave his fingers a squeeze. 'It's what grown-ups say to children to make them behave. Don't worry about it.'

'I'm glad you've come home,' Eddie said softly. 'I missed you.'

Sammy glanced over his shoulder as he mounted the staircase. 'I bet I missed her more than you did.'

'There's no need to argue about it,' Hetty said, smiling. 'I'm home now and I'm never going away again.'

'Do you promise?' Sammy stopped on the second step, holding the lamp so that he could see Hetty's expression. 'Cross your heart.'

'Yes,' Eddie echoed. 'Cross your heart.'

Hetty rubbed her cheek against Natalia's soft curls and was rewarded by a sleepy smile. 'I promise that I will never leave you again. Cross my heart and hope to die.'

This seemed to satisfy them, and after Hetty had settled Natalia in her cot she stayed upstairs to supervise the boys while they washed their hands and faces, making sure they scrubbed behind their ears and cleaned their teeth. She helped Eddie into his nightshirt, and was amused to find that Sammy was shyly aware of his growing body and spurned her offer of assistance. When they were ready for bed, she tucked them in and kissed them goodnight. She lit a candle and left it burning on the mantelshelf in their room, and then made her way downstairs taking the oil lamp with her. It was comforting to be able to pick up the threads of her old life again, and the simple task of putting the children to bed was reassuring in its normalness. At the foot of the stairs, she paused, listening for sounds of pattering feet or the horseplay that often ensued when the boys went to bed early, but all was quiet. Perhaps Granny's dire warnings of bogeymen still played on their minds, or maybe they were simply tired. She headed for the kitchen to find out exactly what was troubling Jane. It was probably something and nothing; Jane loved to exaggerate.

The table was set for supper and Granny was ladling soup into china bowls. Nora had already taken her place at the table and Jane was cutting slices from a loaf. She looked up as Hetty entered the room. 'You took your time.'

'I haven't seen the nippers for almost a month. I wanted to see them safely tucked up in their beds.'

'Sentimental nonsense,' Granny said, holding out a plate filled with savoury-smelling soup. 'Do something useful and pass this to Nora.'

When they were all served and seated round the table, Hetty looked from one to the other with her eyebrows raised. 'Well? What's been going on? And where are Dorrie and the boys? And why isn't Tom here? You haven't called the wedding off, have you, Jane?'

'No, nothing like that,' Jane said, shaking her head. 'Tom is working nights and Dorrie, Wilfred and Stanley are with Miss Heathcote in Berkeley Square.'

'They are? Why? I don't understand.'

Granny dropped her spoon with a clatter. 'Oh, for Gawd's sake, Jane. Tell her the worst and be done with it.'

Jane's lips trembled and her eyes were magnified by unshed tears. 'Miss Heathcote sent a note to say that Dorrie was to live in the big house, and then her man came to take Wilfred and Stanley because Dorrie wouldn't stay without them.'

'But why?' Hetty demanded. 'Why would she do such a thing?'

'I dunno, but that ain't all. This very morning, Cyrus Clench come to the coffee shop and made me hand over the takings. He said Miss Heathcote was going to put a proper manager in and he took the keys off me and he locked the shop up. I run straight to the market to find George and told him what had happened.'

Hetty stared at Jane in disbelief. 'What did he say?' she asked faintly.

'You know George,' Nora said with a grim smile. 'He said he was going to see the old girl and he took off in a great hurry.'

'And that's the last we saw of him,' Jane murmured tearfully. 'I'm sorry, Hetty. I dunno what's got into the old girl, but I ain't done nothing wrong. Honest.'

# Chapter Twenty-Three

Hetty leapt to her feet. 'Why didn't you tell me all this the minute I walked in the door?'

Jane's face paled alarmingly and she clutched her swollen belly. 'Don't shout at me.'

Nora reached across the table to pat Jane's hand. 'Don't get upset, ducks. It won't do the baby any good.'

'It's no use getting at Jane,' Granny said, frowning. 'You shouldn't have gone off like that and left everything to a daft girl like your sister. If you want to know what's been going on you should go straight to the old cow in Berkeley Square.'

'Don't worry, I will, but first I'm going to see George.' Hetty moved swiftly across the room to retrieve her bonnet and cape. She hesitated in the doorway, torn between guilt and anger. 'I know that I'm to blame for some of this, and you were right, Granny. Charles was just stringing me along. All the time he was sweet-talking me he was secretly engaged to his blooming cousin.' Her voice broke on a sob and she fled from the room.

Outside the rain was coming down in a steady drizzle that showed no signs of letting up. Hetty went in search of a cab but without any success, and she ended up walking all the way to Cottage Green. By the time she reached George's lodgings she was soaked to the skin and close to exhaustion. It had not occurred to her that he might not be at home, but when no one answered her urgent summons she stepped back to peer up at the windows. She knocked again, and this time she was rewarded by the soft padding sound of bare feet on wooden floorboards. The door opened and George stood there, half naked, with a towel wrapped round his waist and water pooling on the floor at his feet. 'Hetty! What the hell are you doing here?'

She had received more enthusiastic welcomes but she didn't care. A bubble of near hysteria rose in her throat and she giggled nervously. 'You're wet, George.'

'You caught me taking a bath.' He stood aside, holding the door open. 'You look like a drowned rat yourself. You'd better come in.'

The giggle turned into laughter and then Hetty found she couldn't stop. Clutching his towel about him, George hooked his arm around her shoulders and led her into the kitchen where a tin tub had been placed strategically in front of the fire. He guided her to a chair and handed her a scrap of towelling. 'So you came back then?'

His icy tone acted like a shower of cold water and the laughter froze on her lips. She took off her bonnet and shook out her wet hair. 'Don't look at me like that, George. I know I don't deserve your friendship and I'm truly sorry if I've treated you badly, but I need your help.'

He stared down at her, unsmiling. 'What sort of man allows his woman to wander the streets on a night like this? Where is he then, your Yankee boyfriend?'

The harsh tone in his voice and the steely glint in his eyes were almost too much for Hetty to bear, and she lowered her gaze. 'He doesn't want me,' she whispered.

'What's that, Hetty? Speak up, I can't hear you.'

She rose slowly to her feet. 'You heard me all right, George. I said he doesn't want me. Charles is engaged to someone else and they had an understanding even before he came to London. Are you happy now?'

'No. Of course not. What do you take me for, Hetty? I didn't want to see you hurt any more than I wanted to see you lose your business.'

'Our business, George. I never forgot that it was both our names over the door.' She hesitated, turning her head away while he stepped into his trousers. 'I've been wrong about so many things, but I never meant to hurt you. I don't expect you to forgive me, but you must care about me a little, or you wouldn't have gone rushing off to see Miss Heathcote.' She shot him a sideways glance but her heart sank as she encountered his hostile gaze.

'Don't use my feelings for you against me.'

'You're not being fair, George.'

'You come here begging for my help, all wet and bedraggled, looking like some damned beautiful mermaid and you call me unfair. Do you really think that you can put everything right by just saying sorry?'

'But I am sorry. I am sorry that I took you for granted and that I didn't listen to you.' She grasped his right hand and held it to her cheek. 'I am sorry that I hurt you, and I am sorry that I . . .' Her voice trailed away and she stared at his bruised and scraped knuckles in horror. 'You're hurt. Have you been fighting?'

His bleak expression was chased away by a reluctant grin. 'Let's just say that I've been teaching someone a well-deserved lesson.'

'Who was it? What have you done?'

'When Jane told me what had happened, I went straight to Berkeley Square. I was going to make the old girl see me whether she liked it or not, but as I reached the house who should come slithering down the front steps but Clench and Shipworthy. I knew then where to set the blame and I challenged the bastards. Shipworthy ran off but I caught Clench and we had a chat.'

Hetty ran her fingers lightly over his injuries and she shook her head. 'It must have been a very rough sort of conversation.'

'He had it coming to him. He was just lucky that I'm a fair sort of bloke, otherwise I'd have killed the sod for what he did to you.'

Hetty was momentarily taken aback by the suppressed violence in his tone. She had only seen him this angry once before, and that was when he had pitched Clench into the canal. She brushed his injured hand with her lips. 'You've always been there when I needed you, George.'

'I only did what any man would do for the woman . . .'

Hetty moved closer to him. 'You do still care about me then?'

'Of course I bloody care for you, Hetty. I loved you right from the start but you had your head turned by that Charles bloke, and then you got in with Miss Heathcote. Almost overnight you changed from my little matchgirl who had set her heart on having her own coffee stall to an ambitious young woman who wanted to mix with the toffs and run a chain of coffee shops.'

'I know what you say is true, but I realise now that I was wrong.' Hetty raised her eyes to his face and saw him clearly for perhaps the first time in her life. It was not the cheerful, easy-going fellow who never took anyone or anything seriously she was seeing now – it was a quite different man. This George was a sensitive, kind-hearted and caring person who had stood by her, comforted and protected her. His mask of insouciance had been stripped away, and she was gazing into the eyes of a man who had been deeply wounded by her uncaring indifference to his feelings. It was not just his angry outburst that had brought about the sea-change in her affections. She had been falling in love with George without even real-ising it, and her passion for Charles had been a mere flight of fancy. Maynard had made her think about who she was and what she really wanted out of life, and the answer was . . . 'George.' His name came out in a whisper as Hetty laid her hands on his bare chest. His skin was slicked with water and she could feel his heart beating almost as fast as hers. She slid her arms around his neck, pulling his head down so that their lips met in a tentative kiss. 'George,' she whispered. 'I don't care about the coffee shops; I don't care about making money. All I want is you.'

For a brief but intoxicating moment, he

returned her embrace with an almost savage passion that robbed her of breath, but he was the first to pull away and his eyes were dark and unfathomable. 'No, Hetty.'

'No? But George, I've just told you that I love you. What more do you want?'

He held her gently by the shoulders and his generous lips contorted with pain. 'If you'd said that a month ago it would have made me the happiest man in the world.'

'But I'm saying it now. I do love you, George. I suppose I always did but I was dazzled by Charles, and then I got carried away with the excitement of working with Miss Heathcote. I never meant to hurt you. Honour bright!'

This drew a reluctant laugh from him. 'You're such a kid.'

'No. Indeed I am not,' Hetty cried angrily. 'Don't you dare laugh at me, George Cooper.'

'I'm not laughing at you, and I do believe you mean what you say now, but I'm not going to take advantage of you when you're in this state. You need time to get over that cheating swine and you need to put things right with Miss Heathcote before you make any big decisions.'

She clapped her hands to her hot cheeks. 'Now I feel quite foolish.'

'No, my darling,' he said, reaching for his shirt. 'You may be headstrong and obstinate sometimes, but you are never foolish.'

'George, I . . .'

He stopped her protest with a kiss and then drew away, clearing his throat. 'I'd best take you home, girl.'

Confused by a whirling eddy of emotions, Hetty was about to tell him that she was quite capable of finding her own way when the sound of the door opening made her turn her head. A small thin woman bustled into the room. She was dressed for outdoors and carried a wicker basket over her arm. She stared from one to the other with disapproval written all over her lined face. 'What's going on here, Mr Cooper?'

'I was just taking a bath, Mrs Haynes,' George said, tucking his shirt tails into his trousers.

'I ain't blind, Mr Cooper. You know my rules about not entertaining females in this house.'

'It's not how it looks,' Hetty said hastily. 'I called unexpectedly.'

Mrs Haynes dropped her basket on the table with an ominous scowl. 'And who are you, may I ask?'

'Now Mrs Haynes, dear,' George said, wrapping his arm around her shoulders. 'There's no need to get yourself in a state. This is my friend Hetty. You've heard me mention her, I'm sure.'

Mrs Haynes wriggled free. 'Mention her? You never talk about anyone else, young man.'

'Hetty had some bad news and she came to me for advice. I was just about to take her home.'

'I suppose that's all right then. I'll let it go this time, George.'

He leaned over to plant a kiss on her lined cheek. 'You're one of the best, my duck.'

'Oh, get on with you,' Mrs Haynes said, giggling like a schoolgirl. 'I suppose you'll be wanting supper when you get back?'

'I'll get something at the pub. You put your feet up and rest.'

Mrs Haynes dug Hetty in the ribs with a throaty chuckle. 'He's a one, ain't he? Quite the charmer. I'm just surprised he hasn't had a string of young women running after him.'

'I thought he had,' Hetty murmured.

'If he has he's never brought them here. Not that I would allow it anyway. This is a respectable house.'

George shrugged on his jacket. 'I won't be long.'

Mrs Haynes grinned, exposing a row of blackened teeth, and then she frowned. 'Bathtub.'

'I'll empty it out as soon as I get back.' He put his hand in his pocket and took out a three-penny bit. 'Here, treat yourself to a meat pie or some jellied eels.'

'You'll hang on to him if you know what's

good for you, girl. God broke the mould when he made George,' Mrs Haynes called after them as they left the room.

'You're very free with your money,' Hetty said once they were outside on the pavement.

'I treat her every once in a while. She's a good sort at heart and her old man led her quite a dance until he died in a drunken brawl.' George pulled up the collar of his jacket and jammed his cap on his head. 'Come on, let's get you home, girl. You need a good night's sleep before you tackle her ladyship in Berkeley Square.'

Hetty slipped her hand through the crook of his arm. 'It can't wait that long. If you will just help me find a cab, I'll go straight there and have it out with her.'

'Is that wise, Hetty?'

'Maybe not, but I'm doing it anyway.'

'Then I'm coming with you.'

'There's no point. She won't see you.'

'I'm coming anyway. Who knows what lies Clench has fed her? I warned him that I would take it very unkindly if he didn't own up, but I don't trust the weasel.'

Hetty knew better than to argue with George when he was in this mood. And he called her stubborn! She squeezed his hand. 'All right, but don't say I didn't warn you.'

As luck would have it, they found a cab that

had just dropped a fare off outside the People's Palace. As she settled herself against the squabs and the cab lurched forward, Hetty uttered a gasp of dismay. 'I've got hardly any money left. I don't think I've got enough to pay the cabby.'

'Then it's lucky I had a good day, isn't it? Don't fret, ducks. I'll see you there and home again.'

'You're a brick,' Hetty said, snuggling up against him. The familiar aroma of the market stall clung to his jacket and she laid her head against his shoulder, safe in the knowledge that she had come home. This was where she truly belonged. George still loved her; in her heart she knew that well enough. All she had to do was convince him that she returned his affection tenfold. His arm was around her waist and their bodies swayed with the rhythm of the cab as it sped over the cobbled streets. There was not much traffic about this late in the evening and the journey took a little over half an hour. When they arrived in Berkeley Square Hetty tried to persuade George to wait in the cab, but he insisted on accompanying her. One of the under footmen opened the door and he would have sent them away, but George stuck his foot over the sill. 'The old girl will see us, mate. You go and tell her that Miss Huggins and Mr Cooper are here.'

Hetty nipped inside smartly before the footman could shut the door. 'Where's Hicks?' she demanded. 'Let me speak to him.'

She must have raised her voice, as it echoed round the marble hall and Hicks emerged from one of the reception rooms looking distinctly put out. 'There's no need to shout, miss.'

Hetty stood her ground. 'Hicks, we must see Miss Heathcote. Please tell her that we are here.'

'I'll tell her, but I don't think she'll see you, miss.' Hicks inclined his head in a polite bow and walked off with a maddeningly slow gait. Hetty paced the floor. She was nervous now and quite dreading a hostile encounter with Miss Heathcote.

George stood by with his hands in his pockets, scowling at the footman. 'Keep calm,' Hetty whispered. 'You won't impress her with strong-arm stuff.'

'I won't start anything, but I'm not letting you face this alone,' George said in a low voice.

'Miss Heathcote says she will see you, miss.'

Hetty turned to see Hicks standing at the top of the staircase and she squeezed George's hand. 'There, I knew she would. I'll soon have this sorted out.'

He made as if to follow her, but Hicks held up his hand. 'No, sir. Just Miss Hetty.'

In the icy splendour of her drawing room,

Miss Heathcote was seated in her chair by the fire with Dorrie standing by her side. Hetty was relieved to see Dorrie looking so well, and she longed to rush over and give her a hug, but there would be time for all that later. She approached Miss Heathcote cautiously. 'Thank you for seeing me,' she began hesitantly.

'Come closer,' Miss Heathcote said in a querulous voice.

Hetty moved nearer, standing with her hands clasped behind her back as if she were a recalcitrant schoolgirl facing an angry head-mistress. 'I would like to know what I'm supposed to have done wrong, ma'am.'

Miss Heathcote's eyes narrowed and she leaned towards Hetty with a disbelieving sneer. 'As if you did not know. Don't act the innocent with me, girl. I have proof that you were fiddling the accounts and taking money for yourself.'

'That's utter nonsense,' Hetty cried angrily. 'Apart from anything else, why would I do that? The business was mine. I would have been robbing myself.'

'Are you forgetting my part in all this?'

'No, Miss Heathcote, of course not, but you said that you were not interested in profit. Naturally, you wanted the capital sum repaid, but your main concern was to prove to the men who manage your father's estate that you were their equal.'

'That is true, which makes it even more difficult for me to understand why you acted in such an underhand way. I trusted you, Hetty. And you let me down.'

'No. No, I did not. I was scrupulous in attending to the accounts and banking the money. I was in America when all this happened anyway, so how could I be the culprit?'

'Yes, you were away chasing after that man.' Miss Heathcote laughed but there was no humour in the sound. 'You returned very quickly, so I assume that the scoundrel let you down. Don't say I didn't warn you.'

'Yes, everything you say is true. Charles was just toying with my affections and I made a complete fool of myself. Does that satisfy you, Miss Heathcote? Do you enjoy seeing me suffer as you did all those years ago?'

'Oh, miss,' Dorrie cried, clapping her hand to her mouth. 'I am so sorry.'

'Be silent, girl,' Miss Heathcote snapped. 'Speak when you are spoken to and not before.'

'Are you happy here, Dorrie,' Hetty demanded, ignoring Miss Heathcote's frown. 'If not you can come home with me. You do not have to stay here.'

'I am quite happy here, miss. I got me brothers with me and we have a room all to ourselves with three good meals a day. She's not such a bad old stick when you get to know her.'

'Praise indeed,' Miss Heathcote said sarcastically. 'You may go and get your supper, Dorrie. I shan't need you again this evening.'

'Ta, Miss Heathcote. I mean, thank you, ma'am.'

Hetty caught Dorrie by the hand as she was about to leave the room. 'I will speak to you again soon. I need to be sure that this is what you want.'

'It's all right, miss, really it is. The servants have been ever so kind to us, and Cook's taken quite a fancy to the boys. If she goes on feeding them up like she does, they'll be fat as little pigs before long. They go to school every day and Miss Heathcote says she's going to bring them up to be decent men and not scoundrels.'

Hetty smiled at that. 'But you, Dorrie. What about you?'

'Don't worry about me, miss. I never expected much out of life. I thought we'd end up in the workhouse, not living in a blooming mansion.'

'Supper, Dorrie,' Miss Heathcote said firmly. 'And you, Hetty, come here. We need to talk.'

Dorrie hurried from the room and Hetty returned to stand before Miss Heathcote.

'Answer me one question, ma'am. Who was it who discovered that the books had been tampered with?'

'It was Maitland at the bank, of course. You know very well that he deals with all my financial matters. When it became apparent that Dorrie was too young and inexperienced to handle the responsibility, Maitland sent two of his men to collect the monies and the ledgers for inspection.'

'Would those men have been named Clench and Shipworthy by any chance?'

Miss Heathcote shrugged her thin shoulders. 'I hardly know. I don't deal with minions.'

Without waiting for permission, Hetty pulled up a chair and sat down. 'Let me tell you about those men, and you will understand why I accuse them. If you will just give me a chance, I think I know how we can prove their guilt and my innocence.'

'Very well, but I have yet to be convinced.'

An hour later, Hetty and George were travelling homeward in Miss Heathcote's carriage. 'I must say this is the way to travel,' George said. 'It beats a hansom cab hands down.'

Hetty slipped her hand through his arm and she smiled. 'One day we'll be rich enough to afford one of these, or maybe even one of those new-fangled motor cars.'

'What's all this "we" business, Hetty? I haven't proposed to you yet.'

She couldn't see his features clearly in the dim light, but Hetty knew that he was smiling. She cuddled up to him. 'But you will, George. You love me – you said so.'

'I do, but you risked everything for that fellow in America. I need to know that you love me as much or more.'

'Then kiss me.' Hetty closed her eyes as their lips met in a kiss that seemed to make time stand still, blotting out the past and promising so much in the future. 'There,' she whispered. 'Does that prove anything to you?'

George released her gently. 'I don't want to be second best, Hetty. I don't want just to be the "and Co." any more. If you give yourself to me it has to be heart and soul. I can't live with the ghost of an old love hovering in the background.'

Hetty moved away from him. 'It's not like that.'

'I'm still here for you, and I'll stand by you. Give yourself time to know your own heart.'

Choking back a sob of frustration, Hetty glared at him. 'I love you truly. You are more important to me than making a success of the business, and I'll prove it to you one way or another.'

His teeth flashed white in the gloom. 'Stubborn and obstinate to the last, girl.'

'I shan't throw myself at you again,' Hetty said stiffly. 'But you might like to be present tomorrow at the shop in Artillery Lane to see Cyrus Clench get his just deserts.'

'Of course I want to be there.'

'Two o'clock, sharp. Don't be late.' Hetty glanced out of the window as the coachman drew the horses to a halt. 'We're home. No, don't bother to see me in, George. Milton will do that.'

Hetty went into the house without a backward glance. She would not let George see that she was hurt by his attitude. Why wouldn't he believe her? Were all men as stupid and stubborn? She followed Nora to the kitchen where Jane and Granny were waiting anxiously for news. Hetty barely had time to divest herself of her outer garments before they were clamouring to be told every single detail of her encounter with Miss Heathcote.

Next day the trap was set. Sammy had been sent round to Tipton's Bank with a note for Clench, asking him to meet Hetty at the coffee shop at ten past two in the afternoon, when he would learn something to his advantage. Hetty was not at all certain that he would keep the appointment, but she had bargained on Clench's insatiable greed. At five minutes before the hour, Miss Heathcote and Dorrie arrived at the coffee shop and George escorted them into the cramped confines of the scullery, while Hetty stationed herself behind the counter. She was extremely nervous; so much depended upon Clench admitting his offences in the hearing of witnesses, and Miss Heathcote in particular.

The hands on the clock face barely seemed to move as Hetty waited. She tidied the counter which had been abandoned so hastily, and she placed fresh cloths on the tables. She had wound the clock and set it at the correct time according to George's pocket watch, and now she watched it as the seconds ticked by and then the minutes. At quarter past two, Hetty was convinced that Clench was not coming, but just as she was about to lock up she saw his familiar figure scuttling along on the other side of the street. She straightened her apron and tried to appear calm, but in truth her legs were trembling so badly that she could not stand. She sat down at one of the tables, clasping her hands in front of her until her knuckles cracked; everything depended on the outcome of this encounter.

She looked up as the door opened and Clench burst in on a gust of cold air. 'Good afternoon,' she said coldly.

Clench took off his bowler hat and he glanced around the room. 'Are we alone?'

'As you can see.' Hetty emphasised her words with a casual wave of her hand. 'I wanted to talk to you in private, Mr Clench.'

'It's no use appealing to me better nature, Hetty, because I ain't got one.'

'I realised that a long time ago.'

'Then what do you want? You said it was something to my advantage.'

'I admit defeat, Mr Clench. You've been out for revenge against my family for a long time and I want it to stop now. You've won.'

Clench's grin almost split his face in two as he sidled over to the table and sat down opposite her. 'Well, now. Here's a turn-up for the books.'

Hetty forced her cold lips into a smile. 'Like the books that you fiddled in order to take money from the coffee shops? Is that what you mean?'

He threw back his head and guffawed. 'That was Jasper's idea, and it was one of his best. It was so easy to cream a tidy sum off each shop every week. We've got a nice little nest egg as a result, but I've still got a score to settle with you and yours, Hetty.'

'That isn't fair, Mr Clench. I've repaid you and you signed a note to that effect.'

'I'll say it was signed under duress.' Clench bared his teeth in a lupine snarl. 'I'll take the coffee shop instead then. I'm sure the old cripple will allow you to keep this one for old times' sake. Just sign the lease over to me and we'll call it quits.'

Hetty leapt to her feet. 'Did you hear that, Miss Heathcote?'

Clench shot off his chair and backed towards the door, his face ashen. 'You little bitch.'

'I've heard quite enough, thank you,' Miss Heathcote said, emerging from the scullery with George and Dorrie following close on her heels.

'You can't prove anything. I'll deny it all in court.' Clench made a grab for the doorknob and twisted it frantically, but it was held by Milton who had just arrived with two policemen.

'You won't get away with it this time,' George said, crossing the floor and seizing Clench by the collar.

'Don't hit me again,' Clench cried, cowering against the wall. 'You broke me nose last time. I'll sue you for common assault.'

'Prove it, mate,' George said, dragging him away from the door to allow the police and Milton to enter.

Miss Heathcote limped forward, supported by Dorrie. 'Take this man away, Constable. Arrest him for embezzlement and also his accomplice, a man named Shipworthy who works at Tipton's Bank.'

The elder constable pulled a pair of handcuffs from his belt and clipped them around Clench's skinny wrists. 'Are you pressing charges, ma'am?'

'I most certainly am,' Miss Heathcote said firmly. 'And I'll be happy to appear in court if necessary as a witness.'

'Oo-er, ma'am,' Dorrie said admiringly. 'You are getting brave.'

'I've always been brave,' Miss Heathcote conceded. 'But now I'm just a bit braver. Take him away, Constable. The sight of him makes me feel sick.'

Hetty watched as Clench was dragged from the shop still protesting his innocence. She was stunned by the sudden turn of events and amazed at Miss Heathcote's unexpected show of resilience. She turned to her with a genuine smile of admiration. 'Well done, ma'am. I didn't think you had it in you.'

A faint blush of pink tinted Miss Heathcote's cheeks and she fluttered her silver eyelashes. 'I have my moments, and this was one of them.'

George nodded enthusiastically. 'That was well done. It was a stroke of genius sending your man for the cops, if you don't mind me saying so.'

Miss Heathcote's flush deepened, and at first Hetty thought she was going to put George in his place for being so forward, but she smiled and nodded her head. 'Thank you, young man. I don't mind in the least. After all, it is only the truth.'

'And now you know that I am innocent of any wrongdoing,' Hetty said, eyeing Miss Heathcote warily.

'Of course, and I am sorry that I doubted you in the first place. You are reinstated as from this moment with my blessing.'

George moved closer to Hetty. 'You've got your business back, girl. I'm glad for your sake.'

Hetty met his solemn gaze and realised that she must make a choice which would affect both their lives. If she chose to accept Miss Heathcote's offer she stood in danger of losing George. To reject it would mean beginning all over again. She must either follow her head, or her heart. She could not have it all. There was a moment of silence in the room, except for the inexorable ticking of the clock. Hetty looked from Miss Heathcote's eager face to George's guarded expression. He gave her an encouraging smile. 'You must do what is best for you, Hetty. I won't stand in your way.'

'Thank you, but I know what I want more than anything in the world,' she said softly. She turned to Miss Heathcote. 'I've made wrong choices in the past and lived to regret them. I put everything I had into starting up the coffee shops, but I know now that there are more important things in life than simply making money. I don't want the business, Miss Heathcote. You see, I'm going to marry George, if he'll have me.' She turned to him, holding out her hand with a tentative smile. 'Will you?'

He strode across the room to sweep her into an embrace that left her in no doubt of his answer. 'My darling girl, of course I want to marry you. But are you sure about this?'

Hetty smiled into his eyes. 'I am, George. You are my life and always will be.'

Dorrie sniffed audibly and Miss Heathcote struggled to her feet. 'This is madness. I'm offering you the chance to make a fortune and you are throwing it away for a man?'

Safe in the circle of George's arms, Hetty nodded vehemently. 'I'll go back to my coffee stall in the market place. After all, Jane will be married by the end of the week and with another baby on the way she won't have time to run the stall. George and I will work side by side and that is enough for me. I'll sew pearl buttons on my clothes and be queen to his pearly king.'

'I think that's ever so lovely,' Dorrie murmured with a catch in her voice.

'You haven't heard the end of this matter,' Miss Heathcote said angrily. 'Dorrie, open the door. We're leaving.'

Hetty went to follow them but George restrained her with a loving hug. 'Let her go, sweetheart. She'll come round in time.'

'Yes, I hope so,' Hetty said with a sigh.

'I love you,' George said, gazing deeply into her eyes. 'All I wanted was to know that you felt the same way about me. You've proved it, and if you want to call her back and tell the old girl that you've changed your mind, then that's all right by me. I don't want to rule you, Hetty. I just want you to be happy.'

She raised her hand to touch his cheek. 'I know, but I've made my choice and I'll stand by it. Let's go home and tell the family.'

The only family member who was not delighted with their news was Granny. She made no secret of the fact that she considered Hetty to be doolally-tap for giving up the opportunity of a shining career in the catering trade. She liked George, she said grudgingly, but he was just a costermonger and Hetty could have had her pick of well-to-do businessmen or even a toff with a townhouse and a country estate. Nora told her not to be such a miserable old cow, and Jane was delighted at the prospect of having George as a brother-in-law. Tom slapped him on the back and added his sincere congratulations and Sammy and Eddie capered about the kitchen whooping for joy.

Picking up Natalia and giving her a cuddle, Hetty smiled to herself. What more could she want than all this? She had no doubts about her feelings for George. She could not even consider a life without him, but she was a little sad to think that the businesses she had been building were now going to fall into someone else's hands. She hoped that Miss Heathcote would understand why she had chosen love over money, and that she would not sink back into her former hermit-like existence. Hetty made up her mind that once Jane's wedding was over, she would go to Berkeley Square and make sure that Dorrie and the boys were content to remain there. In the meantime, she would go back to her old stall in Spitalfields market. That would be enough for her from now on.

The day of Jane's wedding dawned cold and foggy but spirits were high in Nora's house. The bridal party walked to St Stephen's Church in Commercial Street, where Tom was waiting with George as his best man. Tom's mother and sisters were already seated in the front pews, and they smiled to see Jane enter the church on Sammy's arm. He stuck out his chest proudly as he gave his big sister away. Hetty cried during the ceremony, but they were tears of happiness. She knew that Jane and Tom were well suited and that Natalia, who sat solemnly on her lap throughout the whole proceedings, would have a kind and loving stepfather. They would be renting rooms from Nora until they could afford to move into a house of their own, which pleased Hetty even though she knew it was a bit selfish on her part. No doubt she would get used to the idea of living apart from her sister when she was happily settled with George, and perhaps having a baby of her own would make it easier to part with Talia. The boys would stay with her and George, there was no question about that, and she could not desert Granny.

Suddenly everyone was standing up as the bride and groom processed down the aisle, and Hetty realised that she had been daydreaming through the last part of the ceremony. She caught George's eye and all her doubts and fears were dispelled in the warmth of his smile. She took his arm and with Natalia holding her other hand she followed Jane and Tom out of the church into a thick, swirling pea-souper.

'Oh! Heavens!' Jane cried. 'I can't see a thing and my new bonnet will be ruined.'

Tom slipped his arm around her waist. 'Don't worry, Mrs Crewe. It's not far to the chop house. I know the way blindfold.'

George bent down to pick up Natalia. 'Best

hurry, mate. We don't want to keep the little 'uns out in this weather.'

'What about me?' Granny demanded. 'I'm not as young as I was, and Nora's rheumatics are playing her up.'

Hetty was about to suggest that they hail a couple of hackney carriages, when out of the fog loomed a pair of matched greys pulling a familiar vehicle. It drew to a halt and Hetty recognised Milton seated on the box. She peered in through the window and saw Miss Heathcote wrapped in furs with a blanket over her knees. The groom jumped down to open the door and Miss Heathcote leaned out. 'Hetty and George come with me. The rest of you can ride in the three hackney carriages following us.'

'Excuse me, ma'am,' Tom said, doffing his hat, 'but this is a wedding party.'

'Do I look simple, young man? Of course I know it's a wedding party. I've arranged to have the reception at my house in Berkeley Square. It's my present to the bride and groom. Now get inside before this wretched fog gets any worse and we're stuck in this godforsaken place all day.'

Tom looked doubtful, but Jane was already heading towards the next carriage. 'Come on, Tom. I'd give me right arm to see inside her drum.'

Hetty knew that there was no point in arguing with Miss Heathcote, and she allowed George to help her into the carriage. 'I don't understand,' she said as she settled down on the seat. 'Why are you doing this and how did you know that Jane's wedding was today?'

Miss Heathcote smiled triumphantly. 'George told me. No, don't look at him like that, Hetty. I sent for him as I wanted to speak frankly and we had a long talk.'

Hetty turned her head to look at him. 'George?'

He took her hand and held it in a warm grasp. 'Hetty, my love, all we want is for you to be happy. Miss Heathcote convinced me that you ought to be allowed to follow your dream. I won't stand in your way; in fact I'll help you. If you'll have me, I'll work alongside you to put the coffee shops on the map of London. Miss Heathcote thinks we'll make a good team.'

'She does?' Hetty said faintly. 'I don't understand. What brought all this about?'

'I had a visit from a certain gentleman,' Miss Heathcote said mysteriously. 'He is an acquaintance of yours, I believe. We talked about many things, but the reason he came to me was that he wanted to invest in the business. With his backing we can begin expanding our chain of coffee shops to cover the lucrative West End.'

'Who is this person?' Hetty demanded dazedly.

'Maynard Kingsley.'

'Maynard! But I still don't understand. Why would he be interested in a few simple coffee shops?'

George squeezed her hand gently. 'He was impressed by you, Hetty. He saw you for what you are and he knows when he is on to a good thing. As I do myself.'

'It sound too good to be true, but I don't know if I can do it, or if it's what I want. It might spoil everything we have together, George.'

'And if you pass up this chance, you will regret it for the rest of your life. You won't be alone, my darling. You'll have me, George Cooper, the coster who can sell anything to anyone. We can't fail.'

Miss Heathcote chortled with laughter. 'Do you know, George, I almost like you. I never thought I'd say that of a man again. What do you think, Hetty? Shall we go ahead with this fine venture?'

Hetty looked into George's eyes and saw her future. They would disagree and they might argue, but there would be love and laughter and maybe a degree of success, although that was almost immaterial. Her feelings for him were mirrored in his eyes and returned in one long look. 'Are you really sure you want this, George?'

'I want you, Hetty. Now and always; forever and ever.'

'That sounds very much like a proposal,' she whispered.

'It is. I was a stiff-necked fool not to have snapped you up the moment you arrived home. You've always had my heart. Will you marry me, Hetty?'

'Of course she will, you stupid man,' Miss Heathcote said, throwing up her hands. 'For goodness' sake kiss her and be done with it.'

'Of course I will,' Hetty repeated, sliding her arms around his neck. 'Kiss me, George, and be done with it.'

# The Constant Heart

## Dilly Court

### Would she risk it all for love?

Despite living by the side of the Thames, with its noise, disease and dirt, eighteen-year-old Rosina May has wanted for little in life.

Until her father's feud with a fellow bargeman threatens to destroy everything. To save them all, Rosina agrees to marry Harry, the son of a wealthy merchant. But a chance encounter with a handsome river pirate has turned her head and she longs to meet him again.

When her father dies a broken man, Harry goes back on his promise and turns Rosina out on to the streets. She is forced to work the river herself, ferrying rubbish out of London and living rough. In spite of her hardships, she cannot forget her pirate and when tragedy threatens to strike once more she is forced to make a choice. But is she really prepared to risk everything for love?

arrow books

---

# A Mot       Gr

## A Guide
## from

### She would do an

When Eloise Cribb receive
has been lost at sea she
manage. With two young ch
almost nothing to live on, s
his estrang

She sets off on the long and
is met with hostility and soor
to return to London. Virtually
faced with her worst nightm
workhouse, or abandon her ch
But she is determined to keep
at all cost

### The recipe

Long before the
remedies to tr
for a tickly co
temperature,
simple and e
would have b
being transcr

Some of the
Did you know
an asthma a
indigestion?
issue repair

But Grandm
home-grow
ntri
study as do
great-grand
was expens
healthcare,
cupboard an
resurfaced t
to collect sp

In these days
to discover h

arrov.

returned in one long look. 'Are you really sure you want this, George?'

'I want you, Hetty. Now and always; forever and ever.'

'That sounds very much like a proposal,' she whispered.

'It is. I was a stiff-necked fool not to have snapped you up the moment you arrived home. You've always had my heart. Will you marry me, Hetty?'

'Of course she will, you stupid man,' Miss Heathcote said, throwing up her hands. 'For goodness' sake kiss her and be done with it.'

'Of course I will,' Hetty repeated, sliding her arms around his neck. 'Kiss me, George, and be done with it.'

# *The Constant Heart*

## Dilly Court

### Would she risk it all for love?

Despite living by the side of the Thames, with its noise, disease and dirt, eighteen-year-old Rosina May has wanted for little in life.

Until her father's feud with a fellow bargeman threatens to destroy everything. To save them all, Rosina agrees to marry Harry, the son of a wealthy merchant. But a chance encounter with a handsome river pirate has turned her head and she longs to meet him again.

When her father dies a broken man, Harry goes back on his promise and turns Rosina out on to the streets. She is forced to work the river herself, ferrying rubbish out of London and living rough. In spite of her hardships, she cannot forget her pirate and when tragedy threatens to strike once more she is forced to make a choice. But is she really prepared to risk everything for love?

arrow books

ALSO AVAILABLE IN ARROW

# A Mother's Courage

## Dilly Court

**She would do anything to keep them safe . . .**

When Eloise Cribb receives the news that her husband's ship
has been lost at sea she wonders how she is ever going to
manage. With two young children, the rent overdue and left with
almost nothing to live on, she has no alternative but to turn to
his estranged family for help.

She sets off on the long and arduous journey to Yorkshire, but
is met with hostility and soon realises she has little choice but
to return to London. Virtually destitute and desperate, Eloise is
faced with her worst nightmare: she must either go to the
workhouse, or abandon her children at the Foundling Hospital.
But she is determined to keep them under her protective wing
at all costs . . .

arrow books

AVAILABLE FROM RANDOM HOUSE BOOKS

# Grandma's Remedies
### A Guide to Traditional Cures and Treatments from Mustard Poultices to Rosehip Syrup

## Cherry Chappell

**The recipes and treatments that have preserved family health for generations**

Long before the advances of modern medicine, families used home-made remedies to treat everyday illnesses. Whether it was onion and garlic syrup for a tickly cough or vinegar and water compresses to bring down a high temperature, the kitchen and garden could always be relied on to supply simple and effective treatments. More often than not, these remedies would have been handed down verbally through the generations, before being transcribed carefully into family recipe books, then reused and refined year after year.

Some of the remedies – even the most ancient ones – work surprisingly well. Did you know, for example, that two cups of strong black coffee will alleviate an asthma attack? Or that chewing toasted fennel seeds will help combat indigestion? Or that lavender has antiseptic qualities and also stimulates tissue repair, which is why it has been used for thousands of years in an ointment for cuts and bruises?

But *Grandma's Remedies* is more than just an intriguing exploration of this home-grown branch of medicine, it also considers how gifted women healers have contributed to medical understanding, despite not being allowed to study as doctors, and paints a vivid portrait of the way our grandparents and great-grandparents lived. In the days before the NHS, sending for the doctor was expensive, reserved only for the greatest of emergencies. For everyday healthcare, it was the women of the family who had to turn to the store cupboard and provide a treatment. This invaluable spirit of resourcefulness resurfaced to great effect on the Home Front, when women were encouraged to collect sphagnum moss, rosehips and conkers that could be turned into dressings, treatments, and tonics for the war effort.

In these days of readily-available antibiotics and painkillers, it is fascinating to discover how people survived when all they had to rely on was a garden, a larder and a healthy dose of common sense.

BOOKS